My Daring Highlander

Vonda Sinclair

My Daring Highlander

Copyright © 2013 Vonda Sinclair

ALL RIGHTS RESERVED

This book may not be reproduced in whole or in part without written permission from the author. This book is a work of fiction. The characters, names, incidents, locations, and events are fictitious or used fictitiously. Any resemblance to actual persons, living or dead, is purely coincidental or from the writer's imagination.

www.vondasinclair.com

ISBN: **1492995851**

ISBN-13: **978-1492995852**

DEDICATION

To my own blue-eyed charmer, my husband.

To my friend, Dana, another Highland adventurer.

The Highland Adventure Series

My Fierce Highlander

My Wild Highlander

My Brave Highlander

My Daring Highlander

My Notorious Highlander

My Rebel Highlander

ACKNOWLEDGMENTS

Special thanks to Sharron Gunn for your Highland expertise.

Special thanks to Vanessa, Terry, Judy, Dana, Eliza, Andrea, and Donna

CHAPTER ONE

Assynt, Scotland, May 1619

Something in the early morn air didn't feel right.

Keegan MacKay rode at the front of the MacKay party of just over two dozen, his gaze scanning the surrounding misty green hills and gray granite mountains. As head guard of the MacKay clan, Keegan took his duty seriously. He was to spy danger before it presented itself.

Had his outlaw cousin, Haldane, returned to kill Chief Dirk and claim the chiefdom for himself? This wouldn't be his first attempt. Although Dirk's youngest brother was but twenty summers, he was a formidable foe and slippery as an eel when it came to capture. Haldane and his band of outlaws had escaped Dunnakeil's dungeon last November. Then, they'd vanished.

No doubt they would come out of hiding again soon.

Wanting to travel as far south as possible before sunset, they'd left Munrick Castle and the MacLeods at daybreak. Though more than two hours had passed, the sun had not yet burned off the thick gray mist rising from the nearby loch.

Their journey had two purposes—Dirk's wife, Lady Isobel, wished to travel to Dornie for a visit with her brothers, and Keegan was in charge of taking Lady Seona Murray back to her home near Inverness. A task he dreaded for he'd grown attached to her.

A prickle of warning passed over Keegan. Was there danger behind them? He glanced back, then guided his horse, Curry, off the narrow muddy trail, turned about and waited until several in their party rode past.

Keegan's gaze settled on Lady Seona. Though she wore a plaid cowl over her head now, he had memorized how glossy her chestnut-colored hair was. More than once, he'd fantasized about running his fingers through the loose strands. They would surely be silky and cool against his skin.

Her dark blue eyes met his, bewitching as always... and so were her Cupid's bow lips. Damn, how he craved kissing her. Like a fool, he had longed for her for months, but he had never dared to touch her. Her chaperone aunt pinned her vicious eagle-eyed glare on him, as she always did.

Keegan had tried to tell himself he was daft for wanting Lady Seona so badly. He was not a chief or titled laird, and her father would never allow them to marry. Cousin of the chief wasn't good enough.

Dirk paused beside Keegan, startling him from his wayward thoughts. "Is something amiss?"

"'Tis only a gut feeling that someone is following us," he said, keeping his voice low.

"Aye. I had the same feeling." Dirk narrowed his piercing pale blue eyes and glared back at the hills they'd just passed through.

People had often remarked that Keegan had eyes like Dirk's and that they were more like brothers than cousins. Keegan agreed with that assessment and highly valued his role within the clan of protecting them and the chief. He was happy Dirk returned last fall to take the position he'd been meant for since birth. He was an excellent chief and a strong warrior.

From the mist behind them, a distant horse's whinny carried on the breeze.

"Did you hear that?" Keegan asked, his gaze searching the murky landscape.

"Aye."

Keegan caught a glimpse of a black horse and dark-clothed rider as they veered off the trail and behind a yellow-blooming gorse bush. "There." Keegan pointed.

"Aye. We're being followed." Dirk moved toward their party, giving quiet orders to the guards to surround the three ladies and their four maids, then he and several guards joined Keegan.

"I wager 'tis Haldane," Keegan said.

Dirk nodded. "He will never give up trying to kill me until one of us is dead."

"'Haps you should wear a cowl so he cannot identify you so easily," Keegan suggested. Dirk's bright copper hair made him easy to spot from a great distance. And an easy target.

"Hmph. I'll not hide from that wily weasel," he muttered.

"I wasn't suggesting you hide, cousin. Merely use caution and disguise yourself so we can protect you better."

"I don't wish for anyone else to be struck with an arrow either. I want Haldane and his whole band of outlaws taken out before he kills someone else." They had murdered two MacKay guards last winter and stolen almost a dozen horses.

Dirk's friend, Rebbie, the Earl of Rebbinglen, halted his horse on Keegan's right. "How many did you see?" he asked, his expression as dark as his eyes and hair.

"One, but I'm certain there are more," Keegan said.

"Without doubt. That damned McMurdo highwayman is likely with him."

"Aye, they have been fast friends since Haldane turned outlaw." None of them held any fondness for Donald McMurdo. They'd had several run-ins with him in the past. For a certainty, Keegan detested the murderer who had slaughtered at least eighteen people in the Durness area, including one of Keegan's cousins.

Last winter, Keegan had scuffled with McMurdo in Smoo Cave, and the old highwayman had kicked Keegan in the groin. He'd fought past the pain and subdued McMurdo by holding a knife to his throat. He shouldn't have been so lenient with the bastard.

Keegan and those beside him stared back at the elevated green hillside. 'Twas too quiet, water trickling in a small burn and the late spring breeze fluttering the leaves of a nearby bush the only sounds. How he wished the mist would clear away, taking with it the outlaws' cover.

Keegan glanced back at Lady Seona, glad to see eight armored guards surrounding her and the other women. They were well-protected. One less thing for him to worry about when the outlaws decided to show themselves.

Isobel held a lethal-looking dagger in her hand. 'Twas one she often carried in a scabbard at her side. Did Seona own a weapon?

Would she even know how to use one? He should've taught her how to use a blade before this journey.

"Ready yourselves," Dirk said, pulling a pistol from his belt.

Four archers on foot nocked their arrows and drew back the bow strings.

Keegan unsheathed his basket-hilt broadsword and held a targe before him to deflect any arrows or sword strikes. His gaze traveled up the green hillside, swathed in vibrant bracken fern where men could easily hide. Plaid flickered in the hazy gray mist. "Look." He pointed with his sword. "They're going to try to ambush us from the hill."

"Move the women over there," Dirk directed the guards, pointing toward an indention in the hillside surrounded by rocks and scrubby bushes. "And help them dismount. Put the horses in front of them."

"Have a care," Lady Isobel said low, but her concerned words to her husband were clear.

"Aye," Dirk responded.

Keegan envied their relationship. 'Twas obvious they were mad for each other. He yearned for that closeness with Lady Seona. But now was not the time to ponder such things. He needed to focus and clear his mind. Lives depended on it.

Movement at the top of the hill drew his attention.

"He may have stones the size of cannonballs," Rebbie said. "But I'd love naught more than to shoot them off."

Dirk snorted. "I hope you get the chance, my friend."

All the men except the archers held swords and round targes, ready for battle.

"'Haps you should move back, Dirk. The last thing we need is for the chief to be hit by a stray arrow." Keegan felt daft even suggesting it, considering Dirk was probably the most capable warrior of them all, tall and broad of shoulder and about the same size as Keegan. They had sparred much over the past few months, training and keeping in practice. Sometimes Keegan won their matches and sometimes Dirk did, proving they were evenly matched.

"Don't worry over me, cousin."

An arrow whizzed down from the hill. All the men lifted their targes. The arrow struck Keegan's and bounced off the central brass boss or one of the metal studs.

"That little bastard," Dirk muttered and dismounted. He led his beloved horse, Tulloch, to a safer spot and the other men did the same, including Keegan, not wanting their horses seriously injured or killed.

"Show yourself, Haldane!" Dirk yelled toward the hill. "Coward!"

A head popped up out of the bracken. 'Twas difficult to identify the person at this distance but he appeared to have red hair like Haldane.

Dirk aimed his pistol and fired, but his target ducked.

"I don't want to kill my own brother, but I will if he forces my hand." Dirk shoved the pistol into his belt. "There he is again! Archers, shoot!"

At this distance, and with the mist reducing visibility, Keegan could not tell if the man was indeed Haldane. If not, he was likely in his gang. Besides that, he'd shot the first arrow, provoking retaliation.

The MacKay archers let fly several arrows.

"Come out and fight like men!" Dirk called out.

Arrows streaked toward them from the hillside. With their targes, they easily deflected or caught each one.

Annoyance twisted through Keegan. He was tired of this cat and mouse game and eager for a good fight. "I'm going after him."

"Not without me," Dirk said.

"Nay, you stay here. The clan needs you."

"The clan needs you as well," Dirk grumbled.

"You are the chief," Keegan argued, matching his cousin's fearsome glare.

"Do you think that matters? Haldane is my problem and I'll deal with him."

"I'm ready to go after him and McMurdo," Rebbie said, eager battle-lust gleaming in his dark brown eyes.

"We'll all go," Dirk said, motioning to a half dozen of his men.

***

Lady Seona Murray watched with sickened dread as Keegan, Dirk and several more men charged boldly toward the hill where the outlaws lurked.

She'd stayed with the MacKays for several months and almost considered them her clan now. They had certainly shown her more care and consideration than her own clan had.

"Dirk," Lady Isobel called, but not too loud. If her husband heard, he ignored her. "He is mad," she grumbled through clenched teeth as the men disappeared from sight, the eerie mist enfolding them. "Haldane will kill him if he has half a chance."

"They are capable warriors," Seona said, knowing she was right, but at the same time realizing they were not invincible. She said a silent prayer for their safety.

"Aye," Isobel said, her dark brows furrowed.

The eight well-armed guards would not let the women move from the cover of the huge rocks surrounding them on three sides.

Seona was equally worried about Keegan, but could not voice her concerns. Her Aunt Patience, standing on Isobel's other side, could never know that Seona held Keegan MacKay in such high regard. All winter and spring he had made a point to greet Seona at every opportunity with a charming smile and a bow. Sometimes she would catch him watching her with an intense focus from the other side of the great hall, but he had not done anything more intimate than usher her to the high table and pull out a chair for her almost every evening.

His pale blue eyes enchanted her, made her feel vibrantly alive. They reflected great interest and longing. She wanted to do naught but stare into his eyes for hours. His thick, tawny mane looked as if it would be soft and silky; her fingers itched to find out. Though he was a tall, broad-shouldered warrior, his size did not intimidate her, for he had an easy smile. The only part of him she had touched was his arm when he escorted her. Each time she slipped her hand around his elbow, she savored the hardness of his well-developed muscles.

A few times this spring, on rare and precious sunny days, she and Isobel had watched the men training with swords in the walled barmkin outside Castle Dunnakeil. She could not tear her gaze away from Keegan then, especially when he grew warm and threw off his doublet. His muscles were obvious through the thin damp linen of his shirt, and his calf muscles beneath the bottom edge of his plaid intriguing.

She only hoped he would be careful as he and the men pursued the outlaws. With each minute that passed in relative silence, Seona's stomach ached more and more. The mist before them, strangely lit from behind by morning sunlight, hurt her eyes.

She squinted against the brilliance.

"Why have they not returned?" Isobel grumbled a quarter hour later.

Having no answer for her friend, Seona shook her head. Indeed, what could be taking so long? Had they been ambushed and killed silently? A chill passed over her.

"Will one of you go check on them?" Isobel asked the bearded guard closest to her.

"Nay. The chief has commanded us to stay and protect you ladies," he said in a brusque tone.

A sound from within the white mist caught Seona's attention and then a movement, low to the ground.

Seona shoved Isobel into her aunt, toward the left side of the stony enclosure. Something struck the sandstone, spraying rock particles over them.

"What on earth?" Aunt Patience squawked.

The women ended up in a heap on the ground. Seona's knee pained her, but she hoped she hadn't injured the others.

Seona looked behind her. "An arrow," she said, pointing to the broken shaft and feathers on the ground where it had bounced off the rocks exactly where Isobel had been standing.

"Men advancing from the rear!" a guard shouted. A *clunk* against wood sounded as an arrow drove into his targe.

The other guards cursed and moved into position to better shield the women.

"Saints, Seona, you saved my life," Isobel said in a stunned voice.

Seona knew not what to say; she'd simply acted on instinct. Isobel had become like a sister to her over the past few months, and obviously she'd help her in any way she could. Just as she wished to return home and help her own sister.

Seona's attention was riveted to the four enemies on foot, wielding swords, storming from the bright mist in front of them, the opposite direction from where Keegan and Dirk had charged earlier.

CHAPTER TWO

Who were the men materializing out of the blinding mist? As of yet, Seona could not see them well enough to distinguish their features.

Four MacKay guards leapt from their horses, drew swords and lashed out at the attackers. Blades clashed and clanged. From her crouched position, Seona caught a glimpse of one of the outlaws—Haldane, with long red hair and a scruffy beard. His face possessed a gaunt, hungry look, and his green eyes glinted wildly.

Seona envied Isobel's dagger for she had naught to defend herself with besides the tiny knife she used while eating. She prayed the older, more experienced guards could easily defeat the young outlaws.

Shouts echoed from the opposite direction, startling her. More enemies? Or the MacKays returning? Behind the tall rocks and horses, Seona was unable to see who was approaching. She and Isobel stood. Abruptly, Haldane and his three cronies fled into the mist. Keegan, Dirk, Rebbie and several more men chased after them on foot, swords drawn, battle-cries echoing.

"Dirk!" Isobel shouted. "They could be hiding in the mist!"

None of the men listened; not that Seona expected them to. She knew how men were—although they might show caution at times, warriors such as these would display no fear or hesitance. They'd charge right in to the midst of trouble with their blades.

Near silence reigned for several minutes.

Seona held her breath, waiting to see what would happen

next. Praying Keegan and the men helping him would not be ambushed in such poor visibility.

Moments later, broad-shouldered, indistinct silhouettes appeared in the bright mist and strode toward them. Was one of them Keegan?

Aye.

When Keegan emerged, walking with Dirk, Rebbie and some of the other guards, she released a calming breath.

"Thank the saints," Isobel whispered.

Seona felt the same gratitude, but could not voice it for her aunt waited beside her, scared stiff.

Sheathing their swords, Dirk and Keegan strode closer and the guards moved aside. Keegan's intense blue gaze was on her but she tried not to stare at him. *Saints!* Anytime he was near, she almost overheated.

Isobel launched herself at Dirk, who caught her and pulled her close for an affectionate embrace and a kiss on the cheek.

Seona admired their closeness, but Aunt Patience let out a gasp, her lightly-wrinkled ivory skin reddening and her dark blue eyes narrowing in disapproval at the public display. Seona wanted to ask her what was wrong with a husband and wife showing love and concern for each other? Certainly Seona's father had never shown any care for her mother. In fact, she remembered him showing utter disdain for her many times.

Isobel drew back. "Seona saved my life."

"What?" Dirk frowned. "What happened?"

"A stray arrow was flying straight toward me, and Seona pushed me to the ground."

Dirk's fierce gaze lit on her. "I thank you, Lady Seona."

She tried to curtsy but her legs were too shaky to perform the motion adequately. "'Tis naught more than I'd do for mine own sister."

Dirk hugged Isobel close again and whispered something in her ear. But Seona's gaze darted to Keegan, standing next to his cousin, and the compelling expression on his face—a proud grin. His blue eyes seemed even brighter than usual as he observed her.

He took her hand in his large one, lifted it, and kissed the back. "You are very heroic, Lady Seona. I thank you for your good deed."

A thrilling heat suffused her and she dropped her gaze.

Heavens! He'd never kissed her hand before, nor should he whilst her aunt was present. She would disapprove. 'Twas not her aunt she feared, but what her aunt might tell her father.

Still, Seona savored the warmth of Keegan's skin against her own and the tingles showering her body.

"No thanks necessary," Seona mumbled, refusing to look at Keegan or her aunt. They could be glaring daggers at each other for all she knew. But at least Patience was silent this time.

After a long moment, Keegan released her hand, but her skin still burned where his firm warm lips and the scratchy stubble on his chin and upper lip had brushed over it. Seona realized Dirk was talking and forced herself to focus on his words.

"When we went that way…" Dirk nodded to the right. "We saw neither hide nor hair of them. They were decoys to lure us away so that Haldane and the others could attack from this side. We couldn't find them when we went that way either and didn't want to risk pursuing them up the mountain in the thick mist."

"There must not be very many of them." Keegan turned aside and crossed his arms over his chest. "Else Haldane would've had more men with him on this side."

"Aye," Dirk said. "Last winter he had around a dozen. No way of knowing whether he's added to his band of outlaws or whether some have died or found more profitable thieving grounds."

"I'm thinking McMurdo has trained them to be as elusive as he's always been," Keegan said.

"Just what we need. A dozen more McMurdos." Dirk shook his head, then glanced at the sky. "After the mist lifts, we'll travel south until we reach a village or until dark, whichever comes first. 'Tis unfortunate there are no castles between here and Ullapool."

They waited for over an hour and, finally, the mist rose further up the mountains.

As they rode south, Seona and the ladies were heavily protected, with a guard on either side, when the trail was wide enough. She wished Keegan would guard her personally, but she knew that wasn't possible. He rode further forward, his head turning right and then left as he scanned the hills and mountains for an impending attack.

***

Although summer days were long, their party was still several miles away from the nearest village when gloaming descended over the Highlands. Seona glanced west. The sun was but a glowing smudge of pink and violet when they stopped beside a stream in a wee glen. 'Twas a beautiful spot with bare mountains all around, some green and some gray granite.

A few of the clansmen built a fire while several others guarded on the outskirts. Soon the scents of roasted rabbit and quail teased her nose and made her stomach growl. Despite her hunger, her full attention had been captured by Keegan on the opposite side of camp where he removed the saddle from his horse.

When Seona noticed Isobel and Dirk approaching her, she curtsied.

"I cannot thank you enough, Lady Seona, for saving the life of my dear wife. Is there anything I can offer you in repayment?" Dirk asked.

Seona swallowed hard for she was momentarily speechless. "'Tis not necessary. Isobel is like a sister to me. I value our friendship greatly."

"Och. Well, I can understand friendship, for I highly prize my own friends," Dirk said. "Still, if there is ever anything you need, and if 'tis within my power to grant it, I will do so. Just let me know."

Seona nodded. "I thank you, my laird."

Dirk bowed, kissed Isobel's hand and moved away from them to talk to the guards.

"You are like the sister I never had." Isobel drew Seona into a tight embrace.

Seona hugged her, then stepped back. "I feel the same. One can never have too many sisters." She grinned, wishing she and Isobel could live near each other, but once Seona went home she might never see Isobel again. Her throat tightened.

"I know what you want, but 'tis not in my power or Dirk's to give it to you," Isobel said.

Seona frowned. "What do you mean?"

"I should've said *who*, not what." Isobel darted a meaningful glance at Keegan across the way. "Why do you not go speak with him?"

Heat washing over her, Seona stared down at her broken fingernails. "I think... that would not be very wise." Surely Isobel knew of the precarious position she was in. Seona would never be allowed to choose her own husband the way Isobel had.

"It appears that Lady Patience is focusing all her attention on that handsome guard, Hugh MacMillan. You might have a few free minutes."

Seona glanced at Patience, laughing and conversing with the guard who was about her age. Seona had never seen her aunt so talkative with a man before. What a transformation. At least she was enjoying life for once.

Seona shifted her gaze to Keegan again, where he brushed his horse while it picked grass at the edge of the camp. Everything about him enticed her—his broad shoulders and strong arms, his tall height and his many other masculine attributes. His plaid was belted about his narrow waist and weapons hung from his belt. Being a guard, he was always heavily armed. But it wasn't just these physical things that appealed to her. He had a charming, friendly and protective nature.

"I wouldn't know what to say to him anyway," Seona said. Despite staying in the same castle for months, they had not truly had a conversation. They had only spoken in a very impersonal manner. A greeting, a curtsy, a mumbled thanks when he complimented her. The kiss on the hand he'd given her that morn was the only time he'd shown so much affection.

"You are in love with him," Isobel whispered.

"Shh." Seona turned to see who might be listening. Thankfully, no one met her gaze. "I certainly won't be telling him that."

"But 'tis true, aye?" Isobel grinned in a teasing manner.

"It matters not. My father would never allow me to marry anyone less than a clan chief or a titled laird. And I wouldn't want to play with such a good and honorable man's affections," she said, glancing at Keegan. "It could be dangerous if my father were to think we've had a tryst."

Her father had slapped her more than once for minor infractions, which was why she had to get her younger sister away from him. She prayed Talia was well and still living with their cousin, Genevieve, but many months had passed since she'd seen her. Talia was eighteen summers and Seona feared her father would marry her off to some violent barbarian before she saw her again.

"I'm not suggesting you marry him," Isobel said as if Seona were overreacting. "And your father will never find out if you

merely have a brief conversation with Keegan. Who knows? You may not even like him when you get to know him."

Ha. That was highly unlikely. She feared she would fall even harder for him if she learned more about him. Some nights she had trouble sleeping because of thoughts and imaginings of him—what it might be like if he kissed her and held her close. He haunted her dreams.

"What is it going to hurt to simply speak to him for a few moments?" Isobel persisted in an innocent tone, reminding Seona of a mischievous fae.

She watched Keegan, crossing behind the horse and brushing the other side. He had removed his dark blue doublet, making the play of his generous muscles beneath his shirt almost visible.

Aye. 'Twas too tempting by far. And speaking to Keegan in private would only make her yearn for more. She could not have him. Her father would never allow it. He had come down hard on one of her past suitors, the youngest brother of a chief. They were of the same social station, in a manner of speaking, but the man had no title or lands. Her father had punished them both for one innocent dance. With Keegan being the chief's cousin and guard, her father would find him even less suitable.

Seona's father had sent her to marry the MacKay chief… whom she'd thought would be either Aiden or Haldane. 'Twas what her father thought, too, but neither of the young men was chief. She was thankful she hadn't been required to marry either of them when their oldest brother arrived and took over the position.

Though Dirk was a handsome man, they were not suited. Besides, Dirk had been in love with Isobel when they'd arrived in Durness. Therefore, Seona was being returned to her father. He would likely find her another chief to wed. She dreaded to see who he chose for her this time and prayed her future husband would not be abusive. She hoped to marry a kind man who would allow her younger sister to live with them.

"You may never again have such an opportunity to speak with Keegan," Isobel said, growing more serious and slightly sad… for Seona's sake.

She gazed across the grassy area toward him… and he was staring at her. Mortified he'd caught her, she quickly shifted her gaze to Isobel. "He is looking this way," she whispered, trying not to move her lips.

Isobel glanced his way, but Seona refused to do so again. She did not wish to lead Keegan on. And she certainly didn't want him to know they'd been discussing him.

"Well, I'll let you decide," Isobel said with a tiny smile. "Shouldn't be long until we can eat." She strolled away.

Why had she ended the conversation so abruptly? Seona turned to watch Isobel approach Dirk.

"Lady Seona?"

She spun to find Keegan behind her. *Saints!* She slapped a hand over her thumping heart.

"Pray pardon. I didn't mean to scare you." He gave a slight, concerned frown.

He was so handsome and disturbing to her, his sandy-brown hair blowing back in the breeze, that she could hardly think what to say.

"Nay." She waved a hand, trying to catch her breath and act normal. "I am well. I didn't know you were there, and I was only a wee bit startled. That's all."

"Good. I but wanted to thank you again for saving Lady Isobel's life. We all know how much she means to Dirk." Keegan's blue gaze was warm upon her.

"There is no need. I merely acted on instinct."

"Well, I must say you have excellent instincts."

"I thank you." She could not look away from his charming smile with a hint of devilment. It bewitched her. "I'm glad you were not injured when you pursued the outlaws." 'Twas true her demeanor was formal and far too stiff, but she knew not how to converse with him, or any man, in a more relaxed way. Besides, he threw her off balance and made her feel strangely feverish.

"I thank you, m'lady." He gave a hint of a bow.

She swallowed hard, trying to think of something else to say. "You are… very brave to defend and protect us."

He grinned, appearing far more relaxed than she was. "'Tis naught more than my duty. And 'twas certainly no hardship to protect you."

She felt humbled and flattered that he'd singled her out. She trusted him to protect her better than anyone.

"'Tis disappointing that we must return you to your father," he said in a lower tone. His gaze grew more intimate and, indeed, his disappointment was clear upon his face.

"Aye. I have enjoyed spending time with your clan." *And you.*

"I wish…" Keegan shook his head, his expression sobering. "I wish you could stay longer, Lady Seona."

A shiver passing over her skin, she savored his deep voice pronouncing her name. "As do I."

His gaze intensified upon her, becoming as hot as a blue flame. He had given her interested looks before, but never one so breath-stealing. She felt near paralyzed. Captivated. But quickly tore her gaze away, her heart thudding loudly. She must protect herself, and him. This delicious enticement could only be destructive. As she had expected, talking to him caused her to want to draw closer to him.

He cleared his throat. "Have you a weapon?" he asked.

CHAPTER THREE

When Keegan's eyes met Seona's this time, the heated passion was banked, and he seemed most solemn. Why had he asked her if she had a weapon?

"Nay," she said, darting a glance toward her aunt. Her back was turned, and she was still conversing with the guard.

"Lady Isobel carries a dagger with her, and you should as well," Keegan said. "You need to be able to defend yourself should—God forbid—something happen to me and the other men."

Seona did not even want to consider such a horrid situation. "You and the other men are strong warriors and guards. I'm certain you will fight off any enemies."

"Aye. I do hope so. But should you ever find yourself alone, 'haps after you return home, you need to know how to fight off an outlaw." His gaze serious, he gave a slight frown. "Come. I want to give you something." He turned sideways and offered his elbow.

"Where?" She sent another quick glance toward her aunt. The guard was giving Aunt Patience something to drink in a wooden cup.

"Just over here," Keegan said. "'Tis in my pack."

"Very well." She curled her hand around his elbow. Just above it, her fingers stroked over the bulging muscle of his upper arm. The times he'd escorted her to the high table, when she'd been at Dunnakeil, were the highlights of her days. His hard, well-developed arm muscles were pleasing to her and, she had to admit, exciting.

Just as she did now, she'd always wondered what his arms would look like and feel like bare. And his chest. She felt overwarm of a sudden, but restrained the urge to fan herself. As well, a fluttering sensation overtook her stomach.

They approached his horse and his belongings on the ground. He bent and took a small dagger in a sheath from his pack. "I want to give you this, Lady Seona. I'll teach you how to use it."

"Oh heavens," she whispered. His deadly serious demeanor chilled her heated skin. 'Twas no wonder he was such a skilled guard. "I thank you, but I'm not certain I will be a good warrior."

"You've already proven you have a warrior's instincts." Keegan allowed a small grin to sneak out and she relaxed a bit. "Now you but need the skills. Besides, I'm not expecting you to be a fully-fledged warrior. 'Tis but for self-defense. I'm surprised your father or some other man in your family did not teach you. Do you have a brother?"

"Nay." Her father would never want her to know how to wield a blade. Likely, he would fear she would use it on him.

"You can carry this small *sgian dubh* on the inside of your forearm, beneath your sleeve," Keegan said. "And I'll show you how to draw it quickly."

"Very well. I shall try."

Keegan was right. She must learn how to protect herself, should the need arise. Aside from that, she relished the notion of spending a few minutes with him for knife-wielding instruction.

She glanced back to see that the clansmen had set up another tent, this one for the chief, between where she stood and the rest of their party, giving her and Keegan a bit more privacy. No one seemed to pay them any mind, and her aunt was still focusing all her attention on the handsome guard.

Keegan motioned her to a flat grassy area in front of the horses and small trees. She moved to where he indicated, her attention shifting to the gleaming basket-hilt of the broadsword at his hip. A foot-long dirk hung on his other side, and she wondered if he had more weapons hidden beneath his clothing.

"If you will raise your sleeve, I'll show you how to put the sheath on," he said.

Her face heating, she untied the cuff of her sleeve and raised it a bit to expose her forearm. Aunt Patience would think it unseemly for her to bare her forearm to a man, but he was trying to help her.

He placed the sheathed knife against the inside of her forearm and pulled the straps around.

"Och, you have wee arms. I'm not certain this will fit unless I alter it," Keegan said, eying the sheath. After removing it and kneeling, he took out the knife and worked on the leather, punching a new hole in both of the straps.

She stood two feet away and glanced back to see if she'd been discovered yet. No one was within sight.

Keegan stood. "Now, let's try this again." He held the sheath against her arm and secured the straps, which were much like small belt buckles. "There now." He smiled at his handiwork.

"It fits perfectly," she said, examining the sheath. The well-worn leather felt foreign against the sensitive skin of her inner forearm. "But I cannot possibly take your treasured knife and sheath."

He waved a hand. "'Tis one I wore as a lad and too small for me now anyway. I was but using it for backup."

She was stunned. He was willing to give her a weapon from his youth? There was no telling how many years he had worn this sheath on his arm. It made her feel closer to him. She caressed the nut-brown leather, tracing the worn Celtic knot pattern, then stroked her fingertips over the decorative handle of the knife, featuring a stag.

"Did you carve this?" she asked.

"Nay, my da did. 'Tis from the antler of a stag the former chief killed over twenty summers ago. I was a wee lad then, but I remember them returning from stalking deer. Everyone was excited and happy about the successful hunt."

Though she had never talked with his father, Conall MacKay, beyond a greeting, she'd often seen him at Dunnakeil and knew him to be a friendly, hearty and boisterous man, quick with a laugh but also quick to defend those he loved.

"The knife is beautiful." She was touched by his generosity, but he seemed unaffected that he was giving away personal items he must have treasured for many years. Or was he merely hiding his emotions? His eyes held no regret, only affection, when he observed her. He made her feel as if… she was special.

She swallowed hard and lowered her gaze. No one had ever made her feel special before. No one had ever cared whether she could defend herself or not.

"I've always wanted a weapon," she confessed.

"In truth?"

She nodded, remembering how she used to dream of having a weapon with which to defend herself and her sister during her father's violent rants. Such a thought was blasphemous, she knew, considering she was not honoring her father. But she had never done anything to deserve his wrath, nor had her sister or their poor mother.

"Why?" Keegan asked.

She could not tell him the truth and instead shrugged. "I admire those who are good fighters."

"Well, mayhap you will be a good fighter when I'm through with you." Keegan smiled.

Heavens! Did he expect her to spar as the men did during practice?

"The first thing you need to learn is how to draw the *sgian* quickly." He moved his right hand near his left wrist and, within a blink of an eye, he held a knife in his hand. "Did you see how I did that?"

"Nay." He'd drawn the knife so swiftly, 'twas but a blur.

Keegan returned his knife to its sheath on his left arm, then pulled back his other sleeve to reveal another on the right forearm. "I never want to be without a knife."

"I see."

"Watch. I'll do it slowly so you can see what I'm doing." He gradually moved his right hand toward his left. His fingertips slipped toward the inside of his wrist and tugged the handle. The knife slid out and he palmed the hilt. With the next demonstration, he repeated the movements a bit faster, but still not with the speed he'd first used.

"You try it," he said.

After relaxing her arms for a moment, she lifted them as he'd done. She pulled at the knife within the sheath on her forearm. It would not budge. She tugged harder and the knife slid out smoothly into her hand.

"Aye. Very good." Keegan grinned and a different expression entered his eyes, darkening them. The way his eyes changed amazed her. Sometimes they were pale and bright as the sky on a clear day. Other times, like now, they resembled the sky at twilight.

She wished she knew what he was thinking so she could figure out why his eyes changed so much.

"I'm proud of you," Keegan said. "Now, return it and draw it again. Often in the Highlands, who lives and who dies is determined by who can draw their knife, dirk or sword the quickest."

Her stomach knotted with the thought she had to be quicker than an outlaw warrior. She did as he'd suggested and returned the knife to the sheath.

She yanked it out again, faster this time.

Keegan stood back, crossed his arms over his chest and nodded. "Keep going."

Concentrating on the task instead of Keegan's intriguingly broad shoulders and muscled arms, she repeated the process several times. She was amazed at how she became much swifter and more proficient each time. She smiled. Of course, she wasn't yet as fast as he was, but she likely never would be.

"Och, lass, you have a beautiful smile," Keegan said.

She halted in the midst of returning the knife to its sheath, her hand shaking.

He quickly grabbed her hand. "Careful. Don't cut yourself."

She released the knife, her hands trembling. That's what he did to her... him and his distracting, complimentary words.

He pushed the knife into the sheath and stepped back. He tried to hide his smile but she saw it easily. The heat rushing over her intensified.

He cleared his throat and sobered. "One thing you have in your favor, Lady Seona, is the element of surprise. Most men won't expect you to be carrying such a stealthy weapon. Likely, an attacker won't strike you with a blade. His main objective won't be to kill you immediately." He frowned, his expression turning lethal. "He'll probably try to restrain you or capture you. He might grab you from behind, or he might rush you from the front."

Imagining such things happening to her, she felt the blood drain from her face and a cold chill pass over her.

Keegan halted, eying her. "Did I frighten you?" he asked.

"Nay." She didn't want him to think her a complete ninny. While thoughts of being captured by a barbarous stranger did scare her, 'twas not more than she could handle. She had never been one to faint or grow frantic. Besides, she wished to be strong like

Isobel. She admired her friend greatly for many reasons. "Go on," she told Keegan.

"If some knave gets his dirty paws on you, you'll want to learn how to make him release you so that you can escape. If you injure or kill him in the process, so much the better."

"Heavens," she whispered, unable to imagine killing or seriously injuring a tough, depraved outlaw. But mayhap she could if she learned how.

"Keep your weapon a secret until you can successfully draw and wield it for your benefit," Keegan instructed.

"'Tis a good idea."

"If a man grabs you from behind, he'll probably put one hand over your mouth to muffle your screams. Then, he'll wrap his other arm around you to restrain your arms while lifting you off your feet."

She nodded, imagining how that could happen.

"If your arms are restrained, you have to make sure your hands remain close together so you can draw your knife. Once he is distracted by looking to see if he's been spotted, withdraw the knife and grip it like this." Keegan held one of his own knives in a backward position with the blade pointing toward his elbow. "Once you can move your arm freely, stab back into his groin or gut if possible. You'll have to put some force behind it and stab deep."

She nodded again, her face heating a bit with the mention of stabbing a man in the groin. But he seemed not to notice.

"Don't try to stab through leather armor. 'Tis too tough for the small blade to penetrate," Keegan said. "Make it count because if the first strike isn't deep, he won't be injured and he won't release you. He'll only get angry, and that's when he'll want to hurt you." Keegan frowned darkly as if simply imagining the violence angered him. "If you stab him deep, he'll shove you away from him."

"Aye," she said, realizing she'd have to practice stabbing if she was to get it right.

"If he then comes back for you again, unarmed, turn the knife around and slash at him. If he takes out a knife of his own, flee. In fact, running is your best defense. Only use the knife if you have to."

"I can run," she said.

"Good." Keegan gave a slight grin. "You've made much progress in a short time. I'll teach you more tomorrow."

"Oh." She was a wee disappointed their lesson was over already, but her aunt would be looking for her soon. "I thank you for the knife and for taking the time to instruct me. You're very generous." She glanced toward camp, not wishing to return. She enjoyed talking to Isobel, but her aunt and the maids were tedious and dull, doing naught but complaining. Whereas Keegan was the most fascinating person she'd ever met. Still, she had best bid him good evening lest he think her a wanton.

"Och. Did you see that lovely waterfall across the glen? I just noticed it." Keegan pointed at a distant granite mountain where a generous waterfall sluiced down over rocks for several hundred yards. The snow at the top of the tall mountain was no doubt melting and feeding the stream.

"'Tis beautiful," she said. The idea that Keegan wanted to show her something lovely warmed her heart. "I wish we could go closer."

When Keegan remained silent, she turned back to find his eyes more intense as he stared at her.

"I wish… a lot of things," he murmured in a low and mysterious tone. His charming grin was gone, replaced by a more serious expression.

"What do you wish for?" she whispered.

His blue gaze, far darker now than usual, slid from her eyes to her mouth and back again.

"Seona?" Isobel said, approaching them between the horses and tent. "Your aunt has noticed your absence."

CHAPTER FOUR

Isobel's unexpected presence yanked Keegan back from the brink of temptation. *Saints!* He'd almost told Seona exactly what he wished for—a kiss. He'd hungered to claim her lips for months, but he couldn't do it now. He wanted to kick himself.

Isobel grinned as she approached. "I hope you can forgive me for the interruption, Keegan, but Lady Patience is looking for Lady Seona. Dirk went to tell her we were taking advantage of the privacy of the bushes for… you know."

Keegan nodded. "'Tis not a problem."

When he glanced back at Seona, her face was rose-colored. She was so lovely when she blushed. He wanted to grin but clenched his jaw instead.

"I thank you again for your generosity," Seona told him as she moved toward Isobel.

Keegan gave a brief bow. "My pleasure."

Watching the lass walk away, he regretted not making use of the brief amount of private time they'd had together and stealing a kiss.

"'Slud," he muttered. Nay, he should never kiss her. He turned away to stare at the waterfall in the distance. The natural beauty of it only made him think about Seona and how he wished she was still by his side. He'd treasured watching the wonder and delight on her face as she'd looked at it. She had wished to go closer to it, and he was more than willing to take her. But that was impossible at the moment. Just as impossible as the two of them being together.

Kissing her would only make him yearn for her more. And that would be of no benefit to him.

Truth was... Seona could never belong to him the way Isobel belonged to Dirk. His chest ached with regret.

"Are you well?" A deep voice came from behind him.

Keegan turned to find Dirk standing there. "Aye."

"Were you doing what I think you were doing with Lady Seona?" Dirk asked. Was he teasing Keegan? 'Twas a rarity.

"Depends on what you were thinking. I didn't kiss her, if that's what you mean."

"Och. Well, you're not as much of a rogue as I thought." Dirk gave a slight grin.

"I wanted to," Keegan confessed. "Damned badly. But that would've been madness. She's a lady and her father will never approve of me."

Dirk frowned, considering Keegan closely for a long moment. "You want... to marry her?" he asked as if realization was suddenly dawning.

"Of course. 'Twould be my fondest dream."

Dirk raised a brow. "When did you decide this?"

Keegan shrugged. "Months ago. I know it seems daft, considering I hadn't actually talked to her much until today. But when you meet the perfect woman for you, you just know somehow. Am I right?"

"Indeed. I respect your honesty. I was not quite so honest with myself when I was falling for Isobel. I thought I was going mad having such feelings for her. But, in truth, 'tis normal. I have never been so happy in my life as I am now." Dirk grinned and glanced back toward camp, most likely hoping to catch a glimpse of his wife.

"I greatly admire what you and Isobel have. 'Tis what I want to share with Seona but..." Keegan shook his head, knowing he was wishing for something he could never attain.

"You never know. Why don't you ask for her hand?"

"Hmph. Everyone has said her father insists she marry a chief or someone with a title and property."

Dirk observed him, his expression serious. "If you truly want her, don't let her go. Isobel was betrothed when I met her, and I was certain she was beyond my reach, too. But 'twas not the case.

Sometimes you must take a chance."

Keegan nodded, though he didn't know how he could marry Seona if her father wouldn't permit him to. What would happen if Keegan stole her away? Although kidnapping a bride was common practice among some clans, surely her father and his men would hunt Keegan down like an outlaw if he dared such a thing. Once he met Chief Murray, he'd know more about how to deal with him.

"I thank you for your advice, cousin."

Dirk nodded and slapped him on the shoulder. "'Tis time to eat."

They headed back toward the center of the camp.

Keegan had been hungry earlier, but after almost kissing Seona, a different sort of hunger gnawed at him. He craved a taste of her beautiful lips. She would be as sweet as flower nectar. He had no doubt of it. She certainly smelled sweet, he'd noticed as he'd strapped the knife sheath on her arm. He'd had a wild impulse to bury his nose in her hair and breathe her in.

As they all sat or stood around the camp, eating roasted rabbit, grouse and bannocks, he tried not to stare at Seona. Suspecting that anyone who caught him observing her would see his desires written clearly on his face, he only slipped a glance her way now and then.

Because she sat by her aunt, she seemed equally determined to avoid eye contact with him.

A quarter hour later, darkness descended a bit more and Dirk approached him. "We'll stay here while 'tis dark and allow the ladies to sleep and the horses to rest. Half the men will guard the first part of the night, then the rest will guard the second half. We'll leave early in the morn, just after daybreak. I'm concerned Haldane and his band of outlaws will attack again."

"As am I," Keegan said, watching Seona and her aunt disappear inside the tent with the maids. At the last second, Seona cast a quick glance his way and gifted him with a wee smile. Joy burst through his chest.

Saints! He was tempted to crawl in after her. To hades with her aunt.

"Are you too distracted to guard?" Dirk asked.

"Nay," Keegan said, perhaps a bit too loudly. He wanted to kick his own arse for allowing Dirk to see he'd been distracted for a few seconds. No one had ever questioned his ability to perform his duty.

"If you are, 'tis naught to worry over." Dirk gave an almost imperceptible grin. "I ken how that can be. Take the night off."

"I'll guard the ladies' tent."

Dirk nodded. "I'm certain you will protect Lady Seona better than anyone else."

Keegan was a bit ashamed he'd allowed a lass to ensnare his attention so completely that it was obvious to the chief, and likely everyone else. But what could he do about it? He'd already tried banishing her from his mind. It didn't work. The more he told himself not to think of her, the more he thought of her.

The men allowed the fire to burn down to coals. With several lanterns around the perimeter of the camp, the guards could see if anyone approached.

Dirk disappeared inside his tent with Lady Isobel. Keegan couldn't deny he was envious they got to sleep together when he could not... ever... sleep with Seona. How could he live never knowing what it would be like to hold her close and sleep with her the whole night through?

***

In the darkness inside the tent, Seona pulled back the sleeve of her smock and placed her hand around the knife and sheath on her forearm. She'd been careful to hide it from Aunt Patience.

The leather sheath still held Keegan's distinctive and entrancing male scent. The knife was like the man himself, sharp and lethal but also protective and comforting. He wanted to provide a way for her to protect herself when he wasn't there. Her heart warmed.

But she didn't want to think about him no longer being there, nor did she truly want to go home. Who would brighten her days with a single glance? No one had Keegan's smiling blue eyes. Every time she looked at the summer sky, she would see his face. How would she survive? She couldn't imagine life without him.

He had been within close proximity for many months. How could he not know how important he was to her? Of course, she didn't have the courage to tell him. It would mislead him into thinking there could be something more between them than was actually possible. She would give anything not to be a lady at the moment... or the daughter of Chief Murray. Of course, the position came with certain privileges, but also heavy restrictions.

She pulled the sleeve of her smock over the knife sheath again. Her aunt could never see it. She would not approve of Seona carrying a weapon. Nor would she approve of Keegan teaching her how to use it, especially in private. Seona smiled, imagining Keegan giving her another knife-wielding lesson on the morrow.

***

Haldane MacKay crouched behind gorse bushes next to Donald McMurdo and watched the lanterns flickering in the distance around the MacKay camp. "You kill Dirk and I'll snatch Lady Seona," Haldane whispered.

He could easily see the four tents and eight or nine guards patrolling the area. Half of them were obviously sleeping now so they could take a later watch. Dirk was canny to bring so many guards, but Haldane could be equally shrewd.

He glanced at the dark blue sky, seeing a scattering of wispy clouds, a full moon and a few faint stars. Summer evenings had a long period of gloaming and it would not be full dark for a while. Although Haldane was not known for his patience, he'd had to learn the virtue over the past several months since his infuriating older brother had taken over Castle Dunnakeil.

Once Dirk was dead and Haldane had Lady Seona in his possession, he would have everything he wished for—he would be chief of Clan MacKay and Seona would be his wife, as she was always meant to be.

"I like your plan," McMurdo said, his voice raspy. His black eyes intensified in the dimness. "When I kill him, you will give me what I asked for, aye? What your father promised me."

"Indeed. The tomb in the church will be yours." Haldane still didn't understand why McMurdo was so obsessed with being buried in Balnakeil Church. Sane or not, the man was a devious assassin. His long gray hair and pock-marked, wrinkled skin said nothing about his lethal cunning. The man was like a well-used, ancient sword—scarred and worn but he could still easily get the job done. At least, Haldane hoped he could. McMurdo had not yet succeeded at killing Dirk, despite a couple of attempts. The first time, everyone had thought Dirk was dead, but then he'd surfaced twelve years later. Haldane didn't want that happening again.

"I want to see his dead body."

McMurdo grunted. "How about his head on a platter?"

"Even better." So long as Dirk was well and truly dead,

Haldane didn't care.

Nolan MacLeod slipped up and knelt beside him. "What's the plan?"

"I'll take two men with me and head toward the tent where Lady Seona is sleeping," Haldane said. "You go with McMurdo and kill the guard nearest Dirk's tent so McMurdo can kill the bastard inside."

"What about Lady Isobel?" Nolan asked.

"What about her? I don't care." Haldane knew Nolan had a bad itch for Isobel. The word was he'd almost raped her, but the lady had bashed him on the head and knocked him out. Haldane could understand his need for revenge, but he didn't want Nolan botching the whole attack because he wanted retribution. Nolan certainly had no feelings for Isobel, not like Haldane had for Seona.

"What if she is carrying your brother's heir?" Nolan asked.

Hell, he hadn't considered that. If she was carrying a male bairn, that child would inherit the baron title and become chief when he grew to manhood. "She'll have to die, too, then."

"Nay. I want her," Nolan said, his eyes gleaming like those of a madman. That didn't faze Haldane. Several of his men verged on madness.

"Have her then, but make sure you kill her when you're done with her. I don't want any of Dirk's spawn running around."

Nolan grinned.

"But you'll have to help McMurdo kill Dirk first. Isobel is in the same tent."

"My pleasure."

"I don't need his help," McMurdo grumbled, glaring at Nolan. "I can kill that whoreson with my bare hands."

"I know you can," Haldane said. "But use your dirk. I always thought it would be fitting that Dirk be killed with the weapon he's named after." Haldane snickered.

A half hour later, Haldane, Finlay and Gil slipped closer to the camp. Gil was the best archer he'd ever seen.

"Take out that guard, the one closest to us," Haldane whispered to him.

Gil hesitated. "I cannot do that. He's my cousin."

"Do you think I give a damn? Dirk is my brother and I'd kill him if I had half a chance." Haldane narrowed his eyes, observing the tent Lady Seona, her aunt, and their maids had disappeared into earlier. Keegan stood in front of it, then paced back and forth. "Looks like I'm going to have to kill my cousin, as well."

"But you hate Keegan. I've never had a quarrel with my cousin. We got on good last time I saw him."

"If you can't do the job I'm paying you for, I'm kicking you out."

Gil had been Haldane's friend for years, but he was an annoying whiner at times. He needed a fierce kick in the arse.

"You've never paid me," Gil said.

"I didn't let you starve this winter, did I?" Haldane demanded in a harsh whisper.

Gil shook his head.

"Besides, I will pay you and everyone who's helped me when I'm chief and wealthy. I'll make you my sword-bearer. You'll have a generous income."

Gil's eyes widened. Even in the near darkness Haldane could tell he was mulling that over. "Come. Let's move closer. Once you kill one of the guards, the others may be alerted. I want to be able to make it to Seona's tent."

Haldane hunched low and crept through the bushes, Gil and Finlay behind him. McMurdo, Nolan and another man were stealing into the camp from the other side. The rest were entering from the east.

Haldane crouched again and peered from behind the bush. "There now, the guard closest to us is Balfour. No kin of yours, is he?"

"Nay."

"When I give the signal, you shoot him."

"Aye." Gil knelt, nocked the arrow and drew back his bow string.

"After you kill him, shoot Keegan next."

CHAPTER FIVE

Seona awoke to men yelling, a shock of alarm ringing through her. At first, she didn't know where she was, then she remembered being inside a tent. She sat up, listening to the running footsteps, curses and swords clanging outside. Cold fear slid through her. What on earth? Had Haldane attacked? She fingered the knife hidden on her forearm, wondering if she should pull it out.

Beside her, Aunt Patience bolted upright. "What's happening?"

"I know not. I think 'tis an attack." Seona crawled forward to peer through the tent flap.

Two blades clashed nearby, sparks popping off them in the near darkness. She could only see the outline of two shadowy figures.

"Haldane!" It was Keegan's voice. "I'll kill you. Have no doubt of it."

God protect us, Seona prayed silently.

More men joined them in battle.

Seona drew back. "Everyone, wake up," she whispered loudly, grabbing her *arisaid* to wrap about her. "We may have to flee."

"Lord, help us. Is it a battle?" one of their maids asked. Someone was sobbing and another of them was praying aloud.

"Aye. Haldane and his band of outlaws have attacked. We must dress and ready ourselves to run," Seona whispered.

A knife blade sliced through their tent's fabric over the maids' heads. Her aunt and the maids screamed as they scrambled toward the opposite side, a couple of them crawling over Seona.

"Remain calm," she said, pulling her legs free of them.

She couldn't draw her knife now or she might inadvertently cut one of the other women in such close quarters. They sat frozen in fear as they listened to the sounds outside—men's angry yells, footsteps thumping, blades clashing.

Someone burst into the dark tent. Seona's heart felt as if it rammed up into her throat.

The maids shrieked and scrambled backward.

"'Tis me, Keegan. Come, all of you."

A couple of the maids were crying in earnest now, one of them frantic.

"Calm yourselves!" Keegan commanded. "Lady Seona, where are you?"

"Here," she said, regaining her breath.

He took her hand and dragged her from the tent. She saw MacMillan and a couple more guards standing outside, holding horses.

"Wait!" Seona said. "I have not—"

"There is no time." Keegan lifted her onto the bareback horse as if she weighed no more than a child, then, grabbing the reins, he leapt on behind her. He wrapped a strong arm around her and kicked the horse into a gallop.

"What about Aunt Patience?" she asked, turning and attempting to look back, but she couldn't see beyond his shoulder.

"The guards will see to her and the maids' safety. Dirk told me to slip you away from the battle and hide you."

Why? Seona wanted to ask, but found it almost impossible to hold a conversation with the horse galloping at such great speed, and her frantic heartbeat keeping the same rhythm. They flew along a trail, opposite the way they'd come earlier that day. Keegan's arm around her near squeezed the breath from her. But she felt safe.

Moonlight reflected off a wide, sparkling burn that flowed alongside the trail. After a few minutes, Keegan slowed the horse to a trot but kept going. Unexpectedly, he guided the horse into a copse of trees. The fresh scent of pine was strong. The horse walked deeper, his breath wooshing in and out.

After a few hundred yards, Keegan stopped the horse and turned it about. They listened to the silence. No hoof beats approached.

"Were you injured in the fighting?" she asked.

"Nay."

"Did you kill Haldane?"

"Hmph. He fled like a frightened rat." Keegan's arm tightened around her again, tugging her back against the hard wall of his chest. "He's trying to steal you away," Keegan whispered, his warm breath stirring her hair.

"What on earth? Why?"

"He said you were meant to be his."

A shiver of revulsion passed over Seona. The last person on earth she would want to marry was Haldane. "'Tis because of the marriage contract the MacKays had with my father."

"That cannot be the only reason. I'm thinking he's greatly smitten with you."

She was not flattered. Haldane was like a half-grown feral mongrel. She had always hated the way he'd leered at her at the high table or across the great hall. That was before he'd left the clan. Now that he'd turned outlaw, she was certain he'd be a hundred times worse.

"I thought he was trying to kill his brother," she said.

"Aye, that as well. Two birds with one arrow." Keegan leapt down, then helped her dismount. He tied the horse's reins to a small tree. "I want to move you away from the horse in case he makes a noise and alerts the outlaws."

"Very well," she whispered.

Keegan lifted Seona, one arm beneath her knees and one at her back. She gasped in surprise, but he ignored her and carried her a few yards away. His warmth felt wonderful against her in the chill night air. When he stopped, he continued to hold her close, as if shielding her with his body.

His fierce protectiveness made her chest ache with tenderness. "I thank you for keeping me safe," she whispered.

"You're welcome."

She wanted to say more, but could think of naught that didn't sound daft. She would have to keep her thoughts to herself and focus on the danger of the situation. The leaves of the trees provided darkness and cover.

"Is Chief Dirk safe?" she asked, distracting herself from how Keegan's powerful body affected her in a strangely exciting way.

"I know not, but I'm certain he can take care of himself and Isobel." He turned his head this way and that, on high alert, listening for any enemy who might approach.

The silence stretched out and, with each moment that passed, she became more and more aware of Keegan's fiery body supporting her.

"I can stand on my own two feet, you know," she whispered.

"I thought you were barefoot."

"I am, but what of it? You certainly cannot hold me the entire time."

"I don't mind." His deep whisper in her ear was sensual and seductive.

Her rebellious body responded to his in shocking ways. Tingles moved from her breasts downward. The only time she'd ever felt like this was when she thought of Keegan in scandalous ways, such as when she imagined him kissing her.

"I insist," she said, fighting down her disturbing reaction to him. "You cannot wield a sword while holding me."

"Och. Very well, then."

When he lowered her to the ground and released her, she missed his warmth. His body had obviously been overheated from the exertion of battle. She tried to ignore the pine needles prickling her feet and the spongy wet ground beneath them.

They stood in silence for a few minutes. An owl hooted in the distance. How far were they from camp?

Seona shivered, her teeth chattering, and she realized she wore naught but an ivory linen smock. Though the material was somewhat thick, the night air was cool. She'd not had time to belt her *arisaid* about her before Keegan dragged her from the tent. Besides, some of the maids had been sitting on it, and she'd had to leave it behind.

"Och, Lady Seona, you're cold."

In the near darkness, the rattle of Keegan's belt startled her. What was he about? A moment later, a warm wool plaid surrounded her like a blanket. He pulled it around her and attached it beneath her chin with the brooch that had been fastened at his shoulder.

He had disrobed for her? Her face heated. "I cannot take your plaid."

"Aye, you can and you will. I'll not have you freezing to death on my watch." He belted his weapons about his waist again.

"I wouldn't freeze this time of year." Though it was May, late spring in the far north of Scotland was much cooler than it was further south, where she'd grown up.

Keegan still wore a long linen shirt that reached almost to his knees, but to have taken his plaid… she couldn't be so stingy.

"We could share this plaid," she suggested.

She could only see an outline of him and the dim glow of his shirt in the night, but somehow she knew he was observing her, or trying to.

"I'm plenty warm," he murmured, his voice husky. He withdrew his sword from the scabbard and turned his head. "Tell me if you hear anything."

"Very well." She knew he needed to concentrate on listening for enemies, but the time they had alone was rare and precious. After several minutes of peaceful silence, she felt it safe to whisper, "Earlier, you were going to tell me what you wished for." She but wanted to know more about him, to learn who he was on the deepest level.

He turned to face her, his breathing close. She perceived his outline in the dim moonlight, but not his features or expression.

"I shouldn't tell you," he finally said.

"Why not?" Now, her curiosity was piqued. She wished to know all Keegan's secrets.

"I'm not sure you would like it," he murmured in a warning tone.

"Why? Do you wish to be an outlaw?" Could he have such shocking aspirations?

He gave a brief, low chuckle. "Nay."

"What, then?"

After a long, tense moment of silence, he stepped closer and placed a hand on her shoulder, then ran it into her unbound hair. He drew nearer still, his breath teasing the skin of her face.

"Seona," he whispered against her forehead, then kissed her there. "This." Slowly, he kissed her temple, her cheek. "This is what I wish for."

All the breath left her and she could not draw more in. The kisses on her face created tingles that spread quickly throughout her entire body.

Lightly, he brushed his warm, tempting lips over hers. Her

eyes slid closed for surely she had drifted into a dream world.

With his thumb, he gently stroked her face and jaw line. His lips were firm, but at the same time, soft and smooth. The short, rough whiskers on his chin scratched against her tender skin, but it wasn't painful; it excited her and made her realize how very masculine he was.

His insistent lips compelled her to return his kiss, though she knew not how. She had never been kissed before, but she followed her instincts, pressing her lips against his and mimicking his movements.

"Mmm," he breathed and kissed her more firmly. His lips nipped at hers, snatching her thoughts and scattering them to the breeze. When he touched the tip of his tongue to her lips, as if he wanted to taste her, a sound escaped her before she could stop it. *Heavens!* His tongue felt wicked. She wished he would do it again.

Trying to figure out how kissing worked, she parted her lips. He growled and darted his tongue into her mouth. That sultry move stole the strength from her legs, but she held on around his neck. Her breasts and other, lower, parts of her body tingled with a strange magic. What was happening to her?

Keegan tore his mouth away from hers. "Listen." He turned his head toward the north.

She held her breath, trying to listen. With her heartbeat thumping in her ears, she could perceive naught.

Finally, she heard it. In the distance, horses' hooves pounded, louder and louder with each moment that passed.

"Someone's coming," Keegan whispered, putting her behind him. The sword in his hand glinted in the faint moonlight, straining through the leaves overhead.

She was glad he'd been paying attention to their surroundings during the kiss, for 'twas almost as if she'd been transported to another world, one where sensation ruled. Her hands trembled as she clutched onto the back of his shirt. Not from fright, but because his kiss had disturbed her so much.

The quick hoof beats drew closer and closer, making her heart thump at the same frenzied pace. Were the outlaws searching for them? She peered around his shoulder.

Two horses galloped past the wood along the narrow trail, a hundred feet away, their silhouettes a dark blur against the moon's reflection in the flowing stream.

A woman screamed.

"Who is that?" Seona asked, icy fear slicing through her.

A war cry sounded not too far away. Horses neighed.

"What the devil? Get on my back," Keegan commanded, then leaned down in front of her.

"Nay. Why?"

"Do it, Seona!" he growled low. "'Tis Lady Isobel. I have to help her, but I'm not leaving you here."

Isobel? Saints!

Seona climbed onto his broad back, holding onto his shoulders. He wrapped one arm around her thigh and, with his other hand, he carried his unsheathed sword. Moving nimbly, he ran through the wood past his horse, weaving among the trees. With the rough pace, she jolted against his back. She could not believe his fearsome strength.

On the trail just beyond the trees, blades clashed and clanged. The silhouettes of two warriors in a sword dual moved this way and that.

"Nay!" a woman yelled. "Cease!"

"Indeed, that is Isobel," Seona whispered, the sensation of chilled water flowing in her veins.

"Leave him alone, you bastard!" Isobel yelled.

"Go, Isobel! Run!" a man commanded. Though enraged, his voice sounded familiar. Dirk?

Aye, he was one of the men fighting, yelling scathing Gaelic insults and curses at his opponent.

CHAPTER SIX

Quietly, Keegan carried Seona on his back through the trees and closer to the edge of the dark forest. Loud shouts from the two warriors and the clangs of their blades filled the night air.

"'Tis Chief Dirk, fighting with someone," Seona whispered into Keegan's ear.

"Aye." But he couldn't tell which of the outlaws challenged him. Dirk could take care of himself, but protecting Isobel while fighting would be much harder. "Wait right here, behind this tree," Keegan whispered, lowering Seona to the ground next to a larger tree. Hopefully, wearing his dark plaid, she would be well-hidden behind the trunk. He wanted her close-by so he could protect her should the outlaw flee Dirk's wrath. "I'll get Isobel."

"Have a care."

"Aye."

Keegan rushed to the perimeter of the wood. He didn't wish to distract Dirk, but he had to be sure Isobel remained safe, especially since she hadn't run like Dirk had ordered her to. Stubborn woman. She stood thirty feet behind Dirk, well out of range of the two fighters, but still too close for his comfort.

"Isobel. 'Tis me, Keegan," he said, still hidden in the shadow of the trees, though likely his pale linen shirt could be seen in the moonlight. "Come."

She gasped and sent a quick glance his way. "Nay. We must help Dirk!"

Keegan crept closer, unable to recognize Dirk's opponent in

the low light. "Who is he fighting?"

"Nolan MacLeod."

The bastard who had tried to rape Isobel last year? Keegan had never met him, but he'd seen him from a distance.

"Dirk can handle him. Come into the wood where you can hide with Seona."

In the next instant, Nolan's sword flew into the air and he fell backward, yelling and grabbing his throat. He sprawled down the embankment, his head almost in the water of the stream. After a few moments, he grew silent and still.

Dirk's loud breaths were the only sounds in the darkness. Isobel ran to him and he drew her close with one arm.

"Are you injured?" she asked.

"Nay," Dirk said. "Are you?"

"Nay."

"Thank the saints. When he snatched you from the tent and took off, I thought my life was over." Dirk pulled Isobel tighter against him and kissed her.

Keegan moved out of the tree line and closer to the unmoving body of Nolan MacLeod. An ugly dark gash marred his throat.

"Is the bastard dead?" Dirk asked.

Nolan's eyes gleamed wide and sightless in the moonlight. "Aye. Looks that way."

"Justice is served," Dirk said.

"Indeed," Isobel agreed, staring solemnly at the dead man's body. "I wanted to kill him myself but... he was too strong for me."

"Nay, 'twas my duty and responsibility," Dirk said. "Any other whoreson who hurts you—or even tries to—will meet the same fate."

Dirk could have lost his beloved wife so easily tonight. He had to be relieved to finally be rid of the MacLeod knave. Keegan could only imagine how he must have felt when Isobel was seized. 'Twas the same gut-wrenching feeling he would have if someone kidnapped Seona. Keegan strode back into the wood and found her where he'd left her, wrapped in his plaid and standing behind the tree.

"All is well now. Nolan MacLeod grabbed Isobel and made off with her, but Dirk killed the blackguard. Neither Dirk nor Isobel is hurt."

"'Tis good news. I would like to see Isobel," Seona said, excitement evident in her tone. "What of Haldane?"

"I know not yet. Come." After sheathing his sword, Keegan lifted Seona into his arms and carried her through the trees. Though he would never tell her, he was enjoying the sensation of carrying her slim, lithe form in his arms. Once he emerged onto the trail, he set Seona onto her feet but stood between her and Nolan's dead body. She didn't need the additional scare.

"Och. I see what happened to your plaid, then," Dirk said in a light tone.

"Aye. I am ever the gentleman." Keegan gave a mock courtly bow.

"I'm not certain of that, but you are generous." Dirk grinned. "Where's your horse?"

"Hidden in the trees. I'll go retrieve him."

While Dirk guarded the women, Keegan returned to the forest for Curry.

A few minutes later, they were all mounted and traveling slowly through the dimness, Keegan's horse behind Dirk's. The faint light of dawn gleamed over the dark mountains and white morning mist floated from the burn.

Thankfully, the echo of blades had gone silent and Keegan hoped each member of the MacKay party was unhurt. He wanted to ask Dirk if they'd lost any men, but he and Isobel were sharing a kiss up ahead. Far be it from him to interrupt, but their actions made him crave another taste of Seona.

Her innocent kiss had completely seduced him. From the first time he'd seen her last autumn, her full, bow-shaped lips had driven him mad. He'd been fantasizing about kissing her for months, and now that he knew how delicious her kisses were, he yearned for more. *So much more.*

Those two minutes had been the most stunning of Keegan's life. He had to find a way to keep her.

Now, he held her slender form with one arm around her midsection. Her curvy arse pressing against his groin was even more tempting than the floral scent emanating from her long, glossy hair. Every aspect of her lured him, but he managed to restrain himself from brushing his lips across her ear. For the moment, simply holding her close and knowing she was safe was enough.

He focused on guiding the horse along the side of the burn toward camp.

Dirk stopped and waited for Keegan to catch up. "I hope the guards have run the rest of the outlaws through," Dirk said.

"Aye. Do you ken if any in our party was killed?"

"Nay, I don't."

A horse nickered nearby. Halting, Keegan snatched his sword from the scabbard and Dirk did the same. Keegan's gaze searched the vicinity for the rider. He detected no other movements. The animal dropped his head and continued picking grass.

"Nolan's horse," Dirk said.

Keegan eyed the animal in the faint light of dawn. The pale gray horse looked familiar, although scrawnier than the last time he'd seen it. "He may have been riding it, cousin, but 'tis one the outlaws stole from Dunnakeil last winter."

"Indeed?" Dirk asked.

Since his cousin had only just arrived in Durness last November, he was not yet familiar with their horses. "He's near starved it to death."

"Aye. Any man who mistreats women and horses deserves what Nolan got," Dirk muttered.

"Agreed." Keegan leapt down and took the horse's bridle, then, after he was mounted again behind Seona, led it back toward camp.

As the light grew brighter, visibility was not improved for the thick haze gleamed white, giving their surroundings a mystical quality. It seemed unreal, just as it had to kiss Seona in the wood. Like a dream. One he never wanted to wake up from.

"Chief!" a man yelled from the depths of the mist. They halted. A guard named Boyce appeared.

"Aye?" Dirk responded.

"Are any of you hurt?" The brawny man's dark gaze skimmed over them.

"Nay. We're well," Dirk said. "Did everyone in our party survive?"

"Aye. Three men have injuries and are being patched up."

Dirk nodded. "Were any outlaws killed?"

"Aye. One I've never seen before. The rest fled."

"Make that two. I killed Nolan MacLeod."

"'Tis good news, m'laird. We're well rid of the outlaw."

"What of Haldane and McMurdo?" Keegan asked.

"Escaped." Boyce lowered his bushy dark brows.

"We'll get them." Keegan was determined to stop Haldane from attaining either of his goals. To Keegan, Dirk was like a brother, and the clan needed him as the chief. As for Seona, she was growing more precious to Keegan each day. He wished he could've found a way to talk to her months ago. But he'd thought there was no hope for anything between them. Now, the time they had left together grew short.

"I only regret we didn't take them down before we started on this journey with the women," Dirk said in a low voice.

Keegan nodded, feeling the same intense concern.

"Send three men to bury Nolan MacLeod's body in the wood and mark the grave with stones. But first, search him and bring his weapons and possessions to me. I'll make sure his brother gets them," Dirk told the guard.

"Aye, m'laird." Boyce bowed and hastened back toward camp.

"I'll let Torrin MacLeod know where his brother is buried," Dirk said. "I'd want to know if it was my brother."

"Aye," Keegan said. Although he didn't know the MacLeod chief well, he didn't think the man would be angered that his outlaw brother was killed at Dirk's hand. In fact, he should've expected it, given what Nolan had tried to do to Isobel.

The four of them rode into camp where the men were packing up the tents and readying everyone to travel. Keegan was disappointed that his ride with Seona was over. Holding her close to him was one of the best feelings on earth. He dismounted, then lifted her down from the horse. Her dark blue gaze met his in the faint dawn light and her lips curved up in a tiny smile that bewitched him. Damn, how he wanted to kiss her again.

Her haggard-looking aunt appeared and dragged Seona away. She glanced back at him once, her expression dejected. He wanted to chase after them, but that would be daft. His chest ached. He led the recovered horse toward one of the two grooms traveling with them and instructed him to give the gaunt animal extra oats and also check it over for injuries.

Glancing down, Keegan realized he was still only half dressed, though he was fully covered. Hopefully, Seona would return his plaid after she put on her own clothing. The men were sure to tease him about losing his plaid.

Behind him, a man roared as if in pain. His hand flying to his sword hilt, Keegan spun around expecting a surprise attack. But no one moved. "What the devil?"

"Rebbie cauterized Marston's badly bleeding wound," Dirk said nearby.

Keegan finally noticed the injured guard, lying on the ground beyond several more men who either stood watching or helped hold him down. "I hope he will recover quickly." Keegan accepted a cold bannock from their cook, Oran, a tall hefty man with a short gray beard and a bald head. "I need another bannock for Lady Seona."

Oran nodded and handed him one. Keegan headed toward the bushes where most of the women were gathered. Apparently, Seona was behind a bush, dressing, with the help of her maids.

"Halt right there, Master Keegan," Lady Patience said, her critical glance darting down his shirt-clad body. Aye, he knew very well he was not dressed properly, but at least his private parts were concealed. Besides, it could not be helped. He'd needed to give Seona his plaid for warmth. They were in the wild Highlands and had just survived an ambush. Men often threw off their bulky plaids to fight more easily in battle.

Keegan held up the bannock. "Lady Seona has not yet broken her fast."

Lady Patience grabbed the oat cake from his hand. "I'll give it to her."

Annoyance drove through him. "I thank you." He gave a mock bow, but waited where he was.

"That will be all," Patience said, with a flick of her hand.

His annoyance grew into full blown irritation and he crossed his arms over his chest. Obviously, he wasn't a laird, but neither was he a servant. "Lady Seona was cold, and I allowed her to borrow my plaid. Do you ken if she's finished with it?"

Lady Patience narrowed her eyes and hastened behind the bush. After a few moments, she returned, holding his plaid between her thumbs and forefingers as if it contained vermin. Grinding his teeth, he snatched it from her and strode away. He wanted to call her a vile name, but somehow restrained himself. The lady had been like a thistle pricking his arse all winter, glaring at him when he merely glanced Seona's way.

Somehow, he had to catch Seona away from her again and

give her another lesson in knife fighting. And 'haps steal another kiss. Anticipation rushing through him, he suppressed a grin.

As he belted his plaid into place, Dirk approached him at a determined pace. "We have a problem."

Keegan tensed, his attention focused. "What is it?"

"The coins are gone," Dirk growled in a hushed tone.

Keegan frowned. "Which coins?"

"I told you about the money I was going to pay Lady Seona's father for breaking the contract he had with my father. 'Twas a large amount." Dirk lowered his voice further. "Five thousand merks."

"Hell. One of the outlaws must have stolen it. Was it on Nolan's body?"

"Nay. I asked the guard who brought his weapons to me. The bag of coins was in my tent, but when I took off after Nolan and Isobel, the money was left unguarded." Dirk released a long, frustrated breath. "Now what am I going to pay Chief Murray with?"

Keegan thought for a moment, but had no ready answer. They were too far away from Castle Dunnakeil now to return and get more money. Nothing else they carried with them would be as valuable, beyond the horses. "Mayhap you won't need to pay him," Keegan suggested.

"Well... nay, I don't have to pay him. 'Twas only an act of goodwill to keep peace between our clans."

"'Haps the horse will be enough," Keegan said, motioning toward the finest horse to ever come from the MacKay stables.

Dirk shrugged, then eyed Keegan. "Or... if you ask for Lady Seona's hand and he agrees, no payment will be necessary. In fact, you'll receive her dowry."

A flash of excitement lit within him. 'Twas what Keegan yearned for more than anything. And he didn't even care if she came with a dowry. "If only I could be so lucky."

"Isobel and I will go with you to the Murrays'. 'Haps we can help convince her father."

"'Twould mean the world to me, cousin." Keegan smiled and shook Dirk's hand, a thrill of exhilaration moving through him that he might have a chance with Seona. He didn't think she would be opposed to marrying him. Of course, he hadn't asked her. 'Twould have been premature. But after that kiss, and the sweet but sensual way she responded, he was convinced she felt as drawn to him as he was to her.

He had to find out for certain.

***

Haldane MacKay rode north across the moor as if the devil himself chased him. Although Dirk MacKay was not half as fearsome as a devil, he had a large force of men with him. More than Haldane had. That was why he hadn't succeeded in his mission.

He hungered for revenge so badly he could hardly sleep at night. That bastard, Dirk, had murdered his mother, and then taken the castle and chiefdom from his brother. Aiden no longer wanted to be chief, so Haldane would take the responsibility off his hands. 'Twas what his mother and father would've wanted.

He would not rest until Dirk was dead.

Glancing back through the dawn light, Haldane saw only six of his men following. Donald McMurdo was right behind him. Gil and Finlay followed, along with the others. Two were missing. They must have been injured badly or killed.

Haldane paused, allowing the others to catch up.

"Where are MacLeod and Quinn?" he asked McMurdo.

"Nolan MacLeod got into the tent while I was trying to kill Dirk. When he noticed Nolan making off with his woman, he chased after him. That gave me a chance to get the hell out of there."

"You didn't kill Dirk. Furthermore, you ran instead of helping MacLeod. I thought you were an assassin."

McMurdo spat on the ground and narrowed his dark eyes, looking as mean as ever. But Haldane was less than impressed with him at the moment.

"That bastard Dirk is big and a fearsome fighter. I doubt *you* could take him down, laddie," McMurdo said with a smirk. "I'd wager Nolan MacLeod is a dead man about now. Dirk didn't want his woman messed with. If you think I'm risking my life for that MacLeod whoreson, you're wrong."

"Never mind him," Haldane snapped. He was no closer to achieving his objective than he had been yesterday, and now he was minus two men. "What about Dirk? 'Tis your job to kill him if you want payment."

"Aye. I'll kill him." McMurdo nodded confidently. "We'll

catch up to them afore long. They'll be out in the open and exposed for many more miles now."

"I don't want to follow too closely," Haldane muttered, still annoyed that McMurdo hadn't done what he'd promised. But Haldane couldn't kick McMurdo out of the group. He was more experienced than any of them. He'd taught them things over the past few months. And he was the one who could most easily kill Dirk, given his experience. "I've lost two more men. Only seven of us left now. Dirk has almost two dozen."

"Aye, but we ken well how to be canny and wily. Nobody said we had to fight fair."

Haldane nodded. "I like it." He couldn't wait to see what kind of crafty ideas McMurdo had in mind. The old highwayman had lived this long somehow, despite a life of crime. Haldane wanted to be like him, wanted to learn everything he could from him.

"I say we head south again," McMurdo said. "Once the sun burns off the fog, one of the lads can climb the hill just north of their camp to see if the MacKay party has packed up and left. I'm thinking they'll head out with all haste because of the ladies."

The ladies. Aye. Haldane pictured Lady Seona and her lovely dark blue eyes. If only he could've lopped off Keegan's head, he would've had Seona. She'd make a fine wife and lady of Dunnakeil.

Nolan had told him 'twas a long way to Teasairg Castle, where the MacKay party was likely headed. Lady Isobel had grown up there. Haldane and his men would have plenty of opportunities to attack them again. Next time, they'd use a different, more successful strategy.

"I agree. We head south." Haldane glanced at the six men waiting around him, then kicked his horse into a trot.

Something jangled behind him as it fell to the ground. Sounded like a purse of coins. He stopped and turned to see McMurdo dismounting. He grabbed a leather purse from the ground and shoved it into his ragged doublet.

"What is that?" Haldane demanded, riding back.

McMurdo's eyes narrowed and, for a second, he looked ready to run Haldane through. The man was intimidating, but Haldane held the upper hand; he possessed the thing McMurdo wanted most, including gold. The burial tomb in the church.

"Is that gold coins?" Haldane asked.

McMurdo let out a resigned breath. "Gold and silver," he

admitted grudgingly.

"Where did you get it?"

"I found it in Dirk MacKay's tent after he followed MacLeod."

"Let me see." Haldane held out his hand. "Any MacKay money is my money, in truth, for I'm the rightful heir to the chiefdom and barony."

McMurdo glared, his lip twitching in a near snarl, but he handed over the leather pouch. 'Twas heavy and it filled Haldane's palm. He pulled open the drawstring to find it full of gold and silver coins. "Saints! 'Tis a fortune."

McMurdo nodded. "Just a little more than I paid for my burial place in the church."

"Since you turned this over to me, you will still have your beloved tomb. We can use this to hire mercenaries. With more men, we'll be able to take down Dirk and anyone else who gets in our way."

"'Tis a brilliant plan. If you can find skilled mercenaries. Not too many of them in the wilds of the Highlands," McMurdo muttered.

"I'll find men desperate for work. Have no worries."

McMurdo shrugged and mounted.

Haldane was well aware McMurdo would've kept the money a secret, but he had to admit the old man was incredibly lucky and canny to have found it. Now, they but had to catch up to Dirk and his party again. A new plan was forming in his mind.

CHAPTER SEVEN

The MacKay party moved south as quickly as they could without overtiring the horses. Although Keegan was tired and his arse numb, Seona had to be feeling a hundred times worse from the effects of their long journey. They needed to put a lot of ground between themselves and the outlaws and arrive at Teasairg Castle as soon as possible. The only problem was few castles existed in the many miles between Munrick and Teasairg. The MacLeods and the MacKenzies each held substantial amounts of land.

Midafternoon, ominous black clouds crept over the mountains from the west and the breeze picked up.

Dirk glanced back at Keegan. "The sky is looking a wee unfriendly, cousin."

"Aye. 'Haps we can make it to those cliffs ahead before the worst of it hits. That might block most of the wind."

Dirk nodded and called out, "Quicken your pace! Gale storm coming."

The riders kicked their horses into faster trots and gallops. The cliffs looked deceptively close because of their massive size. By the time they neared the cliffs, the sky overhead was black. The fierce wind flung a few raindrops sideways and almost pushed their mounts off the narrow trail. Thankfully, the horses were accustomed to unexpected gales and didn't get overly spooked by the storm.

The drops stung Keegan's face but he ignored them, trying to ride closer to Seona where she was hunched in the saddle, the wind whipping her wool plaid *arisaid*. He'd noticed before 'twas a high quality tight weave that would keep most of the moisture out.

One of the lead horses reared, drawing Keegan's attention to the herd of red deer that tore out and fled by the cliffs.

Within moments, the deer had disappeared from sight. Keegan turned his attention back to Seona, but her black mare had become unruly, tossing her head about, then she bolted off the trail and across the moor.

"Saints," Keegan hissed, kicking his horse into a gallop and following her over the uneven terrain. He prayed she would hold on. After a shouted command at the horse, she hadn't uttered another sound that he could hear above the brutal wind. He was proud to see she leaned low over the horse's neck and held the reins tight.

She was good with horses, but apparently the mare she'd brought with her to Dunnakeil last fall was skittish. If he'd known, he would've let her borrow a different one.

Keegan kept pace about twenty feet behind her. He needed to approach without spooking the daft horse further. Seona's cowl had been blown off her head and her long dark hair whipped out behind her.

"Whoa!" she ordered the horse, which promptly ignored her and continued its panicked run.

Pushing his larger mount harder, Keegan gradually gained on her. "Seona! Come. Get on in front of me," he called, his words whisked away in the chill, punishing wind.

She turned her head, quickly glancing at him. "I cannot!" Then, she focused her attention on trying to get the animal under control. She truly was a skilled rider.

But who knew how long it would be before the moor turned boggy or… Something up ahead caught his attention—a wide stream near overflowing with spring thaw. *Saints!* The horses couldn't jump that. Likely, her horse would stop abruptly and toss her in.

Guiding his horse closer to hers, Keegan placed the reins in one hand and offered his free hand to her. "There's a wide burn up ahead! You can't jump it. Give me your arm. I'll pull you onto my horse."

When she noticed the swollen stream, her eyes widened and

she looked near frantic. Her gaze darting back and forth between him and the burn, she held out her hand toward him.

He grabbed her arm and dragged her from her mare and onto Curry, while her horse kept going. Holding Seona tightly around the waist, he slowed Curry and guided him toward the left and away from the stream. Likely, she wasn't in the most comfortable position, because of his saddle, but at least she was safe.

"Saints, Seona. You scared the devil out of me," he grumbled loudly to be heard over the wind.

"'Twas not my fault," she responded, trying to gather her wildly blowing hair into one hand. Her skin was still pale, but thankfully she hadn't gone to pieces in terror. He admired her strength.

"Nay. Your mare went mad." He glanced about for shelter. They were some distance from the rest of their party now, and he couldn't even see them beyond the hill. Further along, he noticed a rocky outcropping and kneed Curry into a trot, the wind and rain lashing them.

He drew up beside the rocks that appeared stable enough and helped Seona slide to her feet, before he dismounted. He guided her toward the stones which blocked much of the fearsome west wind that pounded them and led Curry behind him. Keegan glanced upward, determining the stone was solid and that nothing would fall on their heads.

Immediately they were out of the wind and rain. He turned back to watch the gale rage across the moor behind them, the grasses, bushes and plants twisting and almost lying flat at times.

"There goes your horse," he said, pointing. Seona's mare was a distant black spot, running along the burn. The animal likely wouldn't calm down until the gale had passed. "We'll recapture her later."

Following his gaze, Seona nodded.

"This is a decent shelter." He was glad to get her out of the wind and rain.

"Aye," she said, her breathing still elevated. Arms wrapped around herself, she shivered and her teeth chattered, though she tried to hide it.

"Come. I'll warm you." He took her into his arms, but he knew it wasn't only the temperature of the chill wind that made her shiver. 'Twas also the waning of the extreme fear she must have felt taking a wild ride on that daft horse, tearing across the countryside. "'Tis all right, lass," he murmured in her ear. "You're safe now."

Her body still trembled, but she nodded. He would do anything to keep her safe. Did she not know that?

His face against her cool damp hair, Keegan closed his eyes and drew in her sweet scent. She felt perfect against him, but he fought down his need to pull her even closer, to feel her body completely aligned with his.

Finally, her shivers diminished and her breathing returned to normal. Reluctantly, he removed his arms from around her and backed up a step. "Better?"

"Aye. I thank you for helping me. I don't know what got into Juliana."

"Juliana?" he asked.

"My mare."

"'Tis a fancy name for a mare," he said, unable to hide his amusement. But his main reason for smiling... he was thrilled she had not been injured.

She grinned, her dark blue eyes gleaming with happiness. *Saints!* He had never seen her look more beautiful.

"Did you know your eyes are the color of bluebells?" he asked.

She glanced away, but her smile widened and her cheeks turned an adorable pink, replacing the earlier paleness. She bit her lip, making him wish he could do the same.

Finally, her eyes met his again. He had the urge to tell her how incredibly beautiful she was, but he feared he might overdo it.

"You are mad to say such things," she said. He barely heard her above the roar of the wind overhead.

He held up his hands in surrender. "I speak the truth."

Seona felt her face burning despite the icy wind, but she forced herself to meet Keegan's gaze. There was so much she wished to tell him, but fear held her back. He was perfect... or he would be perfect for her, at least. Simply gazing into his enchanting sky-blue eyes made her feel happy. And his grin was naught but charm and seduction. Most impressive of all, he was a strong, heroic man who didn't fear anything.

"You are..." What should she say?

He moved his head closer to hear her better, and turned

slightly so one of his ears was near her mouth.

"You are very brave and heroic. You saved my life," she said, finding it easier to talk to him when he wasn't looking directly into her eyes. "Twice."

He pulled back a few inches, his lips twisting into a lopsided grin. "I thank you, m'lady," he said. "I could never allow you to be injured." He shook his head. "Over the past few months, I have wanted to talk to you or... dance with you but... you ken your aunt doesn't like me."

"Nonsense," she said to be polite. Truth was Aunt Patience didn't want her to go near him because she deemed him unacceptable as husband material for Seona.

"Come now, Lady Seona, you ken I speak the truth," he said in a light tone. "Her glares are like sharp blades."

She nodded. "My aunt is much like a guard dog."

"Well, she has a right to be. You're a beautiful *lady* and I'm..." He shrugged. "Just a guard."

She frowned. "You are much more than that."

'Twas obvious he was trying to maintain his pleasant expression, but a hint of sadness crept into his blue eyes that near broke her heart.

He shook his head. "Nay, I fear when it comes to you, Lady Seona, I'm naught but a knave and a rogue. I've hardly been able to concentrate today because of memories of that amazing kiss." After shoving his fingers through his windblown, damp mane, he backed away and stared out at the blowing rain. "I must behave myself," he muttered, as if to himself, but she heard it despite the roaring wind.

She could not take her eyes off him and the stunning passion in his gaze. He was right... completely and unequivocally right. He should never touch her again. She should've never allowed him to kiss her the night before, but she could not have stopped him any more than she could've stopped breathing. Speaking of which, her own breaths were now short and shallow. Her chest ached with the need to be closer to him. To touch him.

His gaze shifted to her. "Hell. Seona, don't look at me like that."

She pressed her eyes closed, the moisture gathering there burning. Why did she feel the urge to cry? 'Twas insanity. She was not normally a very emotional person. She should face facts now—

she could never have Keegan. Even though he had owned her heart for months.

His warm, rough fingers touched her face. Her eyes popped open and she sucked in a sharp, surprised breath.

Standing an inch in front of her, Keegan frowned down at her. "Don't you dare cry."

She shook her head. "I'm not," she said just above a whisper, her throat tight. 'Twas a lie, she knew, even as more tears formed in her eyes. She didn't want to cry and didn't understand why she was. She simply felt overwhelmed and confused by her own surging emotions, added to her earlier fear of the bolting horse. And Keegan's close proximity only made everything more powerful.

When tears spilled from the corners of her eyes, she was mortified and tried to avert her face. Surely, he would think her a bairn.

He held her still and brushed his thumb beneath her eyes, catching her tears.

"Shh." He kissed her forehead, his lips and breath warm and soft on her skin.

Feeling both comfort and excitement, she slipped her hands around his lean torso, her palms pressing against his sides. Moving closer to him and pushing her hands around to his back, she found most of the aching pressure leaving her chest. She could not believe how much she needed him and wanted him.

He held her close, pressing kisses to the top of her head. She laid her head against his chest and listened to his heart pounding in her ear. The appealing scent of him—male, spice and leather—was like a bewitching potion to her senses.

'Twas perfection.

Shortly, a bit of her sanity returned. *Heavens!* What must he think of her, embracing him in such a way? She drew back and glanced up at him.

His heavy-lidded eyes searched hers. She was glad he didn't ask why she'd been crying for she couldn't have answered. Merely that her rampant emotions had gotten the better of her, which almost never happened, and she couldn't let him know the depth of her feelings for him. At the same time, his gaze was so spellbinding, she could think of naught but touching him.

Before she knew what she was about, she lifted her hand and

stroked her fingers along his square jaw, delighting in the prickly golden-brown stubble. She had wondered what it felt like—very masculine and harsh, so unlike her own skin.

She raised her gaze and found his eyes darker than before, the color of the sky near gloaming. She dropped her hand, but he caught it and kissed her palm. His lips and warm breath on her sensitive skin fragmented her thoughts. His gaze held hers with that intense, magnetic force she didn't understand. It compelled her to draw closer to him, and she did.

He leaned forward and placed a sweet kiss on her lips. It surprised her and served as a potent temptation.

Unable to quell her enthusiasm, she lifted herself onto her tiptoes and tilted her chin up, hungering for another kiss like the one they'd shared the night before.

"Saints," Keegan growled then took her mouth. His wicked tongue flicked at her lips and she opened for him, completely ready to devour him. But he did not seem in a hurry as he tempted and taunted her. Barely touching his tongue to hers, then retreating.

A sound escaped her and she was shocked to realize it was halfway between a moan and a needy whine. He gave an answering groan and stroked his tongue inside her mouth. It darted around hers, then swirled.

He hummed a soft sound. "So sweet," he whispered.

Whatever magic possessed her increased with each kiss he placed upon her mouth.

She became aware of strands of his soft hair between her fingers. When had she buried her hands in his hair to hold his head?

He pulled her tightly against his hard body, and she had never felt anything so exquisite. This, combined with his kisses, consumed her thoughts with a fiery, carnal sensation. *Oh saints.* She craved his bare skin against hers. She wanted him to touch and kiss every inch of her.

What was wrong with her?

Keegan was thankful his sporran disguised his body's fierce response to her. He was mad to indulge in such luscious kisses with her, but he could not stop himself. Especially when she made it abundantly clear she wanted more.

She shyly flicked the tip of her tongue against his, stirring his lusts into a boiling caldron. *Mo creach!* She was too innocent for him to kiss this way. He was indeed a rogue, as he'd told her. Yet, he could not get enough of her. He feared he was hooked.

"Thank the saints!" someone said behind him. Keegan spun around to find Rebbie behind them, grinning like a devil. "We thought you'd both perished in the storm."

Keegan stepped away from Seona and glanced beyond Rebbie. The gale had passed and the sun was peeking through the clouds. When had that happened? He knew gales could vanish as quickly as they appeared. But had he been so wrapped up in kissing Seona, he'd ignored their surroundings completely?

'Slud! He was daft.

"Nay," Keegan muttered. "We are well."

"I can see that." Rebbie's dark eyes gleamed with amusement. "Where is Lady Seona's mare?"

"I know not. Last time I saw the mad animal, she was running along the burn." Keegan pointed.

Rebbie nodded and hoisted himself back into his saddle. "We'll find her." He rode down toward the burn and three guards joined him.

"Come. I'll help you mount." Keegan glanced at Seona, not expecting her to look so... arousing. Indeed, she was always beautiful, but now her cheeks were pink, her pupils dilated, and her bow-shaped lips red and moist from his kisses. She looked well-loved but... like she needed more. Aye, he could easily imagine her in his bed, looking just like this, her dark hair mussed, her heavy-lidded gaze silently asking him for more.

Lust and need burned through him.

Her mouth was sweet as a wild summer strawberry. He wanted to consume her utterly. He ground his teeth and forced himself to look away.

She moved toward Curry and waited, avoiding his gaze. Maybe that was for the best. 'Twas when she made eye contact that he got into trouble and did things he shouldn't.

He lifted her to the soft roll of woolen blankets behind his saddle. It provided a good pillion cushion. He then hoisted himself into the saddle in front of her. He would certainly much rather hold her in front of him, but it wouldn't be as comfortable for her. Besides that, he needed his arousal to drain away before they joined the rest of the party, and that wouldn't happen if he was holding her in his arms.

But when she slid her arms around his waist from behind and flattened her hands against his stomach to hold on, another wave of desire surged through him. How he would love to feel her hands smoothing over his bare skin.

Even though his rational mind told him he would never have Seona, something inside him refused to believe it.

He kneed Curry into a trot and guided him across the moor toward where their party must be. The breeze was calm and the sun beamed between the scattering clouds. Glancing across the rolling, heather-covered landscape and toward the burn, he didn't see Rebbie or anyone else. 'Twas too bad the heather was not yet in bloom, for the sight would've been lovely.

Glancing up, he noticed something else. A giant double rainbow spanned across the horizon, one slightly dimmer than the other.

"Och." He halted and turned in the saddle. "Have you ever seen such a bonny rainbow?"

Seona gasped. "Nay. 'Tis very bright."

Even lovelier, at least to Keegan, was Seona's smile as she took in the scenery. She was so beautiful his chest ached. Yet… he knew not how he was going to keep her in his life so that he might see her smile every day.

Facing forward, he urged the horse along at a slower pace. No reason to rush. He wanted to enjoy Seona's arms around his waist a bit longer.

"I can't believe how big the rainbow is," she said behind his shoulder.

"Aye. Are you thinking there's a great pot of gold at the end of it?"

She smiled. "Haps. Or maybe something even better than gold."

He wondered what she was thinking. What would she prize more than gold?

He covered her hands with one of his and stroked her silky smooth skin. An idea occurred to him. He turned. "I no longer trust your horse and I'm thinking you should ride with me for a ways."

"In truth? You are right that Juliana has become unpredictable, but I'm not certain my aunt will agree to the riding arrangement."

"She wants you to be safe, aye?"

"Aye, but…"

Out ahead, their party came into view. They appeared to be gathered around someone sitting on the ground. Who was that?

"I wonder what's happened." His heart rate accelerating, he kneed the horse into a trot. As they approached, he saw that it was Lady Patience sitting on the ground on a plaid blanket.

"Is Aunt Patience hurt?" Seona asked, concern in her voice.

CHAPTER EIGHT

Why was her aunt sitting on a blanket on the wet ground with everyone else standing around, Seona wondered. *Heavens!* Had something bad happened to her during the storm?

Keegan drew up a few feet from their party, moved his leg across in front of him and slid to the ground. Next, he lifted Seona down.

"I thank you," she whispered, savoring one last, brief glance into his eyes.

He gave a deep nod and she hastened away to see what was going on.

"Aunt Patience, what has happened to you?" she asked, bending and taking her hand.

"Me? What about you, lass? I feared your horse would toss you onto the rocks and kill you."

"Nay. I am well, as you can see. Keegan rescued me."

"Thank the heavens." Her aunt spared a halfway kind glance up at Keegan, the first Seona had seen her give him.

"Are you injured?" Seona asked her.

"'Tis my ankle. We dismounted during the gale and I stepped on a rock that rolled. I felt something pop in my ankle, then I fell to the ground."

"Did you break a bone?"

"Nay, Laird MacKay examined it and said 'tis more likely I have sprained it or pulled something." She glanced at Dirk where he stood a few yards away with Isobel.

'Twas good news at least that nothing was broken. "Can you stand?" Seona asked.

"I know not. Can you help me up?"

"Aye." Seona grabbed one of her hands, while Isobel rushed forward and took the other. Patience was not a heavy woman, but it appeared Seona and Isobel were supporting most of her weight. Her aunt winced. "Ow! I think I'll not be able to."

They lowered her to the ground again.

Rebbie and the guards arrived, leading Juliana. Seona was glad to see the mare had calmed herself and was uninjured. But Seona was unsure whether she was ready to ride the horse again. She would have nightmares about that frantic ride across the moor.

"We need to be going," Dirk said, loud enough for everyone to hear.

Members of their party strode forward and mounted. Hugh MacMillan lifted Aunt Patience into her saddle.

"I no longer trust Seona's daft mare," Keegan told Dirk, loud enough for her aunt to hear. "She's going to ride with me."

"She should." Dirk nodded. "'Twould be far safer."

Seona felt her face heat, certain her glaring aunt would protest. But she kept her lips sealed tight, apparently thinking better of opposing the chief. But Seona would likely get an earful later.

***

Sitting behind him with her arms around his waist, Seona enjoyed riding with Keegan several miles south. Despite her weariness, she'd never felt more alive. 'Twas the most enjoyable part of the journey thus far, aside from the stolen kisses. Each time she thought of them, her body heated all over and she hoped no one could tell what she was thinking. The fact that she was riding astride with him so close in front of her didn't help. Her body felt strange and tingly, just as it had during the kisses they'd shared.

Though she tried to keep some distance between them, her hands on the firm muscles of his abdomen and waist constantly made her wonder what he would feel like naked. She shouldn't be having such scandalous thoughts; she certainly never had in the past. But they came to her mind and would not leave her be.

Being held in Keegan's arms was one of the few joys she'd experienced in life. And his kiss was pure decadence.

'Twas true that she was a virgin who had never been kissed

prior to the night before, but now she found herself growing more and more curious about physical relations between men and women. No one had seen fit to educate her about such things thus far. Likely, a lot of naïve young ladies were in the same situation, until their wedding night when they found out first hand. She was not sure whether the bedding would be horrible or enjoyable. She suspected, with Keegan, it could only be enjoyable.

The sky was temperamental all day, but no more gales blew in, thank heavens. They rode into the evening. Huge gray clouds rolled in, bringing an earlier gloaming than usual. On the western horizon, sunset illuminated the clouds in bright pink, orange and violet.

She was thankful when they came upon a group of three thatched-roof stone cottages by a small loch so she could stretch her sore legs.

"We'll have to see if we can stay the night here," Dirk said to Keegan as they dismounted. "I want the women safe inside one of the cottages."

"Aye. I like that idea," Keegan said, helping Seona down.

But who knew if the occupants were friendly? Of course, Highland hospitality dictated that Scots be welcomed, especially a chief and his entourage. She hoped that would be the case this time. She didn't relish sleeping in a tent again.

A few minutes later, the smiling crofters welcomed them to stay the night. They considered it an honor to host a chief, his wife, and the rest of the party.

Oran, the MacKay cook, helped two of the women prepare a huge meal from pooled resources. The crofter even cast his net into the small loch and hauled out several trout to add to the small feast.

After they ate, her aunt decided it was time for the women to wash up. They'd gotten muddy crossing the moor after that gale.

"You bathe first, Aunt Patience. I will later," Seona said, then went outside while their maids helped her aunt with a sponge bath. Before their meal, Seona had washed her face and hands in the loch. She couldn't wait to sink into a luxurious tub of hot water, but that was not likely to happen until they reached a castle.

Isobel talked with Dirk some distance away, near the horses. How cozy they looked, holding hands and murmuring. He kissed her cheek. Seona envied and idealized their love so much her chest ached. Isobel was lucky to have found such a deep passion. Seona longed for a happy marriage like theirs. An image of Keegan's face sprang to her mind.

Lest she be caught staring at Isobel and Dirk, Seona glanced away from them and, turning in a half circle, she noticed four guards standing at attention around the perimeter, their gazes scanning the surrounding hillsides while one watched the trail they'd arrived on. They certainly had no time to spare her a glance. She felt much safer knowing they took their jobs so seriously.

A yell and a loud laugh echoed in the opposite direction. But the guards did not seem concerned about it. What was going on? She followed the noise into the low-growing trees and bushes at the edge of the loch, then peered through.

Several of the men were chest deep in the loch. *And naked.* She gasped. Although it was dusk, she could clearly see their skin. Some had chests near hairy as a wolf, while others only had a small amount of body hair, their chest and abdominal muscles showing through.

Her eyes sought out Keegan. Where was he? Someone emerged from beneath the water's surface and flung his hair back. Her breath held, she squinted. Aye, 'twas him. His shoulders were incredibly wide and muscular. She was glad to see he wasn't one of the furry men. His back and arms appeared smooth and sleek. When he turned, she saw that his chest only had a light amount of hair which tapered into an intriguing line down his ridged abdomen.

As he waded toward the bank, his body emerged from the water, inch by glorious inch. His lean lower abdomen, his trim hips, his…. "Oh my," she whispered, then covered her mouth. She had never seen a completely naked man before. The male parts between his legs both shocked and amazed her. The light was too dim to see much detail, but she saw dangly parts that were substantial in size.

"Who are you spying on?" The whisper came from behind her.

She jumped and spun. Only her hand over her mouth prevented her squeal from emerging.

Isobel waited there with a wicked grin.

Lowering her hand, Seona took in a few deep breaths and tried to calm her rapid heartbeat. "You scared the life out of me,

Isobel."

She snickered and sent a quick glance through the bushes. "You are being a very naughty lass."

Seona placed her hands on her burning cheeks. "Aye. 'Tis true. I pray you won't tell Aunt Patience."

"Don't be silly. I would tell her naught. Did you see anything over there you liked?"

Seona left the bushes, heading toward a sheep enclosure out to the side of the cottages. "Don't tease me, I beg of you."

Isobel kept pace beside her. "I cannot help myself. 'Tis too much fun."

"You're incorrigible."

"Dirk thinks so, too." Once they stopped at the sheep pen, Isobel whispered, "I have been wondering all day whether Keegan kissed you today after he rescued you. When you two returned, you seemed very cozy."

Seona's face felt like an inferno. Thank the heavens for the low light of gloaming.

"I won't tell anyone," Isobel whispered.

"Do you promise?" Seona asked.

"Aye, of course, I promise." She placed a hand over her heart.

Seona nodded. "Aye," she admitted, though she could not bring herself to say *Keegan kissed me*. "Unfortunately, Laird Rebbinglen happened upon us. I pray he tells no one."

Isobel snorted softly. "He may tease Keegan about it, but he won't tell your aunt. That is a fact."

Seona relaxed a bit, hoping she was right.

"And how was it?" Isobel inquired.

Seona considered for a moment, trying to think of the right word. But there was none to describe how she'd felt when Keegan kissed her. "Wonderful."

"Well, 'tis only natural that you'd want to know what he looks like naked, then."

"Shh." Seona spun to see if anyone else was listening. They were alone, thank the heavens. "I heard a noise. I didn't know the men were bathing. What a shock."

Isobel giggled. "Last November, I was in a similar situation, wishing to know what Dirk looked like completely bare of clothes. I was fortunate one night when he needed help with his bath. I volunteered for the task." Isobel bit her lip to hold back a naughty grin.

Seona shook her head, unable to believe how daring Isobel had been. Seona wished to be just as confident. If she was, could she have everything she wanted just as Isobel did?

"That night turned out to be quite amazing." Isobel smiled wistfully.

Seona wanted to ask what she meant, but couldn't bring herself to pry about such a private matter. But maybe she could ask a general question to satisfy some of her curiosity. "My aunt would never tell me anything about... you know... the marriage bed. And my mother passed when I was too young to know about such things."

"I'm sorry to hear this." Isobel appeared pensive for a moment. "My maid tried to educate me about what goes on between men and women, but she did a poor job. She told me sexual relations with a man was the worst thing imaginable. Like torture."

"Was she wrong?" Seona asked, unsure what Isobel meant.

"If a woman is forced against her will, it would be like torture, aye. But with the right man—a man you are in love with—there is naught in the world like a proper bedding."

What did she mean by *proper* bedding? Surely 'twas one of the least proper things imaginable. "Why?" Seona asked.

"How did you feel when Keegan kissed you?"

Seona's whole body flushed and burned. "Heavens. I know not how to describe it. 'Twas like standing next to a bonfire, but at the same time, my mind floated away on the clouds." She would not mention how certain parts of her body awakened with a quickening excitement.

"Indeed. Making love to a man you are strongly drawn to is like that, only a hundred times more intense and exciting. The kisses, the touches. The need to have him fill that void."

Seona held her breath for she was certain she was going to learn more than she'd ever expected. "Is it painful?"

"I will admit it hurt the first time, but only for a minute or two," Isobel said, then shrugged. "After that, there was naught but an overwhelming pleasure that I couldn't have imagined before I experienced it."

When Seona realized her eyes were wide as platters, she blinked and tried to appear nonchalant. She didn't want Isobel to think her a complete idiot. She had seen animals mating and knew human mating had to be much the same. Back at home, she had heard a couple of maids working in a chamber, giggling and talking about a man one of them had a tryst with. They had gone into some detail about his large shaft, but Seona still had a difficult time understanding how things worked.

"What is hard to imagine is how…certain parts would fit," Seona said. 'Twas even harder to imagine since she'd caught a glimpse of Keegan's masculine parts minutes ago.

"Aye, I wondered the same thing," Isobel said in a whisper. "'Tis true when a man becomes aroused, his member becomes larger, harder and it stands at attention."

"In truth? Larger?" Seona was afraid to ask how large.

"Aye, but apparently, a woman's body is designed to accommodate his size, whether he is small or large. When he kisses you, strokes his fingers over you, you will start to feel very warm and tingly in certain places." Isobel grinned.

Aye, Seona could understand that. She'd already marveled at how tingly Keegan had made her feel during their kisses. 'Twas a spellbinding feeling which stole her thoughts and only made her want more.

"A purely primal urge will overcome you and you cannot wait for him to… how should I say this?"

Seona waited, anxious to hear what Isobel would reveal next.

"You will crave having his hard shaft inside you," Isobel whispered. "Once you are past the pain and used to his size, he will start moving and… thrusting. That is when you will lose your mind with the pleasure and not be aware of whether you are crying out or not."

"Lose your mind?" *Heavens!* Seona didn't want to lose control of her responses. Crying out without restraint must be mortifying.

"In a manner of speaking. You won't care what you say or how loud you scream." Isobel grinned and Seona knew she must look horrified. "'Tis naught to worry over. He will keep you quiet."

"How?" Seona was having a difficult time picturing it.

"With his mouth, his kisses."

"Heavens," Seona whispered. Surely kisses combined with thrusting would be overwhelming.

"Aye, 'tis heavenly." Isobel appeared dreamy. "Saints, I wish I could share my husband's bedroll this night. But he wishes me to sleep in the cottage with the rest of the women."

A little laugh escaped Seona before she could quell it. Isobel did indeed appear to enjoy her husband's company. Seona thought of another question. "What does a man expect of a woman? I would have no inkling what to do."

Isobel waved a hand. "He will show you soon enough. Anyway, it will come to you as if 'twas something you'd always known. Accepting his kisses and kissing him back. Touching him. Men love to be touched."

"Where?"

"Anywhere." Isobel snickered. "I remember one thing that surprised me the first time. Although I should have known, considering how men are always staring down at my breasts."

Seona felt her eyes fly wide again, then tried to hide her shock.

"Men love to kiss and suckle nipples," Isobel whispered.

"Heavens, you cannot be serious." Seona felt like the most naïve person on earth at the moment.

"Indeed, I am. That is why they're always gawking at women's breasts, even when they're covered by layers of clothing. They also like to fondle, squeeze, kiss, and stroke them."

Seona cleared her throat. She had never imagined such a thing, but she had noticed men, at times, would stare at her chest when they thought she wasn't looking. But even more interesting, she remembered her nipples had tingled when they'd been pressed to Keegan's hard chest. They had seemed to yearn for something. His touch?

"'Tis enjoyable for the woman, too," Isobel said. "It makes her more ready for his... invasion, so to speak."

"I see." Surely, 'twas sinful to speak of such things, but she had been wondering about them. "I thank you for telling me. I've been curious for some time. And I don't want to be too shocked on my wedding night."

"Well, you won't be... now that you've seen Keegan naked." Isobel beamed a wide, mischievous grin.

"Shh," Seona hissed, wondering if Isobel was mad. She could not marry Keegan, even though 'twas what she wished for most in the world.

"A good eve to you, ladies," said a deep male voice behind her.

Seona spun to find Keegan approaching, his hair still wet

from the dip in the loch. Thank the saints he'd been too far away to hear Isobel's whispered, shocking words of a few seconds before... hadn't he?

"Good eve," she mumbled, feeling a bit tongue-tied.

Keegan was fully dressed in his belted plaid, but Seona was very aware of what lay hidden beneath his clothes. A heated blush covered her skin and she was thankful for the dim light of dusk.

"A good eve to you, Keegan," Isobel said. "I need to discuss something with Dirk." She bypassed him and strode away.

Don't leave me alone with him, was Seona's first thought. Though she knew not why. 'Haps because she still felt mortified, having been caught spying on Keegan naked. Or maybe 'twas because she now knew far more about what happened between a man and woman in bed.

"Do you have time for another knife fighting lesson now?" Keegan asked.

She inhaled a deep breath and tried to forget all the newfound sexual knowledge and conflicting feelings swirling within her mind. The sight of Keegan's naked body had been disturbing yet intriguing to her, but he was the same generous and kind man who was teaching her how to defend herself. He was the same man who had saved her life twice and who kissed her gently.

She loved spending time with him, but she had been outside for a while, long enough for her aunt to have finished her sponge bath.

Seona glanced toward the nearby cottage. "I'm not certain. My aunt may send for me in a moment."

"Is something wrong?" he asked.

"What? Nay." Surely he couldn't detect she had been recently thrown off-kilter. "'Tis only that my aunt..." *Has been bathing and 'twill be my turn next.* Could she say that to him? Nay, 'twould not be acceptable. Besides, it made her recall how he had bathed in the loch.

"Aye?" he asked, his brows quirked.

She couldn't believe how she was bungling this simple conversation. "Will be looking for me," she finished, though she knew she was repeating herself and making no sense.

"How is her ankle?" Keegan asked.

"It pains her."

He nodded. "'Twill take time to heal."

"Aye." There was so much she wanted to say to him, and share with him, but her tongue felt stuck to the roof of her mouth. She needed time to absorb everything she had experienced and learned today.

"Did she say anything to you about riding with me?" he asked.

"Nay." *Not yet, anyway.* But Seona suspected her aunt would complain at the first opportunity.

When the cottage door opened, Seona held her breath. Two of the maids emerged. When they spotted her, they headed in her direction. Aye, just as she'd expected. A few feet away, they paused and curtsied. "Lady Patience asked us to send you inside."

"I'll be there in a moment."

When the two didn't move, Seona glared at them.

"Aye, m'lady." They hastened away.

"Och. I hope you never send such a fearsome look my way," Keegan said with a half grin. "I do believe the heart of a warrior beats inside you, Lady Seona."

She snorted before she could stop herself. "I doubt that." She glanced toward the cottage again, seeing that the two annoying maids were standing by the door, watching her. "Well, I had best go before Lady Patience herself comes to retrieve me on her injured ankle. I bid you goodnight, Master Keegan."

"A good night to you, m'lady." He bowed.

Before Seona reached the cottage, her aunt, now making use of a crooked cane, joined the two maids at the entrance. Her gaze flew past Seona to Keegan, then her eyes narrowed.

"I'll have a word with you inside, Seona." Her aunt motioned toward the doorway.

Seona proceeded into the cottage.

"If you wouldn't mind, I need to have a private word with my niece," Patience told the owner of the cottage and the other two maids who'd remained inside. They all exited silently. Lady Patience could easily intimidate servants, but she didn't scare Seona. Her only leverage was that she would tell Seona's father everything.

Once the door closed behind them, Patience said, "I've been wanting to talk to you about Keegan. I don't like that you have been riding behind him all day. 'Tis indecent."

CHAPTER NINE

Seona knew Aunt Patience would complain about her riding with Keegan earlier that day.

"My mare is unsafe," Seona said. "I was afraid to ride her. She went mad during the storm and bolted, in case you don't remember."

"I remember!" Her aunt paused in her limping trek to the chair by the fireplace to glare at Seona. "Don't be impertinent with me, young lady."

Ignoring her, Seona continued with calm reasoning. "Chief Dirk said I should ride with Master Keegan. Do you wish to naysay a chief?"

"Nay." Patience slumped into the chair by the fire and propped her crooked cane next to her. "But you didn't even protest. I ken what you're thinking, lassie," she snapped, pinning Seona with a perceptive stare. "I see how you blush when he looks at you."

Seona felt her face heat.

"Aye, just like that." Her aunt pointed at her.

How on earth could Aunt Patience see Seona's face in the dim candlelight? She was too blasted observant. Seona sat down in the chair opposite her and didn't comment.

"I'm not daft," Patience said. "I was once a pretty young lass like you are. And I know how men are, especially charming rogues like that commoner."

Immediately bristling, Seona stiffened. "He is no commoner," she said firmly. "His grandfather was a baron and a chief, just like my own father. Keegan is a gentleman of the clan."

"He is a scoundrel," her aunt insisted. "Good for naught but to lure a good lady into sin and ruin her reputation. If you give him half a chance, he will steal your virtue and forget your name the next day. He is not fit to marry, so don't even be thinking of it."

"I'm not." 'Twas a lie, but what else could she say? Her father would never allow it, and besides, Keegan had never mentioned marriage. 'Twas but her own outlandish fantasy.

Her aunt's eyes narrowed. "What happened when you were alone with him during the storm? And last night, when he snatched you from the tent, wearing naught more than your smock? He returned wearing only a shirt. 'Twas shocking."

"As you already know, he let me borrow his plaid because I was cold. Naught more. He saved my life twice. Do you care so little for me that you cannot appreciate that?"

Seona knew she was challenging her aunt, but she needed it. Patience's glare intensified, but Seona held her gaze, waiting for an answer.

"Nay," she finally confessed. "I am thankful he saved your life."

"Did you tell him that?"

"Not yet. But I will," Patience grumbled. "My concern is what happened after the rescue."

"Do you honestly think I'd bed down with a man outside while someone is trying to kidnap me or during a horrendous storm?"

"Well...nay, I suppose not." Her aunt shrugged. "But I don't trust him. He could take advantage of you or force you."

Seona shook her head. "Keegan is not that type of man."

"What type of man is he... since you know so much about him?"

"Kind and protective. He risked his life to save mine."

Her aunt lifted a brow. "Aye, well... he'd best not get it into his head he has a chance with you. Your father would never approve of him."

"I ken it." But her father was daft, valuing wealth and prestige over strength of character.

"Get the maids in here to help me over to the bed. I'm tired," her aunt said.

"Very well." Seona strode to the door, opened it and summoned the maids. After they helped Patience into the bed, Seona took a sponge bath and changed into a clean smock.

While she was getting into one of the four beds, Isobel arrived to spend the night inside the cottage with them.

Seona couldn't sleep, nor could she talk to Isobel about anything of importance with her aunt and the maids so close. She felt safe enough within the stone walls of the cottage, but she missed Keegan... maybe because she'd ridden so close to him all day. The feel of his hard, strong body had become familiar. *Addictive.* Would she be allowed to ride with him again?

***

Two days later, Keegan and the MacKay party were finally drawing closer to Ullapool. He was still annoyed that Seona's aunt had insisted she ride a separate horse both days. He had argued that Seona couldn't ride her own untrustworthy one. They'd compromised and Seona had temporarily switched horses with one of the guards. Keegan didn't like it but he had to live with it. They'd been riding daylight to dark most every day, and everyone was exhausted and short-tempered, especially Lady Patience. 'Haps her injury added to her bad mood.

He put her from his mind and thought of someone more pleasant. He grinned, remembering how he had enjoyed Seona riding with him for those few hours two days before. Now, he simply rode close to her in the event something threatened her safety. He relished the secret smiles she sent his way. But they'd had no more opportunities for a moment alone or for knife-fighting practice.

It had to be around midday but the sky was thickly overcast. The terrain turned from moorland to rough and rocky as they approached the pass through the mountains. Most everywhere he looked now, he saw gray granite and scrubby gorse bushes.

Something struck the ground nearby. *An arrow?*

"We're being shot at!" Keegan glanced up at the cliffs above them and saw a figure with a bow drawn. "'Tis an ambush!" Keegan yelled, raising his targe and urging Curry forward, between Seona and the outlaws. "Archers!"

Their archers leapt to their feet and took up positions. A few fired arrows up toward the cliffs.

Dirk dismounted and slapped his horse on the rump. "Escort

the women further along and take cover behind those boulders," he told Keegan.

"I'll protect them with my life," Keegan said.

"I thank you, cousin." Dirk directed five more of the guards to help Keegan.

Much as he'd love to be at the forefront, fighting the knaves, Keegan knew protecting the women was the main goal.

"Haldane may come after you because he's wanting to kidnap Seona," Dirk said.

"Aye. That bastard," Keegan muttered, motioning for the women to precede him and head for cover. "Get behind the boulders." Once they were beyond the range of Haldane's archers, he and the guards helped them dismount.

Keegan stood peering out, the women and most of the horses behind him. Aside from Keegan, MacMillan, and four other guards, the rest of the men were fighting beside Dirk.

"Surround the women," Keegan told the guards with him. "The outlaws may try to sneak up from behind again."

"What do you see?" Isobel asked. "Is Dirk safe?"

"Aye. Naught is happening yet." At least, nothing that he could see. The outlaws were no doubt doing something sneaky. Keegan wanted to be standing beside Dirk, ready to take down Haldane if he came close. The weasel was likely too afraid to face Dirk and fight hand to hand. Haldane was no match for him, anyway, and he knew it. He'd have his archers do most of the work. But they would run out of arrows eventually.

Keegan glanced around, making certain no one had circled behind them. He had to keep on high alert because Haldane had a powerful obsession for Seona, and he couldn't lose her at all costs.

Facing forward again, he noticed the movement of plaid behind a bush off to the side, near Dirk and the others.

"To the left!" he called out.

Dirk shifted his focus. "Come out, wee cowards, and fight like men," he yelled.

More than a dozen men broke from the bushes, charging Dirk and his guards. *'Slud!* Haldane's force was far bigger than last time, making the two sides more evenly matched. Where the devil had Haldane found more men? Some were several years older than most of Haldane's gang.

Keegan cursed, annoyed he couldn't join in and help protect

the chief. Although, clearly, his cousin could protect himself. He dealt two of them killing thrusts with his sword.

The gray-haired McMurdo engaged Dirk in swordplay. Dirk was the stronger fighter and he drove McMurdo back, while the other guards fought the remaining outlaws.

A movement up the hill caught Keegan's attention. One of the younger men in Haldane's party, Gil, drew back his bow.

"Dirk! Up the hill!" Keegan shouted.

Just after Gil released the bow string, Dirk leapt to the side. The arrow struck Dirk's lower leg.

"Iosa is Muire Mhàthair," Keegan muttered.

McMurdo came back after Dirk.

"Damn the old bastard," Keegan muttered, yearning to charge forward.

"What is happening?" Isobel asked behind him. "Is Dirk hurt?"

"Shh." Keegan waved her back. There was naught she could do about his injury now. If he allowed her to get hurt, Dirk would string him up.

Rebbie moved in to help Dirk, beating McMurdo back. But Dirk was holding his own despite the arrow protruding from his calf.

Two more of Haldane's men fell beneath the blades of the MacKay guards, both of them too young to be seasoned warriors. Keegan knew them, for they had both been part of the MacKay clan before Haldane had gone rogue and led the other lads astray.

Where was Haldane, anyway?

Keegan surveyed the area around himself and beyond. "Keep alert," he told the guards.

Five men emerged from behind a rock formation several yards behind them. Haldane led the charge, his long red hair flying back in the breeze, his teeth bared in a snarl, and his green eyes glinting with pure bloodlust.

"There!" Keegan told the guards.

Placing the women between himself and the boulders, Keegan assumed the guard stance. In passing, he noticed knives in both Seona's and Isobel's hands. He hoped they could protect themselves if need be. But he didn't want it to come to that.

Haldane avoided him and engaged one of the other guards in swordplay. Coward.

Keegan had never before seen the scraggly man who ran toward him. Though he looked scrawny, the first blow from his sword was passable. Keegan was faster and stronger and three strikes later, he ran the man through the abdomen. He shrieked and collapsed, writhing in pain. After disarming him, Keegan turned his attention to the other outlaws. One of the guards had already cut one of the knave's throats. Haldane and the other two turned tail and ran the way they'd come.

He couldn't believe what cowards they were. "Come back, you bastards!" Keegan yelled. He wanted to finish the three of them off.

Once they'd disappeared from sight like terrified rabbits, he glanced back toward where Dirk and the other men were fighting.

Despite his injury, Dirk was still slashing and thrusting.

His blade sliced McMurdo's shoulder and the older man jumped back. Then he fled.

Twenty feet away, he turned back and yelled for the other men to retreat. He obviously knew the outlaws were on the losing side of the skirmish now, even with the reinforcements they'd found along the way.

Rebbie chased after McMurdo, but the old man was quicker than he looked. A few of the other brigands fled to the left, down an embankment and through the bushes.

"Is Dirk hurt?" Isobel demanded, sidling up to him.

Since the outlaws were gone, he could reveal the truth. Still, he grabbed her arm so she wouldn't go running out there too soon. "An arrow struck his calf."

"What? Oh good lord!" She tried to jerk away from him. "Unhand me, Keegan."

Dirk limped in their direction, his face red, eyes wild and jaw clenched.

Keegan released Isobel. Making sure Seona was beside him for her own safety, he moved toward Dirk. Isobel fussed over him, crying.

"Calm yourself, Isobel. 'Tis naught to worry over. Merely a flesh wound," Dirk said, his voice rough. He was obviously trying to hide his pain.

"How do you feel?" Keegan asked him.

"I'll live."

"How will we remove it?" Isobel asked.

"Rebbie will do it. Go over there with the ladies so you don't have to watch. I don't want you to pass out."

"Are you mad? I'll not be passing out."

"Keegan, make her stay with Lady Seona."

"Lady Isobel." Keegan motioned toward the boulders.

"Don't make the man have to carry you, Isobel," Dirk said in a tone that brooked no argument. "I've had far worse injuries than this."

She huffed, her eyes glistening with tears, then proceeded back toward the boulder with Seona.

Keegan followed. "He will be well, I'm certain."

"But he could get infection and fever," she said, trying to suppress her sobs.

Behind them, Dirk growled and Isobel turned to run back toward him. Keegan caught her arm and ushered her once again toward Seona. "Removing the arrow will be painful, no doubt," Keegan said. He'd never been shot with an arrow so couldn't say from experience, but it had to hurt something awful. He glanced back to see Dirk lying on the rocky ground and Rebbie knelt over him, working on his leg. The two had fought battles on the continent together and had been treating each other's wounds for years.

"I want to kill Haldane and his damnable archer," Isobel muttered, striding forward, a glower on her face.

"As do I," Keegan said.

Isobel and Seona sat together on one of the rocks beside the wide-eyed and pale Lady Patience, while Keegan and the other guards kept watch for returning outlaws. Several men stood around Dirk, mostly blocking Isobel's view of his bloody leg. He could certainly understand Dirk's need to keep her shielded from most of it, although she had never seemed squeamish to him.

He was glad to see she took some comfort from having Seona by her side as she watched the proceedings from a distance. Seona was also a bit pale. Her worried gaze met his.

"He will recover quickly," Keegan said. How could he not? He was one of the strongest and most resilient men Keegan knew.

"Aye, he will," Seona said, putting an arm around Isobel's shoulders and comforting her. "All will be well."

A quarter hour later, Dirk's calf was bound in linen cloths, most likely someone's clean shirt that had been ripped up, and most of the bleeding had stopped. Rebbie had poured whisky on it along with some powdered healing herbs he carried with him. Dirk pushed himself to his feet, though his face was ashen.

Isobel ran to him and slipped an arm around his waist. "Lean on me. Don't put any weight on your right leg."

"Don't fash yourself. I am well." He limped forward, gritting his teeth.

"You are lying," Isobel accused.

"Naught a wee dram of whisky won't cure."

"You're in luck. I have some," Keegan said, digging into one of the packs on his horse.

After Dirk had two generous swigs of whisky, he hoisted himself into the saddle using his uninjured leg. Everyone else followed suit.

Keegan helped Seona mount again and they were on their way.

He divided his attention between Seona, Dirk and the surrounding cliffs. He had to make sure Seona was safe, but at the same time, his concern for Dirk grew. Riding the horse had to be jarring his injured leg and causing severe pain. His skin remained pale and his jaw clenched. He couldn't drink enough whisky to kill the pain and stay in the saddle at the same time.

Isobel was right to worry about the infection and fever. 'Twould be the worst part to get through.

***

After riding a couple of hours, they reached Ullapool, a wee village on the bay of Loch Broom.

"Is there an inn here?" Keegan asked.

"Nay." Dirk was sweating and pale when he dismounted, which concerned Keegan a great deal. And 'twas clear he was holding his breath half the time. "One of Isobel's distant cousins, Linden MacKenzie, owns that manor house, there." Dirk pointed at a thatched-roof, whitewashed structure, much larger than a cottage, yet not as large as a castle. "He has a shipping business, transporting goods from the ports down south out to the islands."

"You need to lie down, cousin," Keegan told him.

"Aye. And a half-pint of whisky wouldn't hurt either."

Keegan sent one of the guards to purchase more whisky while Dirk, Isobel, Rebbie and a few of the others went to speak to her cousin about their party staying the night.

Rebbie returned, reporting that Isobel's cousin had welcomed them to stay and had four empty rooms with beds for their use.

The women disappeared inside the manor house, as did Dirk and Rebbie. MacMillan carried Lady Patience inside because of her wrenched ankle.

Keegan and most of the other men waited outside, on the lookout for Haldane or any of his party who might have followed. Since Keegan didn't know the new men Haldane had enlisted, 'twas even harder to spot the knaves. He simply didn't allow anyone near the house. The five-foot stone wall around it might deter petty thieves, but it was too low to provide much defense. The wooden gate was sturdy but open. Hopefully, it would be locked at night. If someone wanted to attack, 'twould be too easy to take over the house. Their guards would have to take shifts tonight, securing the perimeter.

The door of the manor house opened. MacMillan exited and approached him, a frown contorting his dark brows. "Lady Isobel wishes to see you inside."

Saints. Was Dirk worse?

"You and the other guards need to secure the perimeter of the house," Keegan said.

"Aye, we'll be on the lookout for the bastards."

Keegan strode toward the entry, and a servant opened the door.

Isobel awaited him, just inside. She was pale, her brown eyes too large. "Dirk wishes to speak with you upstairs."

"Very well." Cold dread weighed heavily in Keegan's chest. "Is something wrong?"

"Nay. He is the same but wanted to talk to you."

She walked with him up the straight stone staircase, opened the door to the bedchamber, then left.

Keegan entered the room, lit by the late evening sunrays that sliced through the clouds, to find Dirk reclining in a large bed, his leg propped on pillows and several more behind his back.

"How are you feeling?" Keegan asked, moving forward.

"Like my leg is shot full of holes. 'Tis hard to believe there is only one through it." Dirk took a sip of whisky from a small goblet. "Have a seat." He motioned to a straight wooden chair by the bed, then poured Keegan a dram of whisky in another goblet.

"I thank you." Keegan sipped the fiery liquid. "I'm certain

you'll be back to your old self in a few days."

"Aye. 'Tis not the first time I've been shot with an arrow. I took one in the shoulder early last fall in Perth."

Keegan dropped into the chair by the bed, relaxing a bit since Dirk wasn't as bad as he'd feared.

"I want to thank you for protecting Isobel during the skirmish," Dirk said. "She means more to me than my own life."

The sincerity in Dirk's pale blue eyes, as well as the obvious and profound love he held for his wife, stalled out any words Keegan might say in response. He gave a brief nod.

"If anything happens to me, promise me that you will protect her," Dirk said, his eyes fiercely intense.

"Och." With the sound, Keegan released some of the pressure in his chest. "Naught is going to happen to you, cousin!"

"If it does. Promise me." Dirk's gaze remained piercing.

"Aye, of course. You ken I would protect both you and Isobel with mine own life."

"I thank you. That means more than I can say." He relaxed back a bit.

"I'm certain you will be well in a matter of days. As you said, you've been injured many times before."

Dirk nodded and sipped the whisky again. "Haldane is a menace. I had no inkling he would come back with such a vengeance this spring. I thought... hoped... he'd escaped to the Lowlands where he'd stop his outlaw ways and start a new life. But I doubt he will ever change. He has too much of his devious mother in him."

"Aye, that he does."

Dirk inhaled a deep breath and let it out slow. "You're not only my cousin, but also a good friend, as you've been the whole of my life."

"Aye," Keegan said hesitantly, wondering what was on Dirk's mind now. Had the whisky loosed his tongue?

"I've been meaning to speak with you about something," Dirk said. "I've thought long and hard on it. I want you to be my tanist until I have an heir who is of age."

"What?" Keegan frowned. Why would Dirk name him heir apparent to the chiefdom? "Nay. Aiden is tanist, as he should be. He's your brother."

Dirk shook his head. "He doesn't want the position. If

something should happen to me before I sire an heir, Aiden might be baron but he could never lead the clan. You saw the kind of chief he was before I came back. He's not a leader. He's a minstrel and a piper, a very talented one. He's more than happy to simply play music. He told me you would make a better tanist, and I agree."

Shocked to the core, Keegan swallowed hard. This was something he'd never expected. "Well…I thank you. I'm honored you chose me. I'd be more than happy to fill the role, until you have a son, although I'm your cousin, not your brother."

"You're like a brother to me," Dirk assured him.

"And you're like a brother to me as well." Even though Keegan had three younger brothers, he actually felt closer to Dirk. Maybe because the two of them were alike in many ways and near the same age.

"You're a fearsome warrior. A strong leader," Dirk said. "You've been head of the guards for a long while now."

"Aye." Four years, in fact.

"You ken what is expected of a chief. You watched my father lead the clan for years, even while I was away."

Keegan nodded. "He was a great chief, as you are."

"I can only aspire to be as good a leader as he was," Dirk said. "Anyway, I want the clan and Isobel to be safe and protected should Haldane or his men hit their mark next time."

CHAPTER TEN

Keegan left Dirk's chamber feeling gloomy and disturbed, despite being named tanist. Of course, 'twas a great honor and a high position within the clan, just beneath the chief, and he was grateful for it. But he would never wish for anything bad to happen to Dirk.

Keegan met Isobel in the narrow corridor, carrying a tray of food. Her face was still pale and concerned.

He paused. "I hope you'll pardon me for asking, Lady Isobel, but I need to see Lady Seona for a few minutes. Could you ask her to meet me here without her aunt knowing?"

"Aye. Just a moment." Isobel took the tray into Dirk's chamber, then returned.

"'Tis not for frivolous purposes," Keegan said. "I'm teaching her how to use a blade to defend herself. I don't want her aunt to know. She wouldn't approve."

"Aye. 'Tis very kind of you, Keegan. There's a private parlor at the end of this corridor you can use for practice if you wish." She motioned toward a distant closed door. "Also, the cooks prepared food and left it in the dining room below for everyone—you and all the men."

"I thank you. I'll let them know."

She proceeded to one of the other bedchambers. A couple of minutes later, Seona and Isobel moved along the corridor, whispering. Seona looked beautiful, but he knew she had to be exhausted after all the travel.

"I thank you." Keegan bowed when they paused before him.

"I'm glad to help." Isobel went into the chamber with Dirk and closed the door.

Seona glanced back at the door leading to the room where her aunt remained, unable to believe she would have some precious time alone with Keegan. She faced him again, taking in his serious expression in the dim light of gloaming. She knew he was concerned about Dirk.

"I had hoped to teach you more about defending yourself," Keegan whispered. "Things have turned dangerous. Our chief is injured, and it near kills me to imagine you attacked or captured and unable to fight off the outlaws."

Seona nodded, a cold shiver traveling through her when she imagined Haldane kidnapping her. "I thank you for the help. Aunt Patience is asleep, so we have some time."

"I hadn't considered… we've been traveling a long time. You may be too tired."

"Nay." No matter how tired she was, she'd rather spend time with Keegan than sleep. Besides, being near him suffused her with giddy energy.

"Isobel said there's a parlor at the end of the corridor we can use." He motioned.

"Very well." She proceeded in the direction he'd indicated and he followed.

Once they were inside, he closed the door.

A bright fire burned in the hearth, and Keegan lit a few more thick candles. 'Twas a beautiful room with several chairs and settees here and there in groupings. A fine Turkish carpet lay in the center of the polished wood floor.

"How is Chief Dirk feeling?" she asked.

"He's in pain." Keegan frowned. "I pray he recovers."

"As do I." She could not imagine the level of intense fear and worry Isobel must feel right now. She and Dirk had only been married six months. They were near inseparable and so in love.

"He has always been like a brother to me instead of a cousin," Keegan said.

"I can tell. The two of you are close." And she admired this about them. She was also close to her cousins, Genevieve and Malcolm.

Keegan stood at the fireplace, staring into the flames for a long moment. A casual observer would think he was relaxed; yet, to Seona he seemed profoundly tense, as if his thoughts were in turmoil.

"Is something wrong?" she asked.

He faced her, a troubled frown upon his handsome face. "I'll tell you something if you promise not to tell anyone as of yet. It hasn't been announced."

"Of course." Praying his news wasn't bad, she moved forward to stand beside him in front of the hearth. The fire warmed her as did Keegan's close presence.

"Dirk has just named me his tanist until he has an heir." Keegan's expression remained dark and foreboding.

"In truth? That is a high honor." She was happy for him, but concerned that he didn't appear pleased.

"Aye. He realizes Haldane and his band of outlaws could kill him at any moment. That's why he asked me. He said he'd been considering it for a while, but the injury… the threat to his life made him realize his own mortality." Keegan shook his head. "That's what feels like a knife to the gut." He looked tormented as he stared into the flames. He turned toward her. "Och. Pray pardon, Lady Seona. I should not have said that aloud."

"Nay. I'm glad you told me," she said quickly. "I'm glad… you trust me." It meant more to her than she could express.

"'Tis true. I do trust you, Seona." In the firelight, his blue eyes were sincere, yet a hint of his natural charm also slipped through, as if he might smile at any moment. But he didn't.

"God forbid that something should happen to Dirk, but if it did, I know with certainty you would do the clan proud as their chief," she said.

He bent his head in an abbreviated bow. "I thank you for your confidence."

She wanted to touch him, to hold him. It meant the world to her that he'd told her about being named tanist before he'd told anyone else. She considered that an honor.

"I wish Da was here so I could tell him," Keegan said.

"He will be proud when he learns of it."

Keegan nodded. "Enough about me. I want you to practice the knife-fighting moves I told you about last time."

"Very well."

"Did you bring your knife?"

"Aye."

"Well, I also brought this." He withdrew a blunt wooden stick shaped like a small *sgian dubh* from his sporran. "I made it last night to help with our practice."

"'Tis beautifully carved. Are you afraid I'll stab you with the real thing?"

A tiny grin quirked his lips. "I don't want you to hesitate." He removed his sporran and sword baldric—she presumed because he wanted them out of the way while they practiced. "Have you ever stabbed anyone?" he asked.

"Of course not!"

"Well, to do it effectively, you have to put some muscle behind it."

She would never have the muscle or strength he had. That was a certainty. "Show me."

"Like I was telling you last time, if you are grabbed from behind, you'll want to hold your *sgian* like this." He held the knife with the fake blade pointing downward. "And when you have the opportunity, stab backward into his body." Keegan thrust the knife blade behind himself toward an invisible attacker. "Now, you try it." He handed her the carved wooden stick. "Face away from me so I can see your movements."

Trying to imagine being in the grips of an outlaw, she drove the fake knife backward into thin air.

"Aye. Good. Now, I'm going to pretend to be an outlaw capturing you."

Surprised by his words, she glanced around at him. He was going to grab her? *Heavens!* Her skin heated with anticipation. *Tis only for practice*, she told her wayward body.

He paused. "Are you in agreement?"

"Aye. I need the practice."

"Don't hurt me." He grinned.

She lifted a brow and sent him a saucy look. "'Tis a risk you take if you assume the outlaw role."

"Indeed." His smile widened, but he didn't move.

When she faced the opposite wall again, he stealthily moved in behind her, covered her mouth with one hand and wrapped his other arm around both hers, trapping them. She was so stunned by his body heat, she couldn't think or act for a moment. When he lifted her into the air in one second and turned with her, she was amazed at his strength.

Forcing her brain to function, she thrust the wooden knife backward toward him. She missed, but tried again. This time, she met resistance.

He grunted, then murmured in her ear, "Try it again. Harder."

Saints! She didn't want to hurt him. While it was true the wooden knife wouldn't cut him, it might leave a bruise.

"Come now, lass. Show me what you've got," he encouraged.

She shoved the fake knife backward again, driving it against what seemed to be his lower abdomen. 'Twas like trying to drive the stick into granite.

"Again. Harder," he commanded.

She let loose and did it three more times.

Finally, he released her. "Well done."

"Did I bruise you?" She glanced down at his trim waist.

"Nay. Don't worry about me. I simply wanted you to know how it would feel if you stab a man, trying to make him release you. If you'd had a sharp blade, you would've done some damage."

"I did hurt you, then?" She wanted to see if she had left horrible red marks on his bare skin. "You kept saying *harder*."

"Seona." He shook his head and took her hand. His warm fingers surrounded hers, filling her whole body with comfort. "Nay, you did not hurt me." Taking the wooden knife, he stroked his thumb across her open palm, sending tingles up her arm. "Now, I want you to practice slashing. You would do this if the attacker is coming at you from the front. This will give you a little extra time to escape him." He stepped back and swung the knife in a half circle at arm's length. "If he is extending his hand to grab you, you may cut his hand or his arm. You try."

She took the knife and mimicked his movements several times.

"You're a quick learner," Keegan said.

"'Tis because you are a gifted teacher." Moving forward, she offered the wooden knife to him.

Instead of taking it, he encircled her hand with his larger one. A heated sensation poured from where he touched her. "And you are a beautiful, resilient woman who has bewitched me," he murmured, his deep voice the most seductive sound she'd ever heard.

Her breath halted and she couldn't think what to do or say

next. The knife slipped from her fingers and thumped to the carpet. He ignored it and stared intently into her eyes.

What was he thinking? Would he kiss her? Her heartbeat accelerated in anticipation.

Slowly, he moved closer until they were standing toe to toe.

His eyes darkened, entrancing her.

He leaned down and touched his lips to hers.

She knew she shouldn't allow him to kiss her, but how could she stop him when she craved him more than food when she was hungry? The months she'd secretly watched him across a crowded room had whetted her appetite.

And each time he kissed her, she understood more about what he wanted, how she should respond and kiss him in return. She opened her mouth, inviting him to deepen the kiss. She'd never guessed she would be an enthusiast of carnal kisses. But when he brushed his tongue over hers, she wanted to do naught but eat him up. He tasted of whisky and man. Intoxicating.

She entangled her hands in his hair, loving the silky feel of it between her fingers.

He moaned, taking her mouth in another slow, luscious kiss and gently tugging her against him. His hard chest pressing against her breasts, even through their clothing, made her body sing with need.

She noticed something hard against the lower part of her belly. At first, she thought it was a weapon hilt, but then she realized it was that most male part of his body that she had glimpsed when he'd waded from the loch. Isobel had said a man's shaft would become hard when his desires were aroused.

As a lady, she should be shocked. But she wasn't. His arousal awoke something within her on a primal level. She loved knowing she affected him in such a way. She felt a liquid warmth in the lowest part of her belly. She didn't understand it, but it was incredibly spellbinding.

His shaft nestled against her through his plaid and he groaned. Some part of her deep inside tingled and ached for him.

She craved his touch on every inch of her skin.

He tempted her. Captivated her. And made her want to do sinful things. This was why her aunt was such a ferocious chaperone, glaring at any man she deemed unsuitable who glanced her way.

But carnal relations outside of marriage had to be dangerous. 'Twas how bastards were conceived, she realized. Imagining having to face her father and tell him she was with child but unwed sent fear lancing through her. She turned her head aside, breaking the kiss.

"Damn," Keegan whispered, his breathing more labored now than it had been when he'd rescued her from the horse days ago.

"Pray pardon," she said, mortifying heat rushing over her skin.

"I'm the one who should apologize." He drew in a deep breath. "I am sorry. I should not have."

"Nay. Don't apologize."

He remained close, and she felt torn, wanting to press her body against his again and kiss him, but knowing at the same time this would be dangerous. His manly scent tempted her to bury her nose against his chest, but she didn't move. She imagined, quite wantonly, what he would look like if he removed his shirt and plaid. *Oh heavens.* And if she was naked… their skin would brush and slide together in a very carnal way.

She was suddenly aware of an abundance of moisture between her legs. It had to be female arousal, something she'd only experienced when near Keegan. The tingling and yearning only intensified.

He stepped away, bent and took up his sporran, sword and baldric.

Nay. She wanted to protest. His body against her had felt better than anything she'd ever experienced.

"'Twas what I wished for, too," she whispered, torn between need for him and shock at herself. Had she truly said that aloud?

He paused in putting on his sporran and turned his head toward her. "What?"

She should keep her lips sealed tight. Confessing her thoughts and feelings would only make the situation more precarious. At the same time, she would never have what she wanted if she didn't show courage. "'Twas what I wanted…. You are the only man who has ever kissed me."

CHAPTER ELEVEN

Keegan halted, Seona's words spurring fierce desire within him.

Twas what I wanted.... You are the only man who has ever kissed me.

"Saints," he hissed. Of course, he'd expected that she was an innocent, but to know he was the first and only man to kiss her sent possessiveness pounding through his blood.

She was meant to be his... had to be.

His first instinct was to kiss her again, but he forced himself to be rational. Truth was, he wanted to do far more than kiss her... but he couldn't seduce her.

His aching and rebellious body told him he was wrong.

He drew in a deep breath and held it, trying to smother his carnal yearnings. Aye, he'd played with fire when he'd kissed her, but to know she felt the same, to hear that she wanted his kisses... it near destroyed his resolve.

Still, he had to wait and ask her father for her hand.

"Seona, I would love naught more than to kiss you again. To kiss you all night, but 'tis not something I should do."

She stared at the floor. "You're right."

"You're an innocent lady, and I would never want to do anything to ruin your future."

She nodded. "You're an honorable gentleman," she whispered. "Besides, I wasn't suggesting you kiss me again. I only wanted you to know there is no reason to apologize."

Was she angry with him? Or had he hurt her feelings? Hell,

what did he know about women? Keegan's stomach knotted as he tried to figure out what to say. "Aye, well, I simply wanted you to know how I felt. You tempt me beyond reason. And to know that you enjoy my kisses..." He blew out a sharp breath. "Makes me near insane."

Her dark blue gaze lifted to his. The emotion and passion he saw there was like a punch to the gut.

"Iosa is Muire Mhàthair," he muttered, grinding his teeth. How could she affect him so profoundly? He wanted to forget everything and kiss her... lay her on his plaid before the hearth, then make love to her for the rest of the night. He'd have to start off slow and gentle so as not to frighten her.

But he couldn't. Not until she was his, in truth. Forever. Because once he had her, he'd never let her go.

"I bid you goodnight," Seona said, then hurried out the door.

"'Slud," he muttered in the silence and sucked in a deep breath. He could hardly think for the arousal flooding his veins. He should be glad she'd left—'twas best for them both—but at the same time, being without her made him feel lonely and empty.

After blowing out the candles, he exited the room, heading out to check on the guards and see if the outlaws had shown their faces.

***

Seona slipped back into the chamber where her aunt was sleeping. The fire in the hearth provided enough light for her to see what she was doing. Millie, one of the maids, arose from the small cot in the corner and helped Seona undress.

"I thank you," Seona whispered. Wearing her smock, she climbed into the big bed beside Aunt Patience. She was glad to see her aunt hadn't moved. Her deep breaths puffed in and out in the steady rhythm of sleep.

Seona, on the other hand, was too excited to sleep. She turned onto her side, her body still burning from Keegan's touch, from his kiss, and the words he'd spoken to her.

You tempt me beyond reason.

Her heart sped up. Indeed, he tempted her beyond reason, too. In fact, she'd been shocked at her own courage when she'd confessed she wanted his kisses and that he was the only man who'd ever kissed her. He'd tried to hide his reaction to that, but she'd sensed he was suppressing something powerful. Arousal?

Emotion? Or a potent combination of both?

Prior to her talk with Isobel, no one had seen fit to educate her on what to expect in bed with a man. Even though she'd recently learned a lot, Seona remained curious about every aspect of lovemaking. She suspected it might be something she could enjoy. Isobel did; so why not? With the right man, of course.

Before she'd met Keegan, she couldn't have imagined being so tempted by a man. She'd always thought the marriage bed was something to be dreaded and feared. Something violent, painful and humiliating for the woman. And something a man could crow about.

Now she knew different.

Earlier, when Keegan's erection had pressed against her, clear evidence that he wanted her, a primitive need for him had come over her, as if he was her mate and she wished to please him.

She relished his desire, but she admired his restraint and honor just as much. He was a good man, putting what was best for her ahead of his own needs.

She well knew, for ladies and lairds, passion and marriage were rarely experienced with the same person. But wouldn't it be hell on earth to be married to one person and in love with another? She couldn't fathom it, nor would she be able to endure it.

Her heart had never yearned for anything or anyone like it yearned for Keegan.

But she didn't know how she could marry him, or even if he wanted to marry her. Her father would never permit a match between them, anyway, even with Keegan's new position as tanist. 'Twas a waste of time to even contemplate it… but she did. She couldn't help herself.

Seona couldn't imagine all the things Keegan would teach her in bed. He would kiss her and undress her. He might caress every inch of her skin. He would guide her hands and show her how he liked to be touched.

Recalling his broad shoulders, muscular arms, trim abdomen and intriguing masculine attributes as he'd strode from the loch, she envisioned him walking just that way, stripped of clothing, toward her in a bedchamber. Her breathing paused, and heat rushed over her skin. What would that dusting of hair on his chest feel like beneath her fingers? How would his hard shaft feel against her bare skin?

Heavens, I am a wanton lass!

She tried to put Keegan from her mind and sleep, but he walked into her dreams and taunted her with smoldering kisses.

She hoped she did not talk in her sleep.

***

The next morn after breaking their fast, Keegan and the whole of the MacKay party proceeded the short distance to the docks on foot, the guards surrounding the women and their injured chief. Several of the guards had already scouted the village, looking for the outlaws, and seen naught.

Seona's hand rested securely at the crook of Keegan's elbow as they walked along the cobbled street. Feeling protective and 'haps a wee bit possessive, he placed his hand over hers and scanned their surroundings—the mix of gray stone and whitewashed buildings, the green hills, and Loch Broom reflecting the cloud-flecked blue sky.

Linden MacKenzie, Isobel's cousin and the owner of the manor house, had arranged passage for them on one of his merchant ships, a galleon large enough to transport them and some of their horses. The rest of their mounts would be stabled here until the MacKays' return in a few weeks.

Keegan hoped the weather would hold so they could reach Dornie before nightfall. He would breathe a lot easier when everyone was out of danger.

What dampened his mood was the pain Dirk was in, even though he tried not to show it. Two of his men, one under each arm, helped him board the ship while Isobel looked on with a worried frown.

Keegan surveyed the area again, especially the stone-dotted green hills around the northern and eastern edges of the village. Haldane and his men had a habit of hiding on hilltops and raining down arrows.

MacMillan carried Lady Patience on board. She and four of the MacKay guards were prone to seasickness, and this was one reason they'd traveled overland thus far. Also, none of the MacKay *birlinn*s or galleys was large enough to accommodate their entire party plus horses. But now they needed to reach Isobel's brother's keep, Teasairg Castle, as soon as possible for everyone's safety and so a healer could treat Dirk's leg.

Keegan escorted Seona to the small, wood-framed captain's

cabin, where the women would remain until they reached their destination. When Seona's gaze met his for that brief moment, he saw glimpses of secret yearnings in her eyes. He hoped they were the same yearnings he had. After what she'd said last night, he believed they were. He gave her a brief smile and took his leave.

On deck, he and the other guards kept an eye out for enemies until the ship sailed out of the harbor. Maybe Haldane and the few men he had left were off licking their wounds.

Keegan was thankful the sky remained clear most of the day with no severe weather in sight. The gentle but persistent wind in the galleon's giant white sails propelled them the fifty or so miles south, between the Scottish mainland and the Hebrides. At first, the islands and their jagged mountains were hazy blue in the distance, but once they sailed closer, the green hills speckled with white sheep and black cattle were clear. He recognized the largest of these islands, Isle of Skye, for he'd visited a few years ago with Da and Uncle Griff, the former chief.

Keegan wished Seona could join him on deck so he could point out the picturesque mountain ranges, the Red Cuillins and the Black Cuillins, but 'twas much safer for her to remain inside the cabin.

The sun was low in the sky when the oarsmen paddled through a few narrow straits and along Loch Alsh. Keegan was glad they were almost to their destination with no sign of trouble. Of course, this was only a stopover, for he was tasked with taking Lady Seona home. A sinking dread settled into his gut.

The ship anchored just off shore from Teasairg Castle, in the middle of the loch, and they took smaller boats to the sea gate. Keegan, Seona, Dirk, Isobel, three guards and an oarsman were in the second boat.

Once they docked and the sea gate opened, Dirk hobbled up the narrow stone steps under his own power. The guards and Isobel followed. Keegan made sure he could catch Seona if she stumbled on the uneven steps. At the top, Dirk was breathing hard and his face was ashen. Although he wasn't moaning in pain, Keegan knew he was feeling it.

Chief Cyrus MacKenzie, frowning darkly, and his brothers, met them in the cobblestone bailey.

Cyrus eyed Dirk's lower leg below his plaid. "Saints! What on earth happened?"

"Arrow through the calf," Dirk said. "'Twas one of Haldane's men. We had a couple of skirmishes during our travels."

"Show them up to Isobel's chamber," Cyrus told the maid standing nearby, then he turned to one of his men. "Go find the healer and send her to Isobel's room."

"Aye, m'laird."

Isobel briefly greeted her brothers while the rest of their party disembarked from the small two-oared boats. Two guards helped Dirk across the bailey and toward the entrance to the keep.

Leaving Seona with Isobel and Patience, who were surrounded by several MacKay guards, Keegan followed Dirk and the two men into the corner of the almost empty great hall. He trailed after them up the narrow turnpike stair and into Isobel's old chamber to make sure the room was safe.

The maid rushed to the small hearth to start a fire while the two guards helped Dirk into the large bed. He sank into what had to be a thick featherbed. Even if Keegan hadn't known this was Isobel's bedchamber from when she was a lass, the lacy curtains and abundance of floral embroidered pillows would've made it clear.

"I thank you, lads," Dirk mumbled, his words slurred.

"M'laird." One of the guards dipped his head. "We'll wait in the corridor."

"Uh-huh," Dirk grunted, his eyes closed.

"How much whisky have you had?" Keegan asked.

"Enough." Dirk forced a grin but his face was sweaty and pale from the exertion and pain.

Keegan had checked on Dirk several times throughout the day where he'd been lying in a hammock style bed used by the sailors. Half the time, Dirk had been sleeping, most likely due to the whisky, or because he'd lost sleep the night before. At least, if he was asleep, he wasn't feeling pain. Keegan hoped the MacKenzie's healer could help Dirk recover.

Rebbie entered the room, his dark eyes concerned. "How is the pain?"

"No' so bad." Dirk winced as he moved his leg.

"You're a bold-faced liar, my friend, but I'll overlook it this time."

"Aye, you'd best do that."

"I'll send Isobel in. She'll cure what ails you."

Dirk actually grinned at that. "Both of you... update Cyrus on everything that's happened."

"We will," Keegan said. "Get some rest."

"Aye."

Keegan and Rebbie left the room, bypassing Isobel, her two maids, and an older woman, perhaps the healer, just as they arrived. At the bottom of the steps, MacMillan approached, carrying Lady Patience, her face white, eyes closed tight, and her hand pressed tightly against her stomach. Keegan cringed, imagining how miserable her extreme nausea must be. But MacMillan was taking good care of her. Keegan suspected the guard did not mind helping her. In fact, he seemed rather taken with the lady and was greatly protective of her.

Seona followed a few feet behind them. When her eyes met Keegan's, she gave him a brief, shy smile. He had come to depend on those to lighten his mood. He winked in return. Even in the dimness, her blush was evident.

"How is your aunt?" Keegan asked, glancing at MacMillan carrying her up the steps.

"Not so well." Seona shook her head. "She's very seasick and her ankle still pains her."

"I hope she recovers from both ailments quickly."

"I thank you. She will be wondering where I am." Seona hastened up the steps.

He stared after her, wishing they could've talked longer about... anything. The topic didn't matter to him. He simply loved listening to her light, feminine voice and looking into her eyes.

He caught up to Rebbie and they headed toward the great hall. "Lucky bastard," Rebbie mumbled.

"What?" Keegan asked, even though he knew what Rebbie was referring to.

"I saw the way she looked at you with that seductive smile."

Keegan couldn't help but grin in response. "She is lovely."

"And you are smitten, my friend."

"Guilty as charged." Keegan only hoped he would find another opportunity soon to talk to Seona and spend some time with her. Their kiss the night before, combined with that revealing conversation, had kept him awake most of the night.

***

Seona entered the chamber Hugh MacMillan had carried her

aunt into. Patience now lay on the bed and the guard waited a few feet away.

"Is there anything else I can do for you, m'lady?" he asked.

"Nay. I thank you, Hugh, for all your help. I don't know how you put up with me."

"Och. M'lady, 'tis no hardship. Would you like me to get a fire started?"

"Nay. Millie will do that. Where is Millie anyway?"

"Here, m'lady." She rushed in from the corridor along with their other maid, Edwina.

MacMillan left and the two maids fussed over Lady Patience, preparing her for bed.

"Is there anything I can do, aunt?" Seona asked.

"Nay, I just want to rest."

"M'lady," one of the MacKenzie's maids addressed Seona from the doorway. "Would you like me to show you to your chamber?"

"Aye," she told her, happy to see she would have her own room and some privacy. "I will return soon," she told Aunt Patience.

Her aunt waved her off as if she didn't want to be bothered with anything. Seona followed the maid down the corridor to the next room.

"Will this suit you?" she asked.

"Aye, 'tis a lovely chamber." Seona surveyed the blue velvet counterpane and curtains on the bed, and the finely made blue, gold and green Turkish carpet underfoot.

The maid lit a fire in the wood and peat that was already laid in the hearth. "Lady Isobel said you might want a bath." The maid stood and faced her.

"That would be wonderful." Seona almost sighed at the thought of sinking into a tub of hot water and scrubbing herself with a nicely scented soap.

"I will have it sent up. Supper will be ready in about an hour." The maid curtsied and left.

Seona moved toward the small window which offered a splendid view out over Loch Alsh. The orange and gold sunset and the blue-gray mountains reflecting in the water was one of the loveliest sights she'd ever seen. She wished she could share it with Keegan. He seemed to enjoy beautiful scenery as much as she did.

But of course, he could not enter her bedchamber. Although she would like him to.

What would it be like if they were married and allowed to sleep in the same bed?

She shook her head, trying to dislodge the spellbinding but impure thoughts.

One of the MacKenzies' manservants arrived, carrying her large sack of clothing which a pack horse had carried from Durness to Ullapool. Poor animal. Well, the bag weighed no more than a hundred pounds, so 'haps it hadn't hurt the animal overmuch.

"I thank you," she told the servant. When he left, she closed the door.

An hour later, she was bathed and dressed in clean clothing, wondering if she should've asked for a tray to be sent to her room instead of going to the great hall.

Nay, she wished to see Keegan again. 'Haps he would escort her to the high table and she would get to touch him for a few moments. 'Twas one of the few joys in life.

A maid arrived to tell her supper was being served. Her heart rate sped up with excitement. But she would not get to talk to Keegan if her aunt joined them. She knocked at Aunt Patience's door. Getting no answer, she poked her head in.

"How are you feeling, aunt?"

"Awful. Just awful!" she griped from the large four-poster bed. "I thought this blasted seasickness would cease once I got off the water."

"I'm sure it will go away soon. Can I bring you something to eat?"

She groaned. "Nay, the very mention of food turns my stomach. I only wish to sleep."

"Very well." Seona exited, and closed the door. She was truly sorry her aunt was so miserable, but maybe she would get some time to talk with Keegan.

In the great hall, everyone was gathering for the meal. She paused, glancing over the crowded room, and Keegan appeared at her side, as he often had at Dunnakeil.

"A good eve to you, Lady Seona." He offered his arm.

"Good eve." She savored the familiar and comforting motion of sliding her hand around his arm and feeling his hard muscles.

"You look lovely," he murmured.

She noticed his hair was still damp from a recent bath and that he'd changed into his finer clothing—a newer blue and green plaid, a clean white linen shirt, and a green doublet. "I thank you. And so do you."

He grinned. "I look lovely, do I?"

"Indeed." She smiled. "Astonishingly handsome, too."

"Och. Lady Seona, you do ken well how to flatter a man." He lowered his voice to a deep, seductive murmur. "That can get you into trouble."

A heated blush seared her skin just as they arrived at the table. Keegan pulled out the chair beside Isobel's and Seona sat.

"I thank you," she told him.

He gave a wee bow and stepped down from the dais.

"How is Laird Dirk?" Seona asked Isobel, hoping her blush was fading.

A small frown drew Isobel's dark brows together. "He is sleeping now. Earlier, the healer soaked his injured leg in hot water and various herbs, then she put some kind of smelly poultice on it. She assured me it would draw the infection from the wound."

"Oh, I certainly hope it does."

"Aye, indeed. My stomach has been in knots with worry."

"He will likely show improvement very soon."

The chair next to Seona slid out. She glanced up to find Keegan taking a seat beside her. She smiled, but then felt her blasted blush returning. Why could she not stop doing that? He sent her a wee smile.

Everyone else took their seats at the high table, including Rebbie and Isobel's five brothers. She had met four of them when they'd visited Durness last winter. They were devilishly dark and attractive men. But none of them captured her interest the way Keegan did with his tawny hair and blue eyes.

After grace, the meal was served, starting with succulent quail and brown crusty bread with butter. Seona didn't realize how hungry she was until she started eating. Never had food tasted this delicious. She barely paid attention to the conversation going on around her about their journey from Durness and the attacks. Enjoying Keegan sitting beside her, which he rarely did, she focused on devouring her food. Though she tried to mind her manners.

"We would like to stay here until Dirk is recovered," Isobel said, drawing Seona's attention. She would also like to stay here, or anywhere Keegan was, instead of going home, but that was impossible.

"Aye. I wouldn't have it any other way," Cyrus said. He had the look of a formidable chief and warrior, tall and broad of shoulder, with long black hair and penetrating dark eyes. Seona found him to be an intimidating man. But when it came to his family, 'twas obvious he cared deeply for them. After all, he had allowed Isobel to choose her own husband.

"Dirk was planning to go with the rest of the men to escort Lady Seona and her aunt home and take her father a gift," Isobel said. "But now he won't be able to."

"What gift?" Fraser MacKenzie asked. Isobel had told her that Fraser was the second youngest brother. He appeared to be in his mid-twenties, but he had to be younger than Isobel, who was five-and-twenty. Fraser resembled Cyrus, except he had blue eyes and his expression was much lighter and carefree. In fact, almost every time she'd seen him, he'd been grinning or smirking. And he possessed a leaner build.

"The horse," Keegan said. "'Tis the finest ever bred at the MacKay stables."

Seona felt bad that Chief Dirk had to give up such a valuable animal because of her. She thought her father would like the horse, but very few things made him happy.

"Why is he taking him such an expensive gift?" Fraser asked.

"Because Lady Seona was not able to marry the MacKay chief. 'Tis complicated," Isobel said.

All eyes turned to Seona and she was glad she didn't have a mouthful of food at that moment. She blotted the linen square against her lips.

"You stole her husband-to-be?" Fraser asked Isobel with a wide grin, his gaze darting back and forth between the two women. "I didn't know that. You kept that quiet while we were in Durness."

"Nay," Seona spoke up. "In truth, I was never betrothed to Dirk."

"There was merely an old contract between Seona's father and the late MacKay chief," Isobel said.

"Dirk's father?" Dermott asked.

This was the first time Seona had met Dermott, Isobel's

second eldest brother, because he hadn't traveled with the others to Durness last winter. He appeared to be around thirty summers. He possessed dark brown hair and green eyes and was not quite as massive in stature as his oldest brother.

"Aye. He was also Aiden's and Haldane's father. They are Dirk's half-brothers," Isobel said.

"We thought Aiden would be chief and that I would marry him," Seona said. "Aiden was chief for about a month, and then Dirk returned."

"Since Dirk is the older son and a stronger leader, the clan agreed that he should be chief. And Dirk was already in love with me…" Isobel smiled.

"Indeed," Seona said. "I did not wish to marry Aiden or Dirk anyway. And especially not their youngest brother, Haldane." Seona wanted to make sure those present knew she held no grudges. "I'm glad Isobel and Dirk found happiness."

"So… who will you marry, Lady Seona?" Fraser asked with a grin, crossing his arms over his chest and leaning back in his chair.

Seona's face heated and she forced herself not to glance at Keegan to gauge his expression. "That remains to be seen," she said, staring down at her almost empty trencher of food. "As you know, very few ladies are permitted to choose their own husbands." She hoped they would soon be off the subject of her marital status.

"'Haps Keegan would be interested in the position," Fraser said.

CHAPTER TWELVE

Keegan glared at Fraser where he sat at the end of the high table. Aye, Keegan was most definitely interested in becoming Seona's husband, but he couldn't announce it at a meal.

"Any man who marries Lady Seona will be fortunate indeed," Keegan said.

"Don't be such a beastie, Fraser, teasing Seona in such a way," Isobel scolded. She looked as if she'd box his ears if he were closer. "Why don't we talk about who *you're* going to marry?"

"No one," Fraser said, sobering. "And I meant no harm. Pray pardon, Lady Seona. I agree with Keegan. Any man who snares you will be lucky."

Seona's blush was still bright enough to light a dim room and Keegan felt bad for her discomfort. Saints, he wished he could declare his intentions now in front of everyone, but first, he wanted to ask Seona to marry him. Regardless of what her father said when Keegan asked for her hand, he wanted to know if Seona was interested in marrying him. To Keegan, that was the most important thing.

When should he ask her?

***

The next evening, Dirk was well enough to join the others in the great hall for supper, and Keegan was glad of it. He'd hated Dirk's talk of *if something happens to me*. Dirk was one of the strongest men Keegan knew and he didn't want to even imagine him dying.

Life was precious and precarious and Keegan preferred to savor each good moment, as his father had taught him.

Life was especially grand at the moment, for he again found an empty seat at the high table right beside Lady Seona.

"Good evening, m'lady."

"Good evening, Keegan." The shy, intimate smile that he relished peeked out. He loved it because 'twas a smile she only bestowed on him. Sure, she smiled at the others, the ladies mostly, but it was not the same smile. And the way she said his name heated him from the inside out.

"How is Lady Patience feeling today?"

"She is not yet fully recovered from the seasickness, although 'tis not as severe as yesterday. Her ankle is still sore. This whole journey has worn her out."

"I'm sorry to hear it." He truly was, but he was glad Lady Patience's hawkish glare was not pinned on him this evening. He and Seona might actually get some time alone to talk or…'haps he might steal another kiss.

He had been reliving the kisses they'd shared and was yearning for another. He was a rogue, he knew, but he could not stop thinking about her and imagining what it might be like to touch her in ways he shouldn't.

He also had to ask her if she would marry him… if he could get her father to agree. 'Haps he should speak to Dirk about it first to get advice on what to do if Chief Murray refused his suit. The last thing Dirk or Keegan wanted was a clan war. And yet, Keegan could not accept a *nay* from her father.

After Fraser had embarrassed her the night before, she'd soon excused herself, pleading exhaustion, and retreated to her room. He was certain it wasn't simply an excuse. She had to be tired from all the traveling. He was glad to see she was in fine spirits this evening.

After the meal, the music and dancing started. Seona could not believe her good fortune in being allowed to sit by Keegan again this evening. Although she was not happy about her aunt's illness, she was glad to have a bit of freedom. In fact, she liked it so much she was determined to get out from under her aunt's thumb permanently. But how would she ever escape her father's heavy hand?

Beside her, Keegan leaned in. "Would you like to dance, Lady

Seona?"

She flushed, feeling as if she'd been drenched in hot bathwater, but an icy chill quickly followed. Indeed, she would love to dance with him, but she recalled the last time she'd danced with a man. Her father had ordered him tossed out and severely beaten. She remembered the horror of seeing him the next day, his face covered in bruises, his lip split. "Oh... nay, Keegan. I don't think I should."

"And why not?" He sent her the devil's own grin, full of mischief and daring. She had to force her gaze away so she wouldn't get pulled into his charm.

Indeed, half the men who'd been sitting at the high table were now on the floor. Even Isobel was dancing with one of her brothers, since Dirk was unable. He had encouraged it since he knew how much she enjoyed dancing.

Seona could not think of a good reason to avoid the dance floor. Her father was not here and her aunt wasn't watching. Likely no one present would care if she danced with Keegan. But what if one of them told her aunt, or what if the servants gossiped?

Her father, and therefore by extension, his sister, Aunt Patience, would only allow her to associate with certain types of men—those who were titled and wealthy, and who would make husbands they'd approve of. All others were off limits. To their way of thinking, there was no reason to dance with a man if she couldn't eventually marry him.

But... she glanced back at Keegan. He lifted a brow and held out his hand. She could not resist taking it and delighting in his warm skin, roughened from handling a sword and being out in the cold wind so much. He lowered their hands, his thumb stroking her sensitive palm and sending shivers up her arm to her breasts. *Heavens!* What a sinful sensation he sent through her body with no more than a light touch to her hand. She bit her lip and forced herself not to look at him.

"Seona?" he whispered, her name more intimate without the formal title of *Lady* attached to it.

She dared to glance up at him and found that his light and playful gaze had changed to midnight blue.

"Aye. I would like to dance," she said to cover her true feelings, which were far grander than simply wanting a dance. She did not understand the enormity of the emotions and yearnings that came over her. She had never experienced anything of the like before.

Keegan led her to the dance floor where they joined the two dozen other couples, most of whom belonged to the MacKenzie clan. She felt more comfortable dancing among strangers. She could be herself and not worry about anyone telling her aunt or her father she was doing something they wouldn't approve of.

She imagined for a brief time that the man touching her and holding her hands was the one she would marry. Wouldn't that be a blissful paradise?

They danced for two more songs, until Seona was out of breath and sweating.

"I think that is all I can take for the moment," she told Keegan.

As he escorted her back to the table, he leaned over and murmured close to her ear, "Meet me in that alcove just beyond your chamber?"

What? Was he mad?

He pulled out her chair and she sat down. Glancing up at him, she took in his dark blue eyes and intense expression.

He dropped into the chair beside hers and pretended to watch the dancing couples, but she felt his attention on her.

Seona sucked in a sharp breath. Had he meant it? And if so, could she slip from the room without anyone noticing, or suspecting they were meeting? What would he say to her and, more importantly, what would he do in the dark alcove? How did he know where her chamber was? Was his chamber off the same corridor? A shiver of anticipation passed over her skin.

She glanced aside to find Keegan's gaze steady upon her.

Of course, she would love a stolen moment in private with him, but what would the cost be? What if someone saw them?

"I must speak to the guards. A good evening to you, Lady Seona." Keegan bowed over her hand, kissed it, and left the table. He then said a few quiet words to the two guards who stood behind Dirk. Seona watched Keegan carefully to see what he was up to. After speaking to Dirk, he moved toward the exit and talked to one of the MacKay guards stationed there. Then, he circled back, his gaze scanning the room, and went up the stairs. Was he going to the alcove he'd mentioned?

Saints! What if her aunt suddenly felt better, left her room and saw them? Seona could get into trouble. On the other hand, she was tired of playing it safe and following everyone's rules but her own. What about what she wanted with all her heart? Didn't that matter?

Since most of the people who'd been seated at the high table were dancing, aside from Dirk and three more who were deep in conversation, no one paid her any mind. When Isobel headed back toward the table, catching everyone's attention, Seona rose and headed up the spiral stone stairs, her moral side warning her to tread carefully. She would simply check on her aunt. Aye, that was it, she decided at the top of the stairs.

She knocked lightly at Aunt Patience's door.

"Who is it?" The snarl came from inside.

Seona opened the door and stuck her head into the dark room, the low-burning fire in the hearth providing a bit of light. "'Tis only me, aunt. How are you feeling?"

"Same as before. Horrible."

"Can I get you anything to eat or drink?"

"Nay. I told you before, the thought of food makes me want to retch. Earlier, Isobel brought that healer in here and she practically forced me to drink some sort of bitter concoction."

"Maybe it will help." Seona remembered drinking a bitter herbal tea when she was sick as a child, and she had recovered soon after. "Where are the maids?"

"I sent them downstairs. I could no longer abide their fidgeting. I just want quiet."

"I will leave you to sleep, then."

"Aye, please do."

Seona backed into the corridor and softly closed the door. She halted for a moment, holding her breath. Did she dare walk thirty more feet to the alcove? Was Keegan awaiting her there?

She drew in a deep breath for courage, then slowly and silently crept forward, her heart pounding louder with each step. Thankfully, the solid floor boards emitted no sounds.

She stopped and peered around the corner. Keegan stood there, leaning against the wall. Even in the dimness she perceived his charming smile. Though he drew her like a lodestone, fear kept her rooted to the spot. She didn't know if she had the courage to take life by the horns as if it were a mad bull. What if she wasn't strong enough to overcome?

Keegan pushed away from the wall and moved toward her. Stopping a few feet away, in the middle of the generous alcove, he held out his hand and waited.

His captivating gaze broke through her paralysis and she approached him. Unable to wait to touch him, she placed her hand into his. He pressed a warm, sweet kiss to it, then drew her back, deeper into the dimness and further from the lantern's glow down the corridor. The only light outside the window was a torch far below.

"Seona," he whispered in her ear and embraced her. She sucked in a surprised breath at the sensation of his hard physique pressed to her body. She nestled closer, her breasts flattening against the granite-like muscles of his chest.

"Oh," she sighed. She had forgotten how delicious he felt.

His hand slid around her waist and pulled her tighter to him. He kissed her temple. Although it was a chaste, friendly kiss, heat seared her. Her hand fisted in the plaid draped across his shoulder and inadvertently drew him closer. He kissed her cheek, his lips hot and firm but also seductively soft. Another kiss, closer to her mouth. Her breath fled as Keegan's mouth hovered over hers. He had kissed her before, and she recalled everything about those blissful moments, but this was different somehow. A fire burned in her chest...a fire that both terrified her and compelled her to lean into him and take everything he would give her. She trembled with the force of the strange emotions.

"Seona?" He lifted his hand to gently tilt her chin up and caress her cheek. His breath teased her lips and his nose touched hers briefly.

"Aye," she responded.

His masculine scent and that of spices from the mulled wine stole her thoughts. When his lips touched hers like a light brush of silk, she was ensnared and her breath remained trapped in her chest.

Some instinct within her surged to the surface and she pressed her lips firmly against his, then she shocked herself by flicking out her tongue to taste his lips.

He growled deep in his chest and embraced her more firmly, one of his hands around her waist, the other cradling her face. She opened her mouth to him, wishing he'd devour her completely. And he did... almost. She certainly felt like a feast he might be having, the way he sank his tongue into her mouth and tormented her. Her body melded to his, and she thought she might drop to the floor, for her legs lost all strength. But he held her up.

"Mmm, Seona, you are sweeter than a strawberry comfit."

What nonsense was he speaking?

She buried her hands in his long, thick hair and wrapped it about her fingers. She wanted to be completely ensnared by him.

Keegan raised his head abruptly as if listening. And then she heard it, voices in the corridor. He moved her deeper into the corner and put her behind him. She recognized the voices... Dirk and Isobel, along with Rebbie, helping his friend to his chamber. Seona held her breath, but it wasn't long before Rebbie bid them goodnight. The door closed and footsteps receded.

Seona relaxed, thankful they'd not been caught. Even though she knew Isobel would keep the secret. In fact, she'd probably encourage Seona to steal more kisses from Keegan. And Rebbie had already caught them once; she was fairly certain he would say naught.

Keegan slipped forward, peered around the corner, then returned. "One of Dirk's guards is stationed in the corridor," he whispered against her ear.

Mo creach!

"I'll go tell him not to say anything, and you can go into your chamber."

"Very well," she whispered, although she truly didn't want to. She'd much prefer to indulge in several more kisses with Keegan.

He kissed her forehead, his affection warming her heart, then turned and strolled down the corridor. Low murmurs reached her as he talked to the guard.

She peered out and Keegan motioned to her. She rushed down the corridor and the guard pretended not to know she was around. How much would Keegan have to pay the guard for that? She silently opened her bedchamber door and hurried inside. Wanting to feel more secure, she barred the door.

Well... that was close. But she smiled at the excitement rushing through her veins. She would've never guessed she'd enjoy taking such risks. Was she mad?

Nay. Keegan was worth any risk.

Seona struggled out of her clothing without a maid's help and crawled into the high, comfortable bed. After lying awake more than two hours it seemed, she realized she would never be able to sleep after Keegan's seductive kiss. Most likely, she would have disturbing, sensual dreams of him all night, and those would keep her half awake.

She craved another of his kisses.

Daft lass. She knew she was foolish and wanton for responding to him. She could never be with him. Her father wouldn't allow it. Her aunt had sent him a missive months ago about Seona being unable to marry the MacKay chief. Even now, her father probably had another chief waiting for her to marry. She prayed he wasn't some ancient laird with rotted teeth. If that was the case, how could she endure it? 'Twould be like torture to receive his attentions in the bedchamber. She cringed just imagining it. An abusive younger man would be just as bad.

A knock sounded at Seona's door, making her jump. *Heavens!* Who could that be? She got up and cracked open the door. Millie stood in the corridor holding a candle, the wide-eyed Edwina beside her.

"What is it? Is Aunt Patience worse?" Seona asked, apprehension slithering through her.

"Nay, m'lady. She is much improved and asked for some food," Millie said.

Seona sighed with relief. "I'm glad she is feeling better."

"Aye. We need to go to the kitchen and find her something to eat, but Edwina refuses to go unless someone comes with us. She's afraid of the dark in this unfamiliar castle."

"Very well. I'll go with you. Let me put on my *arisaid.*" Seona quickly belted the wool plaid around her waist, secured the brooch at her chest and joined the two maids in the corridor.

"I'm sorry to bother you, m'lady. I simply didn't know what else to do."

"'Tis no bother. Do you ken where the kitchen is?"

"Aye, we were there earlier, but 'tis a long trek."

The door where the guard was stationed opened and Isobel stuck her head out. "Is something wrong?" she whispered. "I heard noises out here."

"Nay. Aunt Patience is hungry," Seona said.

"Good. She is improving, then. Wait just a moment." Isobel returned a minute later, also wearing her *arisaid.* "I will show you where the kitchen is. I'm certain there must be some leftover bread and cheese. I need to go down there anyway." Carrying a lantern and a small flask, Isobel led the way.

Seona knew Isobel hated whisky, but maybe Dirk needed more.

"Is Laird Dirk feeling well?"

"Aye, he is sleeping now but when he wakes up he may want more wine or whisky for pain."

The four descended the spiral stairwell, took two turns along a corridor, then descended another stairwell. Finally, they entered the stone-vaulted kitchen. The fires burned low but the room was still cozy. Seona had always enjoyed visiting kitchens because of the warmth and scent of fresh baked bread or savory stew.

Isobel placed a wooden tray on the high cook's table, then moved about the kitchen gathering food items—a wooden bowl of venison broth, bread, hard yellow cheese, and mulled wine.

"Is something wrong, ladies?"

Seona turned to find Keegan behind them, holding a thick candle. Heated excitement rushed over her. "Nay," she said. "'Tis only that Aunt Patience is finally hungry."

His brows lifted. "Ah, 'tis good news, then. Her seasickness must have passed."

"How did you know we were down here?" Isobel asked.

"MacMillan is on guard duty, and he saw the four of you sneak by his post at the bottom of the steps. He told me immediately."

"Where was he? I didn't see him," Isobel said.

"Come now, ladies. Surely you pay more attention than that to what is around you."

"Nay, we depend on you men to do that for us." Isobel smirked.

"Aye, treat us all no better than guard dogs, then."

Seona snickered, and Keegan grinned in response.

"There now," Isobel told Millie. "Take that tray to Lady Patience. If she needs more, feel free to come down here and get it. There is naught to fear, Edwina. This castle is safe. As a child, I used to wander all over it, even at night. Indeed, sometimes I would wake up and find myself here, in the kitchen."

The timid maid nodded, but didn't appear convinced.

"I thank you, m'lady," Millie said. "Come, Edwina. Carry the candle."

The two proceeded up the steps.

"What are you doing up this late, Keegan?" Isobel asked.

"I was playing cards with three of your brothers."

"I hope you beat them."

"Aye, I won a few. I'll be glad when Dirk is recovered enough to play a few hands."

"He feels better, but his leg still pains him greatly. That reminds me… I need to get a bottle of mulled wine and fill up the whisky flask." Taking the small lantern, she disappeared down a short corridor and into the storeroom off the side of the kitchen.

Seona could not stop her gaze from wandering back to Keegan. He was already watching her, his normally light blue eyes much darker in the dim room, lit only by the low-burning kitchen fire and the candle he had brought with him and set on the scarred table.

The kiss they'd shared in the alcove upstairs burned through her mind. *Saints!* He had made her weak with powerful yearnings and emotions she didn't understand.

"I'm glad your aunt is much improved," Keegan said. "Likely, she will be kicking up her heels tomorrow."

Seona held back a grin. "I don't know about that, but at least she is craving food again."

"You will escort Seona back to her room when you are done talking, will you not, Keegan?" Isobel asked, startling Seona.

What?

"Aye, of course."

CHAPTER THIRTEEN

Seona stared after Isobel as she disappeared up the steps, a bottle of wine and flask of whisky in one hand and the lantern in the other. What was she up to, leaving Seona alone with Keegan in the kitchen?

Well… Seona knew Isobel wanted her and Keegan together. She encouraged her at every opportunity, because she wanted Seona to have a happy marriage like she had. But Seona did not see how that could happen.

Her gaze darted back to Keegan. He watched her as an osprey watches a salmon, with a concentrated focus that might be called hunger. Aye, she hungered for him as well.

His brows quirked in a wee, concerned frown. "Are you afraid?"

"Nay." Did she look afraid? She tried to smooth out her features. She certainly didn't fear Keegan. Only what he represented—everything she wanted, standing before her, just waiting. She still wasn't sure she was brave enough to grab hold and face down all the obstacles.

"Good. I would never want you to be frightened of me, Seona." His deep, soothing voice was spellbinding.

"I'm not. I trust you more than anyone." 'Twas the truth and she was not shy about admitting it to him.

"That means more to me than I can say," he whispered. "But 'haps you shouldn't."

His words should have alarmed her, but they didn't for she suspected she knew what he was about to say. "Why not?"

His gaze grew more penetrating. "Because I wish for things I have no right wishing for."

Another kiss?

"When I'm alone with you…" he said, shaking his head, "I find I want to…" He blew out a sharp breath and glanced away. "Hell, why am I telling you this?"

"I want you to tell me." She yearned to know his every thought. "I couldn't sleep." That was her confession. Surely he would understand her meaning—she couldn't sleep because thoughts of him kept taunting her, especially after he'd consumed her mouth earlier.

"Would one more goodnight kiss help?" His expression remained serious. Passionate.

Her heartbeat thumped in her throat. "Aye." 'Twas a lie. The kiss would not help her sleep; it would keep her awake the rest of the night. But 'twas the one thing she craved most, as a starving person craves bread.

Gradually, he moved closer to her, stroked his warm hand along her cheek, leaned down and pressed his lips to hers… twice, completely seducing her. She slid her hands around his neck. Each kiss was more lingering than the last, then he flicked his tongue against her mouth, sparking fiery yearnings within her. She parted her lips, inviting a deeper kiss. With a soft moan, he indulged her. He tasted faintly of spiced wine, but mostly, he tasted like a man she wanted to devour.

Before she knew what was happening, the passion exploded. She could not get close enough to him, and he seemed equally determined to bring her body as tightly as possible to his. Her knees grew weak and her feet left the floor. The sensation of flying suffused her with dizziness. He was carrying her, she realized, awareness of his strength only fueling her desire for him.

A moment later, she felt him kick a door closed behind them. Opening her eyes, she could see naught. The room was pitch black and the air smelled of spices and flour. The storeroom?

Saints! Would he seduce her in truth?

If so, she was ready. Life was short and she needed a few precious, sparkling moments to bring her joy during the dark days of the future.

"Lady Seona?" he whispered, his breathing harsh and unsteady as he held her against the door, her toes barely touching the floor.

"Aye."

"You are not frightened, are you?"

"Nay." In the darkness, she stroked her palm along his bristly square jaw, then kissed his lips, eliciting a groan from him.

He grazed his tongue between her lips. That move shattered her thoughts and her composure. Her hands fisting in his hair, she drew him closer and welcomed his tongue invading her mouth.

Oh, how she craved this man, the taste of him, the scent and feel of him. He was tall, his shoulders broad and thick with muscle. His chest and stomach were hard against her, as was a lower, male part of him. She knew little about men's bodies, but since the evening she had seen Keegan walking naked from the loch, she had been fascinated. Through their clothing, his hard shaft pressing against her lower belly enthralled her.

"Mmm," he hummed quietly and consumed her mouth. That sensation she'd felt before when he'd kissed her was now besieging her ten times stronger than before. It had to be the arousal Isobel had told her about. She had said the kissing and caressing a man did would make a woman eager for the bedding. Seona had never experienced this before Keegan had kissed her that first time. But now she knew, she wanted his naked skin brushing against hers.

She wanted him to bed her.

But she couldn't. If her father found out, he'd surely beat her. At the same time, she could not refuse Keegan anything he wanted, because she wanted the same things. She wouldn't turn away from him.

"I want to touch you," Keegan whispered between little kisses, his hand skimming from her waist to the side of her hips.

"Aye," she agreed, perhaps a bit too eagerly. She didn't know where or how he would touch her, but she craved it, his hands, his mouth.

"I'd never do anything to harm you. You ken that?" he asked.

"Aye." She loved how he was so considerate and protective of her.

Her skin burned, head to toe. She knew not what to do, or what he would do. In the next instant, he unfastened the brooch that held her wool plaid *arisaid* together at her chest.

He was undressing her? She shivered in expectation.

He kissed her again, and pulled her closer. Bending slightly, he placed his hand behind her knee and pulled her leg upward, rubbing her knee alongside his hip. *Heavens!* Her legs were spread in a decadent way that made her crave having him between.

He placed his hand on her calf, then slid it beneath the hem of her *arisaid* and her smock. His hand heated her bare skin as he stroked her calf gently, entrancing her. Tingles traveled up her leg toward her center.

"Oh," she breathed, tilting her head back and allowing him to scatter little kisses down her neck.

He slid his hand to her knee, then higher, his fingertips trailing lightly along the outside of her thigh, delightful and stimulating. She held on 'round his neck, lest she fall over from lightheadedness.

His questing hand moved higher, up her thigh, to the flare of her bare hip. Oh, saints, he was bold.

He purred against her throat and glided his hand down the outside of her thigh again to her knee, then slowly up the sensitive skin of her inner thigh. She held her breath in anticipation while he leisurely stroked his fingertips back and forth, lightly teasing her skin, making her tingle and ache in shocking places. Some primal part of her urged her to spread her legs and allow him to stroke her very core. She gasped. She could not do that.

At least she should not.

But her need for Keegan was too strong to ignore, and she wished to feel his hands all over her. She wanted him to teach her everything about passion and carnal relations.

Using his thumb, he stroked over the upper part of her mound, tickling through her hair. She felt paralyzed, unwilling to stop him, but too afraid to move.

His heated breath fanned against her throat and the upper part of her chest. Her plaid fell behind her, leaving her covered in naught but a linen smock. She shivered, hot and cold at once. Keegan's bristly jaw rubbed against her breast, the course whiskers prickling the sensitive skin of her nipple through the material.

She gasped, for she had never felt such a sensation—raw need and possessiveness.

He moaned and brushed his lips over her beaded nipple, then plucked at it through the fabric.

Breathing hard, she pulled him closer. "Aye," she whispered, needing more. A second later, he slipped his fingers between her legs. *Saints!* A shock cut through her at the same time sizzling pleasure jolted her. She had never been touched *there* by anyone. She even tried to avoid touching herself on that spot. He was lightly but deliberately caressing, bare skin to bare skin. Heat and lust seared her.

"Lass, you are luscious and wet," he murmured low in her ear.

She knew not what that meant... except that she wanted him... craved for him to do something more to her, to appease this powerful need. Oh, how she ached inside.

She clutched his plaid in her fist, pulling him closer. "Keegan?"

"Aye. Do you like this?"

"Aye. You make me feel..." How could she describe something she'd never felt before?

"I ken what you mean," he whispered against her breast, then using his lips, he tugged at her nipple again.

With frantic unsteady movements, she untied the neck of her smock and yanked at it, until her breasts were bared to him.

He muttered a curse and took full advantage, drawing her nipple into his mouth and sucking.

"Oh," she breathed, dizziness storming through her. She clung onto his broad shoulders for dear life.

His wicked fingers teased her beyond bearing. She widened her legs, allowing him access to the mysterious part of her that tingled unmercifully.

He rubbed his fingers over the spot and massaged in a circle. The sensations were startling, blinding, and impossibly pleasurable.

She heard herself cry out.

"Shh, lass. No one must hear us."

"Aye." She bit her lower lip to keep from making noise, but the intense, delightful feelings almost overcame her.

His mouth covered hers again and she eagerly sucked at his tongue as his fingers tormented her. He slipped one of his fingers further between her legs. Oh, that was where she ached for him! He must have sensed what she wanted. She widened her thighs more.

He hissed a curse, stroking in and out, very shallowly. "Seona. You feel so good."

Unbidden, a high-pitched cry came from her. Realizing what she was doing, she forced herself to be silent again, no matter how incredible it felt.

He slid his fingers to the tingling, sensitive spot and teased it again. She had become very moist and needy, craving his attention. She wanted to push him to the floor and climb atop him. She did not understand it. Nothing made sense, and she could not think anyway.

She pressed her hip more firmly against his shaft where it stood upright toward his stomach. He moaned. That hard appendage was what she craved stroking her instead of his fingers. She knew it was designed to slide inside her.

Her hips moved wantonly but she could not stop them. He turned her so that her back was to him more. With her derriere pressed against his shaft and her legs spread wide, he held her tight, his hand caressing her.

He kissed her neck, then urged her to turn her head toward him. He locked his mouth to hers and rubbed her more firmly and persistently. She cried out at the intensifying sensations, but he caught the sounds with his mouth. She found herself arching her back, yearning for something more.

A strange, otherworldly feeling overwhelmed her—shivers hurtling through her body and converging on her center. Primal pleasure seized her. She could not breathe, or think. "What…?" she gasped. Keegan's mouth covered hers, and she felt she was leaving the earth, shooting straight up into the stars. Every muscle in her body contracted over and over, wishing to clutch onto Keegan, but she couldn't. She yanked at his clothing, trying to show him what she needed, but he was in the wrong place. She could only arch her back and grind her derriere against his stone-hard shaft.

He groaned in her ear. "Aye, Seona, lass. That's it."

Near suffocating, she gasped for breath, trying to regain her reasoning abilities. What had happened? Her whole weakened body trembled in the wake of that storm of sensation.

A fist banged at the door, breaking through the sensual fog in her brain.

CHAPTER FOURTEEN

Another knock sounded at the storeroom door. Keegan froze, his body pressed close to Seona's. "Shh," he hissed in her ear, then lowered her smock. He was unable to see her in the absolute darkness of the storeroom, but he knew she had to be horrified that someone was pounding at the door not five seconds after he'd brought her to climax. How could someone interrupt one of the most amazing experiences of his life?

"'Twill be all right," he whispered, then directed her behind the door. He felt her struggling to adjust her smock and *arisaid* into place. He'd love to help her, if only he could see, but everything had to be done by touch in this windowless room.

He felt to make sure his own clothes were still straight and in place, then he cracked the door open.

Fraser stood outside. His frown shifted to a mischievous lopsided grin. "What in blazes are you doing in there, Keegan?" he asked, keeping his voice quiet.

"Drinking ale." Or maybe mulled wine would've been a better lie.

"In the dark?" Fraser snorted. "I don't think 'tis ale you're drinking."

Heat washed over Keegan. Aye, he'd been caught, and he'd never been able to lie his way out of anything. "How did you know I was in here?"

"One of the kitchen servants came down to start baking bread and heard a noise. I was talking to the guard when she reported it."

He grinned. "Which maid do you have in there with you?"

"Damnation," Keegan muttered. "You must not tell anyone. Promise me." He hoped his worried gaze communicated the seriousness of the matter.

Fraser sobered. "Of course I won't. I ken well how awkward it is to be caught with a lass."

Keegan gave a brief nod. His stomach clenched for he knew not whether he could trust Fraser. He had only known him a short time. He seemed like an honest and trustworthy man, about a year younger than himself. But Fraser was a rogue who thought of little beyond finding another lass to bed.

"No one can know she is down here with me."

"Very well. I'll help you slip her out. Just a minute." Fraser turned and moved toward the stairs again. "'Tis two huge rats," he called up to someone waiting at the top.

"Oh heavens!" the female said. "I shan't go down there until they're gone."

"I'll get them, Mary. You go back to your chamber for about a half hour." He then told the guard to return to his post. "I'll be right back," Fraser whispered to Keegan, then disappeared up the steps. He returned a couple of minutes later. "All clear up to the second floor." His eyes narrowed as he looked over Keegan's shoulder. But of course, he could see naught. "Why do I get the feeling 'tis not one of the servants you've seduced?"

"I didn't seduce anyone." Keegan frowned, hating that Fraser would think the worst of Seona once he learned she was behind the door.

"Not enough time, aye? That can be damned frustrating."

Keegan's face heated, though he knew not why. He was not one easily embarrassed. Although he didn't have a reputation as a gallant or a rogue, he had bedded a few lasses over the past few years. Even then, he would not say he'd *seduced* anyone. Usually it was the lasses who'd seduced him, in a manner of speaking.

Aside from that, he had not planned to take Seona, anyway. Indeed, he would like to but... he could not endanger her uncertain future.

Fraser chuckled. "Come on, man. Bring her out so she can return to her sleeping quarters. She must be exhausted since you've kept her up half the night."

"Can you hand me that candle?" Keegan motioned to the one

sitting on the cook's table."

"Aye." Fraser retrieved it for him.

"I thank you." Keegan closed the door, set the candle on the floor, and turned back to Seona. Finding her wide-eyed and pale, he took her hands. "I'm sure you heard, 'tis only Fraser," he whispered. "He's promised he won't tell anyone and that he'll help get you back to your room. I never meant to endanger your reputation. I simply wanted—"

She rose onto her tiptoes and kissed his lips briefly. Arousal riveted him along with a generous helping of affection.

"Och, Seona, lass." How he wanted her in every way. But this might be their last private moment together. He leaned down, claiming her lips again. Though the kiss started out soft and slow, it quickly grew to burning and volatile. Arousal demanded that he press her against the wall and have his way with her... but he couldn't do that.

Forcing himself to pull back, he cursed and clenched his teeth. How passionate she was. She had to be his, always.

After taking her hand, he led her to the doorway. As soon as he opened it, Fraser turned toward them.

"I thought you were—" His words stalled when his gaze landed on Seona. He smiled and shook his head. "I should've guessed." He shoved Keegan's shoulder as he emerged from the tiny room. "You dog. Defiling ladies?"

"Well, I wasn't... exactly." He couldn't tell Fraser how much Seona meant to him.

"Aye, indeed. Not to worry. I've defiled a few myself." He chuckled.

"Fraser," Keegan chided between his teeth and sent him a meaningful frown, trying to convince him not to embarrass Seona any more than she already was. Her face was dark red, even in the dimness of the kitchen.

"Very well. I'll behave myself." At the base of the stairs, Fraser said, "Wait here." He ran up the steps, then returned seconds later and motioned. "All clear."

Keegan climbed the steps first, holding Seona's hand and pulling her up behind. That way, if they ran into someone, he could conceal her.

"Are you well?" he whispered back to her as they moved along a corridor.

"Aye." Her response was barely above a breath.

Fortunately, they reached the upper corridor where her bedchamber was without meeting anyone. Of course, Dirk's guard was still on duty, but once he recognized them, he again pretended not to see Seona.

"Have a good night's sleep, m'lady," Keegan whispered.

Seona gave a brief curtsy and hastened down the corridor and into her room. If Fraser and the guard hadn't been there, she might have allowed him another kiss. But that was impossible now. With regret, he turned to leave. He doubted he could sleep much after that, even though 'twas past midnight.

"Come, let's go have a wee dram," Fraser said. "I'm thinking you need it. Or another lass."

"A wee dram, aye. Another lass, nay." Keegan followed him down the stairs. Another lass was the last thing he would ever want.

At the bottom, Fraser gave him a questioning look, then shook his head. "You have the sickness, man."

Aye, he knew Fraser was right, but he remained silent until they entered the small room off to the side of the great hall. Fraser took a decanter of whisky from the shelf and poured a bit into two small, expensive crystal glasses, then offered him one.

Fraser clicked his glass to Keegan's, then downed the shot.

Keegan took a large sip and savored the burn. He only drank whisky on rare or special occasions, and he supposed this was one. Or maybe not.

"Do you not have the sickness?" Fraser persisted. "You are smitten with the lady."

"Aye. 'Tis true," Keegan admitted. He didn't regret it, nor was he ashamed. "I've never met anyone like her before." Every time he saw her, his mood lifted. When she smiled, it was like a hundred suns were shining inside him.

Fraser dropped into his brother's huge chair behind the desk. "What will you do?"

Keegan shrugged and sat across from him. What could he do? "I want to marry her, but I suspect her father will not allow it."

"Marry? Saints! You are mad." Fraser's blue eyes gleamed with humor.

"I am mad for her," Keegan said in a matter-of-fact tone. "But I thought you agreed with me, that any man would be fortunate to marry her."

"Aye, she is beautiful, but marriage seems like…" Fraser cringed. "Being trapped in a dungeon."

"Nay, my friend. One day you will understand how I feel when you meet that one special woman."

"I don't see it happening, unless a witch casts a spell on me or something equally horrible." Fraser rose, retrieved the whisky and poured more for both of them.

"I have to take her home to her father in a few days." Keegan's stomach knotted and ached with the very thought. 'Twas the last thing he wished to do. He wanted to take her north to his home, not east.

"So… why not ask her father for her hand?"

Keegan nodded. "I will. 'Tis what Dirk suggested. But I ken my chances are slim."

"Well, maybe her father will force you to marry her since you've…"

"I've not done what you're imagining," Keegan said. "She is still an innocent lady."

"Only because I interrupted." Fraser gave a broad grin. "And maybe you should. Ruin her and her father will have no choice but to force you to marry her."

Nay, the thought did not set well with Keegan. It felt underhanded and dishonorable. "I'm thinking that would not work. He insists on her marrying a chief or titled laird. 'Tis my suspicion that if he thought she was no longer a virgin, he would marry her off to the first eligible laird that came along, no matter his age or disposition."

Fraser's dark brows lowered into a frown. "He sounds like a right ogre."

"Aye. And if I don't take her back to him, 'twould be inviting an attack from the powerful Murray Clan."

Fraser nodded. "'Tis a bad position to be in."

Keegan swallowed another generous sip of whisky, the burn reminding him of how much he yearned for Seona. "Dirk has named me his tanist."

Fraser sat forward. "Well, there you are! 'Tis a title. Second in line to be chief is an important position."

"Aye, and I am honored. 'Tis more than I'd ever imagined, but 'tis doubtful her father will consider it a high enough position. I own no property."

"'Tis better than naught. I want to come with you."

"Where?"

"To see the lass's father. I'll ask Dermott to come along, too. He has met Chief Murray. Dermott is tanist for our clan."

"Very well. Dirk is not well enough to go as he'd planned." His injury deeply concerned Keegan.

"We know most of the clans between here and Murray's holdings. We can easily secure lodgings each night of our travels."

"'Twould be a great help to us." Keegan had never before traveled this far south on the mainland and had met none of the chiefs or their men. If he was to be Dirk's tanist and right hand man, he had to make good connections.

Plus, he would need all the help he could get to convince Seona's father to allow them to wed.

***

Seona threw off her *arisaid* and climbed into the high, four-poster bed. She snuggled down and drew the covers over her head, her face still burning. *Heavens!* What had just happened to her? Isobel had been right—Seona could've never imagined such intensity of sensation and carnal pleasure was possible. 'Twas almost like magic when Keegan had touched her. And he hadn't even made love to her. He had simply used his hands and his mouth. Surely, the full bedding experience would leave her passed out on the floor.

But to have Fraser catch them... how humiliating. He must think her a harlot. She hoped he would tell no one, else she would be in deep water.

Seona wished she could talk to Keegan now and ask him about what she'd experienced. She was certain he would be patient in explaining the sensations and teach her how lovemaking worked. He'd already taught her shocking things about her own body. She had not known she was capable of feeling such things. Her physical body had been dormant and asleep until he'd awakened it with a simple touch.

Feeling calm and satiated for the first time ever, she floated off to sleep, only to be awakened what seemed a moment later by loud knocking on the door. But it couldn't have been a moment, for bright sunlight beamed through the small window.

Saints! Had she slept half the day?

***

Haldane MacKay and his remaining ten men had spent all night traveling from Kyle of Loch Alsh, where they'd disembarked from a galleon. He'd had a devil of a time securing passage in Ullapool. Linden MacKenzie certainly wasn't going to allow it. In fact, he'd sent the constable after Haldane and his men. They'd escaped and hidden out for several hours.

Then, the night before, Haldane had paid a captain employed by a different shipping company a handsome sum for passage. That bag of gold and silver McMurdo had lifted from Dirk's tent was proving useful. Haldane had hired several men with it, though he hadn't paid them in full yet. They'd have to complete the job first. But he was well aware he had to watch his back closely or any of the new men might murder him for the pouch of money.

Haldane doubted McMurdo would kill him, because he knew if Haldane was dead, his chances of securing the burial spot he coveted within Balnakeil Church would be nonexistent. In fact, McMurdo seemed like his own personal bodyguard.

Haldane grinned as he climbed the bush-covered hill near the edge of Loch Long, McMurdo scrambling up behind him. Once they'd ascended far enough to see over the trees, the top of a gray stone castle came into view over the hilltop. Once they climbed higher, Haldane could see that the castle stood on a tiny island at the point where three lochs met.

"Is that it?" Haldane asked.

"Aye. 'Tis Teasairg Castle." McMurdo breathed hard from the exertion.

"It appears they have strong defenses," Haldane muttered, watching the guards stationed on the wall-walk and the battlements.

"Without doubt. MacKenzie is a powerful chief."

So… that's where Seona and Dirk were. Since Dirk was injured, he was unlikely to show his face for a good long while… if he survived the wound.

Soon, several of the MacKay men would take Seona and her aunt home, toward the east. Haldane would grab her then and head back to Durness, by ship or *birlinn* if possible, to make it quick. Once he reached Dunnakeil, he and his men would take the castle. The only task left at that point would be killing Dirk. He was still counting on McMurdo to figure out a way to take care of that problem, if an infection hadn't already.

After descending the hill and rejoining the other men, they hid in the bushes and watched the crofter's cottages along the edge of the loch. Several of them showed no signs of activity this morn. Likely, the inhabitants had taken their sheep to the high pastures on the mountains. Some wouldn't be back until autumn.

He and his men slipped to one of the cottages near the edge of the wood, and he forced the door open. He was right. No one inside the fully furnished home. No food either, unfortunately. He and his men would sleep a few hours, then head out later. He didn't look forward to hiring a boat or ferry to take them across the loch. 'Twas money he'd rather spend for something else, but the loch was named Long for a reason, McMurdo had told him, and going around it was out of the question.

Haldane wasn't daft enough to storm Teasairg Castle. They'd merely wait until the party escorting Seona emerged, then follow and find the best opportunity to snatch her.

CHAPTER FIFTEEN

After being startled awake by the loud knocking on her door, Seona rushed across the room, unbarred the door and opened it a crack.

"Is something wrong?" Aunt Patience asked, her hand propped against the doorframe, her dark hair coiled into a perfect style.

Seona's face heated as she tried to smooth down her disheveled hair. "What do you mean?"

"Millie said she knocked on your door twice before breakfast but there was no response. When she tried to open your door, it was barred."

"I didn't hear her. I must have been sleeping soundly."

Aunt Patience's dark blue eyes narrowed and inspected her. "I'll send one of the maids in to help you get dressed. 'Tis almost time for midday meal, and Isobel is all in a tizzy about having the meal outside in the garden. 'Tis silly if you ask me. Did we not eat enough meals outside during our travels here?"

Seona shrugged. Judging by the sunlight beaming through her window, it appeared to be a nice, warm day. "It could be fun."

"I suppose," she said, sounding like a snob.

Seona noticed her aunt was without her cane today. "How is your ankle?"

"A bit better." She limped away, then called back, "I'll send the maid for you."

An hour later, the MacKays and MacKenzies gathered around three long tables in the stone paved center of the garden. Red and pink roses climbed the gray stone walls surrounding it, filling the air with a wonderful scent. Standing at the edge of the activity, Seona glanced up at the clear blue sky, with only a few wisps of white clouds, and relished the warm sunlight on her face. 'Twas indeed a rare and spectacular day.

A familiar deep voice reached her. *Keegan.* She turned her head to find him standing near the castle's rear exit talking to the other men. The memory of last night flashed into her mind, bringing scorching heat to her face.

Heavens! She had been shamefully wanton, hadn't she? The way she'd allowed Keegan to touch her in shockingly intimate places. What would he think of her today? She was not certain now that she could face him. She tore her gaze away, turned her back and pretended to be studying the roses against the wall. Maybe he wouldn't notice her and she could slip back inside.

What was wrong with her? She drew in a deep breath, trying to calm her pounding heartbeat. She was no longer a child who could run and hide when she didn't want to face a stranger or deal with a difficult situation. Of course, Keegan was no stranger. But talking to him and looking into his eyes after what they'd shared in the dark... surely she would melt into a puddle of mortification on the stones beneath her feet.

"Lady Seona, 'tis a lovely day, aye?" Keegan said behind her.

She sucked in a surprised breath, praying she wouldn't pass out or do something equally daft, then turned to face him.

"Aye, lovely," she repeated, darting a glance up into his eyes, bright blue, like the sky.

"But not as lovely as you," he murmured in a lower tone, a wee grin lifting his lips.

Her face burned as if she'd stood too long in the sun. "I thank you." Unable to hold his gaze, she stared at the ground. 'Twas too much, too intense. Her heart thumped so loudly she could hardly hear anything beyond it.

He turned aside and offered his elbow. By habit, she slid her hand around his arm and he led her to one of the tables, all of which were already crowded. Each bench was only long enough for two people, or three if they were small. But none were completely empty. He seated her beside Aunt Patience, then proceeded to one of the other tables to sit with a few of the men.

Blast. Much as she'd wanted to hide from him minutes ago, now she missed sitting beside him. Of course, with Aunt Patience there, that might not be possible.

The meal dragged by, but the food was delicious. She was saved from total boredom because Isobel and Dirk sat at the same table. He had better color today and was grinning more. The way he and Isobel interacted with such affection, humor, and care made Seona's heart yearn for something she might never have. What would it be like to be married to the person who made your heart sing? It seemed pure fantasy.

After the meal was over, Dirk limped away to talk with the men at another table.

"Come, Seona," Isobel said, rising to her feet. "I want to show you something."

Seona followed her to a small doorway cut into the stone wall, then up a narrow dark stairway. They emerged outside on a roof or small terrace of some sort. More plants and flowers grew here and a bench sat toward the back.

"'Tis amazingly beautiful up here." Seona took in the view toward the west, over Loch Alsh, with jagged mountains and islands in the distance. Spectacular. Turning, she glanced southeast over Loch Duich. The surface of the water was so still and glassy it mirrored the blue sky and the vivid green mountains.

"Aye," Isobel said. "My mother loved gazing out over the lochs so much my father had this terrace built for her. Down in the garden, 'tis impossible to see over the high defensive walls. Then, she planted a few wildflowers up here. I would often find my mother and father up here on nice summer days."

Bittersweet tears burned Seona's eyes for she knew Isobel's parents had both passed a few years ago, but they'd shared a great love. 'Twas what had inspired Isobel to find her own true love. Seona's parents had been the opposite. Her father had cared naught for her mother. She, in turn, had lived a miserable life, having been forced to marry Chief Murray at a young age. At all costs, Seona did not want to share her mother's fate. But how could she prevent it?

"Did you and Keegan talk in the kitchen last night?" Isobel whispered, sending Seona an impish grin.

Seona hated the way her cheeks burned. How could she stop

blushing whenever Keegan was mentioned? "Aye, we talked for a few minutes."

"Well, I hope he was a gentleman."

"Indeed. When is he not?" Seona was unsure if his actions had been gentlemanly or not, but he hadn't taken her virtue. Was that what Isobel had meant? However, the things he had done with his wandering hands, and his wicked mouth, had not been proper behavior at all. But she had reveled in it.

"Speak of the devil," Isobel murmured with a grin.

"What?" Seona turned to find Keegan emerging from the small doorway leading from the stairwell.

"I have to go see what trouble Dirk is getting into." Isobel strode toward the doorway as Keegan approached Seona, one hand behind his back. Was he hiding something?

"What are you about?" she asked, eying him suspiciously.

He grinned and brought his hand from behind his back. In it, he held a small bundle of bluebells.

She drew in a sharp breath and glanced up into his eyes, his expression filled with happiness.

"These bluebells match your eyes so perfectly, I had to bring them to you." He held the flowers out to her.

"I thank you," she said just above a whisper and accepted them. The two dozen or so stems were bound together by a strip of plaid material. Had he ripped this from his own clothing? She pressed her nose into the bluebells and sniffed, catching a faint sweet fragrance. "Where did you find these?"

"By the loch shore." He nodded toward the south.

No one had ever given her flowers before. Emotion grabbed at her throat but she pushed it back. She refused to let Keegan see any tears from her in such a public place. "You are too kind."

"I think not. You deserve far more, Lady Seona." He lowered his voice. "I wish I could give you the world."

"I don't want the world. This is all I want." Glancing up into his eyes, she sniffed the flowers again. *Him.* He was what she wanted.

His gaze penetrated her for a long moment, then abruptly he glanced around them, toward the castle and the garden below.

Would he have kissed her if they'd had more privacy?

He motioned toward the bench. "Would you like to sit?"

"Aye."

He dropped down beside her on the stone slab and turned to her. "I hope you're not angry with me because of last night," he said, just above a whisper.

"Nay. Why would I be?" It had been the best experience of her life so far.

"Well... I took liberties, shall we say." His brow furrowed. "I probably shouldn't have touched you the way I did, but—"

"Surely, you ken 'twas what I wished as well," she whispered.

He observed her, his eyes darkening, then he blew out a sharp breath—in relief or growing desire, she was not certain.

"But I worry now that you think me a wanton or a harlot," she confessed, her face feeling scalded again.

He frowned. "Nay. Never, m'lady."

"Master Keegan?" the male voice came from the doorway that led to the terrace. A second later Hugh MacMillan appeared.

"Aye, what is it?" Keegan asked.

The guard's face appeared flushed. He stared at his feet for a moment. "Lady Patience sent me."

Keegan's annoyed gaze darted to Seona, then back to MacMillan. "And what is her message?"

"She wishes to see Lady Seona."

How had her aunt seen them? Seona's stomach ached and frustration near overwhelmed her. Why could she not have any time alone with Keegan without someone cutting it short?

"Where is she?" Seona asked.

"I took her upstairs. She was tired."

Seona stood. "I thank you again for the lovely flowers, Keegan."

"You're most welcome." He stood, took her hand and kissed it. "I'm going deer stalking with the MacKenzies. I will see you at supper."

"Very well. Have a care," she said, wishing she could spend the afternoon with him instead.

The bundle of flowers in one hand, Seona descended the stairs and went in search of her aunt. If she had seen Keegan within three yards of her, Seona would likely get another scolding.

Taking her time, she climbed the stairs within the castle, then proceeded to her own bedchamber. She placed the lovely little bouquet of bluebells in a pottery vase of water on the windowsill. Her eyes misted because Keegan had been so thoughtful and romantic in picking them for her. He was a treasure. She remembered the first time he'd told her that her eyes were the color of bluebells, during the gale when they'd taken shelter against the rocks. She took a moment to savor how charming and sweet he was.

She truly believed he cared for her.

Unable to delay the inevitable any longer, she strode down the corridor and knocked at her aunt's bedchamber door.

"Enter," she called, though the word was more like a command.

Seona slowly opened the door, went in and closed it behind her. "How are you feeling?"

"Tired." Still fully dressed except for her shoes, Aunt Patience reclined in bed, her swollen ankle elevated on two pillows.

Seona could not miss her aunt's ominous glare or her lowered brows. Had Fraser told someone he'd discovered her and Keegan last night? Had gossip spread? She braced herself for the worst. "You wished to see me?"

"Indeed. I will tell it to you straight, lassie. Your father will beat you if you are carrying Keegan MacKay's bastard."

A slap could not have surprised Seona more. She gasped. "What? I am not!"

"You'd best hope not. I saw the two of you all cozy and romantic on that terrace." She motioned toward her window.

Saints! Seona had not realized the window looked out over the terrace and gardens. Nor had she known her aunt was up here, spying. She'd left her at a table in the garden. MacMillan must have carried her up here while Seona was talking to Isobel and enjoying the views.

"I saw the flowers he brought you," Patience said, her lip lifting as if in disgust.

How dare she think what Seona and Keegan shared was disgusting? To Seona, 'twas the most beautiful and deeply meaningful thing on earth. Mayhap her aunt was jealous because MacMillan hadn't brought her flowers.

"If he hasn't seduced you yet, I'm sure 'tis not for lack of trying. I told you he was a rogue."

"He has not seduced me." 'Twas the truth, and Seona had no problem saying it. "Nor is he a rogue." She had not seen Keegan so much as look at another woman during the months she had known him. That realization riveted her. Every time she had seen him, his attention had been on her or on his duties. Could he be that devoted to her? Her eyes burned.

"He is not good enough for you," her aunt said. "What kind of life would you have?"

A happy one. Moisture welled in her eyes.

"The only home he could provide would be a small cottage," Patience muttered.

That wouldn't be so bad, if Seona could be with Keegan. And if she could bring her sister with her.

Seona blinked hard, fighting back the tears. "A fine castle isn't always the most important thing."

"Indeed?" Her aunt's gaze grew sharper. "Do you not need warm shelter, food and drink? Do you not need the safety of a castle and walls in the event of an attack?"

"Of course." Seona had not considered where they might live if she married Keegan. Dunnakeil was a huge castle. 'Haps Dirk and Isobel would not mind if they lived there, too. After all, Keegan and Dirk were close family, and Keegan was tanist.

"There is no way in hades your father will allow you to marry him, so don't even imagine it."

"I'm well aware." Seona ground her teeth and stared at the ceiling, for none of this was news to her. Besides, her aunt didn't need to know Seona was imagining what it would be like to marry Keegan. But he had not made it known whether he wished to marry her. Mayhap he thought it just as impossible as she did.

"Stay away from him," her aunt warned. "He is naught but a guard."

Fury built within Seona's chest, but she drew in a deep breath to dispel it. "He is Chief Dirk's tanist."

"Do you think that will matter to your father?"

Seona shrugged. Of course it wouldn't. Her father was like a stone monolith when it came to sentiment. "What about the guard you have been spending so much time with?" Seona asked, her heart rate speeding up with her bold words.

Her aunt narrowed her eyes until they were like sharp blades. "My ankle is near broken and he is but helping me get about. Besides, how dare you question me and my actions?"

"You are a lady, just as I am," Seona pointed out innocently. "What about your reputation?"

"I am a widow," her aunt snapped. "Not a virgin. There is a vast difference."

"I doubt my father would approve, either way."

"Are you threatening me?" her aunt demanded through clenched teeth.

"Nay," Seona said mildly, lifting her brows into what she hoped was a pleasant expression. She was tired of obeying her grouchy, snobbish, hypocritical aunt and ready to give her a taste of her own bitter medicine. Seona's father provided financial support to her aunt. That was why she'd agreed to be Seona's companion and chaperone during this journey. What would her father do if he knew his sister was *interested* in a guard, someone he would see as far beneath her? Would he cut off her funds?

"You'd best watch yourself, lassie." Patience pointed a finger straight at Seona. "I will tell your father everything. You ken how he is when angered."

Indeed, she did. She well remembered his red-faced tirades, his arms flying about, his big hands hurling objects. And worst of all, those same meaty hands slapping her face so hard the imprint of his fingers left a red mark for two days. Seona had to get her sister away from him. Was Talia well? Had he abused her already? Seona's heart thudded with sudden concern.

"Are you listening to me?" Patience asked.

"Aye. You would enjoy watching him strike me again, would you not?"

"Of course not! I don't enjoy it. But it would be nothing less than you deserve in this case. Dallying with a bodyguard."

"I am not dallying." At least she hoped that wasn't what it was called. 'Twas true Keegan had touched her in scandalous ways, but he had not taken her virtue. She was immensely grateful for that now. Although at the time, she hadn't been. She'd wanted something she couldn't name. She'd craved for Keegan to claim her in every way and make her a woman. *His* woman and his wife.

"The way he always watches you with lust in his eyes tells me loud and clear that he wishes to bed you," Patience said.

Seona's face burned, but she ignored it. Aye, she hoped Keegan did wish to bed her. 'Twas her fondest desire.

"Your father will find the man he wishes you to marry, and it won't be Keegan."

Clearly her aunt loved naught more than rubbing salt into her wound. She was a woman too; how could she not understand Seona's feelings? If only Patience could visualize how much better Seona's life would be if she could marry Keegan instead of some old barbarous ogre mayhap she wouldn't be so harsh. Her aunt was a widow, aye, but Seona knew naught about her marriage, for her husband had died when Seona was a small child. "What was your marriage like?"

Patience sent her a severe frown. "My marriage is none of your concern. That was fifteen years ago. We are talking about you."

"I was merely curious," Seona said in a benign tone. "Although your marriage was brief, I wondered if it was a pleasant experience."

"Nay. 'Twas not. But I know not any woman who has had an enjoyable marriage. 'Tis a part of life. You must grow accustomed to it."

There was something very wrong with that. People in her society married for money, property, alliances and prestige. Not for love. Never for love. But if love could enter into it, wouldn't the marriages be more happy and enjoyable? Wouldn't life be worth living?

Isobel had told her that her parents had loved one another, despite their arranged marriage. And 'twas abundantly clear that Isobel and Dirk loved one another. She often caught them whispering and giving each other affectionate smiles at dinner. A few times at Dunnakeil, she'd accidentally seen them kissing passionately in a stairwell or an out of the way place.

"'Tis obvious Lady Isobel has a happy marriage," Seona pointed out.

"Hmph." Patience glowered. "The way that marriage came about was highly unusual and bordering on scandalous. Dirk stole her from the MacLeod."

Seona shrugged. "Everyone is happy with the outcome. And the MacLeod did not seem to mind so much."

"Well, it matters not. Don't expect the same thing yourself. You should be angry that Isobel stole Dirk from you."

Seona frowned. Was her aunt insane? "She didn't steal Dirk from me. I was never betrothed to Dirk."

"You were betrothed to the next MacKay chief, and who is that? Dirk."

Seona shook her head. "I was betrothed to Aiden. He was chief for a brief time before Dirk arrived."

"'Tis a tangled mess, and your father will not be happy about it. The MacKays broke the contract."

Seona was glad, for she'd never wanted to marry Aiden or Dirk. And especially not Haldane. The way the dirty little knave used to stare at her all the time made her skin crawl. Nay, their cousin, Keegan was the only MacKay to catch her attention and steal her heart.

"If Keegan has taken your virginity, your father will kill him. You ken this is true," Patience said. "I'm certain you remember what happened to the unsuitable young man you danced with last year—MacSween's youngest brother. Your father had him beaten."

"I remember." And she'd felt horribly guilty for agreeing to the dance.

"What you may not know is that young MacSween met an unfortunate end not long after that," her aunt said.

"What?" The sensation of ice cold water washed over Seona. "Someone killed him?"

"Aye. It happened in Inverness. He was stabbed and robbed."

Waves of horror and disbelief crashing over her, Seona could scarce breathe. "Did Father order this done?" She forced the words out.

"No one would say for certain, but there was a rumor among the men that MacSween had kissed you and tried to force himself on you."

Outrage burned through her. "That is not true! We danced and that was all."

"Well, you know how men are; they like to boast. Once a story gets started, it becomes exaggerated."

Seona paced, tears stinging her eyes. What in heaven's name? Had her father really done this? She'd never known her aunt to lie. In truth, her father was violent and brutal, and more than capable of ordering someone killed.

"Keegan is tasked with taking us home, once I'm well enough to travel," Patience said. "You ken your father has far more men than the MacKay guards who are traveling with us. He could easily have Keegan killed."

The image of the bruised and battered MacSween man appeared in her mind and blended with Keegan's handsome and precious face. If her father killed Keegan, she would not want to live. She loved Keegan more than life itself. She would gladly endure a lifetime of unhappiness and beatings if that meant Keegan lived a full life, too, even if he was far away from her.

She imagined what might happen—when Keegan saw he was being attacked, he would draw his sword. But he would be outnumbered by her father's men, and they'd all have swords and dirks, too. He wouldn't be able to fight them all.

They'd kill him.

Her throat closed up and tears flooded her eyes. She had to stop spending time with Keegan and make it clear to him any connection they'd shared was now over.

CHAPTER SIXTEEN

Keegan rode with the MacKenzies and seven of the MacKay guards through the village and to the edge of the small wood near Loch Long. They dismounted, leaving the horses with three grooms, and moved quietly through the trees. Fraser had told him the stags had been spotted early that morn, halfway up a mountain, above the tree line, gorging on the fresh spring growth.

All was silent in the wood, except for the whispering shuffle of their feet on the wet leaves. Several of them, including Keegan, carried a bow and arrows. Though he was no archer, he was a fairly good shot.

Cyrus and Dermott led the way, Keegan, Fraser and others behind them. Keegan wished Dirk could've joined them, but he wasn't recovered enough yet. Rebbie had stayed behind to keep him company.

Abruptly, Cyrus halted, holding up his hand for silence. Keegan stopped just shy of running into him. Had he seen a deer? Keegan squinted into the dimness of the forest. In the distance, something darted from one tree to another. *Plaid?* 'Twas not a deer at all, but a man.

"Who the devil is that?" Dermott whispered.

Cyrus pulled his sword from the scabbard at his side. "Let's go find out."

Several of the men drew their swords, while others nocked arrows into the bows they carried. Keegan chose his sword since he was far more experienced with it. The lot of them advanced, trying to keep even quieter than before.

Keegan saw naught but tree bark and leaves for several minutes. Abruptly, the man abandoned his hiding place behind a thick tree trunk and sprinted deeper into the wood.

Cyrus and Dermott increased their pace. Keegan and the other men followed suit. Shouts and yells echoed through the trees up ahead.

"What the hell?" Dermott asked. "How many of them are there?"

Realization dawned. "'Slud. That might be Haldane and his band of outlaws," Keegan said just above a whisper. A couple of days ago, Keegan and Rebbie had given Cyrus and his brothers a detailed accounting of Haldane, his men, and their crimes.

Dermott glanced back briefly, his green eyes gleaming in the strange light of the forest. "How many of them?"

"Around a dozen at last count," Keegan said. "Unless he's hired more since that last skirmish."

"We're going to find out," Cyrus said. "Prepare for battle, lads."

"Their archer is deadly. Watch out for him," Keegan warned.

None of them carried targes since they'd been headed out for deer stalking, not into battle, and had no way to deflect arrows that might fly at them.

Keegan hadn't imagined Haldane would follow them here, but he shouldn't be surprised, really. Haldane was a canny lad and determined to get what he wanted.

Shouts and running erupted up ahead, some of the men on horseback and others on foot. Most fled north, along the loch's edge, while others scurried up the side of the mountain to the east. The MacKenzies and MacKays pursued those running along the loch's edge. Easier pickings.

"Capture them," Cyrus ordered. "I want to question the bastards."

Keegan was glad to see they were gaining on the stragglers of the group.

One of the scrawny men, red-headed with a stringy beard—but unfortunately not Haldane—glanced back and screamed like a lass. He ran down the bank and into the loch. Fraser took after him, splashing through the shallows, latched a hand onto the plaid at his back and dragged him toward the bank. A struggle ensued, but Fraser, being taller and stronger, quickly disarmed him and shoved him up the bank onto dry ground.

Once Keegan saw Fraser and one of the MacKay guards had the outlaw well under control, he ran ahead to join the MacKenzies. He hoped they could catch several of the knaves.

Dermott threw a rock at another outlaw and hit his mark. With a dull thud, he crumpled to the ground and didn't move.

Only one more was still within sight. He was taller and broader of shoulder with black hair. When he glanced back, Keegan didn't recognize him. Picking up the pace, Keegan joined Cyrus in the pursuit.

An arrow jabbed into the ground near Keegan, spraying dirt and leaves. He jumped aside. "Arrows!" he warned Cyrus. Taking cover behind a tree trunk, he glanced up the steep, tree-covered hillside where the arrow had come from, seeing Gil and Haldane.

"Bastards. They're up there!" Keegan pointed, then sheathed his sword and nocked an arrow. Aiming and drawing back, he let the arrow fly. It sailed through the trees a good distance but then stabbed into a tree trunk. "'Slud," he muttered.

Taking cover near Keegan, Cyrus yelled back to his guards. "Shoot them!"

Keegan nocked another arrow, but Gil and Haldane disappeared before he could release it. Keegan ground his teeth. He wanted to chase them down like the vermin they were, but he was ill prepared at the moment. No armor, no targe.

The other outlaw they'd been pursuing along the loch had also vanished.

"Bastards," Cyrus grumbled. "We'll take these two prisoners to the castle, arm ourselves better, then come back and hunt down the rest of them."

"Aye." Keegan was glad Cyrus was also eager for a fight. "I want to hear what these two have to say."

***

Keegan didn't recognize the two scraggly-bearded men being shepherded back to Teasairg Castle, their hands bound behind their backs, but they definitely looked like desperate criminals. No doubt Haldane had hired them.

The portcullis was raised and all of them strode into the bailey.

"Go get Chief MacKay," Cyrus said to one of the male

servants. "Tell him we captured two of his brother's men."

"Aye, m'laird." The servant hurried inside.

Keegan was surprised to see Dirk appear at the entrance a moment later. He must have been in the great hall for he couldn't have had time to negotiate the stairs from the upper floor.

"Aye?" Dirk limped forward on the sturdy cane, his sharp blue gaze cutting to the outlaws. "Are these Haldane's men?"

"Indeed, cousin," Keegan said. "I remember that one from the skirmish we had north of Ullapool." He nodded to the brown-haired one who had been knocked down by the rock. Blood soaked part of his hair and dripped onto his filthy clothing.

"Have they revealed anything as of yet?"

"Nay, I thought I'd let you question them," Cyrus said.

"Did Haldane MacKay hire you?" Dirk asked the two.

Neither man opened his mouth.

"Did you cut out their tongues?" Dirk asked, pretending to be aghast.

"Nay." Cyrus gave a dark smile. "But I will if you want me to."

The men's eyes widened and their faces paled beneath the layers of dirt. "Um... aye... m'laird," the redheaded man stammered.

"What are your names?" Dirk asked.

"Eli Carmichael," the red-haired man said.

The one with brown hair and a bushy beard glared at his companion, then blew out a breath. "Neil MacEldon."

"Well, Neil and Eli—if those are your real names," Dirk said. "What job were you hired for?"

Both men appeared twitchy, their gazes darting this way and that. Keegan studied them, determining they were near terrified. How loyal were they to Haldane?

"Has Haldane paid you yet?" Keegan asked.

Eli glared. "'Tis no concern of yours."

"If he hasn't paid you yet, he likely never will."

"He paid us some," Eli said. "And we ken there's more where that came from."

Keegan and Dirk exchanged a glance. The purse of coins that was stolen from Dirk's tent.

Keegan shrugged. "Just because he has it doesn't mean he's going to give *you* any of it. And yet, he expects you to risk your necks for him. 'Tis not fair, is it?"

"If we do the job, he'll pay us good," Neil said. "He's a man of his word."

Dirk snorted. "And what job is that?"

"Don't know yet. He said he'd tell us."

"He won't be telling you," Cyrus said. "Because you two are going to spend the rest of your lives in my dungeon."

The outlaws paled and exchanged a terrified glance. Were they having second thoughts?

"Any man who attempts to murder my sister and my brother-in-law is going to get what he deserves," Cyrus said, his voice hard.

"We didn't do it," Neil said quickly. "'Twas Gil what shot him with the arrow." He nodded at Dirk.

Cyrus shrugged, looking unconcerned. "You both were on his side, trying to ambush my family, friends and allies. You put my sister's life in danger," Cyrus said, his voice quiet but deadly.

"We didn't ken y-your sister w-was with them," Eli stuttered.

"Now you do. So, tell these men anything they want to know." Cyrus motioned to Dirk and Keegan.

"What are Haldane's plans?" Dirk asked.

Eli squirmed for a moment, staring at the ground, then at the sky. "We heard him murmuring something to McMurdo about…" He dropped silent.

"Aye? About what?" Dirk demanded.

"A lady. Seona—I'm thinking that was her name. She has brown hair and blue eyes, very beautiful. We're to grab her but not hurt her. Then, he'll pay us and head back to Durness with her. 'Twas what he said."

Fury simmered inside Keegan, tensing all his muscles. He wanted to hunt down Haldane and put him out of his misery. "I'll tell you one thing. None of you are getting your filthy hands on Lady Seona. The man who tries it will get his throat cut."

"Aye," Dirk agreed.

"I'm not touching her," Eli promised, backing up. The stone wall behind him halted his progress.

"Nay. Me neither!" Neil's wide gaze darted back and forth among the three men.

Keegan narrowed his eyes, scrutinizing Neil. "What did Haldane say about Dirk?"

"Well… uh… what was it?" he asked his friend. "That he

might die of fever. If not, McMurdo is tasked with killing him."

Dirk gave a brief humorless laugh. "'Tis old news. Tell us something we don't know."

"Aye. How many men does Haldane have now?" Keegan asked.

"Ten, counting us."

"We'll not count you," Cyrus said. "Because you're no longer a part of the gang."

"Aye, well. We're glad to be out," Neil said. Clearly he was lying and only trying to appease them. "He said he would hire more men when he moved east."

"Why east?" Keegan asked.

"'Tis where the lady will be taken… back to her home. Near Inverness."

Hell. Haldane knew their plans. 'Twas probably obvious to him Seona would have to be returned to her father since she didn't marry the MacKay chief. And Haldane obviously knew where their branch of the Murrays was from.

They could expect more ambushes and attacks as they escorted Seona home. 'Slud! He couldn't expose her to that danger.

"Where will Haldane lie in wait?" Keegan asked.

"We know not. We're not from this area."

Once they were finished questioning the two men, Cyrus had them taken to the dungeon.

Keegan ground his teeth. "I want to go out and hunt down Haldane. Now," he told Dirk and the other men. "I don't want to start east with Seona while Haldane and his men are still a threat to her."

Dirk nodded. "'Twould be best to take care of him beforehand."

"I agree with you," Cyrus said. "I ken these hills and mountains like the back of my hand." He nodded toward the north. "I ken where all the hidey-holes are. I'll line up more men and we'll head out in a quarter hour."

***

A knock sounded at Seona's door late that evening. 'Twas almost dark, but she hadn't left her room after her aunt had threatened to tell her father about her and Keegan…. and how Graham MacSween had died.

Seona had to stay away from Keegan.

She prayed 'twas not him knocking at her door now, for she knew not how to tell him to stay away from her. 'Twould break her heart.

Seona approached the door. "Who is it?"

"Isobel."

Seona should've guessed her friend would wonder why she'd missed supper. Millie had brought her a tray. Even so, Seona had eaten little. She was sick knowing she had to give up Keegan, the only bright spot in her life.

Bracing herself for a multitude of questions, she opened the door.

Her gaze concerned, Isobel entered and closed the door. "Are you ill?"

"Nay. I simply... didn't feel like being with a lot of people."

Searching her eyes, Isobel nodded. "Keegan and most of the men went out looking for Haldane and his gang."

"What? Haldane is here?" *Saints!* Even now, Keegan could be in danger.

"Aye, when the men were deer stalking, they ran upon the outlaws in the wood. They captured two of them and got information. Haldane is still bent on kidnapping you. So, the men decided to take care of the threat."

Her throat tightening, Seona shook her head. "Keegan is risking his life for me. And he shouldn't. He's such a good and honorable man." She felt unworthy.

Isobel led her toward the fireplace and they sat on the padded bench before it. "Aye. That's what a man does when he loves a woman."

Emotion caught in Seona's throat and emerged as a sob. Overcome with the sudden and sharp emotions, she covered her face with her hands. "He shouldn't do it," she forced the words out past her constricted throat. "He should not risk his life for me."

"I doubt anyone could stop him." Isobel rubbed her shoulder in a comforting manner. "What is wrong, Seona? Why were you not at supper?"

Swallowing back the emotion and blotting a handkerchief against her eyes, she shook her head. "My aunt saw Keegan giving me flowers. I must stop seeing him. I fear my father will kill him if he has half a chance. Aunt Patience thinks Keegan has... compromised me, and she's going to tell my father if I don't stay away from him."

"What a meddling battleax," Isobel muttered.

"Aye. I agree. I care for Keegan too much to put his life in danger."

"Well, I know he cares for you, too." Isobel patted her hand.

"Last year, I merely danced with a man named Graham MacSween. My father deemed him 'not good enough' and had his men beat him horribly. My aunt just told me today that someone murdered MacSween shortly after. My father probably sent his men to do the horrid deed. They made it look like a thief killed him in Inverness."

Isobel's mouth dropped open. "Saints! In truth?"

"I've never known my aunt to tell a lie. And she didn't know for certain my father had it done. But knowing him like I do, I wouldn't put it past him."

Isobel shook her head and appeared in deep thought. "I wish there was some way to get you away from your father so you and Keegan could be together. You could come live at Dunnakeil."

Seona's heart ached for that would be her fondest wish. "I would love that, but I fear 'tis impossible. I must go home for my sister. I fear Father will beat her if she talks back to him."

Isobel frowned. "Has he beaten you?"

"Aye." Seona had never talked to anyone about this, other than her aunt or the people back home who knew about it. "He's hit me several times. Sometimes for no true reason other than he was angry and I happened to be there."

"'Slud!" Isobel muttered, her face tightening. "I had no idea he was so brutal. Does Keegan know this?"

"Nay. And you must not tell him. You know he would do something drastic and put his own life in terrible danger."

Isobel nodded. "Keegan is a lot like Dirk. Neither of them would stand for such injustice and abuse, especially to someone they care about. You must get away from your father."

"I had hoped to marry a decent man who was not cruel and bring my sister to live with me."

"'Tis a good plan."

"It isn't too much to ask, is it?"

Isobel put an arm around Seona's shoulders and gave her a comforting hug. "Nay, of course not. Not only do you deserve a good man, but also a man who loves you."

"That would be a dream come true, of course. But I doubt that I'll be as lucky as you are."

If only she could be. The image she had in her mind of being married to Keegan was so beautiful it brought tears to her eyes.

"Indeed, you might be luckier than anyone," Isobel said. "It can't hurt to imagine it. And it will give you comfort."

"I'm not certain of that. 'Tis something I'll likely never have, so why imagine it might come true? I would only be torturing myself."

"I disagree. Last year, I thought I would have to marry another man I didn't care for, but I didn't. I stopped thinking of Torrin. I could think of naught but Dirk after he rescued me and took me to Dunnakeil. I couldn't help falling for him or thinking about him all the time."

"Aye, but your older brother is far more lenient than my father. Besides, Dirk is a chief. Your brother knew he was suitable for you. Keegan is not a chief, but I… that doesn't matter to me."

"Of course it doesn't matter. He isn't exactly penniless. He's Dirk's tanist. 'Tis the highest position within the clan, aside from chief. Keegan will have a good income, and he is welcome to live at Dunnakeil always. As is the woman he marries."

Seona's face burned for she truly wished to be the woman he married. But the reality was, each time she talked to Keegan, and especially when she kissed him, she was putting his life more and more in danger. Especially if he was the one who took her home. But she knew not how to convince him to stay here and allow someone else to escort her home.

"You must not reveal to Keegan what I've told you," Seona said. "Promise me."

"If you will tell him," Isobel said. "He deserves to know everything you've told me."

Seona shook her head. "If he knows what kind of man my father is, that he is abusive and violent and probably even a murderer, Keegan may not allow me to go back. You ken as well as I do that could have terrible consequences. It could mean a clan war. My sister could be in danger. And Keegan, most of all, would be in danger."

CHAPTER SEVENTEEN

Two nights later, Keegan and the other men dragged into the great hall of Teasairg Castle just as supper was ending. They had searched endlessly for Haldane and his outlaws over much of MacKenzie territory for miles around. Keegan was hellishly annoyed none of them could be found.

His gaze scanning the great hall for Lady Seona but not locating her, Keegan strode toward high table, then slumped into a straight wooden chair beside Dirk. Keegan wanted to immediately ask where Seona was, but didn't want the others to ken how much he thought about her. The servants rushed to bring the newcomers food, which Keegan appreciated greatly for he was near starved.

"Let me guess—you saw neither hide nor hair of Haldane," Dirk said.

"You have the right of it. We climbed mountains on foot and searched more glens than I can count," Keegan said. "We took a galley to the end of Loch Duich and searched part of Glen Shiel, while some of the MacKenzies took another galley up Loch Long. The bastards have vanished."

"Hell," Dirk muttered. "McMurdo has taught them to be as cunning and illusive as he is. They could be lying in the bracken somewhere and 'twould be easy to walk right past them."

"Aye." Keegan sighed. "Or they may have left the area. 'Haps they went east to await us at the edge of Murray's holdings."

"That's a good possibility," Dirk said. "Damnation, I want to be out there searching with you lads."

"Not until you're recovered. How's your leg?" Keegan asked, digging into the trencher of venison stew the servant placed before him.

"Improving."

Isobel, sitting on Dirk's other side, leaned forward. "What he neglected to tell you is that he still has fevers sometimes, especially at night. And look how swollen it is, Keegan."

"Och. I'm getting better," Dirk muttered.

"Aye, you are better than you were," Isobel agreed.

Keegan drank a long swallow of heather ale. "You must take care of yourself, cousin."

"I am. And I have the best healer in the world." Dirk put his arm around Isobel and drew her closer.

She smiled and kissed his cheek.

Saints. Keegan missed Seona. He could use a kiss from her right now. Though he'd need a bath and a change of clothes first. And some privacy, away from her aunt, who sat further down the table, talking to MacMillan.

"Where is Lady Seona?" Keegan asked in a low tone, making sure her aunt couldn't hear. With all the noise in the great hall, 'twas doubtful she would hear him even if he asked in a loud voice, but he didn't want to take any chances.

Both Dirk and Isobel merely looked at him for a long moment. Finally, Isobel said, "In her bedchamber."

Alarm rushed through Keegan, not because of Isobel's words but because of the somber look in her eyes. "Is something wrong?"

"Nay," Isobel said, glancing away.

She was lying or being evasive. What was she hiding?

"'Tis only that Lady Seona has not been to any meals since the one we had outside," Dirk said.

What?

Isobel poked Dirk in the ribs and gave him a severe frown.

Dirk caught her hand. "Well, 'tis true."

"Has anyone seen her?" Keegan demanded, imagining the worst. Had she slipped out and run away?

"Aye, Keegan. Calm yourself," Isobel said. "I've talked to her several times in her chamber."

"And?" He waited, anticipation near consuming him.

"She is not ill. She simply doesn't want to be around a lot of people. She is a private person who prefers spending time alone, sometimes." Isobel shrugged.

Keegan frowned, knowing full well Isobel was behaving strangely. Aye, Seona was a quiet lass who didn't mind being alone, but he'd never noticed her avoiding meals. Was it simply because he hadn't been there? Or something else?

Isobel was keeping a secret, and he intended to find out what it was. "Are you saying she hasn't been out of her room for two days?"

"I don't know if she has or not," Isobel said with a neutral expression.

Irritation welled up inside Keegan's chest. "Is she eating?"

"Aye. The maids take her food."

"Isobel said she was worried about you going after Haldane." The look in Dirk's eyes said he understood the turmoil and worry Keegan felt.

The idea that Seona was worried about him eased Keegan's mind a bit. Maybe the anxiety had gotten the best of her and that was why she wanted to be alone.

He had to see Seona. Would Isobel help him with that as she'd done in the past? Something had changed, and he didn't like it.

After the meal, he asked the servants to bring him a bath, then proceeded to his small bedchamber in the same wing as the MacKenzie brothers'. Once Keegan had bathed and put on clean clothing, he proceeded through the castle, trying to think of a place where he and Seona might talk in private. Though it was late, the castle was still abuzz with activity.

He proceeded up the steps to the corridor where Seona's chamber was. If he ran into anyone, his excuse would be that he was going to talk to Dirk, whose chamber was a couple doors down. But luckily, no one was about in this part of the castle. He hurried to Seona's door and knocked lightly.

As the silence extended, the foreboding inside him grew darker.

Isobel had told him Seona wasn't ill. She simply wished to be alone. But he knew something was wrong. Had he offended her in some way? Angered her?

He knocked again, a bit harder.

"Who is it?" Seona asked from the other side of the door.

He released his held breath. The sound of her voice both calmed him and excited him at the same time.

"'Tis me. Keegan," he said, low, then glanced back along the empty corridor.

Staring at the door again, he waited for her to open it. But it remained closed.

"Seona?" he asked "Are you ill?"

"Nay."

"Why won't you leave your bedchamber?" He had not considered it might be *that* time of the month for her. But surely if this was the case, she would at least pretend to be ill.

"I cannot see you again," she said, her voice strained and barely audible.

"What?" Surely, he'd misheard, but still… her words sent a shock of confusion and denial through him. "Why would you say such a thing?" he asked, trying to keep his voice down.

"'Tis dangerous, Keegan. My father is a cruel man."

Hell. She had been crying. He heard it in her voice.

"I do not fear your father," he said.

The silence on the other side of the door frayed his nerves and sliced at his composure.

He leaned closer to the door. "I want to see you, Seona. I *need* to see you." He had thought of naught but her during the past few days. 'Twas why he'd spent two days searching for Haldane… to keep her safe from the knave.

"Seona?" He didn't want to try the knob and enter without an invitation, but she sore tempted him to do just that. With his luck, she'd barred the door.

What seemed to him a long while later—though it could have been seconds—the door opened. Seona's tear-filled, dark blue eyes tore at his soul and stirred his protective instincts. He pushed his way inside the door and closed it back.

"Nay," she whispered, backing away. "You cannot come in here." Though her words were quiet, they were intense, her eyes wide but reddened from crying. "What if Aunt Patience should see you?"

"Seona, why are you suddenly so distraught? Tell me why you said what you did." He couldn't even bring himself to say the words, for he couldn't imagine never seeing her again. Never touching her. Never kissing her. *Nay.* Such thoughts were like dagger stabs to his heart.

"I told you," she said. "My father is a cruel and brutal man. If he finds out we have talked and kissed and... other things, I fear he will kill you." She closed her eyes and tears ran down her cheeks.

At the moment, he didn't care if his life was in danger. All he wanted was to see Seona, to touch her, to hold her.

"He is not here," Keegan said.

"Nay, but his sister is. Aunt Patience will tell him everything. She was spying on us. She saw you give me the bluebells."

This was all caused by the bluebells? *Saints!* Lady Patience was a she-devil.

"It doesn't matter," he said. "What matters is—"

"Nay. I cannot see you or talk to you," Seona insisted. "You have to leave."

Keegan's chest ached and his possessive urges rose to the surface. Nobody was taking Seona away from him. To do so was the same as ripping out his heart. He couldn't live without his heart... nor without Seona.

If *she* was the one rejecting him, that was something altogether different. But he didn't think that was the case. She was crying because she cared about him.

Seona backed away. "Go, Keegan," she whispered.

But he didn't. He watched her retreat. This spurred his instincts to pursue her, to capture her, to make her see he would never abandon her.

He took a step closer. "I fear no man, not even your father."

"Well, you should." She retreated behind a chair.

"Why are you so afraid of him?" Keegan's own father was a loving, jovial man. Of a certainty, Conall MacKay could be vicious in battle, but with his family, he was warm. However, Keegan knew all fathers were not like him. Evidently, Seona's father was just the opposite.

"He could have his men *kill* you, Keegan. Do you understand what I'm saying?"

His muscles tensed at the potential threat and the challenge. "Not without a fight. And I wager I'd take a few of them out before they did me in." He stepped forward again.

"Keegan, please." She squeezed her eyes shut and shook her head.

"The MacKay guards always watch my back." He hoped that

would ease her mind... though he was well-trained in protecting himself.

She looked down, appearing suddenly defeated, her unbound hair shielding most of her face. "I didn't want to tell you this, but you leave me no choice."

Warning prickled at the back of his neck. "What?"

"Last year at home, I danced with a man, the youngest brother of the MacSween chief. My father disapproved because he did not see him as suitable. Aunt Patience said there was a rumor started that MacSween kissed me and it grew out of proportion. MacSween was murdered a short time later, in Inverness. My father probably ordered it done. Do you understand what I mean now?"

"Aye, your father is ruthless, and he will not approve of me." Keegan had already guessed her father would have a negative opinion of him, since he was not a chief or titled. Still, that would not dissuade him from asking for her hand. If her father attempted to kill Keegan for his boldness and his interest in Seona, then he'd best be ready for retaliation.

"When I go home, I want you to stay here," Seona said.

"What? Are you mad?" Annoyance gored Keegan. "I would never do that. Do you take me for a coward?"

"Nay! I'm trying to protect you."

"Well, I intend to protect you. And I can't do that if I'm here and you're traveling across the country with Haldane on your heels." His words were low but firm. The last thing on earth he'd do was stay here, safe, while she faced danger. Though her idea irritated him, he understood why she'd suggested it. She worried about his safety because... mayhap she cared about him a great deal. He hoped.

"I'm sorry," she whispered, tears welling in her eyes again. "I should've never..."

"What?"

"I didn't mean to lead you on... and lead you into danger. I should've never allowed you to... kiss me."

"Saints, Seona." Could she not see that he cared for her? 'Twas not as if he merely wanted beneath her skirts. She had stolen his heart.

She stared at the floor, her blush evident in the candlelight. "I ken I acted very... wantonly. That was wrong of me."

He ground his teeth. Aye, he knew he shouldn't have touched

her in the most intimate of places but... he ached. Not only his groin, but his chest and his whole body ached for her. He sucked in a deep breath, trying to dispel his need but naught helped.

"I should not have teased and tempted you," she said.

"You didn't. I am the one to blame for leading you astray. You're an innocent and I shouldn't have touched you." He forced himself to say the words, to be a gentleman. 'Twas true he *shouldn't* have touched her, but he did not regret it. Nay, he wanted to touch her again, more than anything, but he would keep his hands to himself if that was what she wished.

She watched him, her blue eyes darkening in a most tempting manner. Was she thinking of how he'd touched her? He could think of little else, himself. Her skin was so soft and silken his fingers itched to trail over her again. When he tried to sleep at night, he had burning, erotic dreams about stroking, kissing and licking her... everywhere. Imagining being naked with her in bed made him yearn so intensely he could scarce breathe.

"I shouldn't have... given you pleasure," he said, remembering how she'd shattered in his arms. He loved how passionate she was.

Her skin turning bright pink, she licked her lips. How he craved another taste of them. He moved closer to her, thankful to see she didn't move back.

"I was wrong to... slide my hand up your thigh beneath your skirts," he whispered, feeling like the most debauched rogue, but unable to stop himself. Aye, he wanted to tempt her as much as she tempted him. He wanted her to remember the pleasure he'd given her.

Her breathing altered but her stare never wavered from his. She swallowed hard.

"I should not have touched you and felt how wet you were... how aroused," he whispered in an intense tone. "Because now I cannot forget it. 'Tis all I can think about."

Her eyelids were growing heavy and her gaze more heated by the moment.

"You have no inkling how you make me ache," he went on. Indeed, at the moment he was so hard he was almost dizzy with arousal. "I want you, Seona. Always." Knowing it was time for him to be completely honest with her, he drew in a deep breath. "I love you."

"Keegan. Nay," she breathed, shaking her head and squeezing her eyes shut. More glistening tears leaked out.

Though her reaction was like a punch to the gut, he shoved the chair out of his way and drew her into his arms. "Don't cry, lass. I'd hoped... you might like to know how I feel."

"Aye." She looked up into his eyes. "I love you, too, but— "

"That's all that matters." Bittersweet joy latched onto him. Aye, if she loved him, he would do anything to have her. He'd move heaven and earth to make her happy, to keep her safe, to keep her by his side always.

She shook her head. Grasping the plaid across his upper body, she buried her face against his chest and sobbed.

God, she ripped his heart out. He pressed his face against the thick softness of her unbound hair. He relished the sleek feel of it. Her hands tugging at his plaid made him want to rip the material from his body and revel in the warmth of her smooth skin against his. Her stomach pressed against his hard shaft. He forced himself not to respond, not to grind into her as his instincts urged.

He kissed her temple. "Please, I beg of you, stop crying and tell me why you're so upset."

She sniffed and wiped the tears from her eyes with a handkerchief. "You."

"Why?"

"You overwhelm me. You make me feel... things I never thought possible."

"I feel the same way." Just as overwhelmed in her presence, especially if he touched her, or held her as he was now. He never wanted to let her go. 'Twas almost as if she was a part of him. And to be away from her felt as if a piece of him was missing.

Embracing him tighter, she pushed her lower belly against his erection. Grinding his teeth, he barely quelled a moan. His hands slipped from her waist to her hips and tugged her closer. The feel of her delectable body sent arousal and raw need pouring through him.

He was glad to see she'd stopped crying. He needed to ask her something very important, but she turned her face toward him. So tempting he could not resist. He captured her lips to taste her sweet and salty kisses.

"Mmm." He wanted to devour her.

An almost imperceptible click sounded behind him, and then

a shriek rent the air. He spun.

Lady Patience stood on the threshold, her hand over her mouth, her eyes wide as platters.

CHAPTER EIGHTEEN

"You beast!" Lady Patience rushed forward with a limping gait, grabbed an embroidered pillow and swung it at Keegan, catching him on the shoulder. "Get your hands off my niece and get out!"

"Calm yourself, m'lady," he said. "I've not harmed her." 'Slud, why hadn't he barred the door? Now he'd gotten Seona into trouble.

Her aunt persisted in swatting his arm with the pillow. Daft woman. If she truly wanted to do him harm, she'd have to find a better weapon.

"Get out!" Patience demanded.

"What is happening in here?" Lady Isobel asked from the open doorway.

Thank the saints. Maybe she would be the voice of reason. "I was but talking to Lady Seona," he said.

"Liar!" Patience yelled, whacking him with the pillow. "You had your mouth on her, you swine!"

"You're right," Keegan admitted, seeing the perfect opportunity. "I have compromised the lass. Now, I will have to marry her."

Lady Patience froze, her mouth hanging agape, eyes wide. Isobel and Seona looked much the same. Speechless.

"I will do the honorable thing," he said. "I take my responsibilities seriously."

Their expressions were so comical he almost grinned, but forced himself not to. He was not joking.

With renewed fury, Patience resumed bludgeoning him with the pillow, which he easily fended off with a lifted elbow. Isobel smiled wickedly.

"You are mad," Seona whispered, blushing bright pink.

"What the devil is going on?" Dirk asked from the doorway, his guard beside him.

"Keegan has compromised Lady Seona and now he will be forced to wed her," Isobel said, grinning.

Dirk's brows lifted. "Could I have a word with you, Keegan?"

"Get out! Rogue! Barbarian!" Lady Patience landed a blow to his shoulder, but not with the pillow this time. 'Twas a fire poker. He grabbed the weapon and yanked it from her, getting his hand covered in soot in the process.

"Damnation!" He strode into the corridor to speak with Dirk, then deposited the fire poker against the stone wall. He glared at the black smudges on his hand and shirt sleeve.

The door slammed behind him, leaving him alone in the corridor with Dirk.

"Harpy," he muttered under his breath.

"Come." Dirk motioned, limping back along the corridor with his cane.

"What are you still doing up?"

"I heard a woman yelling. I couldn't very well ignore it. Isobel rushed to see what was happening and I followed." He opened his bedchamber door and motioned Keegan inside. The room was very floral, lacy and feminine.

"Have a seat." Dirk nodded toward the dainty chairs next to the hearth, then poured whisky in two small stoneware cups. He handed one to Keegan.

"*Slàinte,*" they said at the same time, then Keegan downed half his shot of whisky.

Dirk sipped leisurely, then eyed Keegan with a bit of devilment. "A word of advice—if you're going to slip into a lady's bedchamber, make sure you don't get caught by her chaperone."

Not amused, Keegan sent him a mock grin. "I figured she was in her own chamber, or still flirting with MacMillan in the great hall."

"Well, thank the saints you weren't naked," Dirk said.

"Indeed," Keegan muttered, taking a seat on one of the chairs. "I should've barred the door."

"What was this about her father forcing you to marry her?"

"Mayhap he will. I hope." Indeed, 'twas Keegan's fondest wish.

Dirk dropped into the chair opposite. "Years ago, when I was a wee lad, the MacKays and that branch of the Murrays were enemies."

A cold frisson of dread slithered through Keegan. "In truth?"

"Aye. When Da married my stepmother, that helped smooth it over because, through her mother, she was distantly related to the Murrays."

Keegan nodded. "Now that you mention it, I remember my da talking about conflict with them many years ago, when he was a young man."

"Aye. I'm hoping the Murray chief doesn't get riled up again because of what's going on with Lady Seona. Not that I fear him or his clan, but his second cousin is the Earl of Tullibardine, leader of all the Murrays. He has a massive army."

Keegan hadn't meant to put the whole MacKay clan in danger. But he couldn't help falling in love with Seona. And he was glad he'd finally told her. He'd loved her for months.

"Peace is important to me," Dirk said. "I don't want the MacKay clan crushed because of some minor offense."

"You mean because I've been caught with her?"

"That and the fact she was not able to marry the MacKay chief as her father had arranged."

Keegan nodded. "Nor do I wish to put our clan in danger. I hope you don't think me a fool when I say—" Hell, could he tell Dirk that he loved Seona without appearing completely mad? Dirk loved Isobel, and he'd told Keegan as much. Anyway, 'twas obvious to anyone who saw them together.

"Aye?" Dirk prompted.

"I cannot help that I love Seona, and I cannot live without her now. Surely, you of all people understand how I feel."

"Of course, I do. I would've fought twenty men single-handedly, if I'd had to, in order to keep Isobel."

"I would do the same for Seona."

A knock sounded at the door.

"Aye," Dirk called.

Rebbie stuck his head in. "I thought I heard a woman's screams."

Dirk motioned him forward. Rebbie entered and closed the door.

"'Twas this scoundrel who caused it," Dirk said. "He was discovered in Lady Seona's chamber."

"Och." Rebbie grinned. "You are naught but a stag in rut, aye?"

Keegan's face burned and he rolled his eyes. "'Tis not the way of it."

"Watch him blush," Rebbie said. "'Tis obvious he's your cousin."

Dirk frowned. "What's that supposed to mean?"

"Remember when you had to spend the night in that wee cottage with Isobel? The next morn you were blushing the same way."

"You're daft."

"Nay. Your face was as red as your hair." Rebbie dragged another chair forward and sat down.

"Pay him no heed," Dirk muttered.

"So… are you going to marry the lass?" Rebbie asked.

"Indeed," Keegan said. "If her father will allow it."

"Well." Rebbie sat back and crossed his arms. "I like that. A decisive man."

Dirk nodded. "'Twould be an ideal match, if only Keegan can gain her father's permission."

Rebbie hissed a breath between his teeth. "Ambrose Murray is a wee cantankerous."

"You know him?" Keegan frowned. This was news to him.

"Not well. When I was a lad, he came to our home to buy a horse from my father. They argued for half the day about the price. Murray got a bit vexed at my father, although in a veiled way. I remember him saying 'with all due respect, my laird,' several times. My father was the Earl of Rebbinglen at the time. 'Twas before his father passed and he gained the marquess title. And Murray was newly chief and Baron of Gillenmor."

Isobel burst into the room. "Keegan, I cannot believe what you did." She smacked him lightly on the arm as she passed by, like a sister might. "Seona is mortified. Lady Patience is having a fit."

He caught a glimpse of the smile she was trying to hide,

realizing she was halfway teasing. Still, his face burned. "I am sorry. 'Twas not my intent."

"It never is," Rebbie muttered.

"I but wished to speak with her. She'd locked herself in her room for two days. I feared she was ill. I ken you said she wasn't," he told Isobel. "But I had to see for myself. I also wondered if she was angry with me, or if I had offended her in some way."

"Considering all the ruckus, I hope you had time to steal at least one kiss," Rebbie said.

Keegan narrowed his eyes at the devilish earl. Aye, 'twas all a grand jest to him.

"He did," Dirk said.

Rebbie smiled, then quickly sobered. "How about this? I will go with you to take her home and I'll put in a good word with her father. I'll tell him what an exceptional husband you will make for the lass."

"I like the sound of that," Keegan said. Indeed, Rebbie enjoyed needling others, but he was a good man who wished to help when he could. "Do you think he will listen?"

Rebbie shrugged. "He is no doubt a stubborn man, but I outrank him. I don't think he will tell me to go to the devil."

Keegan relaxed a bit. "I thank you for your offer of help."

Aye, perhaps the earl could convince her father to see reason.

"And I thank you as well," Dirk said. "If you two would take the stallion to her father as a gift from me, I would appreciate it." He glanced down at his swollen calf. "With this injury, I fear traveling that far would be a problem."

"Aye, send me to soothe Beelzebub himself while you remain here in this floral and lace bower, coddled by this lovely lass." Rebbie waved a hand toward Isobel.

Dirk grinned. "Not to worry, my friend. One day you will have a sweet wife to see to your wounds."

"Och. Not a wife. Nay."

"You will need a wee Rebbinglen heir, will you not?" Keegan asked.

"Aye." Rebbie grimaced, then shook his head. "I pity the lady they saddle me with. I pity myself as well, for she may be as homely as George."

Imagining Rebbie's lanky servant dressed up as a woman, Keegan chuckled.

"Why do you not find your own wife?" Isobel moved to stand behind Dirk and placed her hands on his shoulders.

"Ha. Are you thinking my father would allow that?" Rebbie asked. "He's been scheming and searching for a bride for me for at least a decade, mayhap longer. 'Tis his favorite pastime. Gushing fathers and mothers with their lasses constantly parade through his great hall, bringing him grand gifts. Why do you think I never go home? He'd find some way to leg-shackle me to one of them."

"Well, you never know. One of them might be beautiful and sweet," Isobel said.

Rebbie lifted a brow. "If she is, I'm certain my father would send her away. He will want me to suffer greatly for what I've put him through over the years."

"All the more reason for you to start searching out a bride yourself," she said.

Rebbie shrugged. "If I find a lady that meets all my requirements, aye."

"And what are your requirements?" Keegan asked.

"Beautiful, buxom, sweet, accommodating, a lady… but she should also have a wild side, someone who is not too serious or aloof. Of course, my father will demand that she be from a prominent family."

"'Tis what every man wants," Dirk said.

"And some of you get it," Rebbie muttered.

"I am a lucky man." Dirk grinned, taking Isobel's hand and kissing the back.

"Forget requirements, Rebbie," Isobel said. "You need someone to fall in love with, who will love you back."

"Hmph. Not all of us can live in fairy-land as you do, m'lady."

"'Tis not fairy-land. What Dirk and I share is real."

"Aye. I have no doubt of it. But I can count on one hand the people I know who have a marriage based on a love match. For the rest of the kingdom, marriage is a political arrangement. You got lucky. I fear I will not be."

Keegan feared he would not be as lucky as Dirk either. And that realization was like getting gored in the stomach.

"Lady Patience is saying she wishes to leave in the morn," Isobel said. "I tried to calm her down but 'twas no use. I feared she would fall into a fit of apoplexy."

"In the morn?" Keegan asked. "But we have not yet found

Haldane and his outlaws."

"I'm not certain they will be found until they wish to be," Dirk said. "'Tis the way McMurdo has always been. Haldane is becoming just like him."

"Aye." Keegan stood, the urge to see Seona again near overwhelming him. He might not get to be with her much longer. But he still could not conceive of giving her up. "I should go apologize to Lady Seona and Lady Patience."

"Nay, not now," Isobel said gently. "'Haps in the morn."

He nodded, annoyed that he had made such a grand blunder, getting caught in Seona's room. "Very well. I bid you all goodnight."

They responded in kind and Keegan let himself out into the corridor. All was quiet and Seona's door was closed. He had to leave now, else Lady Patience might attack him again with a fire poker. He strode to the end of the corridor and took several steps down the spiral stair. A door opened and closed behind him. He inched back up far enough to see who it was. Lady Patience. She disappeared into her own chamber. Excitement lit within him. Dare he go back and speak with Seona again?

If he did, he would get into deeper trouble, for he didn't simply want to talk to her. He wanted so much more, and all involved physical contact.

***

Seona covered her head with the counterpane and blankets, so glad Aunt Patience had finally exhausted herself with that rant and gone to her own room. Seona's head throbbed painfully from the woman's shrieks.

Aye, she knew her aunt would report all the scandalous news to her father, but she didn't want to think of the horrid consequences right now. She'd already tortured herself with those for the past two days.

Keegan loved her—that was all she could focus on now. He'd said the words—*I love you* in that deep, spellbinding voice. The look in his eyes had been serious, passionate and emotional. He'd meant what he said. 'Twas what she'd hoped for during the past few months.

She did not know the exact moment she'd fallen in love with him. It had happened gradually with each smile he'd bestowed on her. Each lingering gaze. Each touch of her hand on his arm.

"Please, God," she whispered. "Help me to make Keegan my own. My husband. He is a good man."

She knew Keegan would protect her always and treat her like a queen. She imagined what life could be like with him. They would share a bedchamber at Dunnakeil and sleep together every night. He would kiss her until she was dizzy and begging him for something she didn't fully understand.

They would talk, laugh and make love. She would never tire of gazing into his spellbinding blue eyes.

She knew now—she'd always felt his love in his kisses, from the first. Closing her eyes, she relived that last one. His lips on hers created magic that sent her into another realm, one where only the two of them existed.

But they couldn't remain there long.

Aunt Patience was insisting they leave tomorrow and head for home. However, the castle where Seona grew up was not truly her home. 'Twas a prison, and her father the warden.

How would she and her sister escape? How could Seona keep her father from knowing about her and Keegan? She had to find a way to protect him.

CHAPTER NINETEEN

The next morn, Keegan noted that Seona did not eat at the high table with everyone else. But her annoying aunt was there, giving him the evil eye every minute or two. If he were to rise from the table and head for the stairs, she would no doubt follow and try to bludgeon him again. He sighed and ate the porridge, eggs, bacon, and oat cakes without enthusiasm. His stomach ached with dread, for today he had to take Seona home.

An hour later, everyone gathered in the back courtyard, near the sea gate, preparing to board two of the twenty-oar *birlinns* which would take them to the other end of Loch Duich. Their horses had already been transported on larger *birlinns* and would be awaiting them so they could ride east through the glen.

Keegan glanced up at the overcast sky, gray as his own mood, but no rain fell.

Seona emerged from the keep, and when her enchanting blue eyes met his, his heart somersaulted in his chest. If her aunt hadn't been beside her, Keegan would've approached her.

Isobel hugged Seona and they spoke quietly. His stomach knotted for he knew his time with Seona would be short unless he figured out a way to convince her father of his own worthiness as a husband. If the man was as stubborn as Rebbie had indicated, likely even *he* would not be able to get through to him.

"Why are you looking so grim?" Dirk asked beside him. He had not even noticed his cousin approaching.

"I'm sure you ken. I have a near impossible task ahead of me. And why are you out here? Does your leg not pain you?"

"Aye, but a warrior must pretend pain does not exist."

Dirk did appear a wee bit pale, and Keegan feared he was not as recovered as he acted.

"You must take care of yourself and mend," Keegan said.

"I'll do my best. Hopefully, you will be back within a fortnight—with your new bride—and we'll return to Durness in the large *birlinn* the MacKenzie is giving me as part of Isobel's dowry. 'Tis an impressive vessel, far larger than our others."

"Aye." Keegan could only hope and pray Seona would be his bride by then. But if her father said *nay*, what would he do?

"You must be ever vigilant for Haldane," Dirk said. "Rest assured the only way to stop him from his goal is to kill him."

"Although I don't wish to kill my cousin, I will if I have the opportunity, for you and for Lady Seona."

"I appreciate that," Dirk said, looking disappointed. Keegan knew 'twas because of how Dirk's brother had turned out.

Keegan could only imagine how he would feel if one of his younger brothers or sisters became a murderous, thieving outlaw.

"Godspeed and have a safe journey." Dirk grasped his hand in a warrior's handshake.

"I thank you."

While Dirk spoke to Rebbie, Keegan stepped away and surveyed the courtyard. The two MacKenzie brothers and ten of their men who would be traveling with them had climbed aboard one of the *birlinns*. Over a dozen MacKay guards stood by, one of whom helped Lady Patience into the boat. Her face was set in grim lines. Seona stood alone by the sea gate. He headed toward her.

"Lady Seona." He bowed. "A good morn to you."

She blushed and curtsied. "Good morn."

He glanced around to see who might be listening. No one was close. "I must apologize for what happened last night."

Her face grew even redder. "Nay. Do not worry over it." She smiled, giving him an intimate glance. It reminded him of the kiss they'd shared the night before.

"Make haste, MacKay," Fraser called out with a teasing grin.

Keegan darted a glare at him, then turned to Seona again. "Would you like me to help you board?"

"Aye and I thank you."

After she slipped her hand around his elbow, he led her to the galley, then took her hand and helped her aboard, wishing he didn't have to release her so soon. Nay, he wished he could lift her into his arms and carry her off to a very private bedchamber where they would not be disturbed for a few days.

But that was not going to happen anytime soon—if ever.

***

Seona sat beside Aunt Patience and their two maids within the polished wood hull of the *birlinn*. Keegan took a seat with Fraser and Rebbie somewhere behind her and to the left. Listening to his deep voice as he talked to the other men, she closed her eyes, wishing she could watch him, for she found each day his face, his hair, his eyes, his body... everything about him fascinated her more and more. The beautiful words he'd spoken to her the night before haunted her... *I love you.*

The *birlinn* rocked and swayed upon the water as the last of the men stepped aboard. The oarsmen set to work, rowing the two large boats away from the sea gate and along the loch.

Seona waved to Isobel, tears burning her eyes, her throat tightening. She hoped she would see her good friend again very soon. She'd never had a friend as close as Isobel, whom she could tell anything and trust her to keep it a secret. Of course, Seona was close to her sister, but since Talia was younger, there were many things she couldn't talk to her about. With Isobel, she could discuss anything.

Besides that, Isobel was a genuine, caring person. Seona would miss her greatly.

"Oh heavens," her aunt muttered a few minutes later, pressing a hand to her stomach.

"Do you feel seasick?" Seona asked.

"'Tis starting."

"This calm loch surely can't be as bad as the rough sea was."

"Nay." Aunt Patience swallowed and appeared to be focusing on not growing nauseous.

They moved smoothly along the dark, glassy surface of the loch, the oarsmen singing a song in rhythm to their rowing. She'd always found rowing songs to be very soothing.

When the wind picked up, the crews of each vessel raised the square sail, making the trip far faster and easier for them.

Just over an hour later, they disembarked at the end of Loch

Duich.

For two days, their party traveled, sometimes on horseback and sometimes on ferries or *birlinns* along the lochs, and each night they were fortunate enough to obtain lodgings in a castle or manor house. Fraser and Dermott knew the important people of the area.

Though Seona wished to speak to Keegan far longer than the brief greetings they exchanged in passing, her aunt watched her even more closely than she had before she'd found Keegan in Seona's room. Sometimes his gaze caught and held hers for a long moment when no one was watching. His eyes were so expressive she could almost read his thoughts. When his eyes darkened, he seemed to be envisioning something passionate and intense; other times, his light blue eyes emanated happiness and mischief.

Her own emotions were tossed upon a stormy sea. Simply to look at Keegan filled her with giddiness, excitement and joy. But thoughts of her future, her home, and her father shrouded her in a smothering darkness.

On the third evening, a misty rain fell, and they arrived at a large fortified castle held by the Mackintosh Clan.

Seona was glad to escape the rain and eat a warm meal in the great hall. Though she wasn't fortunate enough to sit by Keegan, he wasn't too far away and she slipped a few glances his way. Once, his gaze caught hers and he smiled, heating her from the inside out.

Afterward, she and her aunt were shown to a large bedchamber containing two beds and a large pallet for their maids.

Seona and the other women were so exhausted, they went to bed early and slept all night. The rain continued and grew harder the next morn. The men of their party decided to stay another night, which Seona was glad for. Though she needed to see about her sister, she was thankful for any sort of delay that kept her from home. Once she arrived there, her time with Keegan would be very short.

***

Haldane led his men east, through the green glens and along the lochs, toward the Inverness area. He only had eight men now. Damn Keegan and the MacKenzies for seizing two of them. Though annoying, their capture didn't put a damper on his plans. The two miscreants had been his least valuable men. As warriors, their skills were sorely lacking, and he was glad he hadn't paid them much.

"'Tis there," McMurdo said, pausing on top of the small rise and pointing at the sizable castle in the distance. "Gillenmor Castle."

Haldane and the rest of the men stopped in the middle of the well-worn, muddy road.

"'Tis impressive," Haldane said. The fifteen-foot, gray stone walls surrounding the castle appeared to be impermeable. Several guards patrolled the battlements, visible above the high wall. A fitting place for an admirable lady like Seona to have grown up. A good-sized village lay only a short distance from the castle.

Thanks to his mother and McMurdo, Haldane knew about the general area where Seona's branch of the Murray clan lived. Along the way, he'd asked two people the exact location of Gillenmor Castle. And now, here they were.

He suspected they'd arrived a few days ahead of Keegan's party, at least he hoped so. McMurdo was an expert at finding concealed spots where they might hide and wait for the MacKays.

Haldane's gaze scanned the surrounding area—a vast expanse of arable farm land with mountains in the far distance. Vibrant green pastures, cattle and sheep. He'd never seen such gently rolling land, so different from MacKay country. Plentiful bushes and trees grew along the edges of the crops and expanded into a forest.

"Do you think we might hide out in that wood?" Haldane pointed to the left.

"Mayhap," McMurdo said. "We'll need to search it and see if anyone else is using it. See if the Murrays have a gamekeeper patrolling it."

Haldane nodded. "You and six of the men do that. I'll take two with me to the village and look for several trained warriors in need of work. After that, I'll seek out a quick way home by sea."

"The sea is about a half day's ride from here," McMurdo said. "I can handle that tomorrow if you wish. As for now, we need food."

"Aye. I'll bring some back from the village." Haldane well knew hunting game on Murray land would get them into trouble with the chief if he learned of it. They had to remain inconspicuous.

"How far are we from Inverness?" Haldane asked. If he couldn't find men here to hire, he would have to go further out.

"About five miles."

Haldane nodded, hoping he wouldn't have to travel that far. Who knew how soon the MacKay party would arrive in the area? He had to be ready.

"Gil and Rusty, come with me. McMurdo, we'll meet you at the edge of that wood in a couple of hours," Haldane said, then headed toward the village. He would have everything set up and in place, but he had to hurry. When he captured Seona, nothing would delay him and his men from reaching Durness within a few days' time.

He would need at least two dozen skilled warriors to help him take Castle Dunnakeil from whoever Dirk had left in charge. Dirk's sword-bearer, Erskine, had not been with the rest of the MacKays as they'd traveled south. 'Twas evident to Haldane he was the one left in charge.

Haldane's brother, Aiden, was there as well, but he posed no threat. Although Aiden was a couple of years his senior, Haldane considered him his wee brother because he was small in stature and utterly incompetent at fighting. Haldane did not want to hurt his brother, but Aiden had best stand aside or he would find himself in the dungeon or killed.

Same with his infuriating half-sister, Jessie. She would likely put up more of a fight than Aiden. She was near as tall as Haldane and had the same flaming red hair, like their da. Besides that, she carried a wicked dagger on her belt.

Truthfully, none of them concerned Haldane. Dirk, Keegan and the more highly skilled MacKay guards would not be at Dunnakeil when he attacked. No doubt, Dirk had only left a few of his weaker men in charge. Haldane would have an easier time taking back what was rightfully his. The legacy his father had left him, and his mother had so desperately wanted him to have. She'd given her life for him and Aiden.

Once Haldane had Dunnakeil well under control, and Dirk returned a few days or weeks afterward—if he survived the injury to his leg—Haldane or McMurdo would have an easier time killing him. Or Gil might fill him with arrows from atop the guard tower. Haldane grinned, loving his plan. He could see it all unfolding so clearly. His mother, God rest her soul, would be proud of him.

What he had to concentrate on now was the best way to slip Seona away from Keegan and the guards. He must grab her as they approached Gillenmor, because once she was inside the castle walls, removing her would be far more difficult. If he and his men were forced to kill Keegan and several of his men in the process, so much the better.

***

A knock sounded at Seona's bedchamber door, startling her from her imaginings of Keegan as she'd drifted toward sleep. She sat bolt upright. The gray light of gloaming still lingered outside the narrow window, and a soft rain fell beyond it.

Her aunt had not yet returned from supper. Perhaps she had spent extra time with Lady Mackintosh, an old friend of hers, catching up. Could that be Aunt Patience knocking? Why did she not simply enter?

Seona slipped out of bed, padded barefoot across the floor, and opened the door to find Keegan standing in the dim corridor.

Exhilaration darted through her. "What are you doing here?" she whispered. "My aunt could return at any moment."

Holding back a wicked grin, he shook his head. "I asked someone to keep her occupied." His voice was equally quiet.

"Who?"

"MacMillan."

Saints! Was her aunt having a tryst? Seona realized her mouth was hanging open and snapped it closed. "Do you mean… what I think you mean?"

His grin broadening, he shrugged. "Who knows what they will do? Where are your maids? I thought I saw them pass through the great hall not long ago."

"I know not. Aunt Patience gave them the night off."

"Well then, may I come in?" Keegan asked. "I need to talk to you."

Her heart pounding, she glanced toward the stairwell. "What if one of the maids or someone should come along?"

"We'll bar the door. And you can tell them you don't wish to be disturbed."

What he suggested… along with the smoldering look in his eyes, sent hot sparks snapping through her body. If her only joys in life were to be stolen moments with him, she would take them. She stepped back, allowing him entrance to the room. Once she closed the door, he placed the plank of wood into the metal brackets, barring anyone from entering.

He glanced around the dim room, inhaling deeply. "I smell lavender soap."

"I had a bath a short time ago."

"Do you mind if I light a candle?"

"Nay." She would like to see him better anyway.

After lighting a candle from the low-burning flames of the hearth and securing it in a candelabrum on the mantel, he turned to her. His normally light eyes were darker in the meager light. "I've been thinking of naught but you."

She stepped closer to him and took his hand. "I've been thinking of you also," she confessed in a whisper.

He lifted her hand and kissed the back, his warm lips and beard stubble teasing her skin.

"There's something I've been wanting to talk to you about," he said. "The last night we were at Teasairg, when your aunt walked in on us in your chamber, I blurted out something that may have shocked you. But I meant it." He lowered himself and knelt on one knee. "If your father agrees to it, will you do me the honor of becoming my bride?"

CHAPTER TWENTY

Seona could not believe Keegan's sincerely spoken words—*will you do me the honor of becoming my bride?*

He dangled what she longed for most right in front of her. Something that would make her life joyously worth living. Something she'd never imagined possible before she'd met Keegan. The one thing she feared she would never have.

'Twould be her dream come true. But naught was more real than the look of sincerity and intense passion in Keegan's eyes. Her tears welled and spilled over, sliding down her face. Her knees grew weak and she knelt with him. "Keegan, aye, you ken I will. But I fear my father will never allow it."

Keegan released a breath, brushed her tears away, then kissed her forehead. "Nevertheless… I'm going to ask him. And I wanted to be certain 'twas what you wanted." He rose to his feet and helped her stand.

"Indeed, I wish it. More than anything."

"I'm not a laird; I own no property. I hold no aristocratic titles," he said, his tone a bit dismal.

"Do you think that matters to me?"

"I know not."

She shook her head and pressed her hand to his heart. "What matters to me is what's in here," she whispered. "I know you will be a good husband. The best any woman could ever hope for."

"I'm uncertain of that, but I will protect you and cherish you,

Seona. I love you, lass."

"And I love you," she whispered, her throat tightening.

He lifted his hand to lightly stroke her cheek, then bent and kissed her lips, at first sweet and light. But with his soft moan it shifted to something deeper and more profound, a melding of their souls. She locked her arms around his neck as she poured herself into the kiss, accepting everything he would give her.

"Mmm, lass." His hands slid to her hips, only the thin material of her smock separating their skin. When he gently caressed her derriere, carnal yearnings rushed through her. Wanting him closer, she pushed her breasts against his chest.

A low curse escaped him. His tongue teased hers, provoking, inflaming her desires to a higher level.

Gradually, he dragged her linen smock upward, wadding it into his hands. Holding her breath, she could hardly wait to feel his hands on her. When he finally reached the hem of the garment, his warm, rough hands on her bare sensitive skin felt glorious.

"Oh, Keegan," she breathed.

"Seona, you feel so good," he whispered against her ear, his hot breath giving her delicious chills. "I want to see you in the candlelight. Will you let me?"

"Aye." She would've agreed to anything he wanted.

He pulled back and slipped the garment over her head, then tossed it. She drew in a sharp breath, shivering both from the cool air and from Keegan seeing her completely naked in the dim glow of the candle. She knew she should feel ashamed of her sinfully wanton behavior, allowing Keegan to do such a thing, but this felt right. 'Twas almost as if he was already hers. When she gave him her heart, she gave him all of herself.

Would he make love to her now? Did she want him to?

Standing back, he trailed his gaze over her from her eyes to her toes and back again. He released a harsh breath. "Saints, Seona, you are the loveliest vision I have ever beheld," he whispered.

She hoped he would disrobe as well. Instead, he drew her close again and kissed a leisurely trail down her neck, bewitching her with heated yearnings.

He brushed his mouth across her breast, his short whisker stubble rasping her skin. She held her breath in expectation. He kissed her nipple, then drew it into his mouth. Desire and a sharp need for him stabbed her core. She gasped, holding on 'round his neck, cradling his head closer and supporting herself.

"*A ghràidh*," he murmured, his breath hot against her sensitive skin.

My love. His endearment thrilled her.

Her derriere in his hands, he lifted her and moved across the room. He laid her softly onto the bed, still lavishing her breasts with abundant kisses. Her hands tangled in his hair, holding his head.

Though she felt beyond wicked, reveling in these exciting sensations, it felt natural for Keegan to be doing these things to her.

He kissed down her stomach gradually. "You smell so good." At her navel, he dipped his tongue inside.

Shivers covered her. She could not believe it when he moved lower still and kissed the mound at the apex of her thighs. Though she knew he should do no such thing, she hadn't the willpower to stop him. Whatever he wished to do would be better than the last thing. He constantly surprised her with sensual wonders she had not known existed.

When he pushed her thighs apart, she grasped onto the sheets beneath her. He would make love to her, and aye, she was ready. She forced her eyes open to see what he would do. She was disappointed to see he still had not removed his plaid or his shirt. Instead, he lay half on the bed, the lower half of his tall body sprawled toward the floor.

He dropped his head and touched her in a most illicit way. Nay, not a touch. A lick… against a highly sensitive and intimate spot. She jerked in surprise, but at the same time her hips lifted, seeking more. And he gave it. Another lick that sent splendid sensations ricocheting through her.

"Oh," she breathed. She had thought his fingers stroking that place were amazing. His wet, hot tongue caressing it was beyond description, both slick and velvety. She turned her head aside to muffle her moan in the pillow. She was shocked at herself and the way her body moved with such wanton undulations, pushing more firmly to his mouth. Surely this was a most sinful activity but she could not bring herself to make him stop. Nay, 'twas too sublime, the heat rushing through her making her lightheaded.

She felt her hips thrust upward, toward him. He groaned, vibrating her flesh, then his tongue flickered over her. At the same time he pushed a finger inside her.

Again, her body acted of its own volition, her hips shoving toward him. Her breath hissed through her teeth. "Keegan, I beg of you…"

"Aye, lass. Take your pleasure."

He was giving her pleasure; that was a certainty. The tip of his tongue tormented her and drove her mad. Her body bowed upwards. She didn't even try to control it anymore. Isobel had warned her about this. She had not thought it could happen. Not like this.

Seona grasped the pillow beneath her head and dragged it over her face to muffle her gasps and cries for she feared she would not maintain control much longer. Nay, the sensations were becoming overwhelming. She felt suspended, dangling from some cliff face. But there was no fear. Nay. She knew she could fly if she let go.

His fingers wiggled against her overly sensitized flesh and his tongue slid back and forth, then in a circle. A sort of pleasurable insanity seized her, just like last time. She did not understand it but she let go and rode it like a violent gale storm. The pleasure crashed and rolled.

Once the intense sensations ebbed, she dragged the pillow off and gasped for air. She was so spent she could barely lift her eyelids.

Keegan raised his head and stroked her thighs. "That was beautiful." He kissed her knee, then placed a playful bite on her thigh.

He moved up beside her and pulled her tightly into his arms. He tucked her head beneath his chin and stroked her back and her hip. She loved being held in his arms, and the way he always smelled clean and manly.

Why couldn't they lay this way every night? 'Twould be paradise.

"Keegan, I don't understand what happened," she said, hoping he would explain a few things.

"Did you enjoy it?" The smile was evident in his voice.

How could he ask such a thing? "I think you ken I did."

"Good. That's what I wanted. To give you pleasure."

"Why did you want to… use your tongue?" Her face burned, but she had to ask if she wished to know the truth about sensual pleasures.

"To taste you." He growled. "You taste damned good, lass. 'Twas a great pleasure to me."

"I know I'm naïve, but I never imagined people did that."

"Aye, well, not everyone does." He leaned back a bit so she could look up into his face, dimly illuminated by the candle. "One summer's day when I was about eighteen, I happened upon a couple on a plaid in the sand dunes and beach grass. They didn't know I was there, of course." Keegan smiled. "'Haps 'twas wrong of me to spy on them, but how could I resist? They were aristocratic guests of Chief and Lady MacKay—I don't believe they were married either. They'd been swimming in the sea. I could not believe the wicked things they were doing, but I knew those were things I wanted to do one day when I found a woman I wanted to kiss every inch of." He touched the tip of her nose with a finger.

Speaking of kissing every inch of... she wished she could do that to him. "Why do you not remove your clothes?"

He released a harsh breath. "'Tis best that I don't. I must maintain control."

"But you made me lose control."

Keegan smiled. "I'm glad." Aye, indeed he was thrilled he was able to give her such a climax. He hoped she enjoyed it. Of a certainty, he did.

His tarse was hard as stone, but he couldn't take her. Not now. First, he had to know she would be his forever. He couldn't risk getting her with child and then her father marrying her off to someone else. If that happened, he'd be forced to steal her away. And then clan war would follow. Though he might have indulged in too many carnal pleasures with her, he wanted to marry her first... not just to be honorable, but because he wanted her in his life forever.

When Seona's hand trailed down his chest and stomach, between them, to his erection, arousal burned through him even hotter. Through his clothing, her fingers brushed his shaft. Though he ached for her to continue, he gently clasped her hand in his and drew it away.

"You didn't like that?" she asked. "I was told..."

"Aye, I would love it more than I can say but..." He blew out a harsh breath. "Who has been telling you wicked things?"

In the low light, the look of guilt and embarrassment in her bewitching dark blue eyes made him want to grin.

"A friend," she said.

He raised a brow, wondering who she meant. "Isobel?" he asked, remembering the many times he'd seen them whispering together.

"Aye."

"Well, Dirk often has a smile on his face, so I'm certain he is well-pleased with their bed-sport. Has she told you things that singed your ears?"

Seona gave a soft giggle. "A few, but one thing she said was that men like to be touched on... certain places."

"That we do, lass. I love it anytime, anywhere you touch me. But it makes me want you even more intensely."

Her hand had somehow escaped his while he wasn't paying attention, and now it brushed over his hard tarse again. Pleasure and powerful need bounded through him, urging him to roll between her naked thighs and lift his plaid. He sucked in breath and forced himself to remain still. If she wanted to touch him so badly, 'haps he'd let her... for a moment.

Her fingers traced along his rigid length through his clothing. "I don't understand how it gets so hard."

Her naïve interest in his body almost did him in.

"Saints, lass," he hissed. "You drive me mad. I want to... but I cannot."

"What do you want to do?" she whispered, still stroking lightly, tormenting him.

His body was starting to overheat. He groaned, wishing he could rip every last stitch of his clothing off. "In truth? You don't know?"

"Lovemaking. I know that, but I don't know anything about it."

He muttered a curse. Though he'd known she was innocent, he couldn't have guessed how incredibly curious she was. Or how vocal, given her usually quiet nature. But, she trusted him. His chest ached, for he treasured her trust as much as her love.

"Of a certainty, I'll be glad to show you soon, Seona. I want to slide this..." He placed his hand around hers and squeezed his tarse, intensifying the pleasurable ache. "Deep inside you and..." He bit his tongue before he said something too vulgar for her ears.

"How on earth would it fit?"

He growled. Just imagining working on making it fit within her tight, wet heat near took his sanity.

"Och, I'll go slowly. 'Twill fit perfectly." Hell, he could hardly wait for what would be one of the best experiences of his life.

"'Twill hurt though… for me," she said.

He wasn't going to lie. "Aye. For a few minutes. But I will make it good for you before I'm done. Your pleasure is more important to me than mine own."

"You are the most generous person I know." She kissed his chin.

He didn't feel generous at the moment. He felt damned greedy, wanting her to slide her hand up and down and stroke him very firmly.

His primal side threatened to override his rational side and answer all her questions by showing her exactly what he yearned to do to her—push, inch by torturous inch, into her and show her how her body could adjust to accept his.

He would kiss her and love her through the pain, then, once he was fully imbedded inside her, he'd withdraw slowly only to drive deep again. She'd beg him to go faster. He would thrust until they both lost their minds, until she cried out her pleasure and he released his seed inside her. He muttered a curse before he could stop himself.

Somehow her hand had sneaked beneath his plaid and long shirt. Her bare cool skin against his… "Saints." Her hand squeezed the tip of his erection and he thought he was going to blast like a cannon.

"Your skin feels so silky and hot," she whispered. "I cannot believe how hard you are."

All he could do was grind his teeth, curse and struggle for control. He gasped for breath. "You're determined to drive me mad."

"Aye. I want to give you pleasure. Tell me what to do."

How could he refuse that offer? Clasping his hand around hers, he showed her how to stroke up and down his rigid shaft. Damn, he was on the edge already. He'd wanted her too long. Months.

He tried to think of something else to distract himself, but 'twas no use. She filled his mind; her scent filled his head. He clasped her to him and kissed her, devouring her lips as she continued stroking without his help. Her tentative, light touch aroused him even more. And then the fuse lit, burning through his groin and exploding with a pleasure more astounding than he'd ever felt. Groaning, he dragged her tighter to him, loving the pressure of her body against his.

How he'd wanted to be inside her when he did that.

He kissed her forehead and pulled in laborious breaths, enjoying the final ripples of pleasure that reverberated through him.

"Oh, that was..." she said in a surprised tone.

"Aye?" He wondered what she'd wanted to say. He could only describe how it had felt to him. "Amazing. Spectacular." He finally came back to himself. "And I'm guessing your hand is drenched with my seed." He wiped her hand on the tail of his shirt. "See? That's what happens when you take away my control."

"I'm glad." Her teeth flashed white in the dimness. And she actually sounded happy, not afraid or disgusted.

"You are?"

"Aye. I wanted to give you pleasure. I simply didn't know how. I'm glad you showed me."

To have a wife who not only enjoyed bed-sport, but wished to boldly seduce him, would surely be heaven on earth. Of course, that wasn't the only reason he wanted to marry her, but 'twas certainly a delightful bonus.

"Hmm. Later, I'll show you more." Once they were married. And he was determined this would happen. He kissed her lips. "I'd best make my escape before your aunt returns. I know not what kind of stamina MacMillan has." He chuckled.

"You are wicked," Seona accused.

"I'm afraid I am." Grinning, he arose from the bed.

"Keegan, wait."

"Aye? I wasn't leaving just yet." He didn't want to leave at all.

Kneeling on the high bed, she wrapped her arms around his neck. He slipped his hands down her back, over the silken skin of her hips and derriere to her thighs. "Mmm," he purred and kissed her. How he needed her in every way... physically, emotionally, spiritually. "I love you," he whispered.

"And I love you."

At her words, his heart pounded harder. Aye, he was determined to have her as his wife no matter what her father said.

Keegan truly did not want to start a war, but he would if he had to.

CHAPTER TWENTY-ONE

"Aunt Patience, I wish to speak to you for a moment in private," Seona said the next morn in the great hall as everyone in their party gathered to leave. "I want to ask a favor of you."

"Aye?" Patience looked mightily *impatient* at the moment. She glanced toward where Hugh MacMillan stood on the other side of the large, dim room.

Seona headed to the small alcove at the back.

Only a little limp left in her step, Patience followed. "What is it?"

When they were out of view and earshot of everyone, Seona said, "I ask that you not mention to my father that I've been talking to Keegan MacKay."

Patience put her hands upon her hips. "You were doing far more than talking to him." Her voice was low but irate. "You were kissing him in your bedchamber. You've been disgraceful."

"He is going to ask Father for my hand in marriage."

Patience snorted. "A lot of good it will do him. He is far beneath you."

Fury burned through Seona. "He is not beneath me. As you well know, he is second in line to the MacKay chiefdom."

"Nevertheless, your father will not allow you to marry him, and he will be most displeased about your association with MacKay. Especially the kissing."

"That's why I ask that you not tell him."

"Your father is my brother and I always tell him the truth."

Her aunt's self-righteous tone made Seona grind her teeth. How could the woman pretend to be a perfect angel when 'twas obvious to everyone she was doing the same things with MacMillan? Probably more, if the truth was known. If Patience told Seona's father that Keegan had been kissing her in the bedchamber, he might fly into a rage and have Keegan killed. She couldn't risk that. She would use the only leverage she had and pray it worked.

"If you tell him about Keegan, then I shall have to tell him about your tryst with Hugh MacMillan, a man Father will see as far beneath you."

Patience's mouth dropped open. Her eyes grew wide. "Why, you little tattle." Though her words were low, they were sharp. When her aunt's hand raised and flew toward her face, Seona lifted her hand just in time to stop the strike. She then locked her aunt's wrist in a firm grip.

"Do not ever do that again," Seona said through clenched teeth, surprising herself. She didn't know she could be so fierce when it came to protecting Keegan. But he was the most important person in her life now.

"How dare you?" her aunt sneered, yanking her hand back. "Your father will hear about this."

"Very well. He will also hear about how you are sleeping with one of the guards."

"You can't prove that."

"I ken the truth of it and so does Keegan. Hugh is always honest with Keegan, his direct commander."

Her aunt's mouth opened and closed as if she would say something, but didn't for a long moment. "You wouldn't," she whispered.

So, 'twas true. Her aunt really had slept with the guard. Seona was relieved. This might be the only way to keep Keegan safe. "Say anything against me or Keegan to my father and find out. He will no longer allow you to stay at Gillenmor and he will withdraw your funds. Where will your food and fancy clothing come from then?"

"You little strumpet!" her aunt hissed.

"No more than you are."

Her aunt stood glaring daggers at her. "You are not the sweet innocent lady I thought you were."

"I cannot say the same about you. I always knew you had a malicious streak." *Just like Father.*

Her aunt's eyes merely narrowed further.

"Do we have a deal?"

"Aye," her aunt said through clenched teeth, then limped away as fast as her sore ankle would take her.

Hoping she'd done the right thing, Seona released a breath and stepped away from the alcove. Her gaze scanned the great hall and locked with Keegan's. Immediately, he headed toward her.

Her heart rate spiked as it always did when he was near. She had hardly been able to sleep last night after the amazing things he'd done to her.

"Are you well?" he asked. "You appeared upset."

"Aye." She briefly explained the precarious deal she had with her aunt about keeping each other's secrets.

"'Tis brilliant." Keegan grinned. "You are more cunning than I realized."

Truth was she'd do anything for him, to keep him safe.

"And you've already proven yourself a lady warrior."

"I thank you." She enjoyed the look of pride in his blue eyes.

Too soon, he sobered. "We'll be heading out in a few minutes. Once we draw nearer to Gillenmor, Haldane will become more of a threat. Do you remember our knife-fighting lessons?"

A chill passed over her. "Aye."

"And you still carry the knife I gave you?"

"Of course." She placed her hand upon the weapon strapped to the inside of her forearm. 'Twas her most valued possession.

Keegan nodded. "I pray you won't need it, but just in case. We suspect Haldane may increase his efforts in capturing you the closer we get to Gillenmor. He may have hired more men. We must be ready for anything."

***

Seona, her aunt, and their two maids rode in the center of the two dozen men in their party. She was happy that Keegan rode to her left most of the way. She often watched him out of the corner of her eye. He and the rest of the guards were ever on alert. Talking was kept to a minimum, the only sounds the horses' hooves striking the ground. She had been through this area a few times and knew they were only a mile or two from Gillenmor. Anguish weighed heavily on her heart with each step they took forward.

Up ahead, the narrow muddy road snaked through a small dark forest. Seona dreaded riding through there.

"Halt!" Keegan lifted his hand. "'Tis likely they are hiding in that wood, waiting to ambush us."

The other men nodded, murmuring their agreement.

"I need ten or twelve of you to scout the wood and kill the outlaws if you find them," Keegan said.

"Aye," several of the men said, their eyes lighting with eagerness.

Fourteen men, both MacKays and MacKenzies, rode swiftly toward the wood. Everyone else waited in silence, watching. The breeze picked up, blowing the vibrant green grasses of the gently sloping meadows where cattle and sheep grazed. Crofters tended their crops in the distance, the soil rich and dark. Stone dykes and low-growing bushes divided up the fields.

'Twas a beautiful, calm area. Seona's home. But it did not feel like home to her anymore. Nay. Now her home was the rough and craggy northern Highlands around Durness. 'Twas a wild and untamed place, filled with rocky terrain, prickly yellow gorse bushes, deep icy lochs and turbulent skies, but its beauty reminded her of Keegan. If she could be with him, she would be at home.

She glanced aside at him. His sharp gaze was fixed on the wood, as if he could almost see what was hidden in the trees. His whole body was tense, as if he was prepared to launch into battle at any moment. She prayed there would be no battle, no ambush or attacks. Why could Haldane not get it through is daft head she would never willingly marry him?

Keegan glanced at her, catching her gaze. The color of his eyes made her think of a blue flame, so intense and practically glowing with vibrant life. He gave her a faint, warm grin, then turned his attention back to the forest. How she loved his protectiveness and his strength of character.

A quarter hour later, the MacKay and MacKenzie men emerged from the forest. She counted all fourteen of them as they approached. Thank heavens no one had been hurt.

"We saw neither hide nor hair of them," MacMillan reported.

"'Slud. Where are they hiding?" Keegan muttered. "We ride on, then. Be ever on alert."

"Aye."

They all urged their horses forward again, at a quicker pace than before, and were soon enshrouded by the forest. Seona had always been afraid of traveling through this area because of how dark it was, with the thick trees blocking out the sun. The air was cool and dank and smelled of rotting leaves. Some even said the wood was haunted because of the many people who had been murdered here. She had never seen a spirit, but she always got chills here.

Thankfully, the men increased their speed even more once within the wood. She was eager to leave it as well.

As they emerged from the trees, one of the guards on her far right yelled out a warning.

"There they are!" Keegan said. "The bastards."

Haldane's archer, Gil, was letting fly his arrows as fast as his arms would move. Two more men were shooting bows as well.

"Kill them!" Keegan shouted.

Most of the men leapt down from their horses and, with swords and targes in hand, charged Haldane's outlaws. The MacKay archers nocked arrows and sent them soaring toward the enemies.

"Protect the women," Keegan ordered, then sidled his horse up next to hers. "Seona, get on in front of me." The look in his eyes was so fierce, she dared not disobey him.

She offered her arm and he dragged her onto his horse. "You hold the reins."

His basket-hilt broadsword was in his right hand and his targe strapped to his other forearm. He locked this arm around her. She felt safer with the shield protecting her chest and Keegan at her back. But he put himself in far more danger acting as a human shield to her. Haldane would want to move the obstacle to get to her.

"Five of you stay with me and help protect Seona," Keegan told the guards. "Haldane has a habit of attacking at the rear."

"Aha!" Rebbie said, off to the left. "Here they are now. Guards!"

Around a dozen men charged them from the opposite direction.

"Saints," Seona hissed. So many. Haldane must have hired more men.

Rebbie and several of the guards met the outlaws thirty feet away. Men who had been fighting the other contingent of

Haldane's gang soon joined them. Chaos erupted, swords clanged, men yelled out battle cries, vulgar names, and howls of pain.

"Come. Let's move away from the skirmish," Keegan called to the five guards surrounding them.

Seona glanced around, wondering where Aunt Patience was... and the maids. Behind her, MacMillan and two other guards had taken the women onto their horses with them. They all quickly moved forward along the road, further from the fighting.

Though Seona hated watching men die, she was glad to see that several of Haldane's men fell under the onslaught of the MacKays and MacKenzies. The brigands were outnumbered. Keegan was canny to bring so many men with them.

Finally, the remaining outlaws gave up and fled, Haldane and McMurdo with them.

"Damnation," Keegan muttered. "I should've killed him myself."

Seona shook her head, not wishing to see Keegan engaged in one-to-one combat with Haldane. Certainly, she believed Keegan could best him, being five years his senior and more highly trained, but she didn't want Keegan in that kind of danger.

"Are you well?" Keegan asked, his warm breath fanning the hair at her ear.

She shivered, relief flooding through her. "Aye. I thank you for protecting me."

"'Tis my pleasure and a great honor."

Six of their men were injured—cuts, stab wounds, an arrow protruding from one man's shoulder—but they all remained on their feet.

"How far are we from Gillenmor?" Keegan asked her.

"About a mile or two. 'Tis over the next rise."

"Does your father employ a healer?"

"Aye, there are two. I'm certain they will help your men."

"Mount up," Keegan called out. "'Tis about a mile or two to Gillenmor. The healer there will see to your wounds. And I thank you for your fearsome fighting skills. You have protected these ladies well."

As they rode forward, Seona savored Keegan's warm, hard body at her back. She prayed this would not be the last time she rode with him.

Once they'd topped the rise and Gillenmor Castle came into

view in the distance, Keegan helped Seona back onto her own horse. The other women returned to their horses as well.

Seona was glad the danger from Haldane was behind them for the moment, but a new danger grew closer with each step they took toward Gillenmor—her father.

CHAPTER TWENTY-TWO

Keegan's stomach knotted as they entered the dimly lit great hall of Gillenmor Castle, but he didn't let his unease show. He tried to focus on doing his job, his duty for Dirk and the clan, and not the fact that he was bringing the woman he loved to a place where he might have to leave her. Nay, he would not. He was taking her out of here, one way or another.

"Well, 'tis about time," a deep, rough voice called out. A man, dressed in the Lowland or English style, stood from his elevated seat at the high table, stepped down and strode forward to greet them. Keegan assumed he was Chief Ambrose Murray, Seona's father. He was stocky, with gray hair. His clean-shaven face was flushed, either from being too close to the fire or too much whisky. With a narrow-eyed gaze, he inspected Seona first.

"A good eve to you, Father." She curtsied, keeping her eyes downcast.

Keegan frowned, his instincts going on high alert for he sensed her fear.

"Seona," Murray said, then lifted his gaze to scan over the faces of those who had come inside. Several of the guards and servants had remained outside, seeing to the horses and making sure the healer attended the injured men's wounds.

"We brought Lady Seona and Lady Patience home in Chief MacKay's stead," Keegan said. "He was injured in a skirmish during our travels. And he sent you a gift."

"Who are you?" Chief Murray asked in a stern voice, his

brown eyes hostile.

"Keegan MacKay, m'laird." He bowed. "Tanist and cousin of Chief MacKay. I'm honored to meet you."

"Ah." He shook Keegan's hand briefly, then turned his attention to the other men. "And who else do I have the pleasure of meeting?"

"This is Dermott MacKenzie and his brother, Fraser." Keegan motioned to them. "They are younger brothers of Chief MacKenzie."

"I stayed here for a couple of nights last year," Dermott said. "Good to see you again, m'laird."

Murray shook both their hands. "Aye," he said in a neutral tone.

Keegan motioned to Rebbie. "And this is Robert MacInnis, the Earl of Rebbinglen."

Chief Murray's bushy gray brows shot up and his demeanor switched, almost as if he were a different person. "Earl of Rebbinglen?" He stepped forward and gave Rebbie a long, solemn handshake while studying him. "'Tis my great pleasure and honor to meet you again, Laird Rebbinglen. I remember when you were a wee lad."

"The pleasure is all mine, Chief Murray."

"You have the look of your father. How is he?"

Rebbie grinned. "Still as ornery as ever."

"Ha." With what might be called a grin, Murray slapped Rebbie on the shoulder, then released his hand.

After scanning the rest of the MacKay party and apparently dismissing them, he motioned those he'd met forward. "'Tis time for supper. Please join us."

Keegan frowned, watching the ladies and the others of their party proceed to the high table, then he followed. Something here was not right and Keegan didn't like it.

"Rebbinglen," Chief Murray said, placing a hand on his shoulder. "Please join me."

Keegan eyed the man, noticing he'd said nothing else to his daughter and had only nodded to his sister, Lady Patience. What Keegan had heard all along was true then—above all, Chief Murray valued prestige. Titles. Wealth. Keegan felt as if a blade had stabbed into his stomach. His chances of gaining the man's permission to marry Seona were going to be nonexistent... unless

Rebbie could soften him up and convince him otherwise. Keegan was suddenly very glad Rebbie had accompanied them.

Keegan approached the high table, and when he saw the vacant seat beside Seona, he took it. He'd be daft not to seize any opportunity to be near her, though he was unsure how Chief Murray would feel about this.

***

Seona couldn't believe Keegan was sitting beside her. With her father only a few seats away? *Saints.* If he perceived that either of them paid much attention to the other, he'd fly into a rage, no matter who looked on. Her stomach knotted and ached. She wouldn't be able to eat a bite. She wished she could take her leave of the table, go to her chamber and rest, but to do so would draw her father's angry attention.

Thankfully, he was too busy entertaining Laird Rebbinglen to notice much else. Rebbie told him of the recent skirmish that had taken place just beyond Gillenmor.

Seona glanced around, not spotting her sister. She was likely still with Cousin Genevieve.

While the food was being served, Seona was able to relax marginally. She had no appetite for the leek and pea soup. Her attention was drawn to Keegan, beside her. From the corner of her eye, she observed his big strong hands, his muscular arms beneath his doublet, and his plaid. She found his manly scent most appealing.

"Are you not hungry, Lady Seona?" he asked in a conversational tone.

"Nay. Not overmuch." She lifted her wooden spoon and forced herself to take a bite.

He removed two slices of bread from the large platter close to him and gave her one.

"I thank you."

Once Keegan had finished his soup, he placed his hands on his thighs. She knew she was mad, but she could scarce eat for thinking what his thighs might look like bare. She'd seen his naked calves often enough beneath the bottom of his belted plaid. They were muscular and lightly furred with golden hairs. Likely his thighs were the same. She had not been able to see them well in the low light when he'd waded from the loch, but she remembered the hard feel of his thighs beneath her when he'd put her on the horse in front of him.

Mo creach! She had to think of something else, but how could she with him sitting so close?

Though she refused to look at him, she felt his attention on her. She prayed he wasn't staring at her. Someone would surely notice.

Beneath the table, he moved his knee against hers and left it there.

She froze, unable to believe what he was doing. She glanced around, making sure no one was watching. They weren't; their attention was on the roasted grouse being served. She released her held breath.

Though she loved sitting by Keegan, she didn't know how much more tension she could handle.

***

After the meal, when the music and singing was underway for the evening's entertainment, Chief Murray rose from his chair and ambled toward Seona. Her heart vaulted into her throat. Had he seen Keegan staring at her?

"I would have a word with you in my meeting room," her father said, motioning her impatiently toward the door.

"Aye, Father." Her stomach felt queasy and she wished she hadn't eaten a bite. She proceeded into the smaller room, just off the great hall, which contained a table covered in papers, a desk, and all sorts of books. The fire had burned down to embers but the room was still warm. Too bad her father was not. Nay, the look in his dark eyes was cold.

He took a seat behind his imposing oak desk. "So, why is it that you return to me unmarried to the MacKay chief?"

Oh heavens. How was she supposed to respond to that without making Dirk out to be a villain?

"He did not wish to marry me." 'Twas the only reason she could think of. And the truth.

"Why?" he demanded.

"I explained in the missive I sent—"

"I had an agreement and a written contract with his father, Griff MacKay! Why did they choose to break that oath?"

Seona drew in a deep breath, then released it, forcing herself to remain calm. "As you ken, Chief Griff MacKay passed last fall. There was some dispute as to which of his three sons would be the new chief. We all thought Aiden was the eldest living son. He, in fact, became chief for about a month. Then Dirk MacKay returned. He is the eldest son, but everyone thought him dead for twelve years. Because he is more suited than Aiden to be a chief and 'twas proven he was indeed the eldest son of Chief Griff, the clan appointed him the new chief."

"And why did you not marry this Dirk MacKay? Why did he not honor the contract his father sighed five years ago?"

"He was already..." How should she say this? Already in love with Lady Isobel? Nay, that wasn't good enough. Emotion held no sway for her father.

"Well, come on, lass. Spit it out! Already what?"

"Already betrothed to another lady," she said. Her chest tightened with the lie. It was the only excuse she could think of at the moment. Dirk had not been betrothed to Isobel at that point, but he was in love with her. That was no doubt a stronger pull for him.

"Already betrothed?" her father thundered.

"Aye."

"To who?"

"Lady Isobel MacKenzie."

"You did not mention this in the missive."

He had a point and she knew not how to counter it. "They married very soon after they arrived."

That much was true. Though it was a few weeks.

"Anyway, Dirk MacKay knew naught of the contract before he arrived in Durness," she added. She'd had to tell the fib about Dirk and Isobel being betrothed; otherwise, her father might grow enraged with Chief MacKay and attack. The last thing she wanted was clan war. She wanted Isobel, Dirk and all the MacKays to be safe. They were like family to her... more so than her own clan. Nor did she want her father to take his wrath out on Keegan, who was acting as Dirk's representative.

But what if Aunt Patience told her father a different story? *Saints!* Had she made a terrible mistake with that white lie? It didn't hurt anyone. In fact, it kept everyone safe. Mayhap the warning she'd given her aunt about exposing her affair with MacMillan would still hold in this case as well. She needed to talk to her again.

"This whole story sounds far-fetched to me," her father grumbled. "The MacKays know not how to keep their word." He rose from his chair and moved toward the door. After yanking it open, he told his personal bodyguard, standing just outside the door, to fetch Lady Patience.

Mo creach! Seona would be in trouble if her aunt told a different story.

Aunt Patience entered and her father closed the door.

"Sister, explain the MacKay situation. It makes no sense to me," her father said.

"I told Father how Dirk was already betrothed to Lady Isobel and this is why I couldn't marry him," Seona rushed to say, giving her aunt a meaningful look while her father's back was turned.

Her aunt sent her a narrow-eyed glare.

"Let her explain it. I've already heard your side," her father ordered.

"Aye," Patience said hesitantly, her expression shifting from angry to pleasant. "I heard that some of the clan thought they were already married when they arrived in Durness. There were abundant rumors that they'd already been intimate and a bairn might result."

"Damned barbarians," her father said gruffly. His gaze shifted between Seona and her aunt for a long tense moment. "That will be all, Seona."

She headed toward the door, then realized Patience hadn't been dismissed. She let herself out, praying her aunt didn't reveal anything that would anger her father. If he knew the truth of it, he would be enraged.

As Seona waited a few yards from the door for her aunt to emerge from the private conference with her father, she thought of her sister, glad she was still staying with Cousin Genevieve. At least she hoped she was, but she would love to see her. It had been many months.

When one of the kitchen servants passed nearby, Seona asked, "Is my sister still with my cousin?"

"Lady Seona." The maid curtsied. "Nay, Lady Talia is in her bedchamber."

What? Seona frowned. Why had she not joined them for supper?

"I thank you for telling me." Seona rushed up the narrow spiral stair to the floor above and knocked at Talia's chamber door. They were so close that normally they didn't knock; they simply barged in. Impatient, she tried to open the door but it didn't budge.

Why had her sister locked the door?

"Talia? Are you in there?" Seona tried to keep her voice low.

"Who is it?" The mumbled response sounded sleepy. Was her sister napping?

"'Tis Seona."

"Seona?" Talia's tone was more excited now. "You are home?"

"Aye. Unlock the door."

"I cannot. Father locked me in here."

An icy shock went through Seona. "Why?"

"I angered him," she said in an uneven voice.

"Are you crying? What happened?" *Heavens!* How she wished she could get inside and see her sister. "Did Father hurt you?"

"Aye," she said low, very close to the other side of the door. "He hit me and I fell."

Seona clenched her teeth. Damn the man. Though she might be breaking a commandment and dishonoring her father, the man was the very devil.

She blew out a breath and tried to sound calm. "How badly are you hurt?"

"The maid said it looks worse than it is."

Dear heavens, it had to be bad, then. "How does it look?"

"I have a bruise on my face," Talia said.

"What else? Any cuts or broken bones?"

"Nay, but I have another bruise on my arm where it struck the bed frame."

Saints! Seona wished she could lash out at her father in the same way, but he was strong and stocky. He had knocked her down before. When she was a wee lass, she remembered him treating her poor mother the same way. She had to get Talia away from him.

"What was he trying to make you do?" Seona asked.

"He wants me to marry Chief Comyn. He is an old man, Seona," Talia sobbed.

Not only that, but the man was notorious for being ruthless and vile. What could she do to help her sister? She well knew fathers in the Highlands chose husbands for their daughters, but hers was determined to find the worst possible husbands for them to ensure their lives would be hell on earth.

"Since he received your missive months ago, he has been hunting a husband for you as well," Talia said.

Dark dread slammed into Seona's gut. "Who has he mentioned?"

CHAPTER TWENTY-THREE

Seona stood outside her sister's door, waiting to hear the name of the man her father planned to marry her off to. Although a title meant naught to her, at the moment she wished Keegan had the grandest title in the land, simply so she'd be allowed to marry him.

"Talia?" Seona asked, moisture burning her eyes. "Tell me who."

"Laird Wentworth from further south. He is a baron."

She didn't know whether to be relieved that he was none of the horrid chiefs she knew, or more terrified of the unknown. "I have never heard of him. Have you seen him?"

"Aye, he visited. He is not terribly old. I would say thirty summers. But you would not like him. He is pompous and arrogant."

"Perfect," Seona muttered, hating her father more with each second that passed.

Footsteps clomped up the stairwell behind her. 'Twas Fleming, one of the guards who had worked here forever. Although his hair was mostly gray, he was still a brawny man. "What are you about? Oh. Lady Seona, welcome home." He bowed.

"I thank you, Fleming. I wish to go in and speak to my sister. Have you the key?"

"Aye, but I must ask Chief Murray."

"Please do."

Fleming disappeared down the stairwell.

Seona turned back to the door. "How long have you been

locked in there?"

"Five days," Talia said.

"Good Lord. Have the maids brought you food?"

"Aye."

"And are you eating?"

"Aye."

Seona was glad for that at least, but she needed to see if her sister had lost weight. When Talia was upset, she would sometimes avoid meals. "Why did you not remain with Cousin Genevieve?" She would've been safe and cared for there, at least.

"I did for several months, but when spring arrived, Father came to retrieve me."

"I see."

"So he could find me a husband." Talia started crying again. "I won't marry the beast!"

Footsteps echoed on the stone steps.

"Shh… the guard is returning. Move away from the door."

Fleming came into view. "Your father said you could visit with your sister." He unlocked the door.

"I thank you," Seona said, then entered the room.

The lock clicked behind her, giving her a cold chill.

Talia lit a candle from the hearth fire and placed it on a nearby table. Seona hurried to her and, when Talia faced her, Seona couldn't believe the bruise covering the left side of her face. Her cheek was purple with tinges of green and yellow. At least it appeared to be healing.

"Oh, heavens, Talia." Tears filling her eyes, Seona stroked the uninjured side of her sister's sweet face. 'Twas almost as if they were wee girls again, huddling in a chamber, hoping their father stayed far away.

Talia grabbed her in a hug and sobbed against her shoulder. Seona embraced her tightly and stroked her back. "Shh, tis all right."

Never had their father given Seona such a huge bruise, though he had slapped her hard four different times. Seona had always tried to protect her younger sister. She regretted that she hadn't been here this time, but she'd had no choice in the matter.

Talia pulled back and wiped her eyes with a handkerchief. "I've decided, if I can get out of this room, I'm going to run away."

"What? Where would you go?"

"I know not. Anywhere."

"Talia—"

"Nay. Do not try to talk me out of it."

Certainly Seona had dreamed of running away, too, but she had never seriously considered it because she had to stay and protect her sister. Plus, as women, they had no means. No money, aside from what their father gave them. They had no relatives in distant villages who might hide them. All their relatives were close-by, and worst of all, they were loyal to her father… or they feared him.

If only Seona could have married one of the MacKays. Keegan, of course, was the man she wanted so desperately to marry, but she feared her father would not even consider it. If she could've married a decent man, she'd hoped to bring her sister to live with her. But now she knew that might not be possible, if her father was bent on arranging a marriage between Talia and the Comyn chief.

Seona's stomach pained her for she was trapped just as she'd always been.

"We must think of a solution," she told Talia.

"I have. I'm running away."

"Do you have a plan? How will you support yourself? Where will you stay? How will you buy food?"

Talia crumpled onto the bench near the hearth. "I know not," she sobbed.

Seona sat beside her and rubbed her back. "Shh. We must think."

Heavens! If only Seona could marry Keegan, she could take Talia with her to Durness and keep her safe. Away from old, beastly chiefs who wanted to marry young girls. Talia would love staying with the MacKays. They were a lively and considerate group. The man Seona loved and her best friend were among them. To think of never seeing them again broke her heart. They were her true family.

Keegan had said he was going to ask her father for her hand. Would he still do this after having met her father? Keegan was a strong, brave man and Seona couldn't see him being intimidated by her father. Although perhaps he should be, given her father's ruthlessness.

If only Laird Rebbinglen could convince her father to see

Keegan's merits. Tanist was no small position within a clan. But more importantly, Keegan was an honorable, protective, and responsible man. Unfortunately, these admirable qualities were not of utmost importance to her father.

Her stomach knotted when she imagined Keegan standing before her father, asking for her hand. She feared her father would fly into an instant rage and try to hurt Keegan.

"I'm tired of thinking about all this," Talia said. "Tell me of your adventures in the north and why you didn't marry the MacKay chief."

There was so much. How could Seona possibly tell her sister of everything she'd seen and experienced since last autumn? "You must promise not to tell anyone."

"Of course I won't tell. I promise."

Seona told her of how beautiful Durness was in the spring, but how harsh and cold in the winter, and how she and their aunt had traveled from Tongue to Durness in the bitter cold. She told her of the friendly, fun-loving MacKay clan and how she envied Dirk and Isobel's love match. She told her of the battles they'd endured on their journey south again and how Haldane MacKay wanted to kidnap her. Seona knew not how long she talked. She could go on for hours about the MacKays and Isobel and how she enjoyed spending time with them.

"What are you not telling me?" Talia asked.

"What do you mean?"

"I can tell you're keeping a secret."

Keegan was her secret. A few of the men knew, of course. But dare she tell her sister? She had always kept her secrets. Talia disliked Aunt Patience's spying as much as Seona did. And how could Seona not tell her sister the most amazing thing that had happened to her—she'd fallen in love with a most remarkable man.

"What is that grin?" Talia asked.

Seona hadn't realized she was grinning. She immediately tried to control her expression.

"Is it a man? You met someone in Durness and fell in love," Talia said in an excited tone, her eyes wide.

"Aye," Seona admitted in a low voice, her face burning.

Talia grabbed Seona's hands. "Tell me about him! What is his name?"

"You must promise to tell no one. Lives could be in danger."

"I promise not to tell anyone." Talia almost bounced upon the bench.

"Very well. His name is Keegan MacKay," Seona whispered. "He is the cousin of Chief MacKay and the clan's tanist."

Talia grinned, her dark eyes alight with excitement. "What is he like? Is he handsome and kind?"

"Aye, indeed. The kindest and most handsome man I have ever laid eyes upon. He protected me during the journey here."

"What does he look like?"

"He has a beautiful, charming smile, pale blue eyes, and tawny-brown hair. He is tall and strong. A warrior."

"He sounds a dream! How old is he?"

"Six-and-twenty. He has told me he loves me."

"Oh, Seona. I'm so happy you found someone." Talia hugged her.

"He asked me to marry him, but I fear Father will not allow it."

Talia pulled back, her expression somber. "'Tis unfair. You must find a way to be with him."

"More than anything, I wish there was a way. Keegan is tanist and next in line to be chief, but you know as well as I that is not enough for Father."

"He is obsessed with wealthy lairds and chiefs."

"Aye, and I fear when Keegan asks him for my hand, he will insult Keegan horribly, or try to hurt him."

***

Unable to believe his good fortune, Chief Ambrose Murray showed Laird Rebbinglen into his private meeting room and they took seats near the warm hearth. During supper, he'd learned that Rebbinglen was unmarried. To have one of his daughters marry an earl would be more than he could've imagined. He poured two small crystal glasses of whisky and gave one to the dark-haired young man. He remembered seeing the lad when he was around five summers. 'Twas hard to believe he was such a big strong man now and obviously well-liked and respected.

"*Slàinte.*" Murray swallowed a generous gulp of the fiery liquid, enjoying the burn and trying to think of the most diplomatic way to bring up this most important subject. "Laird Rebbinglen—"

The earl held up his hand. "I'd be pleased if you would call me Rebbie as my friends do."

Murray smiled. 'Twas almost as if they were family already. "I would be honored. Everyone calls me Murray, friends and enemies alike."

"Murray." Rebbie lifted his glass again.

"Rebbie," he began again, though he felt awkward not calling the esteemed man a more formal name. "I thank you for bringing my daughter home and keeping her safe."

"Well, I—"

"Nay. I ken you will deny it, being the good man that you are. But I'm certain my daughter felt much safer with you than the rest of those men."

Rebbie shrugged. "In truth, I wasn't the one guarding her. 'Twas Keegan MacKay who kept her safe during the entire journey. He is the best of men, highly honorable like his cousin, the chief. They were practically cut from the same cloth."

Murray waved off his humility. Besides that, he didn't want to hear any more about the detestable MacKays—men who couldn't keep their word.

"'Haps you would like Keegan MacKay to join us," Rebbie suggested. "He was the one Chief Dirk MacKay sent with a gift for you."

"What gift?" Murray did remember a gift being mentioned earlier. So, this Dirk MacKay sought to mollify him for breaking the contract of his father.

"A fine stallion," Rebbie said with enthusiasm.

"Aye? Very good." If the earl thought the horse was fine, then indeed it must be. "I will look him over on the morrow. Please send Chief MacKay my thanks."

Rebbie gave a sincere nod. "I will do that."

"You were very generous to travel with the MacKays to bring my daughter home. I'm certain you have far more important things to do."

Rebbie shrugged. "'Twas no trouble at all."

"Are you related to the MacKays, then?" Murray had to figure out their connection.

"Chief Dirk MacKay has been a very good friend of mine for a decade. We attended university together and traveled on the continent."

"Ah. I see. Well, the MacKay party was lucky to have you leading them in the absence of their chief. I'm certain they listened to your decisions. If not, they were daft."

Rebbie gave an enigmatic grin. "Well... I thank you for your confidence in me but Keegan—"

"How could I not have? You're an experienced soldier, an earl, and a future marquess." Murray near had heart palpitations at the thought that one day his daughter could be the wife of a marquess. And his grandson, one day a marquess, too. But first, he must convince Rebbinglen he needed Seona... or Talia... as his wife.

Murray gulped the last of his whisky. "One day soon, you will want fine sons—an heir—to follow in your exalted footsteps."

Rebbie quirked a brow, his dark brown eyes taking on a displeased look.

"I have two beautiful, sweet daughters. You have met Seona and, on the morrow... or the day after, you will meet Talia. She is eighteen summers, and just as lovely as Seona. I am providing them both with generous dowries, including land... not that you have need of it, of course, but 'tis always good to have a few more acres."

Rebbie was already shaking his head and sitting back further in his chair. "I thank you, Murray, but I'm not looking for a wife at present," he said firmly.

Too firmly.

Damn. Murray shoved to his feet and paced, then poured more whisky into their empty glasses. How could he convince the stubborn earl? What did he want? What did he value most?

"Well, I can understand that. You are a young man who doesn't want to be tied down, but it need not be that way." Murray forced himself to stop pacing and sit in the cushioned chair across from Rebbie. "While I was married, 'twas almost like I wasn't really. I was five-and-twenty when I married Seona's mother, but I still dallied with the lasses everywhere I found a willing one. And there were plenty, let me tell you." He grinned.

Rebbie frowned, his mouth a firm line. "You want your daughter's husband, whoever he may be, to be unfaithful to her?"

Murray shrugged. "He will be whether I approve of it or not. Aye?" He laughed. "A wife is for providing heirs. For bed-sport, a man must look elsewhere. The buxom village lasses are far more entertaining betwixt the sheets."

Looking morose, Rebbie stared down into his whisky. What

was the man thinking? His dark eyes made reading him near impossible. He was no doubt a rogue like any other man his age, and the lasses probably chased after him, considering how handsome he was.

"Once you married her and took her to one of your estates, you would only need to see her once a year or so," Murray said.

Setting his unfinished glass aside, Rebbie stood. "I hope you will forgive me, Murray, but I'm tired and would like to retire for the night."

"Och. Of course." Murray leapt to his feet. "Forgive me for keeping you up so late." It wasn't late but he must somehow appease the earl. "Although I'm certain our guest chamber is not up to your standards, 'tis our best one. I'll have one of the bonny maids take you to it." He winked.

Rebbie gave a tight grin. "I thank you for your generous hospitality."

After instructing one of his guards to find Abigail and have her escort Rebbie to his chamber, Murray closed the door. He was a hellishly obstinate man. Murray had to figure out what the earl desired most. Rebbie had shown no interest in the money or land. Nay, he already had plenty of that.

He would have to listen carefully to what Rebbie said from now on. By hook or by crook, he would discover a bit of leverage. Horses, perhaps. Murray had plenty of them. Or could he somehow trick or blackmail the earl into marrying either Seona or Talia? Had he found Seona lacking somehow? Was that why he had no interest in her?

Talia might be a good choice, but he'd already promised her to the Comyn. And she had to stay locked in her room until that ugly bruise healed. How had he sired such fragile, weak daughters? Both of them annoyed him to no end. He wanted them both married and settled with the men he chose so he wouldn't have to deal with them anymore.

***

Lying in one of the four small cots, Keegan was unable to sleep in the bedchamber that he shared with the MacKenzies, but across the room, the brothers were snoozing away.

Keegan could think of naught but Seona. What would he say to her father on the morrow? How would he convince the harsh and unyielding man of his worth? It seemed hopeless.

But he could not fail in this. If he did, how would he face his future without her? She had come to be his life.

A light tap sounded at the door, startling Keegan. He sat up. Before he could get out of bed, the door opened and Rebbie entered, carrying a candle.

"Keegan. We must talk," he whispered.

"Aye, have a seat." Keegan sat on the edge of the bed while Rebbie took the wooden chair nearby and set the candle on the small table. The MacKenzies continued their light snoring.

"I talked to Murray at length," Rebbie said.

A sinking feeling punched into Keegan's gut. "Aye. And?"

"He's trying to convince me to marry Seona or his other daughter. He's the most status-hungry man I have ever encountered."

"'Slud." Of course. Why had Keegan not realized earlier that her father would be drooling over an earl who was still a bachelor?

"He does not care one whit what kind of man Seona marries, so long as he has a title, land, and money. Nor does he care how her husband would treat her. He would even encourage the man to be unfaithful."

"Damn him." Keegan wanted to knock the daft old whoreson on his arse. How could he care so little for his own flesh and blood? "'Tis as I suspected. He's a horse's arse and a bastard. And he cares naught for Seona. Still… tomorrow I will ask him for her hand."

CHAPTER TWENTY-FOUR

"Chief Murray." The next morn in the small meeting room, Keegan bowed briefly, then stood straight and tall before Seona's curmudgeon of a father. One of the chief's bodyguards waited in a corner to Keegan's right. Did the old man fear him?

"Aye, what is it you're wanting?" Chief Murray grumbled from behind his desk, barely glancing up from his papers.

Keegan's stomach ached, but he drew in a deep breath and charged ahead, eager to get this over with as quickly as possible. "I ken you are looking for a husband for Lady Seona and I would like to offer for her hand in marriage." *Saints!* Had he said the right words?

Chief Murray gave a brief, humorless laugh, his dark gaze skewering Keegan. "Are you a chief?" The man knew good and well he wasn't. He was but rubbing his nose in it.

Keegan retained his composure. "Nay, I am the tanist of Chief MacKay, which as you know, means I am second in line to the chiefdom."

"The chief has younger brothers, does he not?"

"Aye, but neither will be chief. The clan won't allow it."

"But one would inherit the title of baron, aye? Not *you*, a cousin," Murray pointed out.

"Indeed." Not unless something happened to Aiden or he forfeited that title as well. And then, of course, Keegan's father would inherit the title first. Keegan did not want the title, nor did he wish to be chief... unless he had no other choice. But he had to somehow make himself look better and more worthy before this bastard.

Murray lifted his bushy gray brows into a snide expression. "And if the MacKay sires an heir—a son—he will inherit. Not you."

"'Tis true." And so obvious no one needed to point it out. But Murray seemed to relish the information.

"Then you have no title at the moment, and will likely never have one. Do you hold lands?"

"Nay."

"Well then, you are not good enough for my daughter."

Keegan had known this would be the outcome, but his ire simmered just beneath the surface. How dare this pompous arse think he was better than Keegan? Keegan was grandson of a past chief and baron, well within the same social circle as Murray and Lady Seona.

Keegan drew in a cooling breath, calming the urge to draw his dirk. Did Murray care even a wee bit about Seona's wellbeing?

"I will take care of her and protect her," Keegan vowed, fighting down his own desperation. "As tanist, I have a good income. And I... care a great deal for her."

Murray snorted. "But you do not have an *earl's* income. Laird Rebbinglen has shown an interest in my daughter."

Keegan knew this was a lie, but rage still burned over him. "Is that so?"

"Indeed and do not dare question me, MacKay."

Keegan would love naught more than to strangle the man. "I am not questioning you," he said firmly. "I but ask you to reconsider my offer."

"Nay. And that is my final answer. Off with you now." Murray shooed him toward the door and picked up a paper as if he were busy.

Fury clawed its way up Keegan's throat and across his shoulders, urging him to take his dirk to the bastard. But he couldn't do that, of course. He turned and left the room, slamming the door on the way out.

When he stormed across the great hall, Rebbie fell into step beside him. "Come outside with me," he murmured.

"Gladly." Keegan needed fresh air. He wished one of the

Murrays would punch him now. He'd love naught better than a good fight. "Damned whoreson," Keegan growled.

Once they were in a deserted corner of the barmkin, near a high stone wall, Rebbie turned to him. "What happened?"

"He said *nay*." Keegan drew in deep breaths of the cool air, trying to smother his fury.

"We expected that."

"Exactly. He claims you have shown an interest in Lady Seona."

Rebbie rolled his eyes. "He is a madman. You ken I have no interest in marrying her or anyone."

"Aye. I knew he was lying." Still, being told he couldn't marry Seona was like glimpsing paradise only to be told he wasn't good enough to have it. A broadsword through the gut.

At the opposite end of the barmkin, the gates opened and half a dozen riders entered, the horses' hooves clomping on the gray cobblestones. The man in front was richly dressed in the Lowland style with brown breeches, tall leather boots, and an elaborate collar at his throat, not a stitch of plaid on him. He wore his slicked-back blond hair in a queue and an English style hat.

"Who the devil is that?" Rebbie muttered. "I'll go find out, while you cool off out here. We must think rationally to find a solution to this problem."

"Very well." Keegan didn't ken who the newcomers were, but he had a feeling they were bad news.

***

"Wentworth." Ambrose Murray shook Baron Wentworth's hand in the middle of the great hall. It had been a couple of weeks since he'd seen the man. He might be a suitable husband for Seona, but Murray would much prefer Rebbinglen, since his titles were far more prestigious and he was likely wealthy as Midas. To imagine his grandson one day being a marquess was difficult to ignore.

"Chief Murray, good to see you again. I have heard a rumor that your beautiful daughter, Lady Seona, has returned home. I hope to meet her," Wentworth said with a mollifying smile.

"Aye, she is here. I'm pleased you want to meet her."

Murray noticed Laird Rebbinglen striding across the great hall toward them. This could be damned awkward.

"Laird Rebbinglen," Murray said. "I'd like for you to meet Daniel Wesley, Baron Wentworth." He turned to Wentworth.

"And this is Robert MacInnis, the Earl of Rebbinglen."

"Ah, a great pleasure to meet you, Laird Rebbinglen." Wentworth gave a tight smile, bowed, then shook Rebbie's hand.

"A pleasure. I knew you must be someone of much import given the beautiful horse you arrived on. You must tell me where you acquired the animal."

"Of course. 'Tis from my own stud farm." Wentworth grinned proudly.

Murray took the two men into the meeting room and poured whisky while they discussed horses for a few minutes, certainly one of his favorite topics. But then, to his chagrin, Rebbie changed the subject.

"I came with the MacKays and the MacKenzies to escort Lady Seona home from Durness."

"Ah. I thank you for bringing her home," Wentworth said. "She may well be my future wife and I would like to get to know her."

Rebbie's black brows shot up, his gaze darting to Murray and back to Wentworth. "I see. You two are negotiating a marriage?"

"Indeed," Wentworth said with enthusiasm. "I hear she is very pleasing to the eye."

"Aye, she is lovely." Rebbie rose. "Well, I don't wish to intrude further. We can discuss horses at a later time." He headed toward the door, but then turned back to Murray. "'Tis fortunate you were able to find another suitor for her. I know you've had a difficult time of it." The blasted earl then disappeared out the door.

Murray ground his teeth until they ached. Had his chances at securing a marriage between Rebbie and Seona just dwindled to naught?

"What did he mean?" Wentworth asked, lifting a blond brow.

"Um... w—well," Murray stuttered, trying to find the right words. "I wasn't sure you would return or that you were truly interested in my daughter. Then Laird Rebbinglen showed up, escorting Seona home. They seemed taken with each other and I thought 'haps he wished to marry her. But now I'm not certain."

Wentworth's face tightened and took on a reddish cast. "Ah. So you thought maybe you could find her a better husband than me, aye? An *earl*."

Murray shrugged. "The man will one day be a marquess. I'm sure you can understand my dilemma. Especially when he is interested in my daughter."

Wentworth narrowed his pea-green eyes. "He did not *appear* overly interested in her. And he said you'd had a difficult time of it. What did he mean?"

"She was supposed to marry the MacKay chief, but he refused."

"Why is that?"

"Apparently, he already had his eye on another woman. 'Haps we should ask my daughter who she'd prefer to marry," Murray said. In truth, he had no interest in knowing whom Seona wanted to marry, but it was a good excuse to keep Wentworth waiting in the wings while he figured out a way to get Rebbie to marry her. And she certainly wasn't marrying that Keegan MacKay nobody.

***

Just before the midday meal, a maid came to take Seona to her father's solar, but she was certainly not looking forward to the meeting.

Seona had spent a few hours with Talia the night before, talking into the wee hours. Once Seona had returned to her own chamber, she'd found it difficult to sleep. Besides, she wanted to see Keegan in the worst way. She replayed the consoling memory of the night he'd come into her chamber and they'd shared one of the pinnacle experiences of her life.

Touching him in such a wanton, sensual way had been amazing. She loved how generous he was, showering her with affection. To know she'd given him the same kind of pleasure he'd given her filled her with joy. How she loved him.

But at the moment, she had to put Keegan from her mind and find out what her father wished to see her about. Had her aunt broken their agreement and spilled Seona's secrets? She prayed that was not the case.

Her stomach clenched as she knocked on the solar's heavy oak door in the dim corridor of the second floor. She hated meeting with her father for he never had good news.

"Enter," he called in his usual brusque tone.

His bodyguard, standing outside, opened the door for her and she went in. The fire in the hearth burned brightly and late morning sunshine beamed through the window. It should have been a warm, inviting room, but the tension emanating off her father chilled her to the core. He stood by the mantel, staring into the flames.

Seona curtsied. "Good morn," she said, trying to use the business-like voice he preferred, though inside her, a storm brewed because he had abused Talia so violently. She wished to confront him about it, but she knew if she did, she'd get the same treatment. She stayed at least five paces away from him and remained standing.

"Why did you lie to me?" He turned to her, his face a mottled red.

Seona was stunned speechless for a moment. "What do you—?"

"You are as sneaky and manipulative as your mother was!"

Angry tears pricked Seona's eyes. Her dear mother was the best of women, not a manipulative bone in her body.

"Chief MacKay was not betrothed to Isobel MacKenzie when he arrived in Durness. Patience told me the truth of it, after I pressed her. Lady Isobel was in fact betrothed to another man when she started warming MacKay's bed."

Blast! How could her aunt do this? Had she also told her father about her and Keegan? Nay, she couldn't have or her father would've brought that up first and been even more enraged.

"What say you?" her father asked.

Well, what could she say but the truth? "Dirk MacKay was in love with Isobel. He refused to consider marrying me."

Her father watched her with a dark, narrow-eyed glare for a long moment. "'Tis about time you told the truth. I want no more lies from you, lassie. Do you understand?"

"Aye." Though she would lie again, if she had to, in order to protect Keegan.

"Forget the damned MacKays. I've found someone else willing to marry you. Laird Wentworth is a baron who holds a large estate south of here."

Although this was not news to Seona, her stomach pained her even more.

"He is here and wishes to meet you."

Her heart rate tripled. "Now?"

"Aye. Now." Her father strode to the door, opened it, and told one of his bodyguards to go fetch Wentworth from the great hall.

Oh dear God in Heaven... What could she do now? She had

never dreaded anything so profoundly in her life. She had thought Keegan was going to ask her father for her hand. Since he hadn't mentioned it, maybe Keegan hadn't talked with him yet. Although she truly doubted he would allow her to marry Keegan, she had to hold onto that hope.

Minutes later, a man, richly-dressed in the Lowland style, entered the room. He was of average height and wore his blondish hair in a queue. His muddy green eyes lit on her briefly before he gave her father a deep bow. "Laird Murray."

"Wentworth, this is my daughter, Lady Seona."

"My lady." The gentleman gave another bow and moved toward her. "'Tis a great honor to finally meet you. Your father has told me much about you."

"Laird Wentworth." She curtsied briefly. After a couple of fleeting moments of uncomfortable eye contact with him, she much preferred to stare at the floor, at her father, or at Wentworth's elaborate collar and silken neck cloth rather than at his face. His sly grin, crooked teeth, and the devious, almost lustful, gleam in his eye gave her a feeling of nausea. Her father would hand her off to the worst outlaw if the man had a title and land.

Wentworth was talking, but she couldn't focus on his words—something about his holdings in Perthshire and his horses.

Thankfully, her father cut off his speech by opening the door. "'Haps you two can get to know each other at supper, then dance afterwards."

"I would like that very much." Wentworth bowed again and exited.

Her father closed the door, then snorted as he paced back to his chair by the hearth. He was acting strangely. Did he truly want her to marry Wentworth? It didn't seem so. She waited to see what he would say next.

He sat down and gazed into the fire for a long moment. "What do you think of Laird Rebbinglen?" he asked.

Seona was startled at this abrupt change in topic. "Rebbinglen?"

"Aye, Rebbie, as he is known to his friends."

What was her father about? "He is a kind and noble gentleman."

A spark entered his eye. "He is an earl, you ken."

Oh Heavens. Nay. He could not be thinking what she feared he was thinking. She pressed her eyes closed.

"Did you hear me, Seona?"

She met his wily gaze. "Aye, Father."

"And why have you not been making doe eyes at him or whatever it is that makes a man fall for a woman?"

Seona's face heated and her tongue seemed a leaden weight. Her father had never suggested she flirt with a man before.

"He would make a perfect husband for you, Seona! Do you not see that?" He grinned, and she was stunned. Her father never grinned, unless it was a sneer.

"Nay," she said. "I had not considered it."

"Daft lass," he muttered under his breath and pushed to his feet. "I have discussed a union with him. He is resistant for some reason. What have you done that he cannot see what a good wife you could be for him?"

"Naught," she said, still near speechless.

"Well, if you don't marry him, you will be stuck with Laird Wentworth. I don't like him near as much as Rebbinglen, but he is the only willing man I've found thus far who would be suitable. We must be discerning, you ken. You want to marry up, not down."

To Seona, the only man suitable for her was Keegan, but she could not tell her father that, unless she wanted to be knocked to the floor.

"Oh, and by the way, Keegan MacKay asked for your hand in marriage."

CHAPTER TWENTY-FIVE

Seona could scarce believe her ears. Keegan *had* asked for her hand in marriage? She held her breath, waiting to see what her father would say or do next.

Chief Murray gave a brief, disgusted laugh. "I told MacKay *nay*, of course. You are far too good for him. He has no title, property, land, money. Naught. He is penniless as a pauper."

Her immediate instinct was to jump to his defense. But she couldn't speak as frankly to her father as she did to her aunt. Seona drew in a deep breath to dispel her irritation. "He is tanist of his clan and no doubt has a good income," she reminded him, desperate for him to see that Keegan was certainly worthy.

Her father narrowed his eyes at her. "Tanist," he repeated.

She nodded briefly. He well knew 'twas a high position within the clan.

"You want to marry Keegan MacKay?" he growled, his face reddening.

Saints! Dare she be honest with him and speak her mind? 'Twas her only chance. Even if he struck her down, he would know the truth for once. And she would stand up for the man she loved.

"Aye. Keegan MacKay is a good and honorable man."

Her father's face hardened and grew more flushed, if such a thing was possible. "What have you done? Have you lain with him?" His voice was low and deadly.

"What? Nay!" Seona could scarce breathe.

"If I find out you have... Lord help you, lass."

Her scalp tingled as if doused with icy water. He was threatening her again, as he always did. She envisioned the knife Keegan had given her; 'twas strapped securely to her forearm. If her father attacked her, would she have the courage to use it to defend herself?

"If your whoring ways cause you to ruin your chances of marrying well, I will be most displeased."

Displeased? 'Twas a grand understatement. "I am not a whore," she stated, looking him squarely in the eye.

Her father turned and paced before the hearth, as if in deep thought. "'Haps that's it. Rebbinglen is friends with Keegan MacKay. He kens MacKay wishes to marry you and that's why Rebbinglen has no interest in you. Damnation, Seona! Why did you not sneak into Rebbinglen's bed, if anyone's? Why a man who is penniless?"

"I have slipped into no man's bed," she said firmly. While it was true Keegan had kissed her and touched her in carnal ways, she was still a virgin. Thanks to his control. If it had been up to her, she likely wouldn't be.

"You think I'm daft?" her father demanded. "MacKay is sniffing after your skirt-tails for some reason. You must have encouraged him. Are you besotted with him?"

Seona's face heated. Did she dare tell her father the truth? "I—"

"Never mind! I don't want to hear it. I don't care if you're besotted with him. Or him with you. 'Tis of nay importance."

Her father was the type who probably took great pleasure in keeping her away from a man she cared deeply about. No doubt he would rather she marry a man who would beat her every day. There was no sense telling him anything about her feelings. 'Twould only anger him more. And any praise for Keegan would fall on deaf ears.

"Here is what I want you to do, girl." Her father gave her a sharp, calculating look. "You are to sneak into Rebbinglen's chamber tonight and seduce the man."

She gasped. "What? Surely, you don't mean it."

"Indeed, I do, lassie. He is in our finest guestroom, of course, and he shares it with no one. 'Twill be easy for you to find him."

"I cannot. He is a good man. I could never trick him in such a way."

"You can and you will."

The image of Talia's battered face flashed in Seona's mind. That, combined with memories of the bruises on her mother's face in the past, unleashed fury through Seona, eclipsing her fear. Her jaw clenched as did her fists hidden within the folds of her skirts. "Or what? You will leave my face black and blue as you did Talia's?"

"Dare you question me?" he demanded, his frown deep and thunderous, but she didn't care.

"Why did you beat her so? She is but a young lass."

"She's a woman, just as you are! You'll both do your duty to me and marry respected, prominent men with titles. Your mother failed in her duty. She never gave me a son. Only whining, frail daughters who are naught but a burden."

Tears blurred her vision. "Mother did the best she could! She could not change God's will."

Her father struck his large fist against the top of a table, sending everything on it smashing to the floor. "Get out of my sight!"

Seona ran from the room, slamming the door behind her. Her heart pounded in her throat and tears blurred her vision as she hurried up the spiral staircase. She'd gotten off lucky—her father had struck the table instead of her.

She would *not* do as he bid and seduce Rebbie. But she must get word to him and Keegan about her father's orders. They needed to know what kind of manipulative, vile man he truly was.

***

Although Seona had wanted very badly to see Keegan at the midday meal, she'd avoided the great hall because of her father and Wentworth.

'Twas early afternoon when she put on her oldest *arisaid*, pulling the dull plaid over her head, and slipped down the back servants' stair to the ground floor. The few maids about paid her no heed. At all costs, she must avoid her father and Wentworth, though she had no inkling where they were.

She needed to talk to Keegan right away.

When she stepped out the kitchen doorway into the barmkin, heavy dark clouds blocked the sun and a faint misty rain hissed through the air.

Rebbie stood just outside the stables talking to one of the MacKay guards. She headed in his direction. Keegan had to be nearby.

She bypassed Rebbie, glancing up at him so he'd know who she was, and moved through the wide doorway into the stables. He excused himself from the guard and followed her inside.

"Are you looking for Keegan?" he whispered.

"Aye. Where is he? I must tell you both something."

"I'll go find him." Rebbie poked his head into an empty horse stall. "You wait in here."

Seona nodded and slipped into the stall, the packed earth floor scattered with straw. It had been recently cleaned. Her father was meticulous about his stables.

Her father. Blast him.

How could he beat her sister and then lock her in for days? Seona's first instinct was to tell Keegan about it, but she couldn't. If he knew how truly violent her father was, he'd likely do something drastic, putting his own life in danger.

She closed her eyes, praying neither her father nor any of his men had seen her slip out and that no one had recognized her. Through the narrow window opening in the stone wall, she listened to the rain falling harder.

The longer she waited, the more her stomach cramped with nerves. Finally, she heard Rebbie and Keegan's deep voices as they approached.

"Thank the saints," she whispered and faced the door.

Keegan, looking more handsome than she'd ever seen him, stepped inside the stall.

"I'll wait out here," Rebbie said.

"Nay," Seona whispered. "You need to hear this, too."

Frowning, Rebbie remained inside and pulled the stall door almost closed.

"What is it?" Keegan asked her.

Her face heating, she drew in a deep breath and stared into Keegan's concerned eyes. "My father ordered me to slip into Laird Rebbinglen's bedchamber tonight. He wants to force us to marry. We have to do something to stop him."

"Saints," Keegan hissed.

"God's wounds. That conniving bastard," Rebbie blurted. "Begging your pardon, m'lady."

"Nay, you are right," Seona said.

Rebbie's dark brows quirked. "Well, I believe 'tis time for me to move to the barracks with the MacKay guards."

"Aye. Good idea," Keegan said.

Seona nodded. "I like it, but Father will suspect I've told you both."

"I shall come up with a story about how I was gambling and drinking with the MacKay men and I passed out for the night in the barracks." Rebbie shrugged.

"Very well," Seona said. "That should work." Still, her father was likely to assume she'd gotten word to him about it. But 'twas the only solution she could think of. If Rebbie stayed in the keep, her father might even drag her to the man's chamber in the middle of the night and toss her into the bed with him. When her father was desperate to get what he wanted, he might do anything.

"I'll wait out here and guard the door." Rebbie exited and pushed the door closed.

"I cannot believe how vicious and manipulative your father is," Keegan said, drawing her into the most concealed corner.

"Aye, he takes the prize on that. I have missed you," she rushed to say, trying to absorb several of the things she loved about him at once—his entrancing blue eyes, his warm and charming smile, his commanding height and broad shoulders.

"I'm certain I've missed you more." Keegan leaned in and pressed his lips to hers.

She slid her arms around his neck, burying her hands in his damp hair, and hung on for dear life, while his hands at her waist drew her closer. She relished each of the heated kisses he indulged her with and the way his tongue teased hers. His masculine taste and scent made her crave more of him instantly. She yearned to rip the wool and linen from his body, wanting him as bare as he'd been that evening he'd bathed in the loch.

Instead of divesting him of his clothes, she pressed her body as close to his as possible, delighting in each hard plane and ridge of muscle.

"Mmm. Seona." He ran his hands beneath her hips and lifted her.

Lightheadedness near overcame her as he consumed her mouth with his wicked kisses. She was shocked to realize she'd immediately wrapped her legs around his hips. Leaning into her, he pressed her against the stone wall. Through their clothing, his hard shaft rubbed against an especially sensitive spot, stimulating her even more.

"Oh, Keegan," she breathed, longing for the feel of his hot skin against hers. How she ached deep inside for him to complete their union and make her his woman. "Please." Oh, saints! She could just imagine how wondrous he would feel.

He lavished her mouth with more sinful and beguiling kisses, making her delirious. Feverish need near overpowered her.

"I shouldn't have brought you back here," he said against her lips, breathing hard, his tone passionate. "I'm going to steal you away."

"What? Nay," she whispered, shaking her head. Icy fear sliced through her desire. "My father would send his men to hunt us down and..." Nay, she did not want to say the horrible words.

"And what?" Keegan set her to her feet, ire glinting in his eyes.

She grasped the plaid that crossed his chest. "He will order his men to kill you, Keegan. You've seen how vile and cruel he is."

The muscle of his jaw flexed. "So, what are you going to do? Marry that Wentworth codpiece?"

"Nay." The very thought sickened her. "I know not. I am trapped."

Keegan stepped away and paced, his actions agitated. "I asked your father for your hand in marriage and he refused."

"He told me." Her heart ached for him, and for herself. "I'm sorry if he was rude to you."

Keegan shrugged. "His words mean naught to me. All I care about is you." The intensity of his eyes was like blue fire. "What if he were to force us to get married because he found us in a compromising situation?"

She shook her head. "He would not. He already suspects we've had a tryst. But if he thought it were really true... or if he caught me here... he would marry me off to someone else. Wentworth or someone with a title."

"He is a weak dandy. Hell, he's practically English."

A pang of nausea struck her, as it did anytime she thought of Wentworth. "Aye, and I sense a vile streak in him."

"I don't care what I have to do," Keegan said. "You're not marrying him."

Voices from outside the stall reached them. "Wentworth," Rebbie said in a loud tone. "I was hoping you would show me your horse."

"'Slud," Keegan muttered, wanting to burst out the door and take his sword to Wentworth.

"Shh," Seona hissed, her eyes wide.

He didn't want to be caught either, but if they were, it might solve a lot of his problems—Wentworth would probably hightail it back to the Lowlands. But being discovered in a stall with Seona would also create new, deadly problems. Her father would no doubt try to kill him. Not that he would succeed.

Rebbie and Wentworth moved away from the door, their voices fading.

Keegan wanted to spend more time with Seona, but 'twas unsafe for her. Besides that, someone was likely to bring a horse back and lead it into this stall.

He slipped toward the door and peered through the crack where Rebbie had left it ajar. The two men stood near the end of the long, straw-littered corridor. Wentworth opened another stall door, his back toward Keegan. Rebbie inspected the black stallion.

"Come," he whispered to Seona. "You need to return to the keep."

They both stepped out into the wide passageway and Keegan tried to keep himself between her and Wentworth. At the entrance, he glanced around, seeing no one about. The rain had diminished to a drizzle.

"I will see you later," she whispered with a fiercely emotional glance. Before he could say anything, she strode quickly across the barmkin toward the kitchens, her head covered with the plaid. Remaining at the stables, he watched her go, praying 'twas not the last time he would see her. *Nay.* She was his life, and he could not go back to Durness without her.

Voices approached behind him. He turned to find Wentworth and Rebbie moving toward him.

"That belted plaid must make it greatly convenient when tupping the maids, hmm?" Wentworth asked with a nasty grin. "Almost makes me want to become a Highlander."

Keegan ground his teeth, his palm itching to feel the horn hilt of his dirk in it. *Maids?* Had Wentworth seen Seona with him and assumed she was a maid because of her old *arisaid*?

"Och! Look at that! The rain has stopped," Rebbie announced, as if this was something monumental.

"Aye. 'Haps we can go for a ride and you can see how the stallion runs," Wentworth said.

"Want to join us?" Rebbie asked Keegan.

"Nay. But I thank you for the invitation."

The two men proceeded into the stables again. "I'll be right there, Wentworth," Rebbie said, then returned to Keegan. "Are you well?"

Keegan nodded. "Did he see her with me?"

"He saw someone. He assumes 'twas one of the maids." Rebbie shrugged. "I'm going to find out all I can about him."

"Mayhap his stallion will break his fool neck," Keegan muttered.

Rebbie snorted with suppressed laughter.

"I'm going to stay here and figure out a solution." At the moment, all Keegan wanted to do was put Seona on his horse and ride as far as they could go.

CHAPTER TWENTY-SIX

Seona paced in her room, knowing supper was being served in the great hall. Wentworth was there, waiting to *get to know her*. Well, she didn't want to get to know him at all. His unnerving smile made her nauseous.

A knock sounded at her door. She jumped, then moved across the floor. Opening the portal, she found Aunt Patience outside, her dark hair styled to perfection.

"Your father sent me to fetch you for supper."

"I'm eating in my chamber." Seona motioned toward the tray of food one of the servants had already brought her.

Patience raised a brow and shook her head. "Your father said if you refuse to come to the great hall, he will send one of the guards to carry you."

Wanting to call her father a vile name, Seona gritted her teeth.

"Very well." She slammed the door on her way out. "I wonder why he won't order Talia to supper so everyone can see all the bruises he gave her."

"You'd best watch your mouth, lassie," her aunt hissed.

"Why did you tell him that Dirk and Isobel were not betrothed when they arrived in Durness? I was trying to protect them. They are my friends."

Her aunt's glare was spiteful. "At least I didn't tell him about finding you and Keegan kissing in your bedchamber."

Icy cold washed over Seona. "And I hope you won't, or we shall both face dire circumstances."

"I'm keeping my mouth shut about that as long as you keep my secret also."

Seona nodded. "Agreed."

They crossed the great hall and several of the men at the high table turned to stare at her. When they drew closer, most of the men stood, Keegan, Rebbie and Wentworth among them. Her aunt rushed forward and claimed one of the chairs. The only vacant seat was between Wentworth and her father.

Blast! She slowed her steps.

"Please, come and sit, daughter," her father said in a forced pleasant tone that gave her sickened chills. "Have some food."

Sending Keegan a longing glance, she proceeded to the chair.

***

Keegan wanted to crawl down the table and beat Wentworth's eyes shut. He detested the smug and lustful way the man watched Seona. Keegan would not abandon her to the bastard even if he had to steal her away tonight.

Rebbie, sitting to his right, lightly elbowed Keegan in the arm, then gave him a lifted brow look.

Aye, Keegan knew he probably looked angry enough to kill someone. But who could blame him? Another man was courting the woman he loved. He drew in a deep breath and focused on his food so no one would suspect the level of his fury.

He needed to talk to her again, right away, but couldn't with her glowering father looking on.

At the end of the meal, the music started and Chief Murray encouraged Seona to dance with Wentworth. How the devil was Keegan supposed to sit and watch this? Murray smirked at him. Battle-lust tore through Keegan's veins. His hand clenched, craving the solid feel of his sword hilt in it.

After one dance, Chief Murray directed Lady Patience to escort Seona from the great hall. Keegan could only assume she was headed toward her bedchamber. To see her there would be a risky endeavor, especially since Chief Murray watched him closely. Without doubt, he had servants spying on Seona, too, in order to see if she would indeed slip into Rebbie's chamber. He wouldn't be there, of course, but Murray didn't know that yet.

'Slud. Keegan wouldn't get to see her this night. Tomorrow night, then. A plan was forming in his mind.

It gored him to realize he was either going to have to betray

Dirk and the MacKay clan by stealing Seona away. Or leave her here to the mercy of a demon chief and his minion.

Dirk obviously trusted Keegan more than anyone else, and that was why he'd made him the tanist. He depended on Keegan to do what was best for the MacKay clan, but taking Seona away from this place was the worst thing he could do for the clan. Murray would seek vengeance.

Keegan's job was supposed to be simple—escort Seona home, bring the gift and smooth things over with Murray. Dirk didn't want conflict. Neither did Keegan. But conflict was exactly what he was going to stir up by protecting Lady Seona. 'Haps even clan war.

***

Seona stood in her father's solar the next morn. He had summoned her again and she was growing exceedingly tired of being treated like his servant. Or his pawn.

"You did not slip into Rebbinglen's chamber last night as I commanded you to do." Her father turned from the fireplace and pinned her with a dark glower.

"It could not be helped," she said. "Someone told me he slept in the barracks with the rest of the men."

"Aye, and *why* did he choose to do that?" her father asked, suspicion written on his face.

"I know not. I haven't talked to him."

"I'll tell you why. Because you warned him of my plans!" His yell echoed off the stone walls.

Staring past her father's shoulder toward the gray light at the window, Seona remained silent. Of course, she'd known he would figure it out. Her father was not only vicious but also canny.

"Did you not?" he asked.

"Nay."

"You are lying again!"

She didn't respond, simply stared past him. She didn't care what he thought of her. If he came toward her, she'd flee out the door. If he caught her... she didn't know. Could she stab her own father?

"Well then, you leave me no choice. You'll marry Wentworth the day after tomorrow. I'll talk to him and arrange everything." His voice hardened. "And you'll *willingly* marry him or you'll find yourself far more bruised and battered than Talia was."

Day after tomorrow? *Mo creach!* She had to find a way to escape her father's plans.

"Next week, Talia will marry the Comyn chief," he said. "That has already been arranged."

"Does she know when she is to be married?"

"Aye. She also knows I will do her grievous harm if she doesn't sweetly go along with the marriage."

Seona gritted her teeth. Damn the man.

"I want you both married and gone from here!"

She would love to be gone from here, but she would not marry the man her father chose for her.

***

That evening after supper, Chief Murray waited in his solar for one of the chambermaids to bring Talia to him. He needed to see if her face was healed so that he might present her to Rebbinglen. If the earl took a fancy to her, mayhap a match could be made. Aye, Murray had already signed a contract with the Comyn chief, but he would come up with a good excuse... the earl compromised her or... stole her away. Out of his control. Besides, who would nay-say an earl?

Talia entered, but remained by the door. His guard outside closed the door back. In the dimness, Murray couldn't see the tone of her skin.

"Come closer, lass."

She inched forward timidly, but her dark, arrow-sharp gaze met his. Aye, she was rebellious, but also brave. He was proud to see she took after him in looks and temperament. Damn, why couldn't she have been a lad? 'Twas the greatest disappointment of his life.

Perhaps her future son might also resemble him. And if the boy was sired by an earl, he'd be a powerful man one day.

Talia paused several feet away.

"Closer," he commanded.

She took a couple more steps. "What is it you want, Father?" Her tone was submissive and he was glad for it.

"To see how your face looks. The bruise is gone, aye?"

"Aye."

"I'm glad. Do not defy me again and you'll not receive another one."

Her eyes narrowed threateningly, and he wanted to snort with wry amusement.

"I'll leave your door unlocked if you promise to conduct yourself as a biddable lady. I'll not have you throwing tantrums like a maddening bairn."

She stared at the floor. "I promise."

"You'll marry the Comyn chief next week... unless you can somehow convince the Earl of Rebbinglen to marry you."

She frowned, her confused but wary gaze on him again.

"I will introduce you to him in the morn," Murray said.

"Very well." She clasped her hands before her demurely.

"Off with you, then."

He was glad to see she quickly vacated the room instead of arguing, as she had done the last time. Aye, 'haps Rebbinglen would find her lovely and lose his head over her. Murray grinned.

***

Just before dark, Haldane and his men lurked outside the walls of Gillenmor Castle. He had lost several men in that last skirmish, but had enough left to get the job done. He'd hired over a dozen in Inverness days ago.

The MacKays had to leave the castle eventually, heading back home, and he intended to kill Keegan and any other MacKay he could. The fewer of them left, the fewer he'd have to fight in Durness. Seona would be the ultimate prize, of course, but he doubted she'd leave the walls anytime soon.

Moments later, his attention riveted on a lass of about Seona's height, slipping out the postern gate. "It can't be," he whispered. She was covered head to toe in a dull plaid *arisaid*, keeping her identity a secret. She had to be a maid or someone of no importance. Didn't she?

Haldane crept through the bushes as silently as possible, the brisk wind helping to conceal his movements. Transfixed, he knelt and watched her in the low light where gloaming meets darkness. The lass moved exactly like Seona. And he should know; he'd watched her often enough back at Dunnakeil last autumn.

When the lass hiked her skirts off her shoes and sprinted toward the village, he tore out after her. He easily caught up and grabbed her around the waist from behind. He covered her mouth with his hand to muffle her screams. He couldn't let her alert the guards. Glimpsing part of her face in the faint glow of the distant torches, he saw that 'twas indeed Lady Seona. Why on earth was she fleeing?

She kicked her heels against his shins. Her sharp elbows drove into his stomach and ribs. Damnation, what a hellcat. No wonder he loved her. He smiled.

"Come on," he growled low to McMurdo as he rushed past where he was stationed. "I've got her. Let's go."

McMurdo and the other men raced after him to the edge of the wood where they'd left their mounts.

"Get something to tie her hands and feet," Haldane said. "A gag, too."

Once they had her bound so she couldn't escape or scream, he climbed onto his horse. "Lift her up to me."

McMurdo and one of the new men named Edgings put her across Haldane's lap. Her light weight felt good there, but he had no time for carnal thoughts. He had to get the hell out of here before anyone realized she was missing.

Though he was eager to leave posthaste, they walked their horses silently a few hundred yards, then picked up the pace, their horses galloping toward the shore. 'Twas time to head for Durness.

***

A soft knock sounded at Seona's bedchamber door. She sat bolt upright in bed. Though 'twas the middle of the night, she had not slept, trying to determine a way out of this trap. Could Keegan have slipped along the corridors of the castle to visit her? She had not seen him all day. Her heart thumped in her ears, with both excitement and fear for his safety.

After belting the *arisaid* around herself over her smock, she moved close to the door. "Who's there?"

"Abigail, m'lady."

One of the chambermaids? What could she want? Although a bit disappointed, Seona was glad Keegan had not risked his life to come to her bedchamber. She opened the door to find a flaxen-haired woman of about her own age standing outside, holding a candle.

"Aye?"

Abigail stepped into the room and closed the door. "Laird Rebbinglen sent me," she whispered, then pulled a folded paper from the pouch at her waist.

A missive? What on earth? Seona broke the wax seal and unfolded the paper.

It is time for us to make our escape. Bring a change of clothing.
It was signed with a K.

Saints! Dare she run away with Keegan now? Right under her father's nose? 'Twould put both their lives in danger, for her father would send his men after them.

But maybe they could hide somewhere far from here. Life on the run with Keegan would be better than any sort of life without him. 'Twas a great risk, but this might be her only opportunity.

If she remained here, her father would force her to marry Wentworth the day after tomorrow. And her father might send the MacKay men away at any time. If she left with Keegan, she had to bring her sister. How on earth would she get Talia out of her locked and guarded chamber? Mayhap if Seona took Abigail with her to visit Talia, the maid and Talia could switch clothing and Talia, with a cowl over her head, could escape, while her maid remained behind.

"Where am I to go?" Seona asked Abigail.

"I know not, m'lady. Laird Rebbinglen simply asked me to bring you to him."

'Haps Keegan waited in the stables. Could Abigail be trusted? Why had Rebbie trusted her? Too many things were left unanswered, but one thing she knew—she had to rescue her sister.

"Would you help me do something, Abigail?"

"Aye, if you wish."

"It might be dangerous."

The maid's face paled, but she gave a little nod.

"I need for you to pretend to be Talia so that I can slip her out of her chamber."

"Her chamber is nay longer guarded or locked, m'lady."

What? "When did this happen?"

"Just after supper. Her father had me to bring her to his solar. Her bruise had faded."

"Oh, I thank you." Why on earth hadn't Talia told her? Feeling a surge of victory, Seona opened the door and stuck her head out into the corridor. No one was about. "Come with me and bring the candle," she whispered.

The two slipped silently to Talia's chamber. When Seona unlatched the door, it opened. She poked her head inside the dim room.

"Talia?" she said in a loud whisper.

"She's not here, m'lady."

CHAPTER TWENTY-SEVEN

"What?" Talia was not in her chamber? Seona opened the door and urged Abigail into the room. Talia's maid, Beth, stood near the fireplace, but the bed was made. "Where did she go?"

"She told me she was going to the attic. She used to hide up there sometimes, you ken?"

Blast! 'Twas true. When she was younger, her sister had a habit of hiding in the unused portion of the attic to get away from their father. At times, it would take Seona hours to locate her.

"Will you two help me find her?"

"Aye, m'lady, but…" Abigail whispered into her ear so Beth couldn't hear. "Laird Rebbinglen said you must hurry down to meet him in the kitchen, otherwise 'twill be too late."

Seona wanted to use some of the frustrated curses she'd heard Keegan mutter. Instead, she clenched her jaw until it hurt. She couldn't run away and leave Talia behind. She would meet with Keegan and tell him that.

"Very well. I must… go on an errand, Beth. But please look for Talia in the attic tonight. Tell her I will have important news and to wait for me here or in my chamber."

"Aye, m'lady." Beth's eyes were wide as platters. The young maid was likely terrified of going into the attic alone in the dark.

"Would you help her, Abigail?" Seona asked.

"Aye."

"'Tis a matter of life and death."

Both maids nodded, their faces growing even paler.

Seona covered her head with her plaid *arisaid*, hurried along the corridor and down the back stairs to the kitchen, trying to keep her footsteps silent.

Laird Rebbinglen waited there, holding a long black cloak. "Here, put this on and no one will recognize you."

"Where is he?" she asked, as he pulled the deep cowl over her head.

"'Tis a secret. Come. We must be quiet but quick." He offered his arm, then opened the door.

Because she trusted Rebbie almost as much as she trusted Keegan, she took his elbow.

At a near trot, Rebbie escorted her along the side of the castle and across the cobblestone barmkin. The only illumination came from two torches secured to the stone walls. When he didn't take her to the stables, she truly wondered where Keegan was.

She considered telling Rebbie about her sister, but she'd rather talk to Keegan about it first. Besides, it would take a while for the maids to find Talia.

Where were the Murray guards? Seona glanced around. All the men nearby appeared to be MacKays or MacKenzies.

Rebbie opened the small iron postern gate and rushed her through. Fraser sat on his horse just outside.

Rebbie quickly lifted her up onto the pillion behind Fraser. "Have a care."

"I thank you," Seona said.

Fraser kneed the horse forward at a slow and silent pace. Four other men... guards... rode at a distance, two in front and two behind.

"Where are the Murray guards?" she whispered.

"We gifted them with three large jugs of whisky infused with poppy. They are all near passed out with drunkenness in the stables." The smile was evident in Fraser's voice. He walked the horse forward, taking his time so as to not create much noise. Less than a quarter hour later, they entered the village.

Fraser stopped in front of the tavern and someone strode from the shadows, their moonlit silhouette familiar.

"Keegan?" she whispered.

"Aye." He reached up and helped her dismount. "Did you not bring extra clothing?"

"Nay." She grasped onto the plaid at his chest. "I cannot run away tonight. I must bring my sister."

"This will be our only opportunity," he said, his voice urgent. "'Twill be impossible to slip you out again. Why did you not bring her?"

"I wanted to, but I couldn't find her."

"Saints," he hissed.

"We must talk," she said.

"Come." Keegan led her toward the tavern door.

"I'll wait out here," Fraser said, then dismounted and moved into the shadows.

"I thank you," Keegan said, opening the door.

Seona had never been into a tavern before, but she supposed it would be a sheltered location where she and Keegan could talk. She had to explain to him why it was so important that she bring her sister.

They entered the dim building, and if anyone was drinking in the tavern at this late hour, she didn't see or hear them. A lantern or candle burned somewhere off to her right providing a bit of illumination.

They climbed the rickety old steps to the next floor. Keegan opened one of the doors and drew her inside the warm room.

She shoved the cowl off her head while Keegan lit a candle from the glowing hearth coals.

"Have you been staying here?" she asked, glancing around the room. She saw none of his possessions but the room seemed lived in, though the bed was neat and tidy.

"Aye, but not long." He placed the candle upon the mantel, then added two small pieces of wood to the coals.

"Why?"

"Your father sent word by one of his servants that I was to sleep in the barracks with the guards and Rebbie. 'Tis very crowded and busy there. I needed time to think, so I rented this room."

Seona was ashamed of how her father treated people. "I'm sorry he has been so rude to you."

Keegan shrugged. "The important thing is we must leave tonight. We won't be able to get all the Murray guards drunk again. Your father may punish them if he realizes they allowed you to escape. Everyone will be even more vigilant." Keegan frowned. "What were you telling me about your sister? You couldn't find her?"

"For the last several years, she's had a habit of hiding in the deserted attic when she's upset."

"Why is she upset?"

"My father has arranged for her to marry the Comyn chief next week. He is a ruthless man who is much too old for Talia. I know marriages such as this are often arranged, but she's only eighteen summers. And the Comyn is at least fifty. Just before we arrived, she resisted and Father beat her so badly, half her face was blue."

"What? That bastard," Keegan growled. "Has he struck you?"

"Not recently. But in the past, aye."

"Damn him," Keegan said through clenched teeth and placed a hand upon his sword hilt. His eyes were so filled with fury, she feared he might storm the castle now and hunt down her father. 'Twas exactly the reason she hadn't told Keegan before. Not because she was trying to protect her father, but because she feared her father's guards would slay Keegan.

Though it might be sacrilege, she didn't care what happened to her father. What occupied her mind most was what would her father do to Talia if he found her first? He might send several of his men to scour the attic, or even the smaller lads to search the nooks and crannies. She couldn't hide forever.

"How will I find Talia in time and get her out?" Tears burned Seona's eyes.

"Shh." Keegan pulled her into a warm embrace. She slipped her arms around him and laid her forehead against his shoulder. His tall, powerful body felt so wonderful and comforting. If only she could draw some of his strength into herself.

Keegan kissed the top of Seona's head and fisted his hand in her unbound hair.

A battle rage such as Keegan had never felt pounded through his veins. He wanted to kill Chief Ambrose Murray. What was wrong with a man who would beat his beautiful young daughters? He had to be a madman.

Keegan pulled back and stared down at Seona's hand within his, so much smaller and more delicate than his own. He kissed her slender fingers, unable to imagine how anyone would want to hurt her in any way. Aye, he knew she possessed great inner strength— she must in order to deal with her detestable father all her life. But

Keegan had to protect her; 'twas his responsibility and his wish.

He'd never even seen Lady Talia, and now he knew why. "Did your father lock your sister in her chamber?"

"Aye. How did you know?" Seona gazed up at him, trust and worry in her dark blue eyes.

"I wondered why I hadn't seen her. If her face has a great bruise on it, he's not going to want anyone to see that."

"Indeed. Just before I left the castle, I learned that my father had unlocked her door after supper because the bruise had faded."

"How will we get her out of the castle?"

Maybe he could ask Rebbie or Fraser to sneak her sister out, but he couldn't let Seona go back. There was too much of a chance her father would beat her.

"What does your sister look like?" Keegan asked.

"She looks much like me, except she has dark brown eyes."

Keegan released her hands and stepped back. "Wait here. I'll go see if Fraser and Rebbie can slip into the castle, find her, and bring her here."

"'Twould be wonderful, but very dangerous for them should my father discover them."

"They live for danger." Keegan sent her a smirk, hoping she would stop worrying so much.

"Very well. Two of the maids, Abigail and Beth, are looking for Talia in the attic right now. I told them to bring her to her chamber or mine when they find her."

Keegan nodded, then hurried down the stairs and outside. "Fraser?"

"Aye." He stepped from the shadows of the building.

"I need for you or Rebbie, or both of you if possible, to steal into the castle and find Seona's younger sister, Talia. Chief Murray beat her recently, leaving her face black and blue. We have to rescue her, too, or he may beat her again. Or worse."

"Damn the man," Fraser muttered. "I agree."

"She has a tendency to hide from her father in the deserted attic. Two maids named Abigail and Beth are searching for her there now. Talia resembles Seona, except Talia has brown eyes."

"We'll find her." Fraser mounted and headed back to the castle.

***

Seona awaited Keegan in the inn's chamber, praying Rebbie or

Fraser could indeed find Talia and bring her here before it was too late. She worried for her sister's safety more than her own.

Keegan entered the room, closed the door, and locked it with a large key. "He said he would do it."

"Oh, I hope they can find her. I thank you."

"You're welcome."

The candle and the fire burned brightly, the orange glow illuminating Keegan's striking face and gilding his hair. She drank in the appealing sight of him, wanting so badly to touch him. To kiss him and show him her gratitude.

"When they find her and bring her here, where will we go?" she asked.

Keegan knelt at the hearth and placed another stick of wood on the fire. "We'll go south with a small group of MacKay guards. The MacKenzies will head back to Teasairg to tell Dirk what's happened. The remaining MacKays will return to Dunnakeil as quickly as possible to prepare the clan and castle for a possible attack from your father. Hopefully, once he knows you're not there, he'll leave."

"This is terrible," she whispered, her stomach aching. "I never wanted to endanger your clan. I love them like mine own."

"I ken it. I wish you'd told me earlier about your father beating your sister."

"I figured if you knew that, you'd also assume—rightly—that my father has beaten me in the past. I feared you might retaliate against him, putting your own life in danger."

He stood and faced her, frowning. "You were trying to protect me by leaving yourself in danger?"

"I suppose I was."

"Seona." He shook his head. "I don't need protecting. *I'm* the protector."

"But you are not immortal," she said fiercely, tears burning her eyes. "I love you, and I could never live with myself if you were hurt or... killed because of me."

"Lass." He moved forward and drew her close. She loved the way his strong arms tightened about her, surrounding her with protection. She felt safer than ever before. He kissed the top of her head, and his affection flowed sweetly through her.

Oh, why could he not be hers?

Sliding her arms around his neck, she rose on tiptoes and

kissed his prickly chin. He bent and captured her mouth with his own. All thoughts scattered from her mind. His lips were so warm and firm, yet also silky soft. Gentle, yet forceful. And his tongue was erotic seduction itself. He tasted of virile male, spiced wine and apples.

Desire for him burned through her and passion exploded like a lightning bolt. His hands cupped her derriere, tugging her closer, tight against his hard shaft. He felt so divine, she couldn't stop herself from rubbing against him. A scorching tingle shot through her, inciting an ache in her lower belly. Somehow, she knew he could relieve the feverish need he always stirred up within her.

"I want you, Keegan," she whispered against his mouth.

He moaned and gave her another deep kiss.

She drew back an inch. "You must show me what love means between a man and a woman."

"Saints, Seona," he hissed. "You drive me mad with your teasing."

"I am not teasing," she said most firmly. "I want you to… show me how to please you… in bed. I want you to take me."

He growled and closed his eyes, his jaw clenching so tightly the muscle in his cheek flexed. After drawing in a deep breath, he opened his eyes. "I need for you to do something first."

"What?"

His blue gaze burned into hers. "Marry me."

CHAPTER TWENTY-EIGHT

All the breath left Seona as she stared into the azure flame of Keegan's eyes for a long, heart-stopping moment. *Marry me*, he had said.

"Now?" she asked.

"Aye. Right now." He dug into his sporran and brought out a gold band. "I went to Inverness yesterday and bought this ring for you, for when we marry. I ken we cannot legally wed without a priest or minister and witnesses, but what matters most are the vows between us, even if spoken in secret. To me, that would be real. You would become my wife, in the ancient way."

She nodded, tears in her eyes, her heart so filled with love and joy she could scarce contain it.

"You agree?" he asked.

"Aye. I want to marry you, Keegan." Even if it was a marriage her father wouldn't recognize… to her it would be a true marriage. The only one she would ever have. Keegan as her husband was what she wanted most in the world.

"Good." Keegan pulled in a deep breath and drew her to stand facing him before the hearth where the firelight was brighter. His face told her many things—that he was suddenly a wee bit nervous, but then, so was she. Terrified, in fact. But it was time to grab hold of what she wanted and never let go. The sincere devotion in his intense gaze made her fall even harder for him.

"Lady Seona Murray," he murmured, his voice deep and strong. "You are the stars in the sky, the warm and bright sun upon my face, the wine I drink, the air I breathe. And I love you." Lifting her left hand, he kissed her ring finger then slid the gold band upon it. "With this ring, I thee wed. I vow to protect you and cherish you the whole of my life. I shall always be faithful unto you. I take you for my wife."

Though she tried to hold back, Seona burst into tears.

He drew her close and kissed her forehead. "Shh."

"That was so beautiful, Keegan," she whispered. How on earth could she find words of equal beauty to tell him how she felt?

Forcing her emotions under control, she wiped the tears away and stood back. Gazing up into his eyes, she knew she had to be the luckiest woman in the world. "Keegan MacKay," she began.

He nodded, a hint of a smile taking away his serious expression.

She swallowed hard. "You are the most honorable and noble of men. Strong and steadfast… the rock I cling to in the storm. I admire you, trust you, and love you more than I could've ever dreamed possible. You bring me joy and happiness such as I have never known. And I vow to forever love and cherish you. I shall always be faithful to you only. I take you for my husband."

His smile broadened, then he kissed her lips. "You have made me the happiest man on earth," he whispered. "I'm never letting you go, Seona."

"I don't want you to." She slid her hands 'round his neck and into his silky hair. "You are mine."

***

Seona's pleading expression told Keegan she needed him in the worst way. In the same way he needed her.

He lowered his head and kissed her lips, her sweet taste and warm breath seducing him instantly. "I could devour every inch of you," he said, then deepened the kiss.

Her arms clasped him tight around his neck. His hands at her hips, he lifted her, relishing the feel of her slight body and feminine curves plastered to him.

He loved her and wanted her intensely, yet he'd restrained himself during each sensual encounter. But not this time.

She ground herself against his erect shaft, sending jolts of pleasure and yearning through him. When she spread her legs and wrapped them around his waist, he near lost his mind. Next thing he knew, he was laying atop her on the bed, his shaft against her crotch. Layers of clothing separated them.

He dug through her skirts. Finally, he reached the silken skin of her thigh above her stocking. His fingertips traced upward.

Slow... take it slow.

He made a fist, restraining himself. Hell, he'd touched her in more carnal ways before, but this time he knew he couldn't stop. He didn't want to hurt her or frighten her.

"Keegan, please," she gasped, tugging at his belt buckle. He caught her hand, halting her. "Make love to me," she whispered.

He growled, wishing he had more control. Wishing he did not crave her so powerfully.

"I want to feel your hot, naked skin against mine," she whispered. "'Tis what I dream of."

Saints! What an image she put into his head. "'Tis what I dream of, too, lass."

When she pulled at his kilt, drawing the plaid upward, something in him refused to stop her. Arousal blazed a trail through him, burning away his restraint. And when her soft fingertips brushed up his bare thigh to his shaft, he groaned.

Launching into action, he unclasped his belt and in seconds threw off his plaid, shirt, and weapons, then kicked off his boots. Next, he removed her belt and *arisaid*. The linen of her smock ripped.

"Damn," he muttered, struggling to unwrap her from all her clothing. Finally, she was nude, the firelight dancing off her pale curves. His chest constricted, seizing his breath. But then he noticed, on her forearm, she still wore the leather sheath and knife he'd given her. The sight of it only aroused him more, told him she was his.

Lying beside her, he traced his fingers along her warm silken skin. "You are delectable," he said.

"Nay, you are," she breathed, her gaze trailing down his chest and abdomen to his erection. Her eyes wide, she bit her lip.

"You are not afraid, are you?" he asked, knowing some women did fear men's bodies... and their first time.

Her sincere gaze met his. "Nay. Of course not. I love you and trust you more than anyone."

His heart near burst from his chest with love for this woman. And when she grazed her fingertips lightly along his rock-hard shaft, showing him how much she wanted him, lust stormed through him.

Moving over her, one of his knees between hers, he brushed his lips over her beaded nipple, then drew the sweet morsel into his mouth. "Mmm." He couldn't resist tasting the other one, too, swirling his tongue around it, sucking it into his mouth.

"Keegan," she whispered. Her hands tangled in his hair, pulling it, holding his head near, her hips lifting toward him. Seeing how much she wanted him, despite her innocence, fired his blood. But he had to take it slow.

"You must relax, Seona."

"I am. I want you. Please," she said against his mouth, then licked his lips. Arousal jolted through his shaft.

Between her thighs, he sat back on his knees and skimmed his hands from her ankles, upward along her inner thighs, spreading them more. When he reached the top, he stroked his thumbs gently along her nether lips, incredibly wet and swollen. "So good."

She gasped and thrust her hips toward him.

With one thumb, he circled that sweet feminine nub that was so inflamed and drenched, it near drove him mad. She cried out his name and words he couldn't understand. Tears glistened at the corners of her eyes.

Leaning over her, he pressed a kiss to her mouth. "I don't want to hurt you but I fear I will."

"Nay. Take me, Keegan… my husband."

A strange primal urge overcame him. Aye, she was his wife. His woman. He must make her his in every way, even though it would hurt. He would try to ease her pain and make it better.

He had to have her now. No more waiting.

He stroked the tip of his shaft up and down along the moist folds of her sex. Saints, he loved the slick feel of her. The more he stroked, the wilder she became, wriggling, thrashing this way and that.

"Oh, Keegan," she breathed, arching her back. "Aye, I beg of you…"

He positioned his shaft at her entrance, teasing her with just the tip. When she lifted her hips, offering herself to him, some instinct overpowered him and he thrust his hips. He found himself lodged a couple inches into her slippery, snug heat. Her inner muscles clamped onto him.

"Ow!" Her nails dug into his arm and more tears glistened on her lashes.

"Shhh, lass," he hissed against her mouth. "I love you."

"I love you, too," she said, her voice intense. "But it hurts."

"I know. Relax your muscles a wee bit right here." He stroked his hand over her flat lower belly. How incredible she felt, gripping him so firmly. Pain was the opposite of what he was feeling at the moment, but he had to help ease her first time, while maintaining some control over his own body. Hell, all he wanted to do was thrust. Hard. And bury himself deeper in her tight body. But he didn't. He kissed her, flicking his tongue against her lips. She opened and sucked at his tongue.

Her inner muscles relaxed a bit, thank the saints. He couldn't take much more of that squeezing.

While distracting her with kisses, he withdrew an inch and pushed deeper.

She cried out, tears dripping from the edges of her eyes.

"I'm sorry, sweet Seona," he rasped, leashing the impulse to drive deeper. "Only a couple more minutes and there will be no more pain. I promise."

"Truly?"

"Aye." He trembled under the onslaught of need. "Just relax, please."

She nodded. "I'm ready."

"Take a deep breath," he said. "And let it out."

When she did, the pressure on his shaft eased.

He listened to her calming breaths. "How does that feel?"

"Not so bad."

He withdrew slightly and thrust again. Aye, that was easier. Very slowly and gently, he moved inside her. She felt so astonishing he feared his primitive side might take over. He did not want to get too rough and hurt her. He'd already caused her enough pain. Controlling his actions, he gradually moved faster, pushing his way deeper.

He groaned with the need to release his seed inside her. But he knew he shouldn't. Besides, he wanted to give her pleasure first. He paused deep inside her, trying to get himself under control. But when he did, her inner muscles caressed him in a most bewitching way, welcoming his invasion now.

"Keegan. More."

He growled, withdrawing and driving in again. She wrapped

her legs around his hips, and he made his decision. She was his. No giving her up now. No turning back. She was his wife and if he got her with child, he would be glad.

He gradually increased his pace, until he was pounding into her. She drew in a deep breath and held it just before her body clamped down on him, squeezing, shoving her hips upward to meet his. He covered her mouth with his to muffle her cries. The more she rode, the deeper he thrust.

"Oh, aye." He yearned to find his release at the same time she did, but something in him forced him to wait, some inner strength he didn't realize he possessed. Some need to give her even more pleasure.

Seconds later, another climax overtook her. She screamed into his mouth, her muscles milking him. Aye, that was it. He could hold back no longer. His release blasted through him like a fuse lighting a powder keg. The explosion of pleasure seared every nerve in his body and snatched his breath. All thought deserted him, leaving him aware of only one thing—she was his. Completely. His soul melded with hers.

When he came back to himself, he was still thrusting, although not as hard, enjoying the last vestiges of pleasure.

Dropping still, he sucked in harsh breaths, then placed a kiss on her lips. "Seona, you are mine now. My wife. I'm never letting you go."

She let out a breathy laugh. "And you are my husband. I love you."

"I love you, too, lass."

Keegan lay down beside Seona and she turned to survey every inch of her gorgeous new husband—the ridges and planes of muscle down his chest and abdomen. Aye, he was even more delectable up close in the firelight than he had been leaving that loch. He'd shown her things and made her feel things she could've never imagined. Such intense pleasures.

'Twas true his initial invasion of her body had been painful, but his sweet words had helped her relax so she could accept him. And then... once the pain had vanished... she could not believe how splendid he felt driving into her. 'Twas beyond comprehension, as Isobel had said.

Seona stroked her hand across his chest, enjoying the light sprinkling of hair, then kissed him there. She loved his warm masculine scent. Glancing up into his eyes, she found him watching her.

"You amaze me," he said.

She smiled and kissed his lips. After a few leisurely kisses, he said, "Let me wash you off." He arose from the bed and went to the pitcher and basin on a table in the corner.

What did he mean? She glanced down, seeing a smear of her virgin's blood on her thigh. And on the sheets. *Saints!* Her face heated.

Keegan returned and stroked the cold, wet linen cloth over her thigh. "I'm sorry I hurt you."

"Nay. 'Twas necessary." She could hardly remember the pain now; the pleasure had eclipsed it.

He pushed her thighs apart and washed between. Her flesh was so sensitive she hissed in a sharp breath. But at the same time, a fresh wave of need came over her.

He returned to the basin to rinse the cloth, then wash himself.

When he came back to the bed, he lay down on his back, grabbed her and dragged her on top of him.

"Oh." How she relished the feel of his hot skin sliding against hers. He skimmed his hands down her back and squeezed her derriere.

He hummed a soft moan against her lips, placing wee kisses there, then slowly exploring her mouth with his tongue.

Beneath her, his shaft gradually grew hard again. An answering clenching sensation echoed inside her.

She shifted and squirmed, trying to ease the itching sensation he was causing. He pulled her knees upward toward his shoulders and she found herself sliding along his shaft.

She gasped at how wondrous he felt. "Keegan?"

"Aye. Do you want more?"

"Indeed."

"Are you not too sore?"

She shook her head. "Nay."

He moved his hand between their bodies to position himself. But first, he teased and tormented her by stroking his erection against her wetness. The burning, prickling need for him increased. She pushed against him. The tip slid in and he groaned. The soreness was more than she'd expected. She paused, but he didn't. She held her breath, hoping it wouldn't be as painful as the first time.

"Did I hurt you?" he asked.

"Nay, I realize I am a wee bit sore."

"I'm sorry." Firmly embedded deep inside her, he drew her close, lavishing her with affectionate and sinful kisses. After a few moments, she forgot the soreness and became highly aware of his sizable shaft inside her. So good. She moaned and felt herself growing wetter. Her body clenched, caressing his.

"Seona," he groaned.

"Aye. It feels better and better."

He held her hips in his hands and moved within her, slowly, but with growing speed and force. The sensations overwhelmed her entire body and mind, but he didn't let up until every muscle in her body clenched onto him. The pleasure crashed within her, taking her breath, snatching her control. His mouth devoured hers.

Astounding moments later, he gripped her strongly to him, ground himself deep and growled into her ear. She savored his climax almost as much as her own.

His breath was harsh, his face sweaty against hers. "I fear I've demanded too much of you for our first time together."

She shook her head. "Nay. 'Twas how I wished it."

His body slipped from hers and he drew her into a warm embrace beside him. "You are more amazing and beautiful than I could ever put into words."

The door crashed open and Seona screamed.

CHAPTER TWENTY-NINE

Haldane and his men dismounted at the harbor near Inverness. He dragged the lass off his horse. She was still kicking and thrashing about, trying to hurt him. Loving the fight in her, he grinned and carried her closer to the torch light at the edge of the docks. He wanted to see his prize. Back when they'd both been at Dunnakeil, he'd loved naught more than looking into her eyes, watching her, fantasizing about kissing her beautiful lips, undressing her.

He stood her on her feet in front of him. "Now listen to me, Seona. I will cut this gag off if you promise not to scream. If you do, I'll simply tie another one on you."

She stood with her head bowed, her long, dark hair shielding her face.

"Are you listening?" Wishing to look into her lovely dark blue eyes, he tilted her chin up.

Seona did not look like herself.

Nay! He felt as if he'd been kicked in the stomach. Her tear-filled eyes were too dark. The shape... different somehow. He had not seen her in a while, but surely he had not forgotten what she looked like. He dragged her closer to the heated light of the torch and searched her eyes, her face, turning it this way and that. With the gag through her mouth, he couldn't see the shape of her lips.

"You're not Seona! Who are you?" he demanded.

She mumbled against the gag.

"I'm going to cut the gag off, and if you scream or call

attention, I'll strangle you. Got it?"

Her eyes widened, but she nodded.

Taking his *sgian dubh*, he cut the cloth at the back of her head and threw it down. The area on either side of her mouth was red and chafed, but most alarming, her lips were not bow-shaped like Seona's, but thinner.

"Who the devil are you?" Haldane snarled.

"Lady Talia Murray. Seona's sister. Who are you?"

Haldane let loose a string of curses. How the hell could he have made such a grievous mistake, stealing the wrong sister?

"Never mind who I am. McMurdo!" Haldane shouted and carried the lass back to his horse.

"Aye?" McMurdo approached.

"We have to go back. This is the wrong lady. I want Seona, not her sister." If he had to, he'd use the sister as bait to lure Lady Seona out.

***

Keegan leapt up from the bed in the inn's chamber and grabbed his sword, keeping his body between Seona and the door while she pulled on her smock. The bastards had near kicked the door off its hinges.

Two men wearing metal-studded leather armor entered, lugging a shirtless Rebbie between them, one of his arms around each of their necks. His head hung as if he'd been knocked out. Blood dripped down his chest.

"What the devil did you do to him?" Keegan demanded, hoping his friend wasn't dead.

They tossed Rebbie on the bed.

Another man with short gray hair and a matching beard entered the room. They were all Murray's men, one of them his personal bodyguard. They turned their attention to Keegan, smirking at his nakedness. He'd had to grab his sword instead of his plaid. He didn't care. He could fight naked just as well as clothed.

All three drew their dirks, long lethal daggers. "Put your clothes on, you whoreson," the black-haired one closest to him demanded.

Keegan slashed his sword at the knave, but he dodged back. Keegan kicked him backward into his friends. Within seconds, they righted themselves and were ready to charge him again.

"You're outnumbered, MacKay," the stout man with a gray beard said. "We have three more men downstairs. Don't force us to kill you. The chief said he'd spare your life if you flee now and don't look back."

"Never." Keegan knew a sword wasn't the best weapon for this small space, but his dirk was in its scabbard on the floor by the bed.

He sent a quick glance at Rebbie, seeing blood glistening on his head. "Is he alive?"

"Of course. Are you thinking we're daft enough to kill an earl? Nay, he's to be Chief Murray's son-in-law." The man gave him a nasty grin. "Nay matter how well-hung you might be, MacKay, you'll never marry that lady. We're dragging you out of here, dead or alive. Your choice."

Three more men stuck their heads in the door, leering and snickering. *Bastards!* Keegan wanted to slay them all, but he doubted he could before they killed him or injured him severely. He'd never gone up against six before.

Think, Keegan, think, he commanded himself. Damn! He felt like he had wads of wool in his head.

"Very well. Allow me to dress." 'Haps he could buy himself some time if naught else.

"Dress, then. We're waiting."

"Wait outside the door."

"Ha. Do you take us for fools?"

"Back away." Keegan waved his sword before the man's face. "How do I ken you won't kill me when I lower my sword?"

"You don't." Graybeard smirked.

A flick of Keegan's wrist sliced the man's arm and he dropped his dirk. Cursing and scuffling ensued. The three men who had been in the doorway invaded the room. One of them tossed a doublet over Keegan's sword blade and grabbed it, while three others tackled Keegan to the floor. He had a quick glimpse of Seona, wearing only a smock, bashing one on the head with the wash basin, a *sgian dubh* in her other hand.

"Release him, you blackguards!" she yelled.

Damn! He was so proud of her.

One of the other men, brown-haired and sporting a goatee, pulled her back, disarmed and restrained her.

"Don't hurt her, you whoreson!" Keegan yelled, intending to

kill him if he left one bruise.

"You'd best be worrying about whether we're going to hurt you," Graybeard said as he bound Keegan's hands behind his back. When they dragged him to his feet and out the door, he glanced back to see if Seona was hurt. She was crying but appeared unharmed.

The man pushed her onto the bed, followed the other men out, and closed the door. At the bottom of the stairs, the two men dragging Keegan shoved him to the floor. Pain shot through his limbs as his knee and left shoulder struck the slate stone floor.

"Bastards!" he snarled.

When he glanced up, a pistol was directed between his eyes and three swords were pointed at him.

"Put these on, you heathen." Graybeard threw his clothes at him.

"Untie my hands and I will."

One of the men cut the rope loose.

After rising to his feet, Keegan slipped the shirt over his head, then eyed them while he belted the plaid about his waist. All six of the men stood around him. Good, they'd left Seona alone in the room with Rebbie. If he awoke, he'd protect her and hopefully get her out of there. The bastards had confiscated all his weapons, and he knew not where his sporran and boots were.

"Outside, MacKay!" The man waved the pistol toward the exit.

One of the men behind him pushed him toward the door. He stumbled outside into the dim gray light. A hint of dawn glowed at the horizon. How the hell was he going to get back in there to rescue Seona? If her father found her and Rebbie in the same room, he'd force them to wed. Even if she already was.

***

When the chamber door slammed, leaving Seona alone with Rebbie, knocked out, bleeding, and half-clothed on the bed, she finished dressing. *Blast!* Her hands shook so badly she could hardly belt her *arisaid*.

"Please don't let them harm Keegan," she prayed, pulling on her slippers and the black cloak. She had to help him escape her father's barbaric minions.

"Laird Rebbinglen?" She shook his muscular shoulder, but he didn't make a sound. "Saints," she hissed. Was he alive? Placing her finger beneath his nose, she felt his breath. Thanks be to God. How could she wake him?

She found the pitcher half-full of cold water on a nearby table and poured it over his head, drenching his black hair and the pillow. Stirring a bit, he moaned and grimaced. He could have a bad head injury. If this was her father's idea of trying to get Rebbie to marry her, 'twas indeed a flawed plan. She had to escape the room before they were discovered together, then find Keegan. Rebbie was a strong, tough warrior, and she had no doubt he would survive.

She grabbed Keegan's dirk, sporran and boots from the floor. Opening one of the window shutters, she looked down in the early dawn light. 'Twas too far for her to jump. She ran to the door, opened it a crack and peered out. The narrow corridor and stairs were empty. Taking Keegan's belongings, she raced down the stairs into the empty tavern then peered out the front door. Several men lingered in front of the building. She went in search of a back door. Once she'd unbarred it, she crept out and headed toward the corner.

A narrow close ran between the tavern and the neighboring building. She slipped down it and hunched to peep out. Men yelled encouragements and two blades clashed and clanged. When a man moved aside, she saw that one of the warriors involved in the sword dual was Keegan. Thank the saints he had a weapon.

She held her breath and watched for several moments. Keegan held his own and appeared the more skilled swordsman, driving the other man back across the grassy field. But then her father, practically running toward the tavern with four more men, caught her eye. What on earth? They glanced at the men fighting in the nearby field, then disappeared from sight, headed toward the entry door. He probably hoped to find her and Rebbie alone in the chamber. She smiled, glad he'd be disappointed.

But how could she get to Keegan and help him? He was barefoot and needed his boots. He might also need his dirk. But if she ran out there, she'd distract him, and her father's men would seize her. She had to slip further away and somehow draw Keegan's attention when he wasn't engaged in a sword fight. She raced along the alley again, then behind the buildings. Dawn was growing lighter.

She sensed someone behind her a second before they grabbed

her around the waist. Terror clawed through her. She screamed, but a big, rough hand clamped over her mouth, muffling the sound.

Who the devil was it? One of Keegan's men or her father's? She couldn't turn her head enough to see him but one thing was certain… he had stinking breath, like rotten cabbage. She kicked, driving her heels against his shins. Keegan's dirk came to mind. *Nay!* She had dropped it. But she still had her own knife strapped to her forearm. What if he was one of the MacKay or MacKenzie guards? She didn't want to stab one of them.

The man carried her, running toward a row of bushes at the edge of the village. From the corner of her eye, she saw the man had long gray hair.

McMurdo? Her blood froze within her veins. *I have to stab him!*

"We have your sister," McMurdo said, his voice gruff and raspy in her ear.

"Talia?" she tried to say, but the word came out muffled. How could they have abducted her sister?

"Come quietly, and we'll let your sister go free. I have proof."

Proof? How had he or Haldane captured her sister? Had they snatched her from Rebbie and Fraser once they'd brought her from the attic?

Keeping his hand over her mouth, he dug through his clothing and pulled out a piece of white linen cloth. "See?" He held it in front of her eyes.

She blinked, trying to clear her tear-blurred vision. The handkerchief's monogram was the initials TEM. Talia Elizabeth Murray. Seona remembered the day Talia had embroidered it in deep red. Nausea rose within her. How had this happened? Had Talia lost her handkerchief and these outlaws found it? If so, would they have known it was hers? She didn't recall that Haldane knew her sister's name. On the off chance McMurdo was telling the truth, she had to do what he said and help Talia.

"Do you agree?" the man rasped in her ear.

Seona nodded as hard as she could.

"Make no sounds or we'll kill your sister."

She nodded again, trying to make him understand she'd do anything to keep her sister safe.

He uncovered her mouth but retained a hold on her arm. She glared at him. *Saints!* He was an alarming sight close up—scars and pock marks mottled his wrinkled face. His hair, brows and short beard were gray, his teeth jagged and half gone. His eyes were black as midnight in Hades, and looking into them chilled her to the core of her soul. He was a murderer, an assassin, his soul as evil as the devil's own.

"Where is my sister?" she asked.

He pointed. "Over there. Stay low and come with me." Hunched, they crept through the bushes toward the forest. Her heart thudded hard. 'Haps she was an idiot for going with him, but she had to free Talia.

Once they entered the trees, McMurdo guided her behind a clump of boulders where several men lurked, some sitting on the ground, others bent and peering between the boulders toward the village.

Haldane stood, his feral green eyes riveted on her with great interest—nay—obsession. He smiled, and her whole body froze.

"McMurdo, you're getting every damn thing I promised you and more." Haldane rushed forward and grabbed her shoulders. He looked different now, less like a lad and more like a man, with the short red beard furring the lower half of his face.

"Where is my sister?" she asked him.

"Seona!" the female shout came from behind another boulder.

"Shut up, wench!" an unseen man said.

Seona bolted toward the sound of her sister's voice and found her lying on the ground, her hands and feet bound. Seona knelt beside her. "Are you hurt?"

Talia shook her head, tears streaming from her eyes.

"Untie her at once," Seona ordered the man.

"I'll release her." Haldane waited behind her. "But you must agree to come with me peacefully. No fighting. And you must agree to marry me."

CHAPTER THIRTY

Chief Murray climbed the stairs inside the tavern as fast as his legs would carry him, the local minister and constable following him, along with two of his men who had assured him everything was set up as it should be.

At the top of the stairs, he strode toward the chamber door. It sickened him to think his own daughter was inside and had lain with that MacKay bastard. He flung open the door to find Rebbinglen sprawled unmoving on the bed. He wore naught but trews. A gash on his head bled on the sheets. And his dark hair was wet.

"Is this the earl?" Constable Winfred asked, his rounded jowls jiggling.

"He's injured," Reverend Lang said in a shocked and concerned tone.

Murray glanced around the room and under the bed. "Where is my daughter?" he thundered.

Rebbinglen groaned and lifted a hand toward his head.

Murray cursed under his breath. He was supposed to find his daughter in this bedchamber with Rebbinglen in a very compromising position. If the minister and the constable had seen the two in bed together, they'd have no choice but to marry. But Seona was nowhere to be found. Never had he wanted so badly to strangle her.

"Did no one guard this room?" he asked his men.

The two dolts looked at him with blank, wide-eyed stares.

"Did you see my daughter in this room with Rebbinglen?"

They both nodded. "Aye, she was here."

But they hadn't made sure she stayed there until he and the witnesses arrived.

"Idiots!" He backhanded the one closest to him. "Find my daughter! Now!"

"Aye, m'laird." They hastened from the room.

"Pray pardon, Reverend Lang, Constable Winfred," Murray said. "My men said they found the two of them together here, but my daughter has slunk away, leaving her lover to fend for himself."

"What's happening?" Rebbinglen asked in a slurred voice, his dark eyes open a crack. "Did you hit me on the head, Murray?"

"Nay, my laird. 'Twas not me. Likely some outlaw did it." Murray turned to the other two men. "I'm sorry I wasted your time, gentlemen. I will handle things from here."

"Well, Chief, clearly the earl has been attacked and robbed," the constable said. "We need to find the culprit."

"Indeed. And I will. I'll not be keeping you. I'm certain you'd rather be at home breaking your fast." He ushered them out the door, then turned back to Rebbinglen.

Lowering his black brows into a menacing scowl, Rebbie squinted, glancing around the room. "Where am I?"

"A room over the tavern."

"Saints!" Scrunching his face into a horrible expression, he sat up. "I'm going to kill whoever hit me."

Murray backed up a few more inches. "Aye, and I'll help you find him. But in the meantime... is it not true that you slipped my daughter out here for a tryst."

Rebbie rubbed his scalp, glaring the entire time. "I assure you that I was *not* having a tryst with your daughter," he said through clenched teeth. "Clearly, someone hit me over the head and brought me here." He glanced down. "Where the devil are the rest of my clothes?" His suspicious eyes turned to Murray.

He held up his hands and remained by the door. "You were like that when I entered the room, my laird. I would never touch your clothing."

"Of course, they took my weapons, too." Growling and holding his head, Rebbie stood. He staggered and braced against the wall. His eyes searched the floor. "Find them, Murray!"

"Aye." Murray hastened to the other side of the bed. "Naught over here."

"Look underneath the bed."

Murray wanted to knock the earl on the other side of the head, but he couldn't get away with it. And now that the man was awake and alert, for the most part, and Seona was not here, Murray couldn't trap him into marrying his daughter. He would throttle the daft men he'd assigned to do this job.

Rebbie turned. "Are they under there?"

Taking the candle, Murray knelt and peered beneath the bed. "Naught but a thick layer of dust and a few mouse droppings."

"You ken who brought me here, do you not?"

"Nay, m'laird."

Rebbie grunted. "Regardless, I am not marrying your daughter."

Rage boiled inside Murray. Where was his daughter? He knew she'd been here with that MacKay bastard. When he found her, he was going to whip some sense into her. Both his daughters were disobedient, daft whores. They were determined to embarrass him and throw their lives away.

"Give me your sword," Rebbie said in no uncertain terms.

"What? Are you mad?" Murray's sword was worth a small fortune and no one used it but him.

"When you recover my sword from whichever of your men stole it, you will get yours back. In the meantime, I require a weapon." Rebbie held out his hand.

"What are you going to do with it?"

The earl sent him a sinister grin. "I'm not going to kill you with it, if that's what you're wondering."

Damn! What could Murray do but give it to him? The man outranked him, and his father was a powerful man.

Reluctantly, Murray drew his sword from the scabbard and gave it to the earl.

"Your dirk, too." Rebbie motioned with his other hand.

"You're disarming me?" Murray grumbled.

"Not intentionally. But I suspect the place is crawling with backstabbers, and I must help my friends."

Glaring, Murray handed the foot-long Highland dirk over and Rebbie slid the two blades into his own scabbards.

"Laird Rebbinglen!" the shout sounded from downstairs.

Who the devil was that? Murray moved toward the door and

opened it. "I've found him up here," he called.

Rebbie's manservant, George, rushed into the room. "Are you injured, m'laird?"

"Not overmuch. Someone tried to bash in my skull, but I'll live, as you can see. Help me find my shirt and doublet. And my weapons. The whoreson who knocked me on the head likely has them." Rebbie headed toward the door, waving off George's offer to assist him down the stairs.

Murray followed them out.

One hand on the rail and one on his head, Rebbie staggered down the steps, George on his heels.

"Are those your clothes, m'laird?"

"Where?"

George ran past him toward one of the tavern tables. "Aye, I believe these are yours."

After Rebbie dressed, they exited the tavern. Outside, mayhem reigned. Several of the Murrays and MacKays were engaged in sword fights. But his daughter was nowhere in sight. Aye, Murray would beat Seona when he found her.

***

I'm already married! Seona almost yelled the words at Haldane, but then realized if she revealed this information, Talia would be in grave danger. The gold band Keegan had placed on her finger was still there, but none of the outlaws had seen it yet. The long sleeves of the black cloak she wore hid her hands.

She had dropped Keegan's belongings at the spot where McMurdo had grabbed her. If she'd known this would happen, she would've strapped the dirk to her side beneath the cloak. Hopefully, if Keegan or any of his men found his things, they'd know she'd been captured.

"Very well." Seona stood and faced Haldane. She'd agree to marry him, or anything, if they'd release Talia.

He raised auburn brows, giving her a skeptical look. "How do I ken you're telling the truth?"

She wanted to box his ears, then kick him in the groin. "Release my sister and allow me to see that she is safe, and I will go with you."

"Nay, Seona," Talia said. "They are madmen!"

"Put a gag in her mouth," Haldane ordered.

"She will be quiet." Seona sent her sister a meaningful look.

"Shh." She then turned to Haldane. "Will you allow me to talk to my sister in private for a minute?" she asked as sweetly as she could, although she wanted to take her *sgian dubh* to him.

"Aye. But I'm keeping an eye on you. Fan out," he told his men as he backed away.

Seona helped her sister sit and lean back against the large stone. At least she was heavily clothed with what appeared to be three layers of wool *arisaids*.

"Have they hurt you?" Seona asked.

Talia shook her head. "Naught but a few bruises from when they tossed me over a saddle."

"How on earth did they capture you?" Seona whispered.

"I ran away... or tried to, but they grabbed me just outside the gate." Tears dripped from her sister's eyes. "They thought I was you for a while, until that one looked at me closer." She glanced at Haldane.

"I'm so sorry you were dragged into this because of me." Seona dried her sister's tears with her cloak sleeve. "Don't cry. Once they untie you, go to the village and hide. When you find Keegan or one of his friends, tell them where I am."

Her dark eyes grew fierce. "I'm not leaving you alone with these barbarians."

It touched Seona's heart that her sister wanted to protect her. She blinked back the burning moisture that threatened to flood her eyes. "Haldane will not hurt me. He thinks he's in love with me."

Talia glared over Seona's shoulder. "Come closer," she whispered.

Seona leaned forward.

"He will force you."

An icy frisson passed through Seona. She knew that was a possibility, but she had to get Talia away from them. None of the brutes cared a thing about Talia. They might kill her if she became a burden or merely annoyed them.

"I believe I can talk him out of it," Seona whispered, not wanting her sister to worry. "I think he wishes to make me happy."

"I want to be released, but I refuse to go back to the castle," Talia said. "Father is going to make me marry the Comyn next week. He's worse than these outlaws."

Seona nodded, knowing 'twas most likely true. "When you're released, hide and slip to the back of the tavern."

"Why?"

"Keegan, Laird Rebbinglen, and their friends should be nearby. But so is Father. You will have to hide from him and his men. Keegan will help you. If we could've found you last night, we would've run away, and already be far from here."

Talia's eyes widened. "In truth? Keegan is stealing you away?"

"Aye, and he agreed to take you, too. But we have to escape these outlaws and Father's men."

"I'll do it. I'll hide behind the tavern and wait for you. If I can find Keegan or his friends, I'll tell them who has taken you."

Seona had pointed out Keegan to Talia from her window when she was locked in, days ago. They had watched him, Fraser, and Rebbie crossing the barmkin. Seona had described a few of the other men to her and the clothing they wore.

"How will you escape these madmen?" Talia asked.

"I'll figure out something." Seona wished she could give Talia her knife, but closely as Haldane and the men were watching, they'd notice. Besides, she might need it to escape them. Hopefully, Talia would be safe if she hid behind the tavern. Even if her father's men found her, they would not harm her. The only dangers to Talia at the moment were Haldane and his men.

Seona stood and turned to Haldane. He moved closer to her. "I'll go with you if you'll untie Talia and leave her here alone, so that she can return to the safety of the village."

He grimaced and shook his head. "I cannot do that, Lady Seona."

Fury tore through her, but she tried to hide it. "Why not?"

"She'll tell your father's men, Keegan's men, and the whole lot of them will be after us."

"Nay, she won't. You will keep this a secret, will you not, Talia?"

"Aye. Of course."

Haldane tilted his head, giving Seona an amused look. "Come now, m'lady. Do not take me for a fool. Here is what I'll do—I'll leave her right where she is, tied up. Eventually, someone will find her. But we'll be long gone by then."

"I thought you wanted me to go with you willingly," Seona challenged.

"You will," Haldane said calmly, but with more of his natural menace creeping out. "Or we can also take your sister with us and leave her deep in the wood."

Nay! Nausea surged through Seona's vitals. She shook her head. "I agree 'tis better to leave her here."

"And you will willingly go with me and marry me, aye?"

She nodded, having no intention of doing anything he said.

"We're heading out," Haldane called to his men and motioned toward the forest.

Clasping her hands together before her, Seona slipped one hand into her smock sleeve and pulled the *sgian dubh* free of the sheath. When she lowered her arms, the long sleeves of the cloak covered her hands and the small knife. Moving her hands behind her back, she dropped the weapon close to Talia. Once they left, her sister would be able to cut herself loose, run to the village and report Seona's abduction to Keegan or one of his friends.

She glanced around at Talia to see if she'd noticed the knife. Her sharp gaze told her she had, plus she had shifted her bound feet to cover the weapon.

"Come," Haldane told Seona, taking hold of her upper arm and leading her forward.

"We're not leaving her, surely," one of his men said, leering back at Talia.

"Aye, we're leaving her. Go get the horses," Haldane commanded.

"Hmm, nice," another of the scraggly outlaws said as he strode by, eying Seona. "I want her after you, MacKay."

Haldane withdrew his dirk and spun. In less than a second, he had the tip of the blade at the man's throat. "This woman is going to be my wife, you whoreson. No one is touching her but me. Anyone who does will get his throat slit. Do you ken what I'm saying?"

The man blanched, his eyes wild. "Aye, m'laird."

Laird? Haldane wasn't a laird. His older brother Dirk was, and obviously Haldane still held onto the fantasy that he would one day take Dirk's place.

"Watch him," Haldane said to McMurdo. "Anyone so much as looks at Seona with lust in his eyes, kill the whoreson."

"Will do," McMurdo answered and followed the others.

Haldane gripped her upper arm again and guided her deeper into the forest behind the other ruffians. She glanced back, seeing that Talia was alone. She prayed no other outlaws would find her before she cut the ropes and freed herself.

Once they were far enough away from Talia, Seona would have to figure out how to escape Haldane and his men. She might grab Haldane's dirk and stab him with it. But he was the one protecting her from the rest of the brutish men. If she killed Haldane, any of his men might rape or kill her. No telling what McMurdo would do... most likely kill her without a second thought.

CHAPTER THIRTY-ONE

Earlier, in the field in front of the tavern, Keegan had snatched a Murray guard's sword, then bested Graybeard, leaving him with several cuts, but spared his life. He'd sent the next one who'd challenged him running away with a deep slice to his sword arm. And now, another of the men who'd invaded their room over the tavern charged him with a sword. He parried and thrust, then drove the other man back several feet.

Keegan darted a quick glance around the field at the crowd of onlookers and noticed Chief Murray a hundred feet away, scowling this way and that, murder in his eyes.

Where was Seona? He must not have found her in the room.

Rebbie stood not far from Murray, looking pale and dazed, his forehead and doublet bloody, but he held a sword in his hand. Keegan was glad he'd awakened.

Fraser, on horseback, rode in behind him, leading Curry. He motioned Keegan forward.

He landed one final blow and sent his opponent's sword flying, then he hastened toward Fraser.

"Haldane took Seona," Fraser said in a low tone.

"What?" A sharp blade of fear and outrage sliced through Keegan. "When?"

"A short time ago. Her sister showed up and told us. Haldane kidnapped her first, then released her when he lured Seona out."

"Which way did they ride?"

"East."

Dermott approached on his horse, tossed Keegan's boots to the ground in front of him, then handed him his sporran and sheathed dirk. "I found these behind the tavern."

Last time Keegan had seen them, they'd been in the chamber. "Seona must have dropped them there." Fear for her life making his hands unsteady, Keegan pulled on his boots then swung into the saddle. "Let's go."

"Lady Talia said they went this way." Fraser took the lead, kicking his mount into a gallop; Keegan and Dermott followed. Hunched low in their saddles, they rode past boulders and into the forest.

Keegan would kill Haldane. To imagine someone harming Seona was like a dagger to the gut. The roughed-up tracks through the leaves and pine needles were easy to see, but when they came onto a muddy road, thick with tracks which forked in two directions, they drew up.

Hoof beats pounded behind them. Keegan glanced back. *Rebbie?* Surely, he was not up to this.

When he halted beside them, Keegan asked, "What in blazes are you doing here? You're injured." Indeed the earl still looked pale, blood matting his hair.

"'Tis naught. When I saw you lads riding like the devil, I knew something had to be wrong."

"Aye, Haldane abducted Seona."

"Saints!" He glanced along the two roads. "North or east?"

Keegan examined the tracks on the muddy ground. "Fresh tracks go both ways. Two of us take one road, and two the other."

Rebbie nodded and rode off toward the east, Dermott following.

Keegan and Fraser traveled north, their mounts charging at full speed. A pistol shot fired somewhere in front of them.

"Who the hell is shooting?" Keegan said between clenched teeth. He prayed Seona was not in the line of fire.

Two horses waited beside the road up ahead, one shifting about anxiously. Behind a stand of bushes, swords clanged.

Keegan pulled back on the reins, leapt to the ground, and drew his sword. He was aware of Fraser following on foot, but he kept his attention focused forward.

Sticking his head through the bushes, he found McMurdo fighting a younger man with a bushy brown beard. Another man lay on the ground, blood pooling around him. What the devil was going on? Where was Seona?

A scream sounded in the distance, ahead but to the left. A female. It had to be her. He raced forward, the prickly gorse bushes snagging his clothes and scratching his skin.

Up ahead, a red-headed man had someone wearing black thrown over his shoulder. *Haldane.* Rushing closer, Keegan saw 'twas indeed Seona he carried. She kicked, elbowed him in the back, and fought to free herself. Even though her hands were tied, she yanked his hair.

"Ow! Damn you, lass!" Haldane bent forward, attempting to dump her to the ground, but Seona held onto his long hair.

Haldane glanced his way just before Keegan reached him. He shoved Seona away and lifted his sword.

She did not appear to be injured, thank the saints.

"Let me have her, Haldane." Keegan forced himself to use a reasonable tone.

"Nay!" He sliced the blade through the air. "Back away."

Seona's ankles were bound as well, but she tried to roll away from Haldane.

"Don't force my hand, cousin." Although Keegan could not say he and Haldane had ever truly been close, they had trained together since they were lads and eaten many a meal together at Dunnakeil.

"You are not my cousin since you are loyal to that imposter you call a chief," Haldane snarled.

Haldane knew good and well Dirk was no imposter, but Keegan wasn't going to argue the point.

"Why did you kidnap Seona?" Keegan knew why, but he wanted to distract Haldane.

"That is none of your concern."

"Aye, 'tis, considering she is my wife."

"Your wife? Ha!" Haldane's pale green eyes glinted with feral energy and he bared his teeth. "Well, if that is true, I can easily make her a widow. She was to marry the MacKay chief, which I will be since Dirk is dead."

Icy cold slithered through Keegan. To imagine Dirk dying was like enduring a strike to his vitals. The man was like a brother to him.

"Dirk is not dead," Keegan assured him.

"How do you know?" Haldane smirked. "You haven't seen him in several days, have you?"

"He's recovering in a safe place."

"You hope. But what if he got a grave fever from that arrow wound?"

Dirk had endured a minor fever, but seemed improved last time he'd seen him. Keegan was not going to worry over him now. Seona was his main concern.

"Release Seona before you injure her."

"Nay." Haldane advanced, sword in guard position. "Back off or you will cause me to hurt her. If she dies, 'twill be your fault."

Fraser stepped from the bushes behind Haldane, snatched Seona from the ground, and kicked Haldane forward. He stumbled to his knees but quickly leapt to his feet, looking about wildly. But Fraser had already disappeared back through the bushes with Seona.

Keegan charged forward, ready to kill Haldane in one-on-one combat. 'Twas not what he wanted, but something he had to do in order to protect Seona and to ensure Dirk's safety.

A glint of fear flashed in Haldane's eyes and he bolted, fleeing through the gorse.

Nay! Keegan chased him. "Coward!" He shoved through the thorny branches after Haldane, running, dodging in and out of the bushes. But after a few moments, all was quiet and still up ahead. He paused. No movements around him. Only the sounds of swords clashing far behind him.

"Haldane!" Keegan shouted. "Come back and fight like a man."

Silence met his ears.

"Bastard." Keeping his sword in hand, he took out his dagger, too, as extra protection should he be ambushed, and proceeded back through the gorse bushes.

Where had Fraser taken Seona?

At the spot where McMurdo had been fighting another man, three scruffy outlaws—he assumed Haldane's recruits—lay on the ground, apparently dead, given their wounds and the blood surrounding them. Keegan was disappointed McMurdo was not among them. Dermott and Rebbie stood nearby, catching their breaths. Dermott held a cloth against a cut on his upper arm. Seeing they were well, Keegan hastened away in search of Seona and Fraser. He found them in the narrow road by the horses.

Upon reaching Seona, Keegan sheathed his weapons and drew her into his arms, her slight, curvy frame conforming perfectly to his. Thank God she was alive. "Are you well? Did Haldane hurt you?"

She shook her head against his chest. "Only a few bruises from his rough handling, I think."

"That bastard." Keegan glanced at Fraser. "I thank you for helping her."

"My pleasure." Fraser gave a slight grin.

Seona pulled back but kept her arm around Keegan's waist. "Indeed, I appreciate the help, both of you. Did you see my sister?" she asked Fraser.

"Aye, the bonny lass was hiding in the brush behind the tavern. She resembled you so much, I knew she had to be your sister."

"Was she hurt?"

"Nay. After she told me you'd been kidnapped, I asked her to wait there with one of the trusted MacKenzie guards protecting her."

"Oh, I thank you."

Rebbie emerged from the bushes, Dermott following. "Did you kill Haldane?" Rebbie asked.

"Nay." Keegan wanted to kick himself for not accomplishing what he needed to. "He ran like the vile rodent he is."

"Coward. He always flees."

"Aye."

"Next time. McMurdo got away, too. He took off when Dermott and I showed up." Rebbie strode toward his horse, then hoisted himself into the saddle.

Keegan glanced down at Seona. "Why did fighting break out among Haldane's men?"

"One of his new recruits decided he... wanted me and attacked Haldane." Seona's face reddened. "Haldane shot him, then his friends joined in the fray. I took advantage of the situation and ran, but Haldane caught me and tied my hands and feet."

Keegan's stomach knotted when he imagined her in such a precarious situation. "Are you certain he didn't hurt you?"

"Aye. I thank you," she said, darting a quick glance from his eyes to his lips and back.

He leaned down and placed a soft, sweet kiss on her mouth, grateful she wasn't injured.

"Where is *my* 'thank you' kiss?" Fraser teased.

Seona pulled away, smiling and blushing.

"Shut your gob, Fraser," Keegan muttered, trying to hide his grin.

A multitude of hoof beats approached from the south, drawing Keegan's attention and darkening his mood. He knew who they were even before he saw them.

A moment later, four of Murray's guards reined in their mounts and surveyed the scene. "We've come to escort Lady Seona back to her father," their leader said.

Keegan stepped in front of her. "I'm taking her."

Smirking, the head guard shrugged. "As long as she goes back to her father, I don't care who takes her."

Seona tugged at his clothing.

He turned to her. "Aye?"

"You stay here," she whispered. "I'll go back with them."

"Why?" Keegan frowned.

"Is it not obvious? I don't want my father and his men to kill you."

"They won't kill me. They may try, but chances are they'll get a blade in the gut."

"Stubborn," she muttered.

"Indeed, I am." Keegan lifted her to his horse and climbed on behind her. He wished he could've stolen her away, but he knew she would never leave her sister behind.

Even though he would enjoy holding her in his arms for a few minutes, he had to figure out how the devil they were going to retrieve Talia, then escape Murray and his men.

***

Seona didn't wish to return to the village or the castle, but she had no choice if she wanted to ensure her sister's safety. And she didn't want Keegan anywhere near her father now that his men had surely told him they'd found her and Keegan in bed together at the inn. Her father would be in a killing rage. She prayed he hadn't already punished Talia for running away.

Riding in front of Keegan, his strong arm around her, Seona turned to him. "We must find Talia."

"Aye, we will," he whispered against her ear, then kissed it.

Delicious shivers slid down her body. She would love naught more than to sink down into the pleasures Keegan knew how to indulge her with, but now was not the time. She had to focus on finding her sister.

Keegan guided his horse toward the back of the tavern, his friends following. But as soon as they rounded the corner, her father, a few of his men, and Wentworth came into view. Nausea rose within her. *Saints!* Exactly who she *didn't* want to see.

As they rode closer, her father's face grew redder.

"Where is Talia?" Seona asked.

"Where have you been?" Murray growled, his glare shifting to Keegan.

"Haldane MacKay captured me. Then, thanks be to God, Keegan and his friends came to my rescue." She gave a quick glance at Wentworth's sullen face, where he stood stiffly by the tavern's back door. Simply looking at him made her cringe.

Keegan dismounted and helped her down.

"Where is Talia?" she asked again.

"Inside. Holed up in the storeroom," her father grumbled. "Go in and talk her into coming out."

"What do you mean *holed up in the storeroom?*"

"She's blocked the door, and she has a knife. She stabbed two of my men in the hands already. She's gone mad!"

"I see." 'Twas true that Talia was belligerent. Even if her actions got her into worse trouble, she would keep rebelling.

Seona headed toward the tavern's back door, Keegan and his friends following.

Her father and Wentworth entered the dim room behind, along with five Murray guards. "I want to talk to you over here, Seona," her father said in a stern tone.

She gave Keegan a quick glance. His firm mouth, hardened jaw, and icy glare said he was ready to stab someone. But none of them had drawn swords yet, thank the saints.

Her father and Wentworth waited twenty feet away, near the tavern's huge cold fireplace.

When she joined them, her father asked, "Haldane, you say? Is he Griff MacKay's youngest son?"

"Aye." The men had already told her father how Haldane had ambushed them several times on the journey here, trying to kidnap her.

"Did he rape you? Seduce you?" her father demanded.

"Nay."

"I don't believe her," Wentworth muttered between his crooked, yellow teeth. "She doesn't have the look of an innocent to me. She probably already carries another man's bastard. I withdraw my suit." He strode from the tavern, slamming the front door on his way out.

Seona's heart lightened with a moment of happiness. Marrying that man would've been hell on earth. But she was surprised to see her father didn't attempt to stop him.

"'Twas not Haldane who compromised you; 'twas that one there." Her father sent a sharp, lethal glare at Keegan.

Seona held her breath, waiting for a battle to break out. But everyone remained silent and still.

"How did Haldane MacKay capture you?" her father asked. "You had to be outside the castle walls. We know the guards were drunk on whisky and not at their posts. You slipped out, did you not?"

"Nay."

"You're lying, you little whore," he muttered, too low for Keegan to hear. "One of the maids saw you slipping out of the kitchen with Rebbinglen. And six of my men saw you in the chamber upstairs with Keegan MacKay. Naked. You sicken me."

We are married. I love him. He is my husband, she almost said. But she couldn't yet. She had to take her sister to safety first.

"Where is Talia?"

"There." He swung his thumb toward an alcove with a closed door. "Get her to come out."

Seona approached the rough door, made of wide planks. "Talia? Are you in there?"

Silence.

Seona knocked. "Talia? 'Tis me, Seona."

"Where is Father?" Talia asked, her voice muffled behind the thick wood.

"Here in the room behind me."

"I'm not coming out," she said in a stubborn tone.

"You cannot stay in there," Seona said.

"I can. There is food in here. I'll let you in and you can stay with me. We won't have to marry the beasts."

Footsteps approached, and Seona turned to find her father

striding closer, a murderous gleam in his eyes. "What is that on your finger?" he yelled.

The wedding band. Fear paralyzed her for a moment, but then she drew in a deep breath for courage, her gaze connecting with Keegan's—intense blue and arrow sharp. Silently, he and his friends moved closer.

"'Tis a ring," she said. "I am married."

CHAPTER THIRTY-TWO

"Married?" Chief Murray's hand flew up and struck Seona's face.

Fury blasted through Keegan's veins. He snagged the back of Murray's collar and yanked him away. The man made a choking sound just before Keegan punched him in the face. The older man bounced off the wall and sprawled to the tavern floor, blood pouring from his nose, curses spewing from his mouth.

Keegan drew his sword to cut down Murray's guards, for they were sure to attack. But Rebbie, Fraser and Dermott were one step ahead of him on that count. Each of them held blades at the ready.

"Halt!" Rebbie commanded the guards.

"Kill them!" Murray snarled, trying to push up on his elbows.

"I wouldn't risk it if I were you," Rebbie warned the guards with a menacing grin and they froze.

Keegan snatched Murray's sword and dirk from their sheaths and tossed them across the room, then stood on the man's scabbard, holding him down. "How many times have you hit Seona?" Keegan demanded.

"You bastard," Murray seethed. "I'm going to kill you."

"I hope you'll try." Keegan went to Seona who still stood by the storeroom door. Her cheek was red and her eyes glinting with fury. "Did he hurt you badly?"

She shook her head. "I'll be fine."

"Hold it right there," Rebbie ordered, drawing Keegan's

attention.

But Murray didn't obey. He'd crawled to his feet. "Give me your dirk," he roared at one of his guards.

"Hell," Keegan muttered.

Rebbie, Fraser and Dermott launched into action, each of them engaging one of the guards, while two charged Keegan. Dodging out of the way, he grabbed a stoneware jug from a nearby table and knocked one on the head. He collapsed to the floor. When the other switched direction and came back for him, Keegan ran him through with his sword. Then shoved him down onto Murray. Keegan kicked the dying guard's sword away, then grabbed his dirk. Glancing around to see who else might be on the attack, he found the other three either knocked out or dead on the floor. None of them moved.

"You lads are lethal," Keegan said, battle rage still coursing through his veins.

Murray struggled from underneath the dead guard and surveyed the scene. His eyes grew wide and his mouth hung open when he looked up at Keegan. Was the man ready to beg for his life? He appeared on the verge. Never had Keegan felt such a sense of victory. But he wouldn't kill Seona's father while she watched, unless he had to. It might prove too much for her to handle.

"Anyone have rope? We'll tie him up," Keegan said. "Them, too." He motioned to the three guards who still showed signs of life. "They'll awaken eventually."

Keegan turned to Seona. "Tell your sister to come out of the storeroom. We're leaving."

Seona banged on the door with renewed vigor. "Talia, come out. Keegan and his friends are taking us. We're running away."

"You damned blackguard," Murray seethed as Fraser tied his hands behind his back. "I will see you dead! All of you!"

"Do you remember who my father is?" Rebbie asked.

Murray merely glowered up at him.

"In case you've forgotten, he's the Marquess of Kilverntay. And, trust me, he has the king's ear. I would hate for you to lose this glorious estate."

"Dare you threaten me, you—?"

Fraser forced a gag into Murray's mouth, then tied it behind his head.

"I'm glad you shut him up," Rebbie muttered.

Keegan turned to see Seona and a dark-haired lass who resembled her a great deal standing with their arms around each other. "Are you both ready to leave this place?"

"Aye." They nodded, eyes wide with eagerness.

Happiness replacing his battle rage, Keegan smiled.

After the four of them dragged Murray and his men into the storeroom, then pilfered some supplies, they headed out the back door and mounted. Seona rode behind Keegan and Talia behind Fraser.

The MacKay and MacKenzie guards awaiting them outside joined them. Keegan could only assume the rest of Murray's men were either still passed out from the whisky or suffering headaches and sickness from overindulging. Of course, the ones who'd sustained injuries during their earlier sword fights had likely gone back to the castle for the healer's assistance.

"Murray and his men will give chase once the tavern keeper discovers them tied up," Dermott said, riding beside him.

"Aye," Keegan said. "We'll ride north for a while to throw them off our trail."

"'Tis a good plan," Rebbie said.

"But we do need to turn west again soon and head back to Teasairg," Dermott said. "Cyrus has a large force of men and the MacKenzies will be glad to help."

"I appreciate it, Dermott," Keegan said.

If they could've slipped away during the night, they would've split up and gone three different directions as planned, but now Keegan thought it best they all stick together because they didn't have much lead time.

During the morning, they stopped once to rest the horses and to eat the tough brown bread and hard yellow cheese they'd lifted from the storeroom. But they didn't tarry too long. They wanted to make good time. Since they were circling around, it would take longer to reach Dornie.

Mid-afternoon, as they rode along a ridge with wide views all around, one of the guards spied a group of riders following in the distance about a half mile back.

"Damnation! They've caught up," Rebbie said.

"Aye, but they'll not get the ladies back." Keegan glanced around, spying a crofter's whitewashed cottage down a short incline and hidden from the view of those approaching. He dismounted and helped Seona to the ground. "Come. Bring Lady Talia." Keegan motioned to Fraser. "MacMillan and Boyce, come with us." The two most trusted MacKay guards and Fraser would protect the women should any of the Murrays get past them. He hastened toward the cottage with Seona and knocked on the rough wood door.

A crofter's wife opened the door, her eyes wide.

"These two ladies, my wife and her sister, need to hide within your cottage, with these three men acting as guards. You will be rewarded for your help. Do you agree?"

"Aye." She stepped back and Keegan entered first. The only other person in the cottage was a young lass.

"Fraser, Boyce, MacMillan, protect them with your lives."

"Aye. You ken we will," Fraser assured him.

"Keegan?" Seona tugged at his plaid sash, and stared up at him with concern.

"You'll be safe in here. Don't fash yourself," he told her.

"I'm not worried about me. 'Tis *you* that concerns me."

"I'll be fine, of course. Do you not ken I'm a warrior?" Forcing a grin for her sake, he kissed her lips quickly and headed toward the door. "Bar the door when I leave."

"Aye," Fraser agreed. "Come back in one piece."

***

Oh heavens! Seona prayed Keegan would be safe as he faced her father and his men.

"I'll stand outside the door and alert you if anyone approaches," Boyce said.

"Aye," Fraser said. Once the cottage door closed behind the guard, Fraser turned to them. "Have a seat, ladies, and try to remain calm. All will be well, I'm certain."

Seona led Talia to a bench by the fire.

"What was this about you being married?" Talia whispered. "I heard Father shout *married* just before the clamorous noise in the tavern."

"Aye." Seona held out her left hand, the gold band gleaming in the firelight. "We said secret and private vows. Though Father may not recognize it as a legal marriage, Keegan and I do. And as soon as we can, we will marry in a church."

"Oh, Seona." Talia embraced her tightly. "I'm so glad you rebelled and followed your heart."

"Aye, well, I couldn't give him up. I love Keegan more than I ever thought possible."

"He is a handsome man," Talia said, then glanced at Fraser, pacing before the door.

"Are you talking about Keegan or Fraser?"

"What? Keegan, of course," she hissed.

"Come now, sister," Seona whispered in a teasing tone. "You must admit Fraser is a handsome man."

"Well, of course he is, but… what of it? I've seen many handsome men before."

"Oh, you have? I didn't realize you were so worldly."

"Cousin Genevieve had feasts and dances. I met a few handsome men."

"Do tell."

"There is naught worth telling."

When Talia's gaze wandered back to Fraser, Seona knew precisely what her sister was experiencing. Obviously, she was intrigued by Fraser, his tall, lean, muscular body. A blue-eyed, black-haired devil with a quick, charming smile. Any lass with eyes would be drawn to him.

Seona simply prayed her own blue-eyed charming husband would be safe.

***

Keegan joined the MacKays and MacKenzie's at the top of the hill, all of them on foot. Rebbie's pistol glinted in the sunlight. Holding targes before them, all the men formed a line, awaiting the approaching Murrays. Keegan fully expected bloodshed.

"Archers, ready yourselves," Keegan yelled. "They could have pistols."

As the riders drew closer, Keegan recognized Chief Murray, traveling at the front and center of twenty other men. Their numbers were about even. Besides, each of the MacKays and MacKenzies could easily take out two men.

The Murrays halted a hundred feet away.

"What have you done with my daughters, you knave?" Murray shouted.

"They are safe from you," Keegan yelled back. "You should be ashamed of yourself, abusing the young ladies, leaving their faces black and blue."

"They are my daughters and I will deal with them as I see fit!

"'Tis none of your concern."

"I made it my concern."

"We all have," Rebbie said. "I'll be reporting you to higher authorities for violently punishing your daughters for no reason. You will find yourself in the tolbooth."

Murray's face reddened but he held his tongue. Rebbie was the only man here Murray respected and feared. Could he talk him into backing away? Murray slowly ran his gaze over each one. Abruptly, he drew his sword and brandished it overhead. "Kill them!" he commanded his men.

Keegan tensed, hoping the chief would challenge him personally.

A few of Murray's clansmen hesitated, appearing startled by his words. Others pulled out their swords.

The MacKays and MacKenzies did the same, the swishing of metal blades against leather scabbards sounded ominous in the Highland breeze.

Two pistol shots exploded. Arrows whizzed through the air and *thunked* against targes. Metal clanged and horses neighed.

One of Murray's personal bodyguards charged Keegan on foot, slashing his blade this way and that. A surge of battle-lust pounded through his veins, making him relish the challenge. Glad to see he was taller and outweighed his opponent by a couple of stone, Keegan easily deflected his blade and launched a counterattack. After a few more parries and thrusts, Keegan's blade stabbed through the man's leather armor and into his chest. He fell to the ground, screaming.

Saints! Keegan turned and noticed that three other enemies had already been felled.

"Retreat!" commanded a younger man who sat on a horse beside Murray.

Some of the Murray clansmen turned tail and ran, while others kept fighting.

"Are you mad, Malcolm?" Murray yelled at him. "Why are you not fighting?"

"Why are you not, uncle?"

Chief Murray charged into the fray on horseback. Malcolm simply shook his head and remained where he was. He was Murray's nephew? Why was he not helping his clansmen?

Chief Murray struck two ineffectual blows at one of the

MacKay guards, then directed his horse toward Keegan, attempting to trample him into the ground. Keegan leapt out of the way, then slashed his sword across Murray's leg. The man yelled out. Blood saturated his trews.

"Bastard!" He turned around, his horse rearing and pawing the air. The more Murray tried to draw the animal under control and head it back toward Keegan, the more unruly it became.

Clearly, the horse was not a trained warhorse, but some fancy expensive breed intended for pleasure riding or racing.

The horse screamed and bolted.

Murray shouted, yanking on the reins. The animal bucked, tossing him into the air. Murray turned a flip and crashed to the ground.

"Saints," Rebbie muttered. "That must have hurt."

The old man didn't move.

Malcolm rode to where he'd landed and swung down. Murray's other clansmen ran toward him, a few of them falling to their knees around him. Others shouted. One headed back toward the MacKays.

"Halt!" Malcolm yelled, and the man obeyed. 'Twas a good thing or he would've been a dead man. All was silent. Still, the old man didn't move.

Malcolm stood, muttered something to his clansmen, then strode toward Keegan.

"Ready yourselves," Keegan told those closest to him and gripped his sword tighter.

The man stopped ten paces away. "Chief Murray is dead."

CHAPTER THIRTY-THREE

Chief Murray is dead. Malcolm, around thirty summers with dark hair and dark eyes, had uttered the words calmly. Keegan had expected a mad attack, but nothing about this man appeared threatening. He had not drawn his sword or any weapon.

Speechless, Keegan eyed him for a few moments. "I'm sorry to hear it," he finally said, though 'twas a lie.

"I'm not. The man was a monstrous bastard."

What the devil? Keegan frowned and sent Rebbie an inquiring glance. Had they both heard the same thing? "Are you Chief Murray's nephew?" Keegan asked.

"Aye. And his heir. I'm Malcolm Murray." He approached and offered his hand.

Keegan hesitated, wondering if this was a trick. Watching Malcolm closely, he sheathed his broadsword but kept his dirk and targe in his left hand, ready for use.

Keegan shook his hand.

"Are you the one who married Seona?" Malcolm asked, stepping back.

"Aye."

"I admire you for standing up to him and rescuing Seona. Talia, too. For years, I feared that he would kill them before they ever married and escaped him. We all believe he killed their mother, though there is no proof. I tried to help the girls, but he wouldn't allow me to live at the castle nor even visit very often. Needless to say, we didn't get along. Where are the ladies, by the way?" Malcolm asked, glancing around.

Going on gut instinct, he believed Malcolm was telling the truth. "In the cottage." Keegan motioned with his head.

"I'd like to have a word with them before they go."

Keegan was again stunned. "You don't mind if we take them?"

He shook his head. "Whatever they want. They've endured years of torture from that brute. They deserve some happiness. If they wish to stay at Gillenmor, they are welcome. Or they can go with you. Since you've married Seona, you will be glad to know she has a generous dowry, including land."

Land? *Saints!* Keegan was almost afraid to believe 'twas true. Not that the land mattered; all he wanted was Seona. But he had never imagined being a landowner.

"Let's go talk to them." He and Malcolm moved toward the cottage. Keegan intended to stay close at hand in the event this was a trick and Malcolm meant the ladies harm. But he didn't think that was the case.

Boyce stood outside. He banged at the door before Keegan arrived.

Fraser opened it and stepped out, eying Keegan and the newcomer. "Is the fighting over?"

"Aye," Keegan said. "This is the ladies' cousin, Malcolm Murray. He wishes to speak to them for a minute."

Fraser frowned. "Is he trustworthy?"

"I believe he is."

"Do you think I'm mad enough to try something with all of you so close at hand?" Malcolm raised a brow, appearing almost amused.

Fraser disappeared back inside, then brought Seona and Talia out.

"Malcolm! You are here? I thought you were away in Edinburgh," Seona said.

"I was, but I returned a week ago." He took each of their hands, his face solemn. "Pray pardon, ladies, but I have sad news. Your da is dead. His horse bolted and threw him. His head hit a rock."

Their mouths dropped open. Keegan took Seona's other hand, hoping to comfort her. But no tears welled in either lady's eyes. And he could certainly understand that.

"You are chief now," Talia said to Malcolm.

"Aye."

"What do you intend to do with us?" Seona watched him warily.

He shrugged. "Allow you to do whatever you wish. You ken I never liked the way your da treated you."

"In truth?" Seona asked.

"Aye. I understand you've already eloped with this unruly MacKay lad." Malcolm grinned.

"I did." Seona smiled at Keegan, her face turning pink. And his heart did a wee somersault.

"Well, then, congratulations." Malcolm kissed both her cheeks.

"And you won't make me marry that old Comyn chief?" Talia asked, her eyes wide with hope.

Malcolm scowled. "Of course not. I have a better way to deal with that cattle thief than giving him my cousin to abuse."

Talia threw herself into his arms and hugged him, tears streaming from her eyes. "I thank you, cousin."

Seona also hugged him. "Aye. Thank you, Malcolm."

He stood back, grinning. "You are both welcome."

Although Keegan would have preferred to take Seona toward Dornie immediately, he knew 'twould be best if she said her goodbyes to her clan and they waited until after her father's funeral. That way, her clan and kin would not question her honor.

After giving the crofter woman all the silver coins he possessed as a reward for her help, Keegan led Seona several feet away to talk in private. "I think we should go back to Gillenmor until after your father's funeral."

She nodded, staring down at their linked hands.

"I'm sorry about your father," he said.

"In one way I am, but in another, I'm not. I'm sad that he never loved us and that he but wanted to use us as pawns to appease his enemies. I'm also sad that he never regretted any of the horrible things he did. But I am glad now that I no longer need his permission to be with you." Happiness shone in her dark blue eyes.

Keegan grinned. "We can marry in a church now, legal."

"Aye."

He leaned forward and kissed her lips. He couldn't help himself. Several of his clansmen on the hill above yelled out ribald comments.

He pulled back and chuckled at Seona's red face. "You will have to get used to those rogues."

***

Two days after Chief Murray's funeral, Keegan, Seona, Talia, Malcolm, Rebbie, Fraser, Dermott and a couple more slipped off to a small kirk near a neighboring village a few miles away.

In her heart, she was already Keegan's wife, but 'twas best to also be married by a member of the clergy. She and Keegan wanted their marriage to be legally recognized without question.

The whole Murray clan was not invited. There was unrest among the clansmen because of the former chief's death, and Malcolm was still reining in the more unruly ones.

But he'd made it clear to her that he wished to see her legally wed before she departed. Her dowry was eight-thousand merks in gold and silver coins, four horses, since Malcolm said he didn't need all the expensive horses her father had collected. He planned to sell most of them anyway. And a hundred acres of farm land, here, bordering Malcolm's holdings. There was no castle on it, only a few cottages, but the crops would provide some income.

All the papers had been signed. Now, Seona and her family members waited outside the charming small chapel, almost hidden amongst the trees. She held a bouquet of bluebells tied with a yellow ribbon. When Keegan had presented them to her earlier, tears had gathered in her eyes.

"Wait! Wait!" Aunt Patience trotted along the flagstone pathway, near out of breath, her face red. MacMillan followed behind her.

"Och, nay," Talia whispered beside her.

"What is she about?" Malcolm muttered.

Seona prayed her aunt wasn't going to cause a fuss.

"I have to be here for this."

Seona frowned. "You're not going to try to stop me?"

"Nay. You deserve happiness." She gave Seona an awkward hug then stood back, tears glistening in her eyes. "I'm sorry I was so… harsh and uncaring before. I only did it because of your father. He'd threatened me. If I'd let you associate with any man he wouldn't approve of, he would've turned me out on the muddy street without a shilling to my name. I hope you can forgive me."

Was her aunt being truthful? She couldn't figure out a reason

Patience would need to manipulate her now. Malcolm would treat her well and provide for her.

Seona was unsure she'd had such a quick change of heart, but she didn't want to argue on her official wedding day. "I'm willing to forgive anyone who's truly sorry for what they've done."

Her aunt nodded with sad acceptance. "I know you have a hard time believing me, but I'll prove it to you."

The reverend motioned them forward. Seona took Malcolm's arm and they stepped into the tiny chapel with its polished oak ceiling and gray stone floor. She found her knees were weak as she stood on the threshold. She had been in this chapel a few times before, but never had the stained glass windows appeared so vivid and colorful.

Keegan waited for her at the front, near the altar. She focused on his smiling sky-blue eyes, shining with love and happiness, as she made her way toward him.

They repeated the vows they'd already said to each other in private days before. If possible, Seona meant the words even more now. Her love for Keegan grew each day.

When the ceremony was over, the minister announced they were man and wife. Keegan placed a quick kiss upon her lips and rushed her out the door. His friends followed, and once they'd exited the church, let loose shrill whistles and made raucous and bawdy comments.

Keegan glanced back, then dragged Seona behind a thick yew bush where he promptly kissed her senseless.

***

A week later, relief flowed through Keegan when they topped a very tall hill and spied Teasairg Castle in the distance. The sun hung low in the sky, casting vivid yellow, orange and pink across the horizon and the loch.

"What a beautiful sunset," Seona said, riding pillion. Although she had her own horse, he wanted her as close as possible in the event Haldane attacked again. And he was simply addicted to the feel of her body against his.

"Aye," he agreed. "But not as beautiful as you."

"You are naught but a charmer," she chided, playfully smacking his arm.

He grinned and twisted around for a kiss. He savored her sweet lips, wanting to drag her onto his lap.

"We'll arrive at Teasairg soon enough and you two can take a private room," Fraser said.

Talia, riding a separate horse behind his, blushed.

"Do you think your brother will allow us to honeymoon there?" Keegan asked.

Fraser snorted. "'Haps. So long as you don't flaunt your marital bliss too much."

MacMillan rode by, Lady Patience behind him. They had secretly married just a few hours after Seona and Keegan. And he was glad to see the lady no longer glared at him. In fact, she had taken on the unusual habit of smiling at everyone. He supposed MacMillan deserved the credit for that. Keegan still didn't trust her, but he hoped she'd truly changed.

He guided his horse forward, wanting to arrive and see how Dirk fared, not to mention eating and taking Seona to bed. Not that he preferred eating food to bedding her, but he would need his strength. He grinned, imagining all the delicious, naughty things he would do to her. They'd had very little private time over the past week and he looked forward to much more.

An hour later, they neared the castle gates. Once the guards recognized Dermott and Fraser at the forefront of their party, they raised the portcullis.

Horses' hooves clomped across the thick wooden boards of the long bridge that led out to the small island where the castle sat.

Guards and groomsmen greeted them in the walled courtyard. Keegan dismounted and lifted Seona down. The smile she gifted him with inspired him to give her another quick kiss.

"What the devil is going on here?"

Keegan turned at the familiar voice and watched Dirk approaching with a grin, hardly a limp in his step.

"Cousin." Keegan took Dirk's forearm in a warrior handshake. "Are you well?"

"Aye. My leg is mended and only a wee bit of soreness remains."

"Thanks be to God," Seona said.

"Chief, I'd like you to meet my wife," Keegan said proudly, his arm around Seona's shoulders.

Dirk's smile grew wider and he bowed. "I'm more than happy to welcome you to the clan, m'lady." He shook Keegan's hand again and gave him a back-slapping embrace. "'Twas what I was hoping to hear. But how could it be anything else since you brought her back, aye? Isobel will be happy to hear this news as well."

"I'll go find her." Seona rushed up the steps and inside, Talia following.

Rebbie strode forward and greeted Dirk.

"What of Chief Murray?" Dirk asked.

"Dead," Rebbie said.

Dirk's eyes widened and darted to Keegan. "What happened?"

"'Tis a long story," Keegan said. "Come. I'll tell you. But first, I will say there is naught to worry over. I signed a peace treaty with Malcolm Murray, the new chief."

"In truth? You did well, Keegan."

"The only bad thing is that Haldane and McMurdo are still roaming free."

Dirk frowned. "Well, they are wily. And I always feel torn about Haldane. On the one hand, he is my brother and I hate to see him dead. On the other, he keeps trying to kill me, so we have to take him out if we can."

Keegan nodded. "I feel the same way. I suspect he and his men have hastened to Durness to ambush us when we arrive back there."

"Saints! 'Tis a good thing I left plenty of men guarding Dunnakeil, including my sword-bearer. I ken Jessie couldn't handle it alone," Dirk said.

"Nay." 'Twas true Dirk's sister was tough, but she was not a fearsome warrior.

"We'll need to return as soon as possible."

***

That night after supper, Seona and Keegan were escorted to one of the nicest bedchambers at Teasairg. Seona had noticed Isobel whispering with the maids during supper. Now, she and Keegan stood just inside the closed door of the chamber. A huge tub of steaming water sat before the hearth, where a roaring fire burned. The covers were turned back on the bed, the clean white sheets glowing in the candlelight. A bottle of wine and two silver goblets sat on a small table along with a vase of bluebells.

"'Tis amazing," Seona whispered, her throat tight. Tears burned her eyes.

"Och." Keegan took her into his arms, his warmth and

strength seeping into her. "Why are you crying?"

"Because I'm so happy. I never truly thought 'twould be possible to have you for my own."

He grinned and kissed her forehead. "Well, maybe I believed it enough for both of us."

She stared up into his blue eyes, turned darker in the night. There was naught she enjoyed more... well, except for kissing him... and making love to him.

He leaned down, claiming her lips with slow sweet kisses that grew hotter and more urgent with each moment that passed. He tasted of spiced wine and she could not get enough.

He groaned and pulled back an inch. "'Tis time for us to indulge in something we haven't yet."

"What?" Seona wondered what else she needed to know about lovemaking. Since they'd only gotten to spend two nights together since that first time, because of crowded sleeping arrangements and various other problems, she was certain she had a lot more to learn about marital relations.

"Bathing each other." He unclasped the brooch holding his plaid together at his shoulder, then unbuttoned his doublet.

She watched, fascinated, as he quickly stripped off each article of clothing—his boots, his belt, his plaid, his shirt. And then he was bare. She held her breath, taking in all his delicious golden skin and sculpted muscles. His chest, his rippled abdomen and the trail of gilded hair that led down to... *Heavens!* He was fully aroused.

And now, so was she.

"What are you doing?" he asked, moving toward her.

She swallowed hard. "Naught."

"Aye, exactly. You were supposed to be undressing." He unbelted her arisaid and let it drop to the floor, then quickly divested her of the rest of her clothing.

When she stood before him naked, she shivered. Not because of cold, but because his gaze was so hot, like blue flame touched to kindling. He lifted her and stood her in the tub, then sat down on the opposite end.

"Come." He motioned her toward him.

When she lowered herself between his muscular thighs and leaned back against his hard chest and hard... other things, she felt almost sinful. But he was her husband, and there was no need for shame or embarrassment.

Taking the soap, he lathered his hands, then glided his palms up her wet arms and over her shoulders, massaging deeply. She sighed in delight. After bathing her neck, he trailed his hands down to her breasts, gently cupped and caressed them. He uttered a breathy moan in her ear.

Once he'd soaped his hands again, he trailed them down to her hips. He drew her onto his lap, turned her slightly toward him and kissed her lips, delicious sinful tongue kisses. The next thing she knew, his hand was between her thighs, stroking over her most sensitive parts. She gasped and widened her legs, craving more of his intoxicating touch.

He groaned. "Aye."

"I want you," she whispered, the ache inside her growing more intense.

"You must bathe me first, m'lady." He grinned and handed her the soap.

What? She could scarce form a coherent thought. But she made an effort.

After scrambling off his lap, she knelt facing him, between his legs. She glanced down to see the tip of his shaft protruding from the water. Heat and arousal drenched her. Dropping the soap, she slid her lathered hands up and down his sleek, stone-hard length.

He muttered a curse and stiffened, his eyes growing even darker. Was he near to losing control? Deciding to tease and tempt him, she took the soap and slicked it over his sculpted chest, around his neck, under his arms.

When he tried to stroke her nipples, she caught his hand and washed his arm but his other hand found its mark, tweaking her already hard nipple.

He pulled her astride his thighs. "Lean back."

"Why?"

"I want to wash your hair." He grinned.

Looking into his mischievous eyes, she wondered what he was about. "How?"

"Do you trust me?"

"Aye, you ken I do."

"Then relax."

When she leaned backward, he dipped her long hair into the water, then pulled her upright. He combed soapy fingers through her hair then rubbed his fingertips against her scalp. It felt heavenly. She sighed, enjoying that and his hard member pressed against her lower belly.

"Time to lean back and rinse," he said. Once she did and her hair was free of suds, he tugged her up again. "That was one luscious sight," he murmured, his eyes heavy-lidded with desire.

She blushed, imagining herself as he must have seen her, back arched, breasts thrust upward.

He captured her lips in a carnal kiss, sliding his tongue inside and taunting hers.

Abruptly, he pushed himself from the tub, supporting her with one arm, and stood.

"We didn't wash your hair yet."

"Later," he said against her mouth and carried her toward the bed.

"My hair is too wet," she said. "'Twill drench the sheets."

He grinned wickedly. "Well, who needs a bed?"

What did he mean?

She had already wrapped her legs around his waist. Now, his shaft rubbed against her in a most enticing way. She hissed. "Aye, Keegan."

"Are you certain?" he teased.

"Aye, I want you. Now."

"Och, you are a demanding wench." He nibbled on her neck and positioned himself. With one hard thrust, he slid to her depths.

She cried out at the sudden penetration. Although she craved him, she was not yet accustomed to his size. It always took her a few moments to adjust.

Holding himself deep within her, he tongued her nipples, suckled them. She moaned and he started moving, sliding in a slow and provocative manner. She sensed something at her back. The door. And his arm. The other beneath her hips. He held her just so, driving himself up into her at a faster pace with each moment that passed. Pleasure ricocheted through her, resounding, overwhelming. How was such intense sensation possible? She held on 'round his neck, her fingers buried in his thick hair, his mouth against hers, breathing hard, devouring. He consumed every part of her and she begged for more.

He moved his hand between their bodies, stroking with his thumb against a highly inflamed spot. Her pleasure shot skyward and she screamed, clutching onto him. Ecstasy crashed through her, rolling her along its violent waves. It stole her breath.

"God, how I love you," Keegan growled against her ear, pushed deep and trembled against her, groaning.

She gasped, tears flooding her eyes. "I love you." Though she wanted to say more, there were not enough words to explain how much she loved him. Because of him, she truly lived.

***

Please look for other books in the Highland Adventure Series by Vonda Sinclair.

Book 1: My Fierce Highlander
Book 2: My Wild Highlander
Book 3: My Brave Highlander
Book 4: My Daring Highlander
Book 5: My Notorious Highlander
Book 6: My Rebel Highlander

Thank you for reading my books!

ABOUT THE AUTHOR

Vonda Sinclair's favorite indulgent pastime is exploring Scotland, from Edinburgh to the untamed and windblown north coast. She also enjoys creating hot, Highland heroes and spirited lasses to drive them mad. Her books have won an EPIC Award and a National Readers' Choice Award. She lives with her amazing and supportive husband in the mountains of North Carolina where she is no doubt creating another Scottish story. Please visit her website to learn more. www.vondasinclair.com

Made in the USA
Monee, IL
22 March 2022